The Limits of Glory

Also by James McDonough:

Platoon Leader

The Defense of Hill 781:
An Allegory of Modern
Mechanized Combat

The Limits of Glory

A Novel of Waterloo

James R. McDonough

PRESIDIO

To my mother and father, Lucy and Gene McDonough.

Copyright © 1991 by James R. McDonough

Published by Presidio Press
31 Pamaron Way, Novato, CA 94949

Library of Congress Cataloging-in-Publication Data

McDonough, James R., 1946-
    The limits of glory : a novel of Waterloo / James R. McDonough.
      p.   cm.
   ISBN 0-89141-384-7
   1. Waterloo, Battle of, 1815—Fiction. 2. Napoleonic Wars, 1800-1815—Fiction. 3. Great Britain—History, Military—19th century—Fiction. I. Title.
PS3563.C3585L58 1991
813' .54—dc20   91-11927
                                     CIP

Maps by Christian Jaupart
Typography by ProImage

Printed in the United States of America

Contents

List of Maps

Acknowledgments

I wish to acknowledge the following people for their contributions to this book:

Mr. Christian Jaupart for his excellent map illustrations. His perseverance through many changes in the original draft deserves special recognition.

Lance Sgt. Lewis Pearch of the Headquarters, Coldstream Guards in London. He provided invaluable assistance in ferreting out the details of the Coldstream Guards' brave defense of the Chateau d'Hougoumont. His knowledge of detail and initiative in locating the enlistment records as well as personal accounts of the Guardsmen were of utmost value.

Lt. Col. Sir Julian Paget, author of *The Story of the Guards*, for taking time out of his extremely busy schedule to provide assistance at Guards' Headquarters in London to verify details of the Guardsmen's role in the battle.

Col. Simon Fraser of the British Army and Wing Commander Gordon Browne of the Royal Air Force for their assistance. Drawing upon their considerable knowledge of the battle through years of study, they provided numerous verifications of details as well as new insights into the battle.

Mr. Rodney Nybroten for the use of his extensive Napoleonic library, which proved invaluable in obtaining out-of-print publications. His detailed personal knowledge of the uniforms of the Napoleonic period proved most helpful.

Mr. Paul Hoogstoel of the Belgian Napoleonic Society, who provided many French and Belgian insights on the battle.

Lt. Col. (Ret.) H. L. T. Radice of the Gloucestershire Regiment for his insight into the Gloucesters' participation in the battles of Quatre-Bras and Waterloo.

Maj. Robert Cazenove of the Regimental Headquarters of the Coldstream Guards for his kind assistance in obtaining permission to use the archives of the Coldstream Guards.

Norman H. Macdonell of Edinburgh, Scotland, a direct descendant of James Macdonell of the Coldstream Guards, for providing personal information on the life of his ancestor.

Dr. P. B. Boyden, Head of the Department of Archives, for allowing access to the files held in the National Army Museum.

Brig. Dermot Blundell-Hollinshead-Blundell of the Grenadier Guards for his valuable guidance, assistance, and encouragement.

Col. John Hughes-Wilson of the British Army for his help in obtaining permission to use various British archives and museums.

Mr. A. van Achter for his kind permission to use the farm of La Haye Sainte to verify details of the battle around this key stronghold.

Mr. and Mrs. Roger Temmerman for their kind permission to use the Chateau d' Hougoumont to verify details and gain perspectives on the fighting in and around the chateau.

Gen. John R. Galvin, Supreme Allied Commander, Europe, for his inspiration in using Waterloo as a vehicle to study command, operations, and tactics. Modestly describing himself as a "student of the battle," he has used his knowledge of it to teach others the lessons of coalition warfare.

Willard O'Brien Richards, to whom I owe my deepest gratitude. His research of the immense detail of the Waterloo Campaign enabled me to write this story. His scholarship, energy, and linguistic ability were of incalculable assistance, as were his friendship and encouragement, neither of which ever wavered throughout the project. Quite simply, this book could not have been written without him.

Finally, I must acknowledge my indebtedness to Michael Shaara, whose book, *Killer Angels*, a novel on the battle of Gettysburg, served as a model for my own work. A brilliant writer, Mr. Shaara set a standard for historical fiction that will seldom be achieved.

Author's Note

Warfare runs along a continuous thread from tactics through operations to strategy; the thread is human. The mind conceives the strategy; men carry out the operations and fight the battle. In the end, human flesh and blood pay the butcher bill for the grand enterprise.

More volumes have been written about Waterloo than any other military event. Some describe the tactics; most analyze the operational and strategic decisions. Both categories of books dwell on technical detail and comprise intellectual analyses of the conditions that applied and the events that transpired.

Yet the whole affair remains a human undertaking. The thoughts that conceived the plans grew amidst the human environment of fatigue, uncertainty, distraction, emotion, and desire. The soldiers who executed the results of the ideas were tired and wet, exposed and vulnerable.

I have told the story across the spectrum of warfare from the human perspective. In so doing, I have tried to be as true to the facts as possible. If this is historical fiction, the fiction is in the thoughts I portray the characters as having. Who knows what thoughts they had at what moments? I have tried, however, to perceive those thoughts in light of what the individuals knew at the time and what actions they took subsequently. Given the logical and psycho-logical relationships of thought and action, action and thought, I hope I am close to the mark.

The conversations, too—for the most part—are fiction, although where possible I tried to find a quote as recorded by some observer at the scene. Memories are inaccurate, however, even in the most placid of times, and the campaign of Waterloo was anything but placid.

Historical events are depicted as they happened, although even here a significant amount of disagreement can be found in various bibliographic sources. Where certainty was impossible, I have presented the interpretation I deemed most plausible based on my own study of war and the human condition therein.

All books take on a life of their own. I began this book in quest of a single protagonist, an heroic figure whose actions in the battle epitomized the highest character of leadership, courage, and sense of duty. Early on, my study led me to James Macdonell, certainly one of the bravest and most inspired leaders at Waterloo. But I found that if I told only his story, then much of the panorama—not only of the battle but of its human drama as well—would be lost. Further research led me to Georg Baring, whose mission, although failed, was as resolutely pursued as any of which I have ever heard. Both men are portrayed as I see them, as professional soldiers of the highest caliber.

But the individual who captured a large sense of the story was quite unexpected. Not a combatant, Lady Magdalene de Lancey played a part as meaningful as any in the drama. Her sacrifice was great, yet she bore it with a nobility that adds a new dimension to anything one might hope to find in the warrior ethic. Her eloquent record of devotion calls to us across the years—a reminder of the limits of glory and the boundlessness of love. Her story stands for the families and loved ones of the forty thousand who fell at Waterloo.

The armies that fought at Waterloo have faded from the soil. Ostentatious monuments stand in their place in and around Mont Saint Jean, among them a gigantic mound of earth that distorts the battlefield and the perspective of anyone who visits there. Of Ligny and Quatre-Bas, barely a marker can be found, yet the memory of the men who fought at these places lives on. This book is one attempt to tell their story.

1

TIRLEMONT: 3 MAY 1815

It was a moaning wind, inarticulate, meaningless—but a distraction
nonetheless. It snapped and blustered over the rolling countryside,
spattering dirt in the rider's face, catching his cape and rippling it across
his back. High grey clouds lent a cheerlessness to the small procession winding along the muddy Brussels-Liège road. Occasionally, the
riders would pass an ugly stone house, one the same as the others,
windowless on any three of four sides, dark looking. And damp! Unhealthy,
unwelcome—sullen like the people they sheltered.

The rider was silent, his followers observing his solitude, respecting
it. He sensed the inhospitality of the land, thought about it, and weighed
it as if it had strategic meaning.

His horse neighed, broke his concentration. It had been a long ride,
four hours so far. The whole time the wind had been cutting at his
face, making it difficult to survey the country or talk to his aides. His
voice was ragged from the shouting he was forced to do to be heard.
Better to be quiet. He didn't need the conversation. There would be
time enough for business later, and polite talk was irrelevant.

His legs were sore from the chaffing. Damn it! He cursed the speed
with which the soldier softens. It had been a pleasant stay in Paris,
and then the posting to Vienna. Yes, the diplomats did go on forever
about trivialities. But that was their way—it was a tactic. They had
the bottoms for it, those dandies. Hour after hour at the table or in
the parlor. No agitation, no spark. Just quiet talk, whining again and

1

again about the same minor point. It wore you down, by God. They had staying power. You had to admire them for that.

And they lived so well. How cosmopolitan Vienna had been. The food, the arts, the accommodations—it had all been so civilized. The thought reminded him of the ugliness of the Belgian countryside and his nose wrinkled in distaste, sensitized again by the smell of feces fertilizing the damp fields. Belgium was an artificial addendum to the Netherlands, a bastard stepchild. Half of the province spoke French, half Flemish. A confusion within a confusion.

He forced his mind back to Austria. The Congress of Vienna had been convened to solve the political differences of the nations of Europe in the wake of Napoleon's abdication. All the important men of the Continent had been there—and many of the loveliest ladies. He lingered on that recollection for a moment, remembered some of the very young ones, then disciplined himself to put aside his memories of the women and review instead the political outcomes of the interrupted Congress.

The duke of Wellington had been sent there as the representative of His Majesty's Government, but Wellington's stay had been brief. Napoleon's reentry onto the Continent had seen to that. The event put the allies in a stir. At first they could not believe the news; they were sure Bonaparte would founder, stopped in his ambitions by a force of his own countrymen, which surely would not let him proceed through the countryside unchecked. Finally, and reluctantly, they had accepted the hard truth. He would have to be fought again, defeated on the field of battle. Wellington would be one of the generals to face him. And so the duke departed the Congress with the title of commander in chief of the British and Dutch-Belgian forces in Flanders. The title sounded nice, but King William of the Netherlands had yet to put his seal of approval on relinquishing command of his own troops. As much as the allies croaked about coalition warfare, they were still guarding their prerogatives carefully. Nevertheless, with luck, the king would hand over command this very day. The only sticking point was his young son, the twenty-two–year–old prince of Orange, who until this moment remained the titular commander of Dutch-Belgian forces.

The duke thought about the Young Frog, so nicknamed by the British because of his oval, flat face and bulging eyes. The prince was headstrong, impetuous, inexperienced. Even if he relinquished command, and he probably would, he would still expect a major posting. Perhaps he could handle a company, but anything less than a corps would be unacceptable to the royal family. That's what coalition warfare got you—a motley collection of ne'er-do-wells from the public houses of the British Isles and an unreliable and ill-disciplined conglomeration of Belgians and Dutch of dubious loyalty, who were led by a bunch of incompetents not of your own choosing. Not quite the best mixture to take into battle against the Tiger.

France considered Belgium to be French, a sympathy shared by many a Belgian. Moreover, virtually every Dutch officer had served at one time or another under French colors. The Dutchmen might fight for a little while, until the winds began to turn against them. Then who knew what to expect? And the other allies. Where were they? It had been a month since Wellington had arrived in Brussels, and still all indications were that the allies were moving slowly.

The politicians in Vienna had promised 1 million men. Wellington would have 110 thousand of them under him once he was given full command in Flanders. But besides them—and the duke had already taken their measure and found them disappointing—only the Prussians, with approximately 120 thousand, were at hand in the area around Liège. Three other armies were allegedly marching now to join them: 200 thousand Austrians approaching by way of the Black Forest, back behind the Rhine; a mixed army of 75 thousand Italians and Austrians coming up into the Riviera; and with full mobilization potentially the largest force of all, but at the moment still under 200 thousand, the Russians approaching the central Rhine. But it would be late summer before the Russians were in position to act as the reserves and July at best before the Austrians were in position to strike. There were the Spanish and the Portuguese as well, but they were back behind the Pyrenees— and would probably stay there until the French were decisively beaten.

In the meantime, Napoleon just might work the magic that could undo the alliance. It was best not to underestimate that man. You could hate him, and the duke recognized that he probably did. But don't underrate him. He was a devil all right, but he was a brilliant devil.

It did not seem likely that Bonaparte could mobilize his own forces before the allies would arise. Certainly he was up against it. A year of exile in Elba and a year for France under Bourbon rule had left his base in shambles. Where could he get an army? How could it be trained, outfitted, commanded? It would take a miracle to do it in short order. Not very likely.

But still! The man was good. He had pulled off miracles before.

The thought left Wellington unsettled. A stiff gust of wind stung his face and forced him to turn into his collar.

I beat the French in Spain and Portugal, on the Peninsula, but I never beat Napoleon. He was never present. It was not the major theater for him. He sent the best of his marshals—Bessières, Ney, Soult, Massena, and others. But he never came himself. France lay sheltered behind the barrier of the Pyrenees. And always I had the sea at my back—an escape route, a way out, if worse came to worse, and a source of sustenance and a means of mobility as well.

It was a desolate, hard-fought campaign for sure. But this will be worse. The French will fight hard. Their survival as a nation is at stake. And Bonaparte will be there. Has he faded? Perhaps. But he was a genius. Elba could not have taken that out of him. He came back, after all. That shows he still has the starch. No, this will be different from Portugal. It will be worse.

That is why this meeting with Blücher is so important, why I have ridden these many hours across this godforsaken countryside. In the short run, the key to our security lies with the Prussians. What a vile thought. The Prussians! A warlike race, bloodthirsty, raucous, unpredictable. But we will need them if Napoleon moves on the Low Countries. I must protect my flanks. The right, my link to the Channel and England, is the most important. I have looked to that myself, but it has caused me to stretch my forces out away from Brussels to the west. Here in the east, on my left flank, there is only the Prussians. And Blücher.

What manner of man is Blücher? I have met him before, but do I know him? I have heard he is crazy, that he thinks himself pregnant. With an elephant no less! Yet I know that he can fight. But can I rely on him? He is old—seventy-two is it? How can someone that old command an army on campaign? Only the Prussians. They are born to it, I suppose. But seventy-two! How can he even sit in the saddle?

He has made it this far, though. That's more than the others have done. Maybe there is a message in that. If I can just convince him to narrow the distance between us. I need him at Namur; he must come forward from Liège. At least Namur. Then we can close the gap if Boney attacks. If I can just get Blücher to give his word. I'm told he keeps his word. We shall see.

A cold drop of rain fell heavily on Wellington's cheek. His aide saw the drop hit and realized others would soon follow, but he made no move to shelter his commander. At forty-six years of age, the duke was in his prime. Lean and agile, Wellington seemed impervious to the elements. Above his aquiline nose the bright blue eyes flashed from horizon to horizon, drinking in the conditions of the countryside. Beneath the edges of his broad hat, thick brown hair bristled in the heavy wind. He seemed in control—of his horse, of himself, of the environment.

The right man for the job, Old Nosey is. The aide kept the thought to himself.

A few miles ahead, in the village of Tirlemont, the old man was waiting. Active as always, he was inspecting the livestock belonging to the farmer whose house his staff had appropriated for the upcoming appointment. Disapprovingly, he noted the lack of care given to the horses. These Belgians seemed callous toward their beasts. Even their dogs were neglected, unkempt mongrels kept ill fed and overworked. He snorted with distaste at the pungent manure smells emanating from the barn. It must not have been cleaned in weeks.

His joints ached from the long ride over from Liège. He called to his aide to bring him a schnapps to ward off the dampness, then proceeded with his inspection of the livery. Now and again he would mutter to himself, let out an oath, chuckle, and move on. He talked to no one in particular, but knew he was being watched. That was half the purpose of his little game. He liked being watched, liked giving a show. He knew his subordinates did not know what to think. Was he mad? Was he merely rambling? Or was there a point to what he was doing? Best to keep them guessing. It kept them on their toes, gave them stories to tell, stories that would be duly passed through the ranks. The men liked that. Let them tell their "Old Forwards" stories. It was good for morale.

Inside the farmhouse his chief of staff, General Count von Gneisenau, had unfolded his maps again and was poring over the markings as if for the first time. That was the way with his chief—he was meticulous, always going over the same things again and again, making sure he had missed nothing. Quite frankly, it bored the marshal. He preferred action to study. Make a decision and move on. The execution was ninety percent of the affair, the planning only ten. Still, it was good to have a chief of staff with an eye for detail, to catch something that was important. Catch it and correct it, that was what chiefs of staff were for. And Gneisenau was a good one. Blücher knew it. He was smart,

that Gneisenau. Didn't come any smarter. With heart, too. Not afraid
to fight—once he had put everything in place. That's where the two
of them were different, though. The field marshal was always ready
to fight, be damned with the details. But Gneisenau kept him in check.
Not too much. Just enough to keep him out of trouble.

Blücher tripped over a harness lying in the straw, stumbled a step,
caught himself, and kicked at the leather apparatus in a fury, cursing
the farmer, his family, the village, the region, and the country as he
did. He caught the sparkle of good humor in his aide-de-camp's eyes
and spiced up his language a bit. The aide broke into a slight smile
before bringing himself back under control and returning to his stoic
watch over his commander. The old man resumed his inspection, feeling
good in the knowledge that yet another colorful story would shortly
be making the rounds.

In the farmhouse, Lt. Gen. Baron von Müffling brought his stout
frame alongside General Gneisenau so that they could both refer to
the map as they spoke.

"You see, my dear Baron," said Gneisenau, "this Wellington that
you like so much has barely moved away from the Channel. He secures
himself at Ostende, directly on the North Sea, and at Antwerp, where
the Scheldt can take him out to sea. In the meantime, we have marched
halfway across Europe. Now he wishes us to move closer to him. I
don't trust him, I tell you. The man is too timid."

Von Müffling patiently heard his friend out. He knew the chief of
staff did not like the English. Never did. And he had a point. The Prussian
lines of communication to the Rhine now extended back through the
Ardennes, rough terrain that would not allow much deployment off
the established roads. If the lines were cut, if Napoleon somehow came
across them, it could be difficult for the Prussian army. Stranded in
Belgium, the individual corps could either fight on alone, without support,
or try to make their way back through the Ardennes, where the French
might be waiting. Neither option was pleasant. Nonetheless, Müffling
decided he could not allow Wellington to be impugned without making
some type of response.

"But General Gneisenau, Wellington must secure his lines to the
Channel. England is a small but mighty nation. The British lifeline is
the sea. It is the source of their strength. England's armies have never
been large. But they can shift them wherever they need them as long
as they have control over the sea and the means to get to it."

"You make too many excuses for them. I think maybe your duke is afraid to fight."

"No, General, he is not afraid to fight." Müffling spoke quietly, determined not to allow his countryman to anger him. "Look at what he did in Portugal. And always he hugged the sea, making the French come to him. He defeated them in detail while husbanding his small forces for a campaign of long duration. It was brilliant, I tell you, positively brilliant."

Gneisenau did not respond. He was too good a strategist and tactician to deny that Wellington had managed well in Portugal. But that had been a long way from France, in rugged, mountainous country. This was Belgium. If they met the French any place other than the Ardennes, it would be open ground. And this time, Napoleon himself would be present to command. That was a different story. In Portugal it had always been one or another of the marshals, and seldom did they get along. Gneisenau kept his eyes on the map, avoiding the gaze of his friend.

Müffling deferred to the chief of staff. "Tell me, good General, do you think Napoleon can attack?"

"Can? Certainly he can attack. Should he attack, however, is another story. I do not see how he could be ready. Certainly not now, and I doubt before August. It takes time to raise an army. And he has been away a year."

"But suppose he could. Would it make sense for him to attack?"

"Truthfully, I think not. How many forces could he raise: a hundred thousand, two hundred, three? And many of them would have to stay in garrison. His country is not without its internal difficulties, its insurrections and dissidents. And even if everyone within his own borders were behind him, he still faces the onslaught of eight hundred thousand or more of his enemies from the rest of Europe. He has to guard his borders. From the Pyrenees to the Alps. From the coast to the Mosel. Those outposts will consume his forces battalion by battalion so that he has little left with which to make war."

"So you think it is a matter of us attacking and him defending?" Müffling was approaching his point and Gneisenau sensed it.

"Yes. I cannot see it any other way."

"Then we must be sure that the understanding between Wellington and us is clear. There is no room for an uncoordinated attack. Napoleon could defeat us in detail."

"You are right there," Gneisenau agreed. "But if I am wrong and he attacks, then we do have a choice. We can only be defeated in detail if we choose to fight. If we attack, our meaning is clear—we will fight. But in the defense, we can choose to decline combat. Sometimes that is more prudent."

"But if an ally is depending on us, how can we choose to decline combat?"

"So we are back to that again, are we? It is a question of trust. Do you trust Wellington to come to our assistance if we are attacked?"

"Yes, General Gneisenau, I do. And we must do likewise."

"That is a decision I prefer to make only at the necessary moment. Until then, I would prefer that we keep our options open."

Müffling would have responded, but the door burst open, bringing with it a strong gust of wind. The aide entered with an announcement. "Wellington is approaching with a small party. Marshal Blücher requests that we all come into the courtyard to greet him."

Gneisenau shot a look at Müffling that said, "Strike no bargains." The baron would have to do most of the talking; neither Wellington nor Blücher could speak the other's language.

As Gneisenau and Müffling went outside, Wellington's small party entered the courtyard. Blücher stood waiting on the ground, rocklike, cunning, his eyes brightly shining above his elaborate mustache.

Müffling was struck by the scene. The wind cut around the sides of the barn and bounced off the farmhouse, sending stray leaves and straw in erratic directions, swirling the hanging capes of Blücher and Wellington, tugging at the shorter coats of the riders. Heavy, low-lying clouds sped by overhead against a backdrop of lighter clouds higher above, casting shadows of varied darkness over the courtyard. Chickens clucked in fear at the approaching horses, stuttering along on spindly legs toward the shelter of the coop. Dogs barked from safe corners of the enclosure.

Wellington recognized the majestic form of Blücher. The duke dismounted with the abruptness and agility of a man half his age, passed his reins to an aide, and strode up to the Prussian. Blücher made a short, stiff bow, then raised his hand in salute. Müffling waited for the two men to shake hands, then closed in beside his commander to do the translation.

"My dear General. It is a pleasure to see you again." Wellington was speaking, the baron interpreting.

"And I you, Duke. We have much to talk about, but first, you must be hungry. Please come in out of the wind. We shall have some dinner."

The two groups exchanged introductions and greetings, then walked toward the farmhouse. The principals entered and moved to the large table; the aides and assistants took their meals outside in the lee of the building.

"How soon do you think you will be able to attack?" Wellington posed the question to Blücher, aware that his own force would need another eight weeks before it could advance.

"I am ready to attack at any time. Today if you like." The field marshal responded cheerfully, knowing that Müffling would not translate it without editing from Gneisenau. He was not disappointed.

Gneisenau quickly added, "Although we are eager to attack, a major advance before July would be ill advised."

Müffling threaded a delicate line between the two statements, transmitting the view that early July would be the best time for an attack.

"I think July would be about right." Wellington was cagey, aware that some difference of opinion had surfaced among the Prussians. His own German-speaking aides would tell him the details later. "We will need the Austrians and the Russians closed up if we are to have the necessary reserves to ensure the total defeat of Napoleon."

"You are right, Sir." Blücher's eyes had narrowed. "It is the defeat of Napoleon that is important. Not the defeat of France. Not the fall of Paris. But Napoleon. Wherever he is, we must catch him and squash him. Like a bug."

"I am told that he most likely will be with his northern army. That is where he is placing the majority of his strength. And it is in the north that he must feel most threatened. If we move on Paris, he will be compelled to defend it. He will no doubt put his strength between us and his capital." Wellington looked straight at Blücher.

"Wherever he stands, we must advance to meet him, with our combined strength. I suggest our staffs meet to consider possible lines of march." The old man surprised Wellington with his thoroughness.

The field marshal continued. "And if he attacks? Do you think he will dare it?"

"General Blücher, I do not think that is possible. But you are correct to consider it. Bonaparte has done the impossible before. If he does attack, then I believe it imperative that we come together to help one another."

Gneisenau leaned forward, stopped chewing. His back and neck tensed, his lungs filled with air, deepening his chest as if preparing for a physical exertion.

"I see it the same way." Blücher's look silenced his chief before he could speak. "There is some risk, however. That French devil is known to delight in falling across his enemies' lines of communication."

"True. But I think this time we are most vulnerable where we have not yet joined—in the center, around Brussels and Ghent."

"We are already a long way from the Rhine. And the roads through the Ardennes are difficult." It was Gneisenau. He was anticipating Wellington's appeal to have the Prussians move farther into Belgium, and he resented the fact that the Englishman would ask it of them when he had so carefully tied himself to the Channel.

Blücher's voice rose slightly. "We will move beyond Liège to Namur. Charleroi seems an appropriate place for an advance guard. How much farther are you prepared to come?"

Müffling softened the tone in translation, but Wellington felt the point of the query nonetheless. "I will bring my center of mass to Brussels." Then he added quickly, "Charleroi is an excellent choice for you. How much are you prepared to bring there?"

"I think a corps will do." Blücher glanced at the map an aide had brought forward on Gneisenau's signal.

The Prussian chief of staff took a chance and interjected, "Are you prepared to cover Mons?" Blücher remained silent, so Müffling translated the question.

"I will cover Mons at Nivelles. Mons itself is too far south. But at Nivelles I can disrupt any French movement until we can come together." Wellington turned to Colonel de Lancey, his chief of staff. "Bring me the map, please."

The food was forgotten as both groups turned their attention to their own maps. After a few seconds, Wellington spoke up. "If Napoleon moves against either Charleroi or Mons, I will advance to Nivelles. But you must come toward me or he will split us."

Blücher looked hard at Wellington, then glanced at the map before bringing his eyes up to meet Gneisenau's. His chief looked concerned but convinced that what the Englishman had said was correct. Without a word with his staff, the old man turned to his ally and replied. "It is agreed. We shall come."

Wellington sensed the depth of the promise. Blücher was not a fool. He was not insane. The reports had been false. Eccentric perhaps, but not insane. And there was more than sanity to say for the man. He was straightforward. He said what he meant, and he meant what he said. These were not light words passing around the table. They were a commitment of tens of thousands of soldiers, of cannon and cavalry, of every ounce of war-making materiel: of the Prussian army itself.

For the first time, a side conversation ensued among the Prussians. It was not agitated. Intense perhaps, but low-key. Blücher merely listened, saying only a few words at the end. Then Blücher looked closely at his subordinates to see if they had anything to add. He closed the discussion with a low grunt and turned to speak to Wellington.

"We have two great armies, united in a common cause—the undoing of the blight of Europe. Many miles separate our headquarters. It would be good if we could exchange a small liaison. I am prepared to offer you Baron von Müffling and a staff to serve you at Brussels or wherever you care to place your headquarters." Müffling translated, excited.

"A splendid idea. I accept, of course, and I offer you Col. Sir Henry Hardinge, an excellent officer. Not only is he highly experienced, he is proficient in German. I will make him and a small staff immediately available."

"Thank you, my dear Duke. But enough of this talk. It wearies me. I invite you to join me for a drink of schnapps and a smoke. There is nothing like a smoke to relieve one's mind of concern."

The two men stood and drank a toast to one another's sovereigns, then moved to the doorway where a pair of rough chairs had been drawn up. Blücher fell heavily into the seat and lit his pipe. The smoke caused his eyes to water as the wrinkled lids pulled closer together, hiding the old man's thoughts behind the double screen of smoke and skin. Wellington sat beside him, quietly waiting for his host to speak. The duke was restless. The business they had come for had been accomplished. The staffs would talk for a few minutes, but he was eager to get back. It would be a long ride, and there was much to be attended to once he returned. Still, it would be best to wait a few minutes rather than to show any rudeness to his host. These Prussians were a funny breed. Warm and mellow one moment, incensed and up in arms the next.

"I have heard that you have never lost a battle, Wellington." The old man's voice was distant, surprising his guest with the directness of the question.

"Everyone has lost some type of battle somewhere or another. But I have been lucky in combat. I have not lost one that would ruin me."

"I have lost many." Blücher spoke softly, then fell silent. "Does that worry you?"

Wellington considered how he might answer such a leading question, then said what he felt. "It matters little if either you or I lose, as long as we both do not. If one of us survives to destroy Napoleon, we will have done our job. That is why we must come to one another's aid. In the end, mutual support will be decisive."

"You are right. Yes, yes. You are right." The old man's voice drifted off, leaving Wellington to think for a moment that he had fallen asleep. Then he shifted in his seat and spoke, "Do not worry, my dear English. I will be there. I will see to the death of that Corsican bastard."

With that the conversation ended. For a few moments Wellington sat there silently, allowing the old man his quiet smoke. Then he stood up and made his farewells. Blücher walked him out into the courtyard, gave him a hearty handshake and salute, and watched him ride away. When the visitors were out of sight, he gave a quick call for a schnapps. He wanted to brace himself before the chief of staff began to express an endless stream of worries about the arrangements they had just made with their allies.

2

THE TUILERIES: 15 MAY 1815

The flickering candles cast an eerie pallor over the silken room. Wavering shadows darted back and forth along the wall in erratic patterns, alternately lighting and darkening paintings and tapestries representing exaggerated deeds of glory. Davout payed no heed to the confused images formed by the candlelight. His attention was riveted on the small hunched figure intently reading the intelligence reports Davout had brought with him to the stifling room.

The reader's eyes were ablaze with an intensity that checked any inclination the marshal had to speak. Not that Marshal Davout was easily intimidated. Time and time again, he had proven his courage on the battlefield. He would speak when it was time; had spoken, in fact, to the very figure now before him about a matter of greatest sensitivity—the necessity of abdication in the face of overwhelming defeat and erosion of support. That had been only a year earlier.

But he didn't want to speak now. He was captured by his study of the man in the chair. He could see the green coloring in his face. Perhaps the yellow candlelight accentuated it, but he had seen it in the morning sun as well. He could see the utter fatigue in his subject's wrinkled forehead, the furrows extending all the way back to the edge of the receding hairline. His arms draped heavily over the sides of the stiff-backed chair, the elbows held unnaturally aloft from his protruding belly. Only the eyes looked alert. The rest of him seemed immobile—barely alive.

It was not the Napoleon that Davout remembered from the years on campaign. Then the face had seemed alive with a dynamism of its own, one befitting the master of the world. It had been a face cast in bronze, unhurriedly gazing over its limitless domain as if in control of time itself. The piercing eyes had held a grip on all with which they had come into contact. There was a regal arrogance in the way the head was set upon its confident shoulders. And the voice! It had been authority itself—firm, direct, at times theatric, at others cold and certain, a little like death.

Now only the eyes retained that glimmer of command. And even they were not constant. More than anything else, that was what unsettled Davout, minister of war and military governor of Paris. He had thrown in his lot with this man. Had it been the right choice? Could Napoleon surmount the challenges before him? Rational analysis had told the marshal that he could not. No mortal man could overcome the difficulties now confronting the leader of France. The citizenry was lukewarm to his return from exile. His public administrators, many of whom he had placed in office before his abdication, were reeking of sedition. The army was understrength, virtually untrained. The treasury, already bankrupt from two decades of adventurism, was straining anew under the burdens of the mobilization suddenly cast upon it. All of Europe was moving to make war—not so much against France as against Napoleon himself. He was the monster; they had isolated him. How could he stand up to all of this?

But he had achieved miracles before. Perhaps he was not a mortal man. Certainly, the clay from which he was molded could not be mortal. All that he had done, all that he had achieved—not just as a military leader, but as a politician and administrator as well—could not have been foretold to be within the capacities of any group of great men; they could not be imagined within the grasp of any single individual.

Even now, his presence in the Tuileries in Paris, the seat of power, was a testimony to his extraordinariness. Only a few short weeks ago the Bourbon Louis XVIII had sat in this very room and received the news that Napoleon, on the first of March, had returned from exile on Elba, landing in the Gulf of Juan in southern France. Bonaparte had barely a thousand supporters. At the time, Davout did not give him a ghost of a chance of surviving more than a few days. But step-by-step Napoleon had marched into the interior, winning the soldiers over to his side and with them at least the apparent support of the peasantry.

He had triumphantly marched into Paris on 20 March, only one day behind the fat Bourbon king's flight to Ghent. It had seemed a miracle.

But it would take more miracles to keep him in power. Davout wondered how many more the great man was capable of producing. He had seen, often enough, the flashes of brilliance as Napoleon efficiently dealt with a myriad of political, military, and administrative challenges. At other times, though, he had seemed disinterested, confused, tired, and ill. Given the work he was doing, it was understandable that he would need to rest from time to time. But in earlier years he had been able to recover his energies after only a few hours' respite. Now he would work diligently for several hours, then grow so withdrawn and lethargic as to appear comatose. The pattern had shaken Davout's confidence.

"These reports are good. They tell me what I need to know." Napoleon's voice startled the marshal, bringing him out of his reverie.

The voice continued. "The rivers and canals around Charleroi and Mons are fordable. I can cross at any number of points. That will be key."

The eyes looked up at Davout, seizing him with their intensity. The marshal did not know what to say—or even if he was expected to say anything. His master did not seem to be asking for comment; he was speaking as if to himself.

"Sit down, Davout. I would like to talk. It is time you understood what I mean to do."

The marshal could feel the sweat dampening his back. A slight chill went through him. Silently he moved to the nearby chair, his eyes fixed by Napoleon's gaze. He did not feel his ankle bump the leg of the table, his sash catch in the tip of his quill. He was oblivious to everything save the fierce look in Napoleon's eyes.

"My enemies have encircled me. They make war on me. Me! Not France. Me! All of them. All of Europe! All of Europe against me." There was an evil ring to the words, a laughter without laughter. A sneer formed on the speaker's lips, as if he savored the compliment their rabid hatred paid to his stature. The civilized world had overcome its own petty differences to do battle with the one being that threatened it. All of Europe against Napoleon, the monster that would not die.

"They fear me! More than they fear each other. More than they fear the mobilized armies of their natural enemies. The nations that would destroy each other for the most minor advantage have put aside their differences to make war on me.

"You know the numbers, do you not, Davout? That British buffoon Wellington sits astride a gypsy army of over 100,000 Dutch, Germans, Belgians, Irish, Scots, and English. The crazy loon Blücher has brought 120,000 of his bloodthirsty Prussians within sight of our borders. The Austrians, under that amateur, the prince of Schwarzenberg, are closing with a force of approximately 200,000, and right behind him comes Barclay de Tolly with an almost equal number of Russians. Give the Spanish credit for 50,000 or so on our southern borders, and General Frimont a command of 75,000 or so Italians and Austrians approaching the Riviera. That is just the start of it. They will find more, and they will send them after me. *Me*." The heat of the fire in his eyes went up several degrees.

"And what can we put against that? The numbers are pathetic. Perhaps 5,000 to hold the Riviera, 7,000 at Bordeaux, and 8,000 at Toulouse to hold the Pyrenees. I've got General Rapp at Strasbourg with barely 23,000 men to hold off the Russians and Austrians." Davout could picture Rapp, fiery and courageous, but of dubious loyalty. It was Rapp who had asked to be sent to shoot Napoleon when he landed on the shores of France. Ney had been sent instead, boasting that he would bring his former emperor back "in an iron cage." The boast had been empty. He had capitulated before the overpowering personality of Napoleon, assisting him on his way and waiting now to be called to the colors at the pleasure of his master.

Napoleon continued. "I have no reserves. Marshal Suchet sits in Lyons with the *Armée des Alpes,* some 24,000 at best. Maybe 10,000 more in the valley of the Loire. You are to hold Paris with whatever you can muster. That leaves me with little more than 125,000, if I include in the *Armée du Nord* all of the local garrison forces. The *armée* is my one striking force, the only mass I have capable of offensive operations."

"Offensive operations, Sire!" Davout reddened at his own spontaneous outburst. He should not have been surprised. The signs had been there that Napoleon was exploring all options. Napoleon's order a few days ago for updated reports on rivers and canals in Belgium implied that operations in that region were under consideration.

"Yes, Davout. Of course." There was an evil glee in Napoleon's face. It frightened the marshal. "What would you have me do? I have offered peace. I have been rejected. The prince regent of England had the effrontery to return my missive unopened. None of them wants peace. They want war. Already they plan to invade. Add up those forces. There are six major armies planning to invade. Every day gives them greater strength, while I must be content to conscript mere babies. Look at the support we get from our own people: They wince every time I tell them we must raise more troops, spend more money. They want to get fat, but they don't want to work for it. They are lazy, slovenly, afraid. They are sheep. They will panic if they see foreign troops on French soil.

"I cannot wait. It is what everyone thinks I must do, will do. But I cannot. To wait is to invite defeat. In time, I will be overwhelmed by sheer numbers, even if our countrymen should hold out against the first invasions—which, as I said, is doubtful.

"I will attack. I will do what they do not expect. I will defeat them one by one. I will break their will for war. I will take the fight to their soil. I will show them that Napoleon is not an easy prey."

The speaker's eyes went to the shadows flickering on the wall and, for a moment, were lost in their wicked dance. Davout seized the opportunity to enter the conversation.

"But how can you attack? As you yourself have said, your troops are barely trained. And you know how poorly they are equipped. Our weapons and ammunition are inadequate. Horses are few; cannon have yet to be procured in sufficient quantity. Even the boots with which we march are in scant supply."

"That is why I have you, Davout. You must obtain for me what I need. You must get me the men, the weapons, the horses, the supplies. You get them; I will direct them."

"But where? Where will you direct them? You cannot fight everywhere at once."

"No. You are right there. I have been considering my options for days now. No, it has been weeks. Come here to the map, let me show you how a commander thinks." Ponderously, Napoleon rose from his chair. A slight sign of pain reflected across his lips, then disappeared behind the fierce eyes as the two men moved to the map table.

"The key is Wellington and Blücher. Foolishly, the allies look to them for leadership. They don't know them as I know them." Davout could sense the arrogance in Napoleon's voice, thought of inserting a note of caution, then dismissed the effort as a futile gesture.

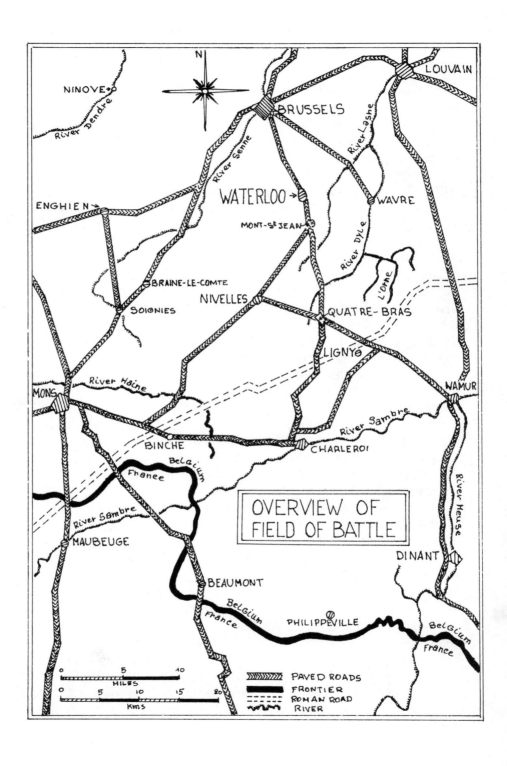

OVERVIEW OF
FIELD OF BATTLE

NINOVE

River Dendre

N

BRUSSELS

LOUVAIN

River Senne

River Lashe

WATERLOO →

WAVRE

ENGHIEN →

MONT-S! JEAN →

River Dyle

L'Orne

BRAINE-LE-COMTE

NIVELLES

QUATRE-BRAS

SOIGNIES

LIGNY

River Haine

WAMUR

MONS

River Sambre

BINCHE

CHARLEROI

Belgium

France

River Meuse

River Sambre

MAUBEUGE

DINANT

BEAUMONT

Belgium

France

PHILIPPEVILLE

Belgium

France

0   5   10
MILES

0   5   10   15   20
Kms

//////////// PAVED ROADS
━━━━━━━━ FRONTIER
- - - - - ROMAN ROAD
∿∿∿∿∿∿ RIVER

Bonaparte continued. "Wellington is afraid to cut his communications from the sea. Note how he has disposed his forces to protect his lines of communication back to the Channel. He has moved out only as far as Brussels, with much of his strength strung out the distance back to the coast. He has not left himself enough forces to effect a linkup with Blücher, who has based his own army in Namur. That old drunk is as afraid of cutting his lines to the Rhine as Wellington is of cutting his ties to the Channel. Blücher has concentrated his forces around Namur. A poor choice. It sits on the edge of the Ardennes, making lateral movement difficult. If pressed, he must either make for Wellington at Brussels or reel back to the Rhine. Either way, his position offers me some possibilities.

"Consider the options. If I wait for an attack, the two of them, Wellington and Blücher, will combine their strength, giving them a force superior to my own in the region. They will invade toward Paris. But if I attack, I can split either one of them from his lines of communication, throwing both armies into panic and keeping the initiative for myself. What do you think, Davout?"

The marshal could sense that Napoleon was playing with him, trying to get him to open up so that he could display his greater intellect. His reasoning was too obvious. How Napoleon liked to belittle his senior subordinates; he thrived on it. Davout feared a trap. He hesitated, preferring not to make comment just yet.

"So. You are thinking about it! Well, let us see what would happen if I cut either from his base. Would that really play out well? If I were to swing wide toward the Channel to cut Wellington, approaching by way of Lille toward the River Scheldt, Wellington would not fight. He would be forced, then, to move toward Blücher, effecting a linkup and shifting his lines of supply farther north, possibly at Antwerp. That would get me nothing. Conversely, if I came at Blücher at Namur from the southeast, I could cut him off from Liège and his lines back over the Rhine. But at the same time it would throw him into Wellington's lap. That is what I do not want.

"I want them separated. I want each of them forced to fight on his own. The only way to do this is to split them with an attack that comes between them. That leaves me two choices. Approach from Valenciennes to Mons, then swing north to Brussels, or come at them by way of Charleroi, crossing the frontier between the Meuse and the Sambre. Which do you think is better?"

Davout could no longer avoid Napoleon's baiting. He glanced at the map. In truth, he had considered the options himself over the preceding days. "The approach from Mons will pit you directly against Wellington. If he falls back to Brussels and then to Antwerp, without a fight, then he retains his strength and an avenue of escape. At the same time, the deeper you go, the more you will be exposing first your flank, and then your rear, to Blücher. If Wellington then chooses to turn and fight, you could be caught from two directions, all the time with the Russians and Austrians closing toward Strasbourg. It seems neither geography nor time are on your side with that approach."

"Good. Good. Your strategy is sound. But we must also look to the operations as well. Look closely at the map. I assume that you have looked at the reports you have brought me. The terrain to the east of Charleroi offers us a greater opportunity for a quick advance. It is undulating, more open, the roads are better, and there are at least three good crossings of the Sambre. Here I can make speed. Speed will preserve our surprise. And with surprise, I can concentrate on bringing us victory before either Wellington or Blücher can react."

Davout took his eyes from the map and once again found himself captured by the intense aura emanating from Napoleon. He made it all sound so simple. As a military man, the marshal knew that inferior forces should normally stay on the defense. Napoleon was proposing just the opposite—a strategic and operational offensive that would force a fight on his terms. From that Napoleon could foresee victory. Based on the numbers, it did not seem plausible. Yet he had done it before. It was a classic Napoleonic concept. Let your enemies come at you, choose the decisive piece of ground, get there with a high-speed march, concentrate your forces, beat the other side to the punch, and allow the opposition to impale itself on forces honed and positioned for the kill.

But as the paunchy little man sagged back into his chair, letting his momentarily animated face go slack, the minister of war allowed himself some second thoughts.

Was France up to it? She had grown tired of war. Her sons had left their blood all over Europe, from Lisbon to Moscow. Their successors did not have the hunger, the zeal that had taken the armies of France through two triumphant decades.

And what of her enemies? The only time they had united before, they had driven the emperor into exile. After Leipzig there had been no chance for Napoleon to regain the initiative. He had fallen back all the way to Paris, where his own marshals convinced him that he must abdicate. Now all the nations of Europe were united against him again. Their numbers were limitless. He might defeat everything his enemies now had under arms, only to see their armies replaced in short order with subsequent levies. Would they break if Wellington or Blücher—or both—were defeated? There were so many: Austrians, Portuguese, Spaniards, Italians, Bavarians, Russians, Swiss. Would they make a separate peace and return to their own internal warring? They detested the man slumped in the chair so much. Not just hated him—they feared him as well. The worst kind of hate, a hatred born of fear! Would they let him remain at the helm in Paris? He had humiliated them time and time again, had ravaged their countries, killed their sons, taken their treasures. Only Wellington was unbowed before him. Britain had never succumbed to his will. Wellington had never been defeated in battle. Yet Napoleon denigrated him so. That seemed unnatural. Should you not respect a man who had beaten your best forces, who had known neither tactical nor strategic defeat? Davout could not resist asking the question.

"Why do you not respect Wellington? He played havoc with us in Portugal and Spain."

Napoleon did not move. His eyes, though open, had taken on a dead glaze. His breathing was deep, troubled. He seemed not to hear the question.

Davout pressed. "Sire, why are you so sure that Wellington is not worthy?"

"Uh?" A stirring. "What? What is that you say? Wellington, that whoremonger, that procurer of young girls, that British dandy! You think he can fight?" The eyes seemed startled. They darted around the room, not looking at Davout, not looking at anything.

"The English are a rabble. They are corrupt. They sit on their island and degenerate. They cannot stand to take casualties. They have no stomach for it. In Portugal they hid behind their defenses. They crawled into the mountains and up against the coast. They paid scum to fall upon our lines, to erode our strength, to murder our agents, and to destroy our roads. And all the time, my marshals bickered among themselves. Junot failed me, Ney and Soult could never come to terms with one another, and Massena diverted himself in his quest for riches and women." Davout bristled at the diatribe. All these were confederates of his. They may not all have been his friends, but to condemn subordinates for failures whose cause may lie elsewhere was a shoddy business.

"Wellington never fought me on the Peninsula. Other matters of greater importance attracted my attention. This time, he will not have that luxury. And look at his troops. What a polyglot! They will never stand together in battle. Even his own British, I am told, are the dregs. They will crack like a nut before my hammer."

"And what of your own generals this time? Who will you rely on?" Marshal Davout was probing, his mood soured by Napoleon's arrogant dismissal of his subordinates' skills.

"Ah, Davout. I will have you remain here. I know you want to come forward. But I need your talents here. We will consume supplies. We will consume horses. And we will consume men. You must replace them for me, no matter how much the public administrators and the mob cry out against it. I trust you to do that and to defend Paris if it comes to that."

"Your chief? Who will be your chief of staff?" The thought had formed at last in Davout's mind. That was a major difference this time. Berthier was not here. Berthier—a marshal since 1804, the quintessential chief of staff, a master of detail and thoroughness—was gone. He had fled upon Napoleon's return. Would he come back? Could Napoleon manage without him? The two of them were a team. Napoleon did not like to admit it. It might imply his own mortality. Time and time again, Berthier's acumen—his anticipation of events—had saved the day for his emperor.

"Soult. I will take Soult."

"Soult will better serve you in the field, Sire. He does not have the patience for Berthier's sort of work. Details escape him. His orders are general, vague. They confuse more often than they clarify."

"Why do you argue with me so, Davout? Do you have doubts? Do you think that I cannot do as I say? Perhaps you wish you were with Berthier. Then maybe you might be safe."

"That is unfair, Sire. I am here, where you want me. I have done everything that you have asked to raise an army. I suggest only that you should have the best men for the critical jobs if you want to proceed as you suggest."

"And what of Ney? How do you suggest that I employ Ney?" Napoleon made no apology for his scathing remarks.

"A minor post, Sire. He is unbalanced. He has not been right since Russia. The strain was too great, the hardship too extreme."

"A minor post? Perhaps, but Ney has something that is still important in battle. He has courage. He always had it. Not moral courage mind you—in that he is wanting. He grovels before all men of authority. Most of all before me. He cannot stand to be chastised. If I want to make his skin crawl, I need only look at him reprovingly." Napoleon let out a mirthless chuckle, as if he received a weary delight in the image.

"No, he has physical courage. That is enough. I may call him forward. But when I think he is ready. When he is beside himself with fear that I will not, I will call for him. Then it will be time. He will want so badly to prove himself. That is when I can best use him."

"Surely you will want more than physical courage in your senior commanders."

"Davout, you have no idea the kind of battle I have in mind. It will be a battle of blood, more ferocious than the world has ever seen. Above all I will want courage. You think you have seen killing. Those sights will be nothing compared to this. Remember, the British do not like to die. They detest large casualties. And the Prussians—just the opposite—as bloodthirsty a race as has ever been put on this earth. I will make a battle that will break both their backs. Even the Prussians will revolt from the carnage, while the British will retreat behind their Channel never again to venture forward onto the Continent. That will be the volume of blood that I will spill.

"What type of leadership will I need for that? It will be the kind of leadership to which blood means nothing. It will be the kind of leadership that relishes the gore, that can only be excited by the flow of it. It must be the kind of leadership whose only fear is the fear of failure and the fear of being afraid. I will have that in Ney.

"You must size up your men carefully, Davout. Look at the boys you are bringing to me. They know nothing of war. I must make them think that the battle I bring them to is the only kind of war. What can do that better for me than to have Ney at the front, showing them how to be brave? Brains! I have no need of his brains. I will be there for that. I need his glory—to inspire, to bring forward, to go in again and again where rational men will not go."

The words frightened Davout. Is this what greatness came down to? Is this what military genius stemmed from: the willingness to expend lives without remorse, without trepidation? What could be worse than Austerlitz, than Jena, than Borodino, than Leipzig? How much killing did Napoleon have in mind? And how could he, Davout, raise the requisite numbers with such cold efficiency? Set a quota; have the provinces meet it. Chastise those that fail. Reward those that succeed. Set a higher quota; create more incentives. Transport the recruits, clothe and outfit them, feed them, train them, then march them to be slaughtered. Then do it again with the next year's crop of children come of age. A knot formed in the marshal's stomach. He wanted to speak; the words formed in his mouth.

Davout checked himself. He had asked enough questions. He would do neither himself nor Napoleon a service by going any further. "It is approaching midnight, Sire. Perhaps you would like some sleep."

"Sleep? I slept enough on Elba. What other reports do you have for me? Leave them here. And call in my scribes. I have some letters that I need to dictate." Again the eyes were alight. But the face remained sunken, listless. Davout withdrew from the room.

Napoleon sat there alone. His head was throbbing. It pained him to sit. Something inside of him was not right. His thoughts returned to his plan. He would make it happen. It was merely a question of will. He had the will, had conquered the world with it. He could do it again.

But there was a nagging self-doubt at the back of his mind. He did not feel well. He found it harder and harder to concentrate. There was a terrible pain in his urinary tract. His piles bothered him. A twinge of indigestion distracted him. Most of all, he felt tired. It had never been like this before. The campaign, the challenge, had always excited him. The more he worked then, the more he wanted to work. He enjoyed seeing the awe in which he was held by those around him. He could work them until they dropped, then work their replacements into the ground as well. Now it was a labor every step of the way. He might have a good hour or two, but then find it difficult to concentrate for several more. Getting up in the morning was harder and harder. He would avoid being seen until he had gathered his wits together. But that was taking longer and longer now.

He looked up with a start and noticed that his secretaries had arrived in force, paper and pens at the ready for his dictation. He closed his eyes and tried to focus on what it was that needed to be said. For a minute or so, his mind remained blank, then slowly the thoughts began to come to him. One by one, he addressed his staff: "Take a letter."

3

PRELUDE TO BATTLE: 0300, 15 JUNE 1815

Lady de Lancey lay quietly on the bed next to her sleeping husband. Soft light from the lamppost in the park square below reflected off the white-ceilinged bedroom, brushing with a gentle glow the two slender human forms on the sheets. Magdalene had parted the curtains fully after their lovemaking, leaving the opened windows to allow some air into the room. She had been embarrassed by the lingering smell of sex and hoped that the night air would dissipate the telltale odor. Not that she minded it. In a way it made the love seem to last, as if enveloping the two of them in a cocoon of warmth and tenderness. But her upbringing had made sex such a private matter. She could not allow any hint of the intensity of their passion to remain by the time her maid, Emma, made up the bed in the morning.

Sir William was breathing gently. She loved to look at him. He was a handsome man, with thick, sensuous lips complementing his strong chin and nose. Even in sleep his face held an intelligent look to it, as if in his dreams he were solving some difficult problem with systematic efficiency. His hair was slightly mussed. A lock protruded onto the pillow here and there, blending in with the semidark with his sideburns, which extended an inch or two below the lobes of his ears.

Unconsciously she reached a small gentle hand out to touch his bare torso, feeling the soft curls of hair compress to allow her fingers to graze his warm skin. His chest and arm muscles were tight across his frame, hardened by years in the saddle on campaign. She thought of his Gold Cross from the Peninsular War. What were all those inscribed names: Talavera, Nive, Salamanca, San Sebastián, Vitoria? What did they all mean? How bad had they been? There were little scars here and there across his chest. Some looked as if a weapon had caused them. They were clean and neat, a straight incision or a small round hole. Others seemed to take random form, as if created by some haphazardly shaped object. Happily, she thought, none detracted from his good looks. If anything, they enhanced the air of mystery that lent so much enchantment to their romance.

He stirred and she withdrew her hand, not wanting to wake him. As quartermaster general of the allied army and chief of staff to the duke of Wellington, Sir William had his share of responsibilities. Fortunately, since his wife's arrival on 8 June, his duties had been light. But at any time that could change, and he would need whatever sleep he had been able to get. For her, the past seven days had been idyllic. From the time she had come ashore at Ostende, she had been captivated by the serenity of Belgium. The journey to Brussels had brought her across a pastoral countryside that gave no hint of impending war. The flat lowlands—with their tilled farmscapes interspersed with small, thickly overgrown streams and serene man-made canals—had given way to gentle hills and airy woods in the vicinity of Brussels.

The count de Lannoy had graciously given the young married couple a suite of rooms in his spacious house on the edge of the park, a square of very beautiful houses with fine, large trees in the center. The count had extended every courtesy and made himself attentive to their needs. But mostly they had been left alone—as they preferred—to enjoy each other's company.

They had been married since only 4 April. The news of Napoleon's escape from Elba had by then traveled to the farthest reaches of the British Isles, so that even in distant Scotland, her native soil, one heard of the impending clash. For most of March the gossip held that he would be stopped, arrested, and driven from the Continent in ridicule. But as the dispatches continued to trace a path that came ever closer to Paris, it became clear to even the dullest that the emperor would soon place himself back on the throne.

Still, that had not worried them. Sir William was in Scotland to be married, and his old commander, the duke of Wellington, was far away in Vienna. Surely there were others who could do the job. After all, Colonel de Lancey had done his duty already. As a recent groom, he would be entitled to some time for himself in which to establish his new position.

She allowed herself to remember the wedding. She had looked so demure in the stunning white lace gown. Yet she knew that she had excited her husband the instant he had laid eyes on her that day. So proudly she had prepared herself for the wedding. Her tight brown ringlets encased her oval face, accentuating the dark beauty in her doelike eyes. Her full lips were lightly colored, holding an ever so slight promise of rapture to come. Her soft shoulders and fine bosom were delicately framed by the finely fitted dress that so seductively presented her figure for his admiration.

And he had been so handsome in his elegant uniform. The eagerness in his eyes had sent sparks across the church and caused her to blush, but not without a feeling of sublime well-being. She had fallen madly in love with this dashing young officer. She could not wait to be his.

The days that followed had been pure joy, dampened only by the continuing news from the Continent. At last, Sir William had brought her the letter from Wellington that asked him to serve as his chief of staff. She had been alarmed, but he had reassured her in his gentle voice that his duties would be merely administrative. He would see to the transport, billeting, and outfitting of the allied army. The fighting, if it ever came to that, would be done by others. And besides, it was a great honor to be called by Wellington to such an important post. Wellington was the finest officer in the British Army—probably the finest officer in anybody's army, for that matter. Moreover, the duke had rejected Sir Hudson Lowe, the next in line for selection as quartermaster general, and insisted that the only man he would accept for the job, as a condition of his own service as commander in chief, was Col. William de Lancey.

In the face of his enthusiasm for the post, she had softened. When he got like that, he so reminded her of a little boy. He was so eager to serve that she had to make his decision easy for him. And he reassured her it would not be an unbearable intrusion on their young marriage. Once the organization was settled and in place, he would bring her to the Continent. There would be no real fighting of consequence. So many of the allies were reacting to Napoleon's return to power that they would mass enough troops from across Europe to compel the French to plead for peace and dethrone their emperor. It was all such a gallant adventure, an opportunity to show his prowess and loyalty, with little risk to his personal safety.

In the end they had parted reluctantly, April passing to May and with it the deepening of the heartsickness and loneliness felt by the two of them. Only a week ago she had returned to his arms. From then on it had been heaven.

They cherished their time together. There was no other word for it. Neither of them would accept invitations to dinner or to the many balls for the aristocracy of Belgium, the leaders of the allied army, and their ladies. Even within the walls of Count de Lannoy's house in the park, they avoided joining the other guests for dinner between three and four in the afternoon. Instead, they took that time for their afternoon stroll, at the traditional dining hour meeting few people in the course of their walk. Then they ate alone at six, Lady de Lancey occasionally meeting an invited friend of Sir William's. Privacy is what they craved more than anything else in the world. They could not get their fill of it. They wanted only each other.

And so it had been that night. They had retired at nine. Not because they were tired, but because they could not contain their passion. The fire had been so intense they could not put it out. Again and again they had devoured each other, until at last in utter joy they had fallen together on the sweaty bedsheets and faded dreamily into a blissful sleep.

But the deep fear within her had awakened her in the early hours. Her mind was racing: What was it that had been in the papers Sir William had received that day? He had gone out with them abruptly but made no mention of their contents. He had promised that he would tell me as soon as he knew anything himself. Perhaps it had been nothing. But then again! . . .

She felt his hand on her forehead and turned toward him with a start. He silenced her with a tender kiss on her lips, one that started softly but quickened with intensity as their lips lingered. She closed her eyes and surrendered her disquieting thoughts to the joy of the moment. His hand went around her shoulder and pulled her into the crook of his arm.

"What is it?" he said as they broke off their kiss.

"Oh, William. I am sorry I woke you. I wanted you to sleep."

"I have slept. And a beautiful sleep it was. But what about you. Why do you lie awake looking so solemn?"

"Solemn. Did I look solemn? I did not mean to. I am so happy. You make me so happy."

"Then you must sleep. If you sleep, our dreams will meld together, and even while our bodies rest we can be together in our thoughts."

He smiled and rocked her toward his chest, kissing her on the eyelids as she rolled into him. He felt them flutter, then sensed a sudden inner chill that raised the flesh in small bumps along her spine.

"There it is again," he said, "you are solemn. What is bothering you? You make me worry."

"It is I who am worried. I saw your face tighten yesterday when the papers came. Then I saw you leave. Did you go to him? Was it something about the campaign that is coming?"

"Magdalene. I promised that I would tell you as soon as I knew anything. The papers I received were just reports. By themselves they mean nothing. But I am duty bound to report their contents to Wellington."

"Reports of what?" Her question was direct, not harsh. She was sure that there was something of alarm in the papers, or else her husband would not have left so abruptly for the duke's headquarters. It was not so distant that he would have had to rush. Only a sense of urgency would have compelled Sir William to go to him that quickly.

"For some days now, the border has been closed. Nothing is moving across it—not merchants, not travelers, not mail, not anything. It is unusual, but it could very well be a defensive action by the French, who do not want us to post advance elements inside France.

"Yesterday, observers from our side of the border reported sightings of large concentrations of French soldiers. Those too may be defensive formations."

"But they might be offensive." She finished the thought for him. So the fighting could come earlier than her husband had said. She knew that when the two sides came together her husband would be in danger.

"They might be on the offensive, but it does not seem likely. The French could not be in any position to move. They have not yet completed the mobilization of their army. And even if they have, the usual tactics don't call for the smaller force to go on the offensive. Don't worry. There is time yet." He smiled that gentle smile of his. She warmed immediately and smothered him with kisses. He responded, and she could feel his lips turn upward into a smile. For a few moments the anxiety left her as both of them lost themselves in one another.

After a while, he spoke. "I must go to the Spanish ambassador's tonight for dinner."

"Yes. I know. You must go. We have probably gone past the point of forgiveness in turning down dinner invitations."

"And after that, there is the ball being held by the duchess of Richmond. Do you have a proper gown ready?"

"Of course. I am told that this will be the gala of the season. All the officers will be there, and all the ladies here in Brussels. Do you think I would let you look upon them if I were not properly attired myself?"

He laughed. "I will not see a one of them. I will see only you."

"Oh, I think perhaps you will notice the others. But I am happy that you should do your dancing with me."

"And I too, Magdalene. I too."

They became quiet. The first light of the early dawn was breaking into the sky. In June in Belgium the day came early and stayed late. A few birds chirped their welcome to the coming light. It was a peaceful sound, and for a moment Magdalene felt completely happy. The deepening breathing of her husband told her that he had drifted off again. She lay still so as not to disturb him.

Her mind drifted to the duke of Wellington. She wondered if he was awake yet in his house only a few doors down. He seemed such a restless soul. She wondered if he ever slept.

Oh, he could look aloof and completely at ease. But if it fooled his men, it did not fool her. Once or twice in the last week she had seen him in the street, from her window. His eyes always seemed so alert, as if he were probing with them, sifting through information, making judgments, analyzing whomever he was talking to at the moment, taking the measure of their worth, trying to see if they comprehended what he was saying to them, and if he should listen to what they were saying to him. A cold one, that one. The thought of him made her shiver, and she eased the sheet up around her neck.

Sir William did not speak of him much, but clearly he admired him. They were good friends, she knew, as much as a subordinate and a senior could be friends. She had heard the gossip about his wandering ways even before she arrived, and had heard it again from the ladies she had spoken to here in Belgium. But Sir William had never said anything of it, and she certainly would not raise it with him.

She wondered, though, if it were true. He was a married man, although from what she had been told there was not much romance in the union. But he was so mature, even stately. Could he possibly seek the companionship of young girls, as so many of the women reported? It did not seem possible. After all, he was the leader of an army; a lord; and, until recently, the emissary of his country at Paris and then in Vienna. People liked to gossip so. And they said such cruel things.

No matter the scandal about the duke of Wellington. Sir William was her husband, and there had never been a hint of scandal about him. How could there be? He was such a good man. She had seen that from the first. If there was anything that drove him, it was his sense of duty. He was so proud to be a soldier and so determined to meet his responsibilities with every ounce of his energy. It was the only thing that took him from her. And she knew that, in time, she would overcome it. Their love would displace everything in the end. Of that she was sure. Contented, she drifted off to sleep at last.

Jamioulx, on the French-Belgian Frontier: 0800

Napoleon's mouth opened into a gaping yawn. A wide draft of air sucked up into his lungs, then came rushing out in a downdraft of fatigue. He shivered in the morning mist and felt his hunger. He spied the abbey to his front and turned his horse toward the churchyard. Perhaps he could find something to eat there. After four and a half hours in the saddle, it was time to have some breakfast.

It was going to be a warm day. He could see daylight trying to burn through the morning mist. The grass was wet and cool to his horse's feet, but soon the sun would dry the dew. The movement of his army would be going forward smoothly if it weren't for the trenches and fallen trees barring the way along the major roads. The allies must have been working through the night to block the advance. The emperor cursed under his breath. It would require work and time to clear the way, and time was of overwhelming importance now. The attack was on. He had to concentrate before the enemy could react.

All in all, though, he was satisfied with the opening moves of the campaign. Closing the frontier had been the essential thing. It had blocked all flow of information to Wellington, save the obfuscations and confusions Napoleon had deliberately seeded into the picture. For that reason the French had been able to concentrate almost one hundred thirty thousand men within miles of the Sambre River, with Beaumont as the center of mass. Wellington and Blücher had kept their armies spread all the way across Belgium from Tournai and Ghent in the west to Liège in the east. Thus, the French force could take on the allied army, almost twice its size.

Napoleon felt satisfied with himself. It had been a masterful feat—pulling together an army, reestablishing political order, appointing his

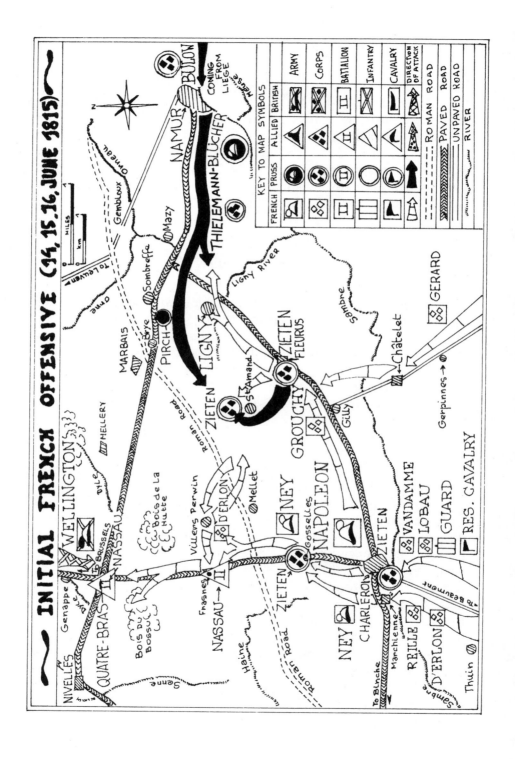

INITIAL FRENCH OFFENSIVE (14, 15, 16, JUNE 1815)

generals and their staffs, calling up the recruits, outfitting them, and moving them into position. And this in the face of overwhelming hostility from the whole of Europe. No one else could have done it. Let those who doubted his continued genius take note. He was yet a force to be reckoned with.

Still, there are some disturbing signs. The Prussians seem to have detected my intentions, at least to some degree. There has been movement during the night—if the spies are correct—and even now they seem to be reacting to the front. That would be Zieten's corps. Too bad. I would have preferred complete surprise. I was hoping that old man Blücher would be too sound asleep to be disturbed. I doubt his staff would awaken him. It must be his chief of staff, Gneisenau, giving the orders. He is a cunning one. Probably has more sense than my own chief, Soult. But Gneisenau is not the commander, and in the end it is command that counts for everything. There I will beat them. Neither Blücher nor Wellington will measure up. One is old, the other weak. They are no match for me singly, and together they will merely reinforce each other's weaknesses.

Besides, complete surprise is not imperative. It only matters that I catch them in the early stages of their concentration. I can do that now. With three columns advancing on Charleroi—Lieutenant General Reille from the west by Marchienne au Pont; Lieutenant General Vandamme in the center, directly along the main road to Brussels; and Lieutenant General Gérard in the east, by Châtelet—I can split the Prussians away from the allied army under Wellington and defeat each of them in detail. Already I can see my good General Pajol's light cavalry corps in the center, advancing on Marcinelle, on the outskirts of Charleroi.

"Good day, gentlemen, and welcome. My name is Abbé Jenicot."

"Good day, Father. You have the honor of welcoming the emperor of France to Belgium." It was Soult speaking.

"*Mon Dieu!* What an honor indeed. Sire, I am completely at your disposal. What may I do for you?"

"Perhaps a small snack. Your emperor is hungry." Napoleon's eyes twinkled. He enjoyed claiming the Belgians as his subjects.

"But of course. And perhaps a glass of red wine to go with it?"

"Abbé, you know how to please. If all goes well on this campaign, I shall make you a bishop."

The priest pulled up his black robe and walked rapidly toward the kitchen, his face reddened by the flattery from Napoleon. The emperor and the skeleton staff accompanying him dismounted. They could hear firing to the north, in the vicinity of Marcinelle. Zieten's Prussians were holding up the crossing over the Sambre, just south of Charleroi.

A rider approached. The guards stopped him and, after a quick discussion, allowed him to advance to the emperor. The chief of staff closed in to hear the conversation.

"Sire, I bring news from General Vandamme." The speaker was General Rogniat, chief of engineers.

"Yes, what is it?" Napoleon looked impatient, apprehensive.

"Sire, he regrets that he received no orders this morning for the movement, and only now has learned what you expect him to do. He says that he will be on the road shortly."

"Shortly! Shortly! He was to be moving by 0330. What does he mean he received no orders? Soult, did you not send the orders?"

"Yes, Sire. I did. I signed and dispatched them myself. In ample time for General Vandamme to receive them, I might add."

"Then why did he not receive them?" Napoleon was curt, angry now. Problems of this sort had not occurred when Berthier had been his chief of staff. But he was dead now, killed in an accident two weeks earlier.

"Sire, the news is that the messenger was injured on his night ride. He fell from his horse and broke his leg. It is only just before I came to you that we learned of this." It was Rogniat.

"Soult, how many messengers did you dispatch? Just one?"

"Yes, Sire. The hour was late, and I had many messages to send."

The emperor bit his lip. It was idiocy. Sheer idiocy. Messages of importance must be sent with several riders. One messenger might fail to arrive. Now there would be no infantry supporting in the middle. The smallest roadblock would set the movement back, if it was defended by troops in any way. No wonder the chief of engineers brought the message. He could not make progress overcoming the obstacles without infantry from Vandamme. And all because Soult did not see fit to send out a second rider. Berthier would not have allowed that. He always sent at least two; often three; and even four, if the message was a critical one. If only Berthier were not dead. He was badly needed now. That Soult is an incompetent. He even forgot to give the orders for the concentration around Beaumont to the four corps of the cavalry reserve. It was only through the intervention of Marshal Grouchy that the error was caught and corrected on 12 June, barely in time to salvage the plan.

"I wonder at the excuse of Vandamme. Did he not realize that troops were moving all around him? Did not anyone on his staff have a curiosity as to why major formations of brigades and divisions were coming down the road, trying to get through his bivouac? What do I have there? A prima donna? If I do not tell him what to do, does he do nothing? Does he not post guards? Does he not make plans? Does he feed himself? Or does he wait until I send him an order?" The emperor's temper was rising. He could feel his blood pounding, caught himself, and stopped his line of questioning.

"Have the Guard pick up the lead in the center. I must have infantry there, and quickly." Napoleon had contained his anger. After all, he had picked Soult as his chief, above his protests. He would stick with him, compensating for his ineptitude whenever necessary. And Vandamme. Yes. He was an idiot. He liked to stand on ceremony. Everyone else was at fault. Never him. But Vandamme had a point. He had received no orders. And it was the middle of the night. The mind plays tricks in the darkness.

"General Rogniat."

"Yes, Sire!"

"Press your men into action. I mean to move forward on all three columns, with lateral communications maintained. I understand that the lack of infantry is a hazard to your men, but you must press on. Time is of critical importance now. We have an advantage, and I mean to keep it."

"Very well, your Highness. We shall do our duty." With that Rogniat bowed and moved out, leaving the emperor staring at the plate of food the priest had set before him. He had that intense stare that seemed to blot out the world around him, a frightening look that made one think the man had lost all touch with reality, all identity with the here and now. That stare was becoming a more frequent habit, the sign of a mood that one dared interrupt with only great trepidation.

After what seemed a long while, Napoleon began to eat. He sipped the red wine. His mood seemed to have lightened. He caught the eye of the priest and raised the glass as if in a toast. The priest beamed, gave a little nod, and reddened again. He, at least, was having a great day.

But there was more bad news to be brought to the commander. Soult had received it while Napoleon sat staring at his food, and he dreaded the moment when he would have to announce it. But Soult was not a coward. He would do his duty as well as he could, even though he had warned that he was better employed as a field commander than as a chief of staff. Soult, above all others, knew that he did not have the acumen for the job. He detested the position with all his soul. But if it was what the emperor wanted him to do, then he would do it as best he knew how.

"Excuse me, Sire, but I have some news."

"Yes, what is it, Soult?" Napoleon's face was almost kindly now. Soult could not know that he had thought through the consequences of Vandamme's delay and concluded that, even though it would slow French progress, it would not be fatal. His forces were still way ahead of the game. Only the Prussians seemed to have noticed there was any movement, and even they had not yet reacted strongly to it. There was still time to catch both armies before they could react.

"Lieutenant General Bourmont, commander of the 14th Division, moving with General Gérard's IV Corps on the right wing, deserted to the Prussians this morning. His entire staff went with him."

"The bastard." It was all that Napoleon could say.

Soult continued. "General Gérard has spoken to the men, who have been shocked by the traitorousness of their commander. He has explained the treacherous act in full detail and gotten them to curse Bourmont's name. They are ready, in fact eager, to march. But the confusion has cost us several hours on the right."

"Yes. Yes. I see." Napoleon kept his thoughts to himself. He was sick of traitors. He considered many of his own marshals in that category. After all, had they not forced him to abdicate a year ago last April? Had not Ney himself, only this March, promised to arrest him after his return from Elba and bring him back to Louis XVIII in an iron cage? There was too much treachery in the French army. What had gone wrong with it? He, Napoleon, had made these men. He had brought them greatness and glory, given them riches and rank, elevated their status from the lowest to the highest level. And what did he get in return? Loyalty? No, not loyalty. They would cut him down the instant things began to go against the French cause. They had no loyalty to France, only to themselves.

But I need them. I cannot do it all alone. I can do much of it, but I am not as young as I used to be. I cannot be everywhere, and when fighting more than one army I will need commanders on the ground at each critical point of the action. For that reason I called up Ney from Normandy a few days ago. Ney arrived at Beaumont on 14 June, without staff and without baggage, and immediately purchased two horses from General Mortier. That was good, because although I have not told him yet, when he joins me today I will give him command of the left wing—two corps of infantry, two regiments of chasseurs, and the lancers of my Guards. And Grouchy—the famed cavalry officer who has contributed so much to the mobilization and concentration effort—he will receive command of the right wing. But I will be with him on that avenue; he will have only nominal command. The emperor commands wherever he happens to be. The trick is to put myself in the right place at the right time. And at that, no one is better than I.

"Oh, Soult. We have our problems. But no move goes forward without its little starts and stops. It is our job to keep pushing. We must force our way between Wellington and Blücher. I do not mind if Blücher comes forward to fight. Let him. By the time he brings his forces together, I will have him crushed. And as of yet, we see no movement by the British. That is all to our favor. If they stay scattered, they can never force a union with the Prussians. They will remain isolated, and then I will defeat them.

"Has my proclamation been read to all the soldiers?"

"Yes, Sire, as you ordered. It was read yesterday morning and was received with cheers of long life to you."

"Bring me a copy. I want to see it again."

Soult sent an aide for his pouch and produced the document. Napoleon donned his spectacles and read.

"Soldiers, today is the anniversary of Marengo and Friedland. Victory will be ours. . . . For all true Frenchmen the time has come to conquer or to perish. . . ."

Good words! Those are good words. Conquer or perish. Yes. That's all there was to it. There was no time for timidity. We cannot sit in France and expect to be victorious. The logical end of defense can only be defeat. It is with the attack that one seizes the initiative, and only then can victory be achieved.

I must defeat my enemies before they can mass against me. It is me they have declared war on. But it is not against me that they make war; it is against the Revolution. They have never seen in me anything but the representative of the Revolution. And that is what they hate. That is what they fear. I will undo them all. They cannot stand up against the Revolution. There is a new order to things. Even to war. And that is where I will beat them. They are too slow. They have never grasped the simple fact that war is movement. They are sloggers. They grapple and hold. I move and smash, smash and move.

"My map. Let me see my map." Napoleon called out to no one in particular, certain that all within hearing would see to it that his order was met. Within a few seconds, his map was placed before him.

Quatre-Bras. There is where I will separate them once and for all. Wellington will mass at Nivelles. He cannot know my plan of attack. Even now, with all the movement against Charleroi, he cannot be sure it is not a feint. He will look to his flank. He will extend out to the Channel, covering his lines of communication. But it will do him no good. I will cut him off from Blücher by seizing Quatre-Bras while I defeat the Prussians wherever they choose to fight. And they will fight. I know those Prussians. I know Blücher. He will not think; he will fight. And then I will have him, for without Wellington he is too weak.

In the end, I have taken the simplest approach. They worried about an attack on the right, an attack on the left. Each of them feared that I would go for their flank. Even now I have reports that Blücher fears that I seek to go around him from Luxembourg. Yet all the while, I come at them by the straightest route. Right up through Charleroi toward Brussels. It could not be more direct.

Yet it will be good enough. For the genius is not in the direction, it is in the speed. Speed breeds surprise. It will happen so fast that they will not be able to react. Even with all these delays, the campaign is mine. For I know how to move, like no other general before me. Certainly better than Blücher or Wellington.

He lifted his glass of wine and drained its contents, then looked up and spied the priest, knowing he would still be standing, watching, waiting. "Yes, Father. You will be a bishop. And I, once again, will be emperor of Europe."

4

LIGNY: 16 JUNE 1815

Blücher shifted his position in the saddle. The sun was past its apex, struggling to cut through the heavy haze that so often obscured the sky over dreary Belgium. But if the sky was obscure, Napoleon's plans were not. Marshal Blücher understood them fully now. After thirty hours of developments to his front, it did not take a genius to figure out what the French devil had in mind.

The old man had to admire the simplicity of the plan. Not a strategist himself, and caring little that others might realize it, he could not appreciate the finer points of his opponent's design. Gneisenau, his chief of staff, would worry about that. But it was clear that the emperor had brought his *Armée du Nord* to fight. Blücher had to respect that. It was what a great general should do, after all.

The key had been Charleroi. The French had massed there the previous morning. They had taken the town from three directions, then driven up toward the Namur-Nivelles road. The army split into two major wings, with large reserves held back in the center. For a while that had confused the Prussian general. Why split your force, especially when facing superior numbers? That would be the tactics of a madman—or a very bold general.

It was the deserter who had made it clear. What was his name? Oh, yes! Bourmont, the commander of the French 14th Division. What a despicable son of a bitch. Blücher spat as if a great distaste had formed in his mouth. The very thought of a general who would abandon his troops as they were about to enter combat was repulsive to the old soldier. Lieutenant General Bourmont had been the commander of the spearhead division of the French right wing. Within hours of the start of the invasion on 15 June, he had abandoned his men to their fate. He had even sent a letter back to his soldiers, the field marshal had been told, with some kind of prattle as to how much he loved them and that he would never give any information that might bring them harm. Yet when he was brought before the Prussian commander, he had been tripping over himself to talk. What hypocrisy.

Ha! I dealt with him as a soldier would—with utter contempt. Gneisenau wanted me to speak to him, to hear him out. That's Gneisenau for you. Anything to help the cause. But not for me. I wouldn't speak with him. My chief pointed out that I should listen, that he was now wearing the Bourbon cockade, an ally loyal to Louis XVIII. "Cockade be hanged," I told him. "A coward is always a coward." Ha! That was a good one. The men heard it. They will pass it on, and they will respect me for it.

And it cost me nothing. Gneisenau got the information that was necessary. That Gneisenau's a sharp one. Thank God for him. He put together the covering action before Charleroi all yesterday, allowing us to concentrate here at Ligny, giving the original orders even before I awoke. That was well done. But he doesn't think about inspiring the troops. Efficiency. Just efficiency. That's his forte. Good. That's what we need—efficiency. Until the battle is brought. Then we need energy, and I give the men that.

Napoleon has us in a tough spot, though. If that bastard French deserter had it right, the imperial runt means to split us from Wellington. Well, it looks like he's done it. Wellington is twelve kilometers to the west at Quatre-Bras. The emperor's pinned him there with his left wing, and he's forming up now to attack me with his right. If Wellington tries to join me along the Nivelles-Namur road, Napoleon will catch him in a lateral move. The same goes for me. The only way we can link up now is by retreating farther to the north, and that will just encourage Napoleon to pursue.

We'll just have to fight him here. That suits me fine. Here's as good as anywhere. We're in a better position than the British and their Dutch friends. They are still forming up. Where was Wellington yesterday anyway? Gneisenau tells me he was escorting some young girl to a cricket match. Those English! Polite little sporting events, and polite little lecheries. Blücher laughed at his own joke, provoking a glance from Lieutenant Colonel Nostiz, his aide-de-camp.

And where were they last night? Müffling reported that they were at a ball in Brussels. A ball! Can you imagine that? These British are a strange lot. It is an interesting way to go to war. They seem almost disinterested, as if battle were just one of a number of frivolous pastimes that competed for their time.

Well, it's not a frivolous pastime to me. It's what I'm all about. If Napoleon is eager to fight, he is no more so than I. Let him come. What can he do? He has split his forces, but I have brought to bear all but one of my corps, and with luck that one will arrive in time for the action as well.

The clarity of thought faded from his mind. His age was setting in again. It happened more frequently now, but he barely noticed it. In the back of his mind would be a slight gnawing as if he should be thinking about something. But there was a great comfort in not thinking. It calmed the nerves, relaxed the mind. Perhaps it was not so bad. As long as one had a good chief of staff to look after the details. And good subordinates as well. Yes, that was a comfort. Good corps commanders: That was what good armies were all about.

The field marshal's mouth softened into a contented smile. Nostiz saw the look, recognized it, and knew in an instant that his commander was no longer focused. His mind had wandered away, lost in the clouds. The aide was pleased about that. It was not good for his general to think too much. It made him irritable, put him out of sorts.

Wellington would be arriving soon. A rider had come in a short time ago to announce that the allied commander was coming for a coordination visit before the battle. Blücher would have to be alert then, but that would be no problem. Wherever his mind had wandered, it was easy to get back. His dimness had not gotten bad yet. Later perhaps, in a year or so, or maybe even a few months. But not now.

Nostiz looked up to the old man, admired him for his daring and courage. Blücher knew his own limitations and understood them. He was ancient, well past any reasonable age for battle. Yet he could fight. Would fight. More than any man in the army, he hungered for combat. It was a game to him—a great game. And he was good at it. Better than men half his age. No, better than men a third his age. He was indomitable. His will was irresistible. Nothing could daunt him. He was like an adolescent, full of zeal and energy, willing to dare all for a glorious cause. He thought himself immortal, like a boy poised on the threshold of manhood, certain he would live forever, eternally young. Always ready for the fray. That was Blücher. Nostiz loved him like life itself.

To the front of the two men, sixty-eight thousand French had taken up their positions. In an amphitheater of gentle hills and small villages stretched over a six-kilometer front, Napoleon had positioned the forty-five thousand men of the right wing of his army under Marshal Grouchy. The remainder of the force, the Imperial Guard, constituted the reserves, which were under command of the emperor himself.

Napoleon had recognized his opportunity. He was looking to find either one of the opposing armies and defeat it in detail before turning on the other. It was the central concept of his master plan. Divide and conquer. That was why he had smashed up through Charleroi, the ideal point from which to split his enemies.

Napoleon had assumed that his first victim would be the British and Dutch under Wellington. But Blücher had presented himself first. The forward Prussian corps commander, Zieten, had put up a brilliant delaying action, but old Marshal Blücher had played right into French hands by rushing forward, then stretching himself thin just south of the Nivelles-Namur road. Exposed along a six-kilometer front on the forward slopes of the small hills—too widely spread to meet normal tactical requirements—the Prussians were offering themselves up for sacrifice.

Blücher did not realize it. He was confident, as always. Gneisenau had told him that they had eighty-five thousand men in the three corps he had mustered around Ligny. Along with their 216 guns, that should have been enough to do the trick.

But the Prussian commander had not calculated on Napoleon. The emperor was in his element—a campaign of movement. Every step so far in the campaign had been brilliant. When he saw the opportunity presented at Ligny, he wasted no time in devising his plan. Already he had ordered Ney to fix the British at Quatre-Bras while he, with the bulk of his forces, hammered away at Blücher. Napoleon himself would fix the leftmost Prussian corps with his cavalry, while his infantry and cavalry wore down the enemy's center and right. Once the Prussians were sufficiently blooded, he would strike with the Imperial Guard, the French reserve, in the center. The result would be the annihilation of the Prussian army and its ultimate retreat from the battle and out of the campaign. A simple plan, but one that the "master of Europe" was confident he could execute.

"Marshal Blücher. Wellington has arrived." Nostiz had spied a small group of riders approaching the windmill at Bussy and recognized them as British by the cut tails of their horses.

Slowly Blücher turned to look at his aide, recognized him, then followed his extended arm and finger in the direction they pointed. At first he did not comprehend what he had been told. Then his mind focused and he remembered the anticipated meeting.

"Have General Gneisenau join us." Blücher spoke quietly to Nostiz, then spurred his horse toward the windmill. He could see Wellington's studied look of disinterest. It was a superb affectation. What magnificent arrogance. A great battle in the offing, and the commander in chief of the allied army was as aloof as he might have been at an afternoon tea.

Riding next to Wellington was the Prussian liaison officer, Baron von Müffling. Blücher was glad to see him. He knew he was a good general staff officer, knew he would do his duty.

"Good afternoon, my dear General." Blücher's face reddened with the exuberance of his cheery greeting.

Wellington nodded, gave a faint smile, and touched his hat. "Good afternoon, Marshal Blücher. It looks as if the French have made their selection. Are you ready for a contest?" The duke had noticed the positions of the Prussians and had not liked what he had seen. They were exposed on the forward slopes, spread among the many villages, the brigades out of musket range of one another. The only mutual support would be artillery fire. Even the reserves were too far forward, in range of the French artillery. Napoleon's guns had the high ground. They would be able to see down into the Prussian positions, and from their greater height, they could range farther than Blücher's guns.

"I am ready, Wellington." The broad smile remained on Blücher's face as Gneisenau came riding up. Wellington saw the chief of staff approaching and noticed the disdain on his face. He knew that the Prussian did not like him, did not trust him.

"Good day, General Gneisenau." Once again the duke touched his cap. The Prussian gave a short bow, jerking his head stiffly toward his chest.

"I believe that Napoleon means to open battle with you. How may I help?" Wellington ignored the distrust in Gneisenau's eyes.

"Perhaps you could send us a few of your brigades. Von Bülow's corps is yet to arrive, and we could use more men." It bothered Gneisenau to admit that he had not fully concentrated all his forces. Though he had performed a Herculean feat by bringing together three of the four corps behind Zieten's delaying action, he was a perfectionist who sensed his failures more than his accomplishments.

"I am afraid that I can spare no men." Wellington answered coldly. "I have little doubt that Napoleon will commit his left wing against me at Quatre-Bras. If he smells the opportunity, he could very well shift his reserves against me there."

"Is that the problem, or is it that your men have not yet arrived in force?" Gneisenau's question was just a little too sharp. Wellington's neck stiffened, and he hesitated before he replied. It was true that the allies had dallied. The duke just had not believed that Napoleon would strike as rapidly as he had. Only at the ball the night before had he realized that the reports he had been hearing since late on 14 June were true. Napoleon had humbugged him. And the damned Prussians knew it.

Müffling seized the moment to diffuse the tension. "My Lord. Perhaps you could concentrate toward Frasnes and open an attack on the French left."

"I would prefer that the Dutch-British forces move along the Namur road to act as reserves for our own forces." Gneisenau would not hold his tongue.

"Somerset, pass me my map if you please." Wellington turned to his aide as he held his temper in check. He would be hanged if he would allow himself to be placed under Blücher's orders. For several minutes he studied the map, seemingly engrossed, while the Prussians talked amongst themselves, irritated with the Englishman's aloofness. At last Wellington looked up and caught Gneisenau's eye, but was careful to appear as if he were speaking to no one in particular.

"It would seem to me that there are some opportunities here to make better use of the terrain. By God, use every hillock, every tree, wall, ridge, and slope for cover. Cheat the enemy's artillery. Make it as difficult for their cavalry and infantry as possible."

He could see Gneisenau redden as von Müffling translated his rapid-fire remarks. Now Wellington turned and spoke directly to Blücher. "Everybody knows their own army best; but if I were to fight with mine here, I should expect to be beat."

Blücher's smile never left his face, even as Müffling interpreted the message, unable to blunt its pointedness. Without hesitating he replied, "My men are assembled as you see them on the forward slopes because they like to see their enemy."

The duke looked at the Prussian commander and his chief and realized that he had been too direct. There would be no moving them now. Even if Blücher reconsidered, Gneisenau would never budge. There was too much hatred in his eyes.

"It remains for us to assist one another if the opportunity arises. My guess is that it will be difficult. I shall come if I am not myself attacked, but I do not think I will have the liberty." Wellington spoke his mind. Arrogance had not worked. He concluded it was best to be honest. He realized that no agreements would be reached as to how best to coordinate their efforts. The most he could hope for was a promise of support. Already too much time had been spent in the meeting. The fighting would be sure to begin soon. He looked again at the poor dispositions of the Prussians. Müffling translated his last statement, and he heard Blücher's response.

At last, the liaison officer spoke. "Marshal Blücher says he is prepared to do battle. If it is possible, he will join you when it is necessary."

So that was it: a tentative agreement to link up—"If it is possible." It wasn't much. Would he really do it? Could you trust these Prussians? Not Gneisenau, that was for sure. But Blücher? Maybe—if he was really in control and his chief did not outmaneuver him. But who could be sure? Well, at least they will fight. I can count on that much. Beyond that it would be best to rely on ourselves.

Wellington nodded his head, tried not to show his concern. "Thank-you, gentlemen. I had best be heading back. Good luck." He spurred his horse and moved out at a steady gait, his staff following behind, silent, not sure what to make of the conference they had just witnessed.

Blücher watched them go. There was something about Wellington that he liked. Much courage there, he thought. An Englishman's courage—controlled, understated, almost gentlemanly. But it was courage, nonetheless. That was good. You could rely on a man with courage. Well, we Prussians have courage too. You will see. You will see, Wellington. Just wait. He turned his attention back to the front. A battery of the French Imperial Guard had just fired three shots. The attack had begun.

All along the line, the French artillery opened up. The first rounds went long. Drums began to beat among the ranks of the *Armée du Nord* as the French infantry started forward. The next artillery volley fell short of the Prussian lines, completing the bracket. Napoleon had directed Vandamme's corps to spearhead the attack on the hamlet of Saint Amand, while the cavalry under Pajol's I Cavalry Corps and Exelmann's II Cavalry Corps moved to fix the Prussian left. It would be a combined-arms attack, in the grandest tradition of the emperor's genius. The artillery found the range on the third volley and began to tear into the Prussian ranks. Men were blown apart before they could fire a shot, before they saw the faces of their opponents. Wellington had been right. It was a duck shoot. Round shot tore into the ranks, bowling men over with a horrible, crushing force. Grapeshot tore through flesh in great hunks, splattering the survivors with the gore of their countrymen. There was nothing to be done about it. Close ranks, look to the front. Then another volley, and more carnage.

The sky rained death, while under it all the infantry closed step-by-step, determined, inexorable. French skirmishers crept up through the rye, driving back the Prussian pickets, trying to break the morale of the defenders. The afternoon sun had broken out, beating down on the combatants below. The cries of the wounded were mixing with the rattle of musketry and the crash of the artillery. Prussian generals worried about the greenness of their troops. They were untested. Raw recruits. Earlier in the campaign, there had been some rebelliousness. Blücher had put it down ruthlessly, meting out soldier's justice in the Prussian manner. It had stiffened the ranks, but that was before the fighting had begun. Would they hold up in the face of this? These were not amateurs coming at them. The French army had been reconstituted from the ranks placed on half pay during the emperor's exile. They were veterans who had known the soldier's lot in peace—neglect, scorn, disuse. They were eager for the spoils of war, for the glory of victory, for the exhilaration of the kill. They were disciplined, coming on in good order, bayonets at the ready, and led from the front by brave officers not afraid to die.

The Prussian artillery tried to find the French guns. It was an uneven duel. Napoleon knew how to move the artillery, and the superior heights of the French guns gave them great advantage. Already the emperor had found the Prussian reserves—positioned as they were on the forward slopes—and picked them apart. Units front and rear were being butchered, and still the French had enough left over to bring the

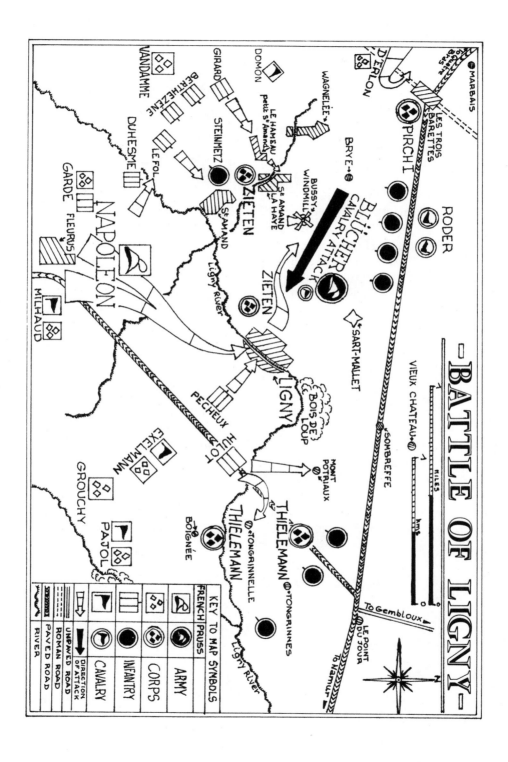

BATTLE OF LIGNY

KEY TO MAP SYMBOLS

	FRENCH	PRUSS	
ARMY			
CORPS			
INFANTRY			
CAVALRY			
DIRECTION OF ATTACK			
UNPAVED ROAD			
ROMAN ROAD			
PAVED ROAD			
RIVER			

MILES

kms

To Gembloux

LE POINT DU JOUR

To Namur

VIEUX CHATEAU

SOMBREFFE

MARBAIS

LES TROIS BARETTES

D'ERLON

PIRCH I

RODER

BRYE

BUSSY WINDMILL

Ste AMAND LA HAYE

ZIETEN

St AMAND

BLÜCHER

CAVALRY ATTACK

ZIETEN

SART-MALLET

STEINMETZ

LE HAMEAU

petit Ste Amand

WAGNELÉE

DOMON

GIRARD

BERTHEZENE

VANDAMME

DUHESME

LE FOL

NAPOLEON

GARDE

FLEURUS

MILHAUD

Ligny River

PECHEUX

LIGNY

BOIS DE LOUP

MONT POTRIAUX

THIELEMANN

ST-TONGRINNELLE

THIELEMANN

TONGRINNES

BOIGNÉE

PAJOL

GROUCHY

EXELMANN

Ligny River

Prussian guns under fire. Disadvantaged in the low ground, Blücher's artillery was blasted apart, impotent, unable to reach the French guns with counterbattery fire.

French voices could be heard above the din. *"Vive l'empereur! Vive l'empereur!"* Again and again the chant rose from ten thousand throats. It was their war cry, an allegiance forged in death and glory, a talisman granting immortality. French musket fire began taking its toll. The Prussians, out of mutual supporting range, were being overwhelmed by the concentrated fire. The standing, unsheltered ranks of the defenders were riddled. They could not move, caught by artillery and infantry, pinned by cavalry. They would have to stand and die, taking as many of the French with them as they could.

The villages caught fire, throwing a scorching blanket over the already stultifying atmosphere. Hurt and broken men could not pull themselves out of the flames. Their friends could not pause in their fighting to help them. The horrible screams of burning men added to the deafening cacophony.

Whipped by the musketry and prodded by the bayonet, the Prussians fell back from the villages. Saint Amand fell. Wagnelee fell. Saint Amand la Haye fell. But the defenders proved they were up to the task and came back, driving the French out from the villages they had just taken. Reserves from both sides bled into the battle. The villages fell again, were retaken once more. Dead and wounded littered every nook and cranny of the dwellings, the slopes, the roads, and fields.

In Ligny the storm was greatest. An entire French corps was committed against the little village, inundating it with death. Locked in hand-to-hand combat, men fought in the church, through the houses, the old castle, and on both sides of the little brook that split the town. Lunging at each other, men tripped over corpses. The wounded cowered behind the dead, hoping the fleshy barriers would protect them from being hit again. The brook became choked with bodies, its reddened water rerouted in countless rivulets as it sought the easiest path around the carnage.

In the west, Ney had begun his attack on Wellington. The Prussians would have to fight alone, and although they were still in possession of the villages by 1700, the French had yet to commit the bulk of their reserves. Lobau's VI Corps of ten thousand men was only now approaching the battlefield. In a great lapse, Napoleon had forgotten to order them up from Charleroi earlier in the day. At 1530 he had realized the oversight and sent the order, but he knew they could not cover the 15 kilometers in time to affect the outcome.

But there were still the eighteen thousand men of the Imperial Guard and eight regiments of *cuirassiers* from Milhaud's corps. The emperor was about to order them in to finish the Prussians when the inexplicable happened. A large mass of infantry, cavalry, and artillery was fast approaching the French left rear near Fleurus. Who could they be? Prussians or French? If French, well and good. But why would they be approaching from that direction? If Prussian, then there was grave danger that the right wing of the French army had been flanked. This could be disaster. Napoleon hesitated. He had to be careful. He would wait for the final attack, allowing forces to shift left to cover his flank—just in case.

Blücher saw the large formation as well, and likewise had no idea what it could be. But what caused Napoleon to hesitate allowed Blücher to rush up still arriving soldiers to strengthen his defenses. The fire was up in the old man. For three and a half hours he had exhorted his men to greater efforts, but he knew that their suffering had been terrible. His hatred for the French burned hotter than any flame on the battlefield. He had looked the other way time and time again as Prussian soldiers took their revenge on captured French. This was a no-quarter battle. There would be no courtesies extended, no mercy given.

The battle had become a fight of dwindling reserves. Grouchy had done his job well on the French right. Cavalry had pushed back the Prussians from the easternmost forward villages, collapsing them in on the center and driving them rearward toward the Namur-Nivelles road. Blücher had concentrated on preserving his own right and center. But to do so he had funneled every spare troop into the fight. He tasked Thielemann's III Corps, barely holding on the left, to send a cavalry brigade over to the right. Pirch's corps, comparatively intact, had been moved forward between Ligny and Saint Amand. They took their pounding in turn.

Confusion had set in over the battlefield. For the next forty-five minutes, men fought their individual battles, oblivious of the bigger picture. Junior officers gave their orders, uncertain of how the fighting was going only a few hundred meters to their left or right. Senior commanders threw more units into the fire, hoping that some good would come of it. Even the army commanders had lost sight of events. A formation of almost twenty thousand men loomed large on the horizon. Whose were they?

No man was more confused that day than Lieutenant General d'Erlon. It was his corps that had mysteriously appeared on the periphery of the battlefield. As far as the general knew, Napoleon had ordered him there. Even though d'Erlon knew that Ney had already begun his attack on the left, he complied with what he believed to be the written order of the emperor and moved toward Fleurus. But he was subordinate to Ney, who was now in desperate combat himself around Quatre-Bras. When Ney learned of d'Erlon's departure, he flew into a rage and dispatched a message firmly ordering d'Erlon to return to the battle at Quatre-Bras. Again d'Erlon followed orders, and just as Napoleon perceived that the unidentified mass on his left rear was in fact one of his own corps and wrote an order for it to move on Wagnelee, it began to fade away to the west.

Blücher learned the identity of the twenty thousand men at about the same time Napoleon did. He watched them moving away, as perplexed as he was when they had first appeared. He turned to Nostiz. "A piece of good luck, I would say. That is quite a force that is doing the French no good in either battle today."

"I do not understand it, Field Marshal." An experienced officer, Nostiz recognized the waste of resources for what it was—utter idiocy.

"Nor do I. But I know that we have gained an hour, and with the dark rain clouds closing in now, we may be able to pull out of this yet to fight again another day."

"General, listen! The French guns have stopped. The only heavy sound we now hear is the thunder off in the distance."

"You are right, Nostiz. Napoleon has reached a decision."

"Sir, I believe he means to commit the reserves. Look, the guns are being prepared for a barrage. It will be on us soon."

"Damn him. He knows how to use those guns. There will be a hot time on these slopes in a minute." The field marshal made no attempt to alert his subordinates. He knew that Gneisenau would have noted the change in tempo, deduced the consequences. Nor did he make any attempt to seek shelter. That was not the style of a hussar general.

What to do? What to do? I have done everything I can today. We have held Napoleon back all afternoon. But I am out of reserves. My ranks are depleted. Wellington will not come. I do not know what shape he is in, but he is cautious. He will hold where he is. Perhaps we can yet link up. Not today, but tomorrow perhaps—or the next day. But the burden will be on me. I told him I would come to him if I could, and I can see that if we survive today, I can yet do that.

I do not think we can hold the French reserves back. My men have fought well, much better than we could have hoped. But they have yet to see the French Immortals, the Imperial Guard. Bastards, all of them. But they never flinch. They have never lost. That counts for a great deal. I will give them a scare, but I do not think we can hold.

The only recourse is to gain the time for darkness to come. With darkness we can withdraw. The French will not pursue, not in the dark, not without having beaten Wellington. And they could not have beaten him yet. There are too many of them here. It is me they mean to destroy today. Thank God for the confusion with d'Erlon. That has saved us. If he is not at Quatre-Bras, then Ney does not have enough there to break Wellington. And if d'Erlon is not here, then I can gain darkness. But we will have to fight hard. And I will have to show my men how.

As one, the more than two hundred French guns opened up. The ground rose under the onslaught. The debris of battle was tossed into the air. Horsemeat and human flesh mingled with muskets, wagons, cannon, cooking pots, and powder boxes. Shattered buildings crumbled further, burying the wounded in mortar and debris. Fires that had almost burned down to nothing sprang up anew, finding new fuel to feed them as the cannonade tossed the living and unliving around like a great macabre salad.

Down into the amphitheater of death marched the Imperial Guard, the steady drumrolls keeping their step, though the sound of the movement was muffled by the greater sounds of competing artillery and thunder. Six thousand men were on the march, their flanks covered by *cuirassiers,* lancers, and hussars. Again Napoleon applied the overwhelming effects of combined arms—artillery, infantry, and cavalry working as one, each compensating for the weaknesses of the others. The French force seized the vulnerabilities of the enemy and pried them open, setting up the final defeat.

Blücher watched the charge of the 21st Prussian Regiment. Gallantly they went forward, only to be cut down by the *cuirassiers,* the French heavy cavalry—big, powerful, heavily armored men who could split a foe in two with a single swipe. An aide came riding up to the old marshal, reporting that the defenders in Ligny were out of ammunition. Blücher—his voice hoarse from the exhortations of the day, his face contorted with determination—rasped that they were to fight on with their bare hands. He yelled at the nearby 2d Squadron, 1st Westphalian Landwehr Cavalry, to charge the attacking Imperial Guard. Off they went, closing to within twenty meters of the French before being cut down by musket fire.

Everywhere, Prussian officers led the ranks of the fallen. On the battlefield alongside their soldiers, regimental and battalion commanders bled, indistinguishable in death from the troops they had led. Lieutenant Colonel Lützow took command of three shattered regiments that included four hundred men of his own 6th Uhlans and led them against the French. His desperate attack stopped their onslaught only long enough for the Imperial Guard to form square and rupture his makeshift unit. A moment later, the Immortals reformed in attack formation and were on the move again. All the while, the French artillery continued to pound the Prussian defenders.

"Nostiz, there is only one thing left to do." There was a fire in Blücher's eyes. "Pass the word that all Landwehr cavalry shall charge to cover the retreat of the infantry and the artillery. I shall lead the attack."

Nostiz stared at his commander, not daring to question the order. The septugenarian had made up his mind; it would not do to try to change it. As quickly as he could, Nostiz dispatched three younger aides to pass the order and returned to the side of Blücher.

The field marshal was already moving up and down the line, oblivious to the cannonade. The darkness was thickening now, heavy drops of rain falling from the black clouds overhead. There was an exhilaration in the man. He had become young again. The saber in his fist felt familiar, comfortable. It had sat too long in its sheath today. The sickly odor of horse and human sweat, the smell of gunpowder and death, the energy of the stallion underneath him, the roar of a thousand hoarse voices—all filled him with a sense of youth and vigor. With an unrestrained smile on his reddened face he turned and shouted to his cavalry, "Forward, my children. Forward!"

Thousands of hooves plowed into earth and bodies alike, thundering down the slope at the oncoming French. The air filled with musket fire, human and animal cries of pain and terror rose from the quickening darkness, leather creaked, saber clashed upon saber. Death was everywhere.

A musket ball tore into Blücher's magnificent mount, catching the stallion's left flank by the saddle girth. Nostiz saw the pop of the flesh, watched the beast gallop forward yet a few more steps, then begin to falter and stumble. He heard the old man call out, "Nostiz, I'm done for now!" and the aide stared helplessly as horse and rider fell to the earth.

The old man was pressed into the mud while his charger thrashed out desperately to stave off death. The horse rolled, tried to get up, then fell back, kicking its legs high into the air as French and Prussian cavalry trampled about, trying to kill anything in their path.

The aide jumped from his horse and ran to his commander. Pulling his pistol, he shot the stallion in the head and by the bridle pulled his own horse in closer, trying to form a break from the wave of cavalry crashing all around. Blücher had not moved from beneath his dead mount. Quickly, Nostiz dropped his own cloak over the old man's upper body and face, trying to conceal his medals from the prying eyes of the French. Drawing his saber with his free hand, Nostiz lashed out at the horsemen reeling all about him. The flow of the battle passed back and forth over the crumpled heap in the mud. For a while, only the French held the ground, but one last charge by the Uhlans brought the Prussians back momentarily.

"Quick there, soldier. This is your commander. You must help him." Nostiz had grabbed the bridle of a nearby Uhlan, who almost sabered him for his efforts. Then Nostiz stopped a half dozen troopers behind him. For a moment they stared in disbelief, but the ferocity of Nostiz's countenance encouraged them to unhorse themselves and remove the dead stallion from Blücher. The old man was still breathing as they threw him over a saddle and sped away in front of the counterattacking French.

Gneisenau knew the battle was lost. There was no chance to hold the ground any longer. Blücher was missing, probably dead. There were no options left. A retreat was the only way out. The chief of staff had himself been thrown from his horse. Bruised and battered, he tried to draw some order from the confusion of the night.

Regiments and battalions were broken, splintered into dozens of fragments. Officers were missing at every level, many dead, even more wounded. Resupplies could not find units; units could not find themselves. Wounded horses whinnied pitifully in the wet night. Broken men moaned or wept silently, some hoping to be found and saved, others hoping only that their misery would end soon. Wagons littered the roads. Drummers moved over the fields, beating the rallying cry of their respective regiments, hoping to draw in scattered units. Fires continued to burn everywhere, attracting the wounded and lost, adding confusion to the mixing and shifting of men. Desertion began to infect the ranks, the disease spreading to up to ten thousand. With over sixteen thousand casualties and with officers lost in the dark and not in control of their units, the least loyal troops, many from provinces until recently under French control, began to melt away. They took with them whatever they could carry, denying desperately needed resources to the army they left behind them and lessening the chances of survival of their fallen comrades.

In the midst of this chaos, Gneisenau faced a momentous decision. He sat with a handful of aides in a ruined building in a small settlement north of the Namur-Nivelles road. The village had been abandoned by its inhabitants. There was no food or water to be had. Wounded lined the walls of the moldy, smelly room, which was lit only by a small, flickering oil lamp. The chief of staff was seated on a barrel of pickled cabbages. Some of the wounded had tried to eat the contents, but the ensuing thirst had only made their condition worse. Their moans filled the room, adding to the gloom already pressing in on the general.

"Do we have any report of Blücher?"

"No, General. The best we have is a rumor that he is dead. Or in the hands of the French."

"What of Wellington?"

"Sir, only that he has been in action all afternoon at Quatre-Bras."

"A fat lot of help he has provided us today. That arrogant English snob. You would think he could have spared us a few troops. We must have had the bulk of the French on us." Gneisenau's eyes seemed black. Wellington was taking the brunt of his frustration.

"Sir, which way do we retreat?"

That was the question. Gneisenau recognized its import. If Napoleon worked his way around the left flank of the Prussian army, they would be cut off from Liège and their line of communication back across the Rhine. It would be disaster. But if the Prussian army fell back on Liège, the move would abandon the allies to the concentrated force of Napoleon. The result would be defeat in detail. And it would not be the promise that Blücher had made.

"What is the condition on the road to Liège?"

"It is a great confusion, General. The French are across it in several places. And to make matters worse, deserters have cluttered it.

Some of our officers have tried to stop them and been murdered for their efforts."

For a moment, the chief of staff stared at the debris-strewn floor of the room. A wounded soldier had soiled his trousers and the stench was overpowering. Flies were everywhere. The aides sat quietly, nervously looking at one another, avoiding the intense concentration in Gneisenau's eyes.

"We will march via Tilly to Wavre." The decision was made. It was not out of love of Wellington that Gneisenau had directed the Prussian army north, on a line parallel with the allies. It stemmed more from an appreciation that a direct move on Liège was now out of the question. It would be better to move farther north, covering their flanks, before pulling away to the east. The main thing tonight would be to gather in the army and get things under control. A retreat toward the Rhine at this stage could result in panic.

At the village of Mellery, seven kilometers north of Ligny, the old field marshal awoke. He felt the pain in his shoulder and leg, and he smelt the weird combination of brandy, gin, rhubarb, and garlic that had been rubbed into his bruises. A doctor hovered nearby.

"So, I have survived after all." Blücher looked delighted at the discovery.

"Field Marshal, you have been badly hurt. And the battle is lost." The doctor was surprised at Blücher's comment, his pleasant demeanor.

"What does the one have to do with the other?" The old man rubbed his shoulder, groaned when he tried to move his leg. "I stink. Give me a drink."

"Sir, you should not drink. It will lower your resistance."

"Resistance to what? Give me some brandy."

"Sir, I am a doctor. You must not drink brandy. If you must drink, then it should be something softer."

"Nostiz, my dear friend. I'm glad to see you are still here. Tell me, what do I have to drink?"

"Some champagne, Sir." The aide was delighted to see the marshal back to his cantankerous self.

"Well, then get me some. And have some yourself. You have probably earned it." Then to no one in particular he said, "Where is Gneisenau? And where is the English liaison officer? What is his name. Hardy? No, Hardinge. That's it. Where is he? I must have news of Wellington."

Nostiz responded. "We have already sent for Gneisenau. He will take a while to find, but I am told that he is well and has taken command of our forces. As for Hardinge, he is here in the outer room. But his condition is not good. His arm was amputated just a few minutes ago."

"I see. Well let the man sleep. I'll speak with him in the morning. Now get that champagne. And find some beer too. We will need it when Gneisenau gets here. He will probably be in one of his dour moods, and his spirits will need lifting."

The old man winked and chuckled to himself. It had been one hell of a day, and no doubt the army had suffered. But it would find itself in the morning, as long as he could get out to the men and share his good humor. The alcohol would help.

5

RETREAT: 17 JUNE 1815

0700

Like a thick fog, the confusion hovering over the twin battlefields of
Quatre-Bras and Ligny refused to yield to the dawn. A scarce 11 kilo-
meters apart, they might as well have been at distant ends of the earth.
The commanders at one had no earthly idea of the situation at the other.

Men lay dying in private agonies. But in the certainty of their death
they possessed knowledge superior to that of the survivors who had
sent them there. At least the dying knew what their future would hold.
They had only to make their peace and wait for the end—some more
eagerly than others, depending on the pain of their wounds.

For the senior generals there was no escape from the heavy responsibility before them. Napoleon knew he had secured a great victory
at Ligny. But how great? Were the Prussians broken? Were they in a
disorganized retreat? And if so, to where? A report just arrived from
Grouchy said that the Prussians were retreating in disorder along the
Namur road. Excellent, that was precisely what he had hoped for. But
should he believe it? And at Quatre-Bras, what had delayed Ney the
previous day? He had dawdled all morning when he should have been
attacking, before the British had reinforced the few Dutch that had
disobeyed orders and moved to hold Quatre-Bras. Why had Ney not
seized the crossroads yesterday? Surely he must have it by now. Wellington
would never offer himself by remaining that far forward once he knew

Blücher was defeated. What would the British do now that their Prussian allies were broken? They could not stay at Quatre-Bras. If they did, they would be easy prey for a quickly reunited French Army, its two wings brought together for a final crushing blow to a foolishly exposed allied army.

A few miles away Wellington knew only that he had held on to the crossroads. Ney's tardiness had saved him. Gradually, the duke had been able to bring in enough British troops to defend against a determined push. Had Ney attacked on the morning of 16 June, the French would have been successful. But Ney hesitated until, in the end, the allies were able to bring thirty-five thousand troops to bear against Ney's forty thousand. But to what end? What had become of the Prussians? Were they defeated? If so, to where would they fall back? Could they be relied on to honor their word and come to join him? Or would they fall back to the Rhine? And what of his own ally, the commander of the Dutch-Belgian forces, the prince of Orange? Could Wellington rely on him? The prince had been a total dunderhead the previous day. Only his subordinates' quick thinking and virtual disobedience of his petulant orders had salvaged any of the fighting. Could the prince of Orange be relied on to command any further? Would his own men follow him? And would the British? All night long the prince's own generals had bombarded the duke with complaints about the young man's childish tantrums and suicidal orders. Who would follow him now?

Nor could Grouchy, commander of the right wing of the French army, understand what was happening. He wanted to pursue the Prussians as early as possible, but instead he had received orders to meet with Napoleon to tour the battlefield at Ligny. What sense was there in that? Ligny was over; it was history now. Better to press on and finish the Prussians before they had a chance to get away. Those Prussians were an unpredictable lot. They lived for war. What would demoralize and break other armies might have no effect on them; they were too thick to understand defeat. Grouchy did not like letting them slip away from the battle unimpeded. He had sent a cavalry force along the Namur road to observe what they were doing, and the force had reported back that Blücher was retreating toward Liège. But was it really the main force the cavalry had seen? Perhaps they had only been deserters— the cavalry had said they were in great disarray. Grouchy had reported a Prussian retreat to the emperor, but in truth there was no way of being sure. Not yet—unless he could put his army on the march. Instead, he would meet with Napoleon and ride around the battlefield. It was absurd. Simply absurd!

Ney did not think; he could only be angry. All day yesterday, Napoleon had irritated him. First the emperor had pressed him into action at Quatre-Bras with the exhortation that the future of France was at stake. Then, when it was time to commit the reserves and take the crossroads, the marshal discovered that the emperor had ordered the reserves—d'Erlon's corps with twenty thousand men—away to Ligny. Madness. Sheer madness. Four thousand men had been lost in the day's fighting, and to no avail. Wellington still held Quatre-Bras. When Ney had learned of Napoleon's usurpation of his own command over the reserves, he had ordered d'Erlon to discontinue his march toward Ligny and return to Quatre-Bras. The corps commander had obeyed, but he had arrived too late. Now his as yet unblooded men sat, along with the rest of the left wing of the *Armée du Nord,* awaiting orders. What were they all to do? What had happened on the right? What did Napoleon have in mind? Where was he? To all these questions, Ney could think of no answer. He could only be angry, waiting to confront his commander when he arrived.

Of them all, only Blücher seemed to know what had happened. He had been beaten. It was that simple. Sixteen thousand men were missing from the rolls; the men were dead, wounded, or deserted. He was knocked out of Ligny and the surrounding villages, back across the Namur-Nivelles road, and away from his lines of communication. The French had interjected themselves between him and Wellington. The allies were split, badly beaten, with the French emperor between them, just where the ogre wanted to be. But it was not yet over. The old field marshal knew that as well. He had made a promise—that he would come to Wellington. He meant to keep it. It was clear that Gneisenau was indifferent to the promise. They had linked up before dawn and discussed the dispositions the chief had ordered in the commander's absence. The march back to Wavre had been merely a convenience, a point on the map that allowed the corps to orient while moving far enough away from the Namur road that they could find a safe place from where to fall back on Liège. But Blücher had changed the reference point to an objective. All the corps would move to Wavre, for it put them on a bearing due north, the only direction in which Wellington could go from Quatre-Bras. Not that the field marshal had heard from his British ally—it was difficult enough merely to coordinate with the scattered pieces of his own army. But it was the only thing that made sense. Surely Wellington could not hold at the crossroads. It would be suicide. So he would fall back toward Brussels, directly north of Quatre-Bras. The Prussians would move in parallel, keeping the distance between the two armies within a march. That way he could keep his word. It was a point of honor.

1100

He snapped out of his self-delusion with a start. Where had his mind been? It was almost noon. The day, which had begun to receive morning light before 0400, was now half spent. And he had done nothing. A great victory had been won over the Prussians at Ligny; even now the British and allied army sat exposed at Quatre-Bras. And he had done nothing!

The emperor backed away from the hastily erected field table and raised his small right hand a few feet from his hip, signaling his entourage to leave him alone. Silently the French general staff stepped away, noting the almost catatonic look overtaking Napoleon's face. He was thinking deeply, they could tell—not posturing for effect as he sometimes did— his face tensing and twisting with the troubling thoughts. Best to leave him alone at a time like this. His aides knew he would be difficult enough when he came out of it. But to interrupt him now would only cause him to turn his wrath upon them. Without speaking, barely daring to move, they sat astride their horses, waiting for Napoleon to complete his mental examination.

Step-by-step he retraced the events of the past night and morning. When the Prussians had withdrawn from the battlefield, he had gone back to Fleurus, where he had begun his day of battle. His orders had been sparse, giving word only that Ney should be there when the emperor arose. Grouchy had followed him to his headquarters and requested orders but had been put off with the response that he would receive his orders in the morning. And so through the night the French commander in chief had slept while both flanks of the army wallowed in confusion, not sure what the next moves might be.

Morning had brought no clarification. The visit by Ney did not occur. Instead an aide had arrived with a handwritten report from the marshal. Ney had failed to take Quatre-Bras. The report went on impudently to complain that the failure was a result of the emperor's usurpation of command of d'Erlon's corps. Napoleon had stared hard at the smudged handwriting, his eyebrows knitted in anger.

In the meantime, the entire *Armée du Nord* eagerly awaited orders, expecting to be told to pursue immediately, in the manner of past French victories. Instead, instructions went out to the victors at Ligny that they were to stand by for an inspection by the emperor. Grouchy again requested orders, receiving for his impertinence the retort that he would get his orders when the emperor was ready to give them.

By 0900 the tour of the battlefield had begun. Napoleon and Grouchy, along with their staffs, had visited the troops and received their cheers while the Prussians slipped away farther and farther from the danger of total destruction. The right wing of the French army was letting its prey escape, the prey it had so bloodily dislodged only the day before.

The realization sank into the emperor's head, startled him. He was dumbfounded by his own lethargy. What was happening to him? Increasingly, he had noticed of late, he was like two people. One was the Napoleon of old—energetic, insightful, quick, restless, able to see several moves ahead, able to catch others up in the force of his will and have them do his bidding. The other was an aged and tired man—apathetic, inattentive, unable to make sense of the many and contradictory reports arriving in random order. He was losing his ability to command.

His mind rebelled at the idea, fled to safer ground, and was brought back by the efforts of his iron discipline. It was true. There was no denying it. His powers were slipping. He could not ascribe the problem to the physical discomforts he had been experiencing. He was suffering pain, but he had been ill before. He could surmount those types of ailments. His will had always been too strong to be subdued. But it was not a question of will. To develop will you must first know what it is that you want. And to know that, you have to understand what had transpired and what could be made to happen. It was as if the comprehension of events—past, present, and future—was not there. Too early he became disinterested, distracted, almost frivolous. He was simply unaware, like a dolt who did not have the sense to appreciate what was going on around him. Until suddenly his mind cleared, as it had right now, and again the Napoleon of old returned.

He was angry with himself. But it was an anger he could not tolerate. His ego would not allow it. Quickly his venom turned toward his subordinates. What had they done to improve conditions? Soult barely seemed to know the condition of the army. His staff work throughout this whole campaign had been nothing short of abominable. He had given no orders, made no sense of the activities of the night, and formed no conclusion about the dispositions of the enemy. How much Berthier was missed! There was a chief of staff. Soult was a poor substitute, a wooden head.

And Ney. Had he moved yet against Quatre-Bras? Last night it did not seem possible that Wellington would stay there. But he had. He must be attacked now, before he got away, while the Prussians were reeling. All day yesterday Ney had dawdled, letting the opportunity slip from his hands. Again and again he had been told to take the crossroads. But he failed. What was wrong with him?

In this manner, the emperor gradually deflected his self-critique. He had not made the crucial errors, his subordinates had. He had given them a victory, but they had failed to capitalize on it. He had devised a brilliant campaign, but they had failed to comprehend it. Must he do everything himself? Could he not rest? Could he not take a night's sleep, a morning's visit to his soldiers to cheer them, to inspire them to yet greater efforts?

He turned his head and glared at his staff. There was the dullard Soult, sitting quietly, his arms folded, idly frittering away crucial minutes. And Grouchy. Why was he not with his soldiers, chasing after Blücher, driving him back on Liège? His eyes hardened. The small entourage a few meters away saw them narrow and braced itself for an onslaught.

"Grouchy, you must be off! Take your thirty thousand men and stay on the heels of Blücher. Don't let him move toward Wellington. I must catch him alone."

"Yes, Sire." The marshal was stunned. All morning he had urged, to the point of insubordination, that he be dispatched immediately to pursue. Fourteen hours had passed since the opportunity of the previous night. The Prussians would have a significant lead.

The emperor continued. "Soult. I will be moving to Quatre-Bras. I want every man and every gun that is not with Marshal Grouchy to be sent to me there. I will not let Wellington escape. Though we have lost time through an inexcusable dalliance, we can yet outmarch the British and their Dutch friends—provided Ney has taken the smallest steps to organize his forces for movement."

Soult, the warrior, felt the stinging criticism implied in Napoleon's words. It was almost more than he could stand. He hated the humiliation, knew that he was inept as a chief of staff, and understood the unfairness of the emperor's implications. Yet he bit his tongue. A riposte at this time would only bring further bitterness between commander and chief, and that was not needed at this juncture of the campaign.

It was not words that had stung the 28th Regiment of Foot. It was grape and shot, saber and lance that had laid low ninety-two men of all ranks. But on 16 June they had held for eight hours in open fields of rye against everything the French could throw at them—artillery, infantry, and cavalry. The North Gloucestershires were that inexplicable collective of individual mortal men who, in the aggregate, assume an air of immortality. They were the stuff of legends, a proud regiment that traced its heritage back over a hundred years of some of the hardest fighting of the British empire.

On their low caps they wore their unit badge, a lion over a crown over the figure "28" with the honors "Barossa" above it and "Peninsula" below. On 28 May they had landed at Ostende on the English Channel and marched to Brussels. On 5 June, Wellington had inspected and commended them. They were a mixed lot. Many were veterans of the tough fighting against the French in Portugal and Spain. Others were raw recruits only recently obtained during their garrison duty in the British Isles. Many of the newcomers were young Irishmen and militiamen who had not yet been able to procure the full uniform of the Glosters.

But if they lacked the clothing, they did not lack the spirit. So effectively had the traditions of the regiment enveloped them that there was little doubt they would fight unflinchingly when put to the test.

That test had begun on the morning of 16 June, when their officers returned from the duchess of Richmond's ball in Brussels. They carried with them the news that Napoleon had invaded. By 0400 they were on the march from Brussels to Quatre-Bras, the drum-and-fife band playing "The Young May Moon Is Shining, Love." They entered the battle early in the afternoon, having marched eighteen miles since dawn as part of General Picton's division.

Lieutenant Colonel Nixon had led them south on the march, but he had relinquished command to Colonel Belson as they neared Quatre-Bras. The orders Belson received had been crisp and delivered by an aide from Wellington.

"Who commands?"

"Colonel Belson."

"Colonel Belson, form square, and take up 42d ground."

Belson issued the order: "28th, prepare for cavalry; ready!" The troops formed square. Belson and the colors were in the center of the formation.

It began with a ripping, heavy sound of hooves slashing through the rye. The enemy was unseen in the high stalks. Then, appearing as if a curtain was being pulled down from top to bottom, heads appeared, then lances, sabers, arms, bodies, and horses. The French were rushing right at the British.

The North Gloucestershires stood silent, waiting—the stoicism of the veterans settling the nervous recruits. The riders looked big, fierce, crouching low in their saddles, lances jutting out menacingly, sabers poised for the slash, horseflesh rippling over galloping muscles. A bloodcurdling yell from the French filled the air, punctuated by the lifting artillery fire.

Closer and closer they came until, at the point that lance closed with waiting bayonet, the command was given.

"Fire!"

Clouds of smoke belched forth from exploding muskets. Horses spun away widely from the noise and pain. Lances lunged into young men barely out of boyhood. Sabers swung from on high. The square shook and held.

"Fire!"

Again the noise and the smoke. Horses could not be made to throw themselves into the barrier of bayonets. Riders had to content themselves with turning aside and swiping at the stationary infantrymen. Men went down on both sides; horses fell into the ranks and kicked out in their agony, smashing and mutilating friend and foe alike. Again and again the cavalry charged. For thirty minutes the carnage went on until, at last, the horsemen pulled away, leaving bent but unbroken the 28th of Foot.

Down came the artillery again, seeking to capitalize on the target of crowded men standing and kneeling in square, the officers on their mounts presenting the greatest profile of all. French infantry formed for attack, hoping to catch the regiment before it could re-form from square. Musket fire and bayonet on an extended front would beat musket fire and bayonet in crowded square. It was a question of simple mathematics: Extend the line and enable more infantry to bring their weapons to bear.

Quickly the Glosters re-formed and beat back their attackers with a disciplined application of fire and movement. But not without cost. The ranks thinned as men fell and sergeants gave orders to close files.

Then the French infantry stood aside and let the cavalry through, trying now to catch the deployed 28th of Foot on line. If the horsemen could work around a flank, they could cut the infantrymen to ribbons. Their only defense was in square, where all flanks were closed and the horses were compelled to face the unwelcome bayonets.

The order was given: "Form square!" Men raced to comply, some attempting to recharge and load their Brown Bess muskets as they ran— a virtually impossible feat. Just in time they made it to the defensive formation, front ranks kneeling, bayonets extended, and two ranks standing. The ranks fired in sequence, dropping the attacking cavalry in its tracks.

More Glosters fell—some lanced, some sabered, some shot or torn by shrapnel. Those that could manage crawled to the interior of the square. Those dead or unable to move were tossed from their positions so that the ranks could close, leaving no entry to the attacker. Men cursed, prayed, sobbed, and followed their orders. Again and again they faced the triple threat of cavalry, artillery, and infantry. Again and again, they shifted formation and fought back, disciplined unto death.

Whenever there was a break in the action, a senior officer would ride up and compliment them, drawing cheers from the ranks. Though the gulf between commissioned and enlisted was great under most circumstances, how grateful each was for the other on the field of battle, where courage and bravery became common traits forged in tradition and discipline and shared by recruit and veteran, officer and soldier.

Finally, as darkness fell and the French were forced to suspend their attacks without having taken the crossroads, the 28th took its first respite since 0400 that morning. They were blooded, tired, and thirsty—but they had lived up to their reputation. Throughout the night they recovered their dead and wounded as best they could, redistributed their ammunition and cleaned their weapons. Some men snatched a few minutes of sleep here and there, but when dawn came again at 0400, they stood ready once more for the onslaught of the French.

But the French did not come. Inexplicably, hour after hour passed without action. By midmorning word came from Wellington that they were to withdraw to Mont Saint Jean, a slight ridge just to the south of Waterloo. In order, the men—veterans all after the bitter fighting of the previous day—prepared their kit for movement. A heavy sky had broken into a downpour, turning the heat of the preceding day into an unseasonable cold. Drenched, grumbling, but unbowed, the regiment moved back with Colonel Belson at their head.

Mont Saint Jean. They had passed through it the previous day, but it meant nothing to them, just a small village by a crossroad—not at all significant.

But at Mont Saint Jean on the following day, Colonel Belson would be succeeded in command of the Gloucestershire Regiment by Lieutenant Colonel Nixon. Nixon, when he fell, would in turn be succeeded by Captain Kelly, who would fall and be succeeded by Captain Teulon. With these officers would fall another 160 or so of all ranks, depleting the 28th of Foot by 40 percent over the two days of fighting. But the Glosters would continue to exist, the regiment bigger than life itself, immune to death.

1300

"Why have you not taken the crossroads? Why have you not smashed Wellington?" Napoleon's face was flushed, his neck bulging over his collar in purple rage. His eyes seemed to lash out and whip Marshal Ney where he stood.

The red-haired marshal felt the blood rise in his veins. He wanted to strike his emperor. Here was the man who had confounded his victory, the man who had denied him his reserve at the critical moment, ranting at him for Napoleon's own poor generalship.

"I cannot attack. Wellington has been able to reinforce. He has too many troops."

"Nonsense! He wishes only to escape. He cannot hold at Quatre-Bras. Even now the Imperial Guard is marching to join you. You should have been attacking all morning, not allowing him to escape. You should have forced the fight so that the guard could administer the coup de grace." The emperor was livid, almost unable to bring himself to explain the simple rationale of fixing an exposed enemy in place while maneuvering superior forces against him.

"We had that opportunity yesterday. But you took d'Erlon away from me. As a result, Wellington was able to hold while his forces arrived." It was out now. Ney's words had taken a direct slap at the emperor. His statement was the embodiment of Ney's chagrin at being overruled, denied the use of his forces, and then heaped with blame for the failure to beat the allied army.

"How dare you, Ney." Napoleon's voice lowered, menacingly. It frightened the marshal, cowed him, as no combat could ever do. "Only now have I come across d'Erlon's corps preparing lunch, as if there were no more important thing in the world for them to do than enjoy a good meal. For that you countermanded my orders yesterday? For that you pulled them from Ligny at the very moment in which they would have crushed Blücher once and for all? Oh, Ney! Ney! You have failed me. You have cost France a victory. Now you are about to hand it a defeat. Do not speak to me of denial. You have denied me. You have denied your emperor. And you have denied France."

The marshal felt as if he would fall over. The world was spinning. He had lost his sense of balance. The words smashed into him like so many blows, reddening his face, churning his stomach, weakening his legs. Ney, the bravest of the brave, was a frightened child before the scolding accusations of Napoleon.

The emperor continued. "I have already ordered d'Erlon to move against Wellington. Since you could not find the words to give the order, I have had to do it for you. Your unthinking dalliance here today is inexcusable. But there is still time to salvage the disaster you have bought with your inaction. Now we must march. Wellington shall not escape."

Ney retreated. Shamed and confused, afraid and angry, he passed the orders for the left wing of the *Armée du Nord* to advance. Aides rode in all directions, ordering the regiments, battalions, squadrons, and batteries to prepare to move. Campfires were extinguished; food hastily swallowed. Wagons were readied; horses harnessed and saddled. By 1400 the French army was at last formed to move. Ten hours of daylight had already been lost, but there was still time to catch the Dutch and British; no army could outmarch the French. Not when Napoleon himself was directing the move, exerting his will and his energy to catch his prey.

But Wellington would not make it easy for the French. Through much of the morning he had braced for Ney's onslaught. As the hours passed and it did not come, he saw his chance. At 0900 a messenger had arrived from Blücher, reporting that the Prussians were moving to Wavre, still intact and able to fight.

So, the old man meant to keep his word. Good. That would make all the difference. The allied army would retreat to Mont Saint Jean, just south of the Forêt de Soignes. It was good terrain from which to defend. There was a ridgeline just high enough to make it difficult for the French infantry and cavalry to attack up but gentle enough so that counterattacks could be easily controlled. The defenders could remain hidden behind the crest, out of sight of enemy artillery, but still be able to be brought into formation quickly enough to affect the battle at the right moment. The woods behind the ridge were open enough to allow a retreat if necessary. Wellington was sure of that. He had reconnoitered them himself, dispelling his staff's concern that fighting with a woods to your rear was tantamount to denying yourself an avenue of retreat.

But the greatest advantage of all to Mont Saint Jean was that it put the allied army on a line with the Prussians. If Blücher would come to the sound of the guns, then there was time to join forces and overwhelm Napoleon. If only Blücher would come. And if only the allies could hold long enough for him to make the march.

The first challenge, though, was to disengage from Ney. If the French marshal realized the forces before him were being thinned, he might attack and catch them in their weakened condition before they could pull out. That would be a disaster. Defeated in detail and scattered before a vigorous pursuit, the allied army would have no possibility of massing for a defense at Mont Saint Jean. It was risky business. Stealth, deception, and discipline would be the order of the day. Most of all discipline. Every unit would have to do its job. Not one could afford to panic. Not one could pull out precipitously to save itself. There must be a rearguard action the entire route back if the bulk of the allied army was to fight another day. The French must be held at bay.

Could it be done? The withdrawals had begun before noon, and for a while the allies' luck held. The smoke from thousands of cooking fires indicated that the French had not yet found their spirit. But shortly after 1200 that had all changed. One by one the fires died. Movement could be seen. Reports came in that Napoleon was on the scene, that d'Erlon's corps was forming up, and that the Imperial Guard was marching toward Quatre-Bras. It would be a race now.

By 1400 the action had begun. Wellington had stood beside the Brussels road, cheering his men as they retreated. But he had kept one eye on the rearguard action. It seemed to be going well. The French formed,

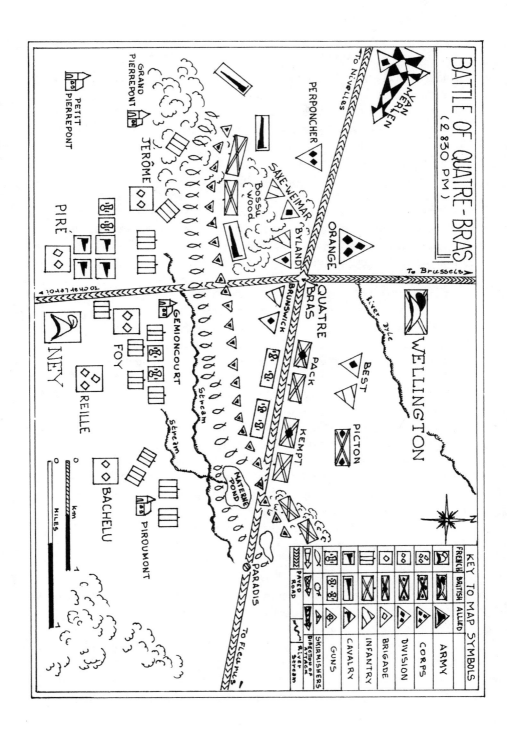

BATTLE OF QUATRE-BRAS
(2 830 PM)

KEY TO MAP SYMBOLS

	FRENCH	BRITISH	ALLIED	
ARMY				
CORPS				
DIVISION				
BRIGADE				
INFANTRY				
CAVALRY				
GUNS				
SKIRMISHERS				
PAVED ROAD				
DIRECTION OF ATTACK				
RIVER-Stream				

VAN MERLEN

PERPONCHER

TO NIVELLES

JERÔME

GRAND PIERREPONT

PETIT PIERREPONT

SAXE-WEIMAR

Bossu wood

BYLANDT

ORANGE

PIRÉ

To Brussels

QUATRE-BRAS

BRUNSWICK

River Dyle

WELLINGTON

PACK

BEST

PICTON

KEMPT

NEY

FOY

GEMIONCOURT

Stream

REILLE

TO CHARLEROI

Stream

MATERNE POND

BACHELU

PIROUMONT

PARADIS

To Fleurus

N

MILES

km

0

0

attacked, were met by a barrage of fire, and forced to pull back to form again. In the brief interim, the allied units scrambled back a few hundred yards, fell into defensive positions once again, and delivered another delaying blow to the pursuing French. The discipline was holding. There was no panic.

And there was good fortune. It came in the weather. Darkening skies had overtaken the precarious retreat. As far as the eye could see, a blackness had clouded the earth. The first few drops signaled the seriousness of the storm. Large, thick drops of water fell heavy on grimy uniforms, the wetness seeping into the dank material, showing no inclination to spare the wearer any discomfort. Quickly the rain intensified, soaking the combatants and forming rapidly running rivulets on the sloped Belgian fields. The heavily traveled roads turned into quagmires. Before long the deluge was the major preoccupation of both attackers and pursued. It made their lives miserable, more miserable than the fatigue and hunger, more miserable than the fear and exertion. Boots filled with water, were tugged at by the mud. Eyes were awash with a cold, beating downpour. The rain collected on headpieces, finding paths of least resistance down inside collars, streaming onto backs and into armpits, and collecting in cold pockets in the constricted waistbands of the soldiers.

Men cursed. They stared at their feet, following the slogging boots in front of them. The weight they carried increased with every glob of mud that attached itself to them. Hands turned white, then purple, from the immersion in cold water. The temperature plummeted; the wind picked up, changing the angle of the deluge from vertical to horizontal. Heads hunched deeper into shoulders chafed and cut by their soldiers' loads. Individuals withdrew into themselves, oblivious of everything but the sheer misery of the sodden march, chilled to the bone, and devoid of any hope of finding a dry article of clothing into which to change later. Most of the allied troops had not eaten for two days, but even the gnawing hunger of stomachs devoid of food took second place to the discomfort of the unrelenting rain.

But the same rain that pelted those retreating fell on those pursuing. They too were blinded by the storm. They too suffered the misery and confusion of trying to move massed forces over muddied fields and roads. And all the while the allied rear guard harassed them, making them cautious lest they stumble into determined resistance in the misty fogbanks to their front. Slowly, the Dutch and British widened the distance between themselves and the French. Yard by yard the two main bodies separated; minute by minute the day passed toward a gloomy darkness, hastened by an ever darkening sky, an ever deepening deluge.

By 1900, Napoleon, who had led much of the pursuit himself, pulled in to a small wayside inn on the Brussels road. The lettering over the door read "La Belle Alliance," an unhappy thought to the emperor. He was soaked to the skin, sore from hours in the saddle, and chilled to the bone. But he did not think of himself. His only concern was Wellington. Where was he? Where would he stop? In the distant haze, he could barely make out a ridgeline scarcely one kilometer to the north.

"Send a cavalry force forward. I must know Wellington's intentions." An aide raced away to pass the order.

A few minutes later, General Milhaud was moving his cavalry up the road, taking with him several batteries of horse artillery. The swampy conditions caused by the rain made the fields impassable. Only the road afforded an avenue of approach.

Suddenly, sixty cannon exploded from the ridgeline to their north. Wellington had revealed himself. He would hold at Mont Saint Jean. The emperor allowed himself a small smile of satisfaction.

"Have all the troops take up positions and we will see what happens tomorrow." D'Erlon took the order from his emperor. He was glad that the exhausting march had at last come to an end.

2300

Lady Magdalene had not eaten all day. Before the rain began, she had heard an occasional boom in the distance. It was impossible to tell how far away the cannon were. All the preceding day she had heard intermittent fire. It was clear that there had been a great battle. But how far was it from Antwerp? Some of the other ladies told her that if they could hear the cannon, it could not be far. Others had explained that there was no way of telling. Sometimes the atmospherics played tricks, obscuring sounds only a few miles away while echoing events much farther distant.

As 16 June passed, it became increasingly clear that a great battle was taking place. Late in the afternoon a few soldiers had appeared in the city, their purpose unclear and rather suspicious. They told of a great defeat for the allied army. At first the rumors had frightened her, but again some of the more experienced wives waiting with her in the "safe haven" of Antwerp echoed Sir William's warning that the first to bring news of disaster were deserters who embellished the reports of ruin to justify their own cowardly departure from the field of battle.

Still, it had been a disconcerting day. By nightfall there had been no official word from the front. Emma, Lady Magdalene's maid, had become increasingly fretful, full of gossip about the plans of various ladies to set sail for England, in accordance with prearranged instructions from their soldier-husbands. Magdalene would have no such talk in her tiny apartment. At last, in exasperation, she told Emma that if she desired to sail then she could do so immediately, but that there would be no more talk on the subject.

That had been enough to silence the maid. Still, both women remained unsettled. Once Magdalene had passed in front of the small mirror on the bureau in the bedroom. She glanced at the waxy pallor and darkened eyes in her reflection and thought how unbecoming they were. If Sir William were to see me like this, she thought, he would send me off to England himself, with little haste in following me. She remembered then their penultimate night together and found reassurance in their passion. He would not send me away, she concluded. Not at all.

But the comfort had lasted only a brief minute or two. Anxiety fast replaced it—not as to how she looked or whether the battle being fought was lost or won, but instead for the safety of her husband. As darkness fell, the casualty figures had grown from hundreds to thousands. Those were just impersonal figures, however; no names were attached to them. The ladies said that another day would pass before lists were produced. Until then they would have to rely on haphazard reports— accounts given by witnesses, sometimes passed on second- or thirdhand— that a husband had been seen alive and well at a certain time and place in the battle. Or reports that he was not so well. Even then, they should not be believed. So many facts were twisted in the confusion of battle. It was best to pray and trust to God, until a note in the handwriting of the loved one arrived with news that he was safe. That was the best reassurance, until he could return in person.

No note had arrived that night—not for her or any of the ladies. A few, though, had received word-of-mouth reports. Regrettably, some had borne bad news. The ladies rushed to each other for support. Still, anxieties were raised all around. Bad news for one might imply bad news for another. What was happening at the battle? Is my man safe? It was all so frightening, so maddening.

There could be no sleep. Night brought such pessimism; the worst fears appeared in graphic detail. The dark hours passed slowly. By the time dawn had returned on 17 June, a weakened and frail Lady Magdalene could barely bring herself to face another day of anxiety.

And now, late in the day, still no news. Again darkness was falling, hastened this time by the endless rain. Her mood deepened. More and more of the ladies had been told that their husbands or their sons were hurt. Some had been told of deaths. They sat stunned, disbelieving. The others averted their eyes, lest they betray their own relief that so far they had been spared such terrible news.

Suddenly, a rider appeared at the front door, and Emma rushed to receive him. A note was passed and Emma walked briskly to Lady Magdalene, who held her breath for the time it took the maid to travel the few steps to her mistress. Trembling she took the damp envelope and stared at the smeared writing on its front.

"Lady Magdalene." It was enough. It was his handwriting. He was alive. He could write. He was conscious. He still had his right hand. Quickly she tore the envelope open. Like a mother inspecting her newborn baby, she examined the note for signs of any defects in the object of her love.

"I am well and in great spirits. We have given the French a tremendous beating." A flood of joy overwhelmed her. She felt faint, her heart was beating audibly. Tears formed in her eyes. He had posted it "Genappe, 16 June."

Suddenly her terror returned. He had written this last night. He was well then, but what had transpired today? Anxiety returned, then shame at her selfishness. It was enough to know that he had survived the battle on the sixteenth. There had not been as much cannonading today. At least she had not heard much—hardly any at all since the rain had begun, except one time around seven o'clock. But if he had survived a great battle on the sixteenth, surely he would survive a lesser action on the seventeenth. She tried to reassure herself, to draw strength from his note, and to go out and bring solace to her acquaintances who were receiving less welcome news. She walked to the mirror again and straightened her hair. Her hand shook visibly.

Midnight

De Lancey loosened the grip around the ink quill and let it slip from his hand. Hour after hour he had been dispatching messages, trying to bring order to the bedlam that was the allied army. His hand ached, the small muscles at the back of his forefinger and thumb bunched from their continual contraction around the tip of the quill. Dark circles rimmed his otherwise boyish eyes. De Lancey's shoulders hunched forward as if to ward off the fatigue trying to overwhelm him. It had been an endless day of desperate effort to move the army to Waterloo.

Early in the morning Wellington had dispatched him to mark positions to which the army might withdraw south of Waterloo. The reconnaissance followed a night not unlike the one he was struggling through now—a night of drawing up orders, seeking information, checking maps and reports, moving stores, arranging for medical support, providing ammunition, and performing the countless other tasks a quartermaster general looks after. Yet the greatest single decision he had made that day was a tactical one: the rejection of the ridge at La Belle Alliance for the main line of defense and the selection, instead, of the ridge at Mont Saint Jean. Wellington had suggested the former, but when de Lancey arrived there he determined that the terrain would overextend the formations. Mont Saint Jean was tighter, and although it placed the Forêt de Soignes close to the rear of the troops, it seemed a better position from which to defend. The relationship between the chief of staff and his commander was close enough that de Lancey risked overriding—or at least giving broad interpretation to—his orders. He had sent word back to Wellington of his decision; then, after a decent interval and in the absence of a countermand, he had proceeded to mark positions as he determined best.

It may have been the only clean decision he had made that day, the colonel reflected. The rest of them had been made on a hope and a prayer. No matter what he might direct, who knew what was happening out there? It was one thing to write an order for the ammunition wagons to be positioned at a particular spot; it was another for the messenger to find the wagons and for the wagoneers to move them over the muddied, crowded roads; find their designated location; and distribute their stocks. And even if all that could be managed, could the troops to be resupplied make their way in the confusion and weather to their prearranged positions, dispatch an ammunition detail, find the correct wagons in the miserable blackness, and struggle with their load back to their own formations—which had no doubt been shifted back and forth by the orders of the commanders, who honed the fine points of tactics?

Likewise, the chief had little chance of bringing order to medical services. Getting the wounded back from Quatre-Bras was a hopeless task. If they could walk, they would have to get along as best they could with the formations struggling up the Brussels road. If they were unable to move under their own power, they would have to trust to whatever impromptu arrangements could be made. They would get little special treatment. Many would die where they lay. Others would be less fortunate—tortured by their wounds; exposed to the cold, driving rain; and looted and savaged by the local peasantry, who robbed indiscriminantly from the fallen of both sides. It would be dawn before anyone even inquired after a wounded man, and only then because his absence would be noted at morning roll call.

And as for feeding the masses of men streaming back toward Waterloo, it was an impossible task. A battle had just been fought, the weather was atrocious, and another battle was sure to come on the following day. Only the essentials could be provided, and right now essentials meant troops, artillery, horses, and ammunition. A man would have to eat whatever he was carrying or attempt to forage, and there would be little time for either. The quartermaster general knew that the movements of the last forty-eight hours had precluded a resupply of rations. Most of the army would go hungry.

De Lancey himself had gone without food, even though for him it was readily available. The press of work had allowed him to put the thought of it from his mind, although by now the insistent noises emanating from his stomach could not be ignored. Perhaps he should take a bite, he thought to himself. After all, he would have to be alert if any progress was to be made in organizing the army. But how could he allow himself to be fed when he could not provide for the troops out in the countryside? He rejected the temptation. It was enough, he told himself, that he was dry. Only a few could claim that comfort this night.

He picked up his quill and returned to his writing. After a few minutes his thoughts drifted back to Magdalene. He hoped she had received his note from Genappe on the sixteenth. It had told her enough—that he was unharmed. It did not tell her how close he had come to being harmed. There was no need for that. Again and again in the preceding weeks he had assured her that, as quartermaster general, he was removed from the fighting. She had believed him, and for that half-truth he felt a little guilty. It was true he was a noncombatant, the man charged to bring together all the details of the operations of the army—the intelligence, the orders, the supplies, the replacements. But his position in battle was close to Wellington so that he could receive his commander's orders and translate them into the necessary instructions. Wellington, however, was often in the thick of the fighting, near enough to observe what was transpiring and to inspire the soldiers as the need arose. Artillery and musket fire was a constant hazard. There was even the chance of a cavalry charge catching them too far forward. But Magdalene did not need to hear of that. There was already enough for her to worry about.

He could see her face in the flickering candlelight—soft, innocent, seductive. His heart quickened; the wrinkles on his brow eased. He was at that stage of fatigue where daydreams blend into night dreams, the line where consciousness and unconsciousness blurs. A trace of a smile curled his lips as he reflected on the unlikeliness of the union: he, the New York City–born son of American loyalists, educated in England and a lifelong soldier in the king's army; she, the highborn daughter of the famed Scottish scientist, Sir James Hall of Edinburgh. Twelve years separated them in age, twelve years in which he had seen much combat and, in consequence, acquired much worldliness. Yet her youth, her exuberance, and her vivaciousness fanned in him his own idealism. She was what he had always imagined in his boyhood dreams—a warm, beautiful, passionate woman, enamored with him, yet independently strong, intellectually confident, and resolved in every way to be a loving wife.

He would like to be with her tonight. What a blissful sleep it would be to lie next to her! She had brought him to understand that there is more to living than adventuring far from home and that a soldier's life, no matter how romantic or epic, is not necessarily the only fulfillment of manhood. He was still a young man, but she had made him realize that there is a greater meaning in life than glory. She had given him a greater wisdom—without saying a word, without instructing, without effort. Just by being there, she had enlarged his sense of being. He did not want to be away from her—not for a day, not for an hour. All of this soldiering, he admitted to himself, was a poor second to being in her company.

Reluctantly, he tore himself from his musing and focused again on the paper before him. He dipped the quill in the inkwell, reread his sentence, and continued with his writing: "You are to advance after 0400 by the Nivelles road to the extreme right wing of the line. The ammunition for your artillery will be posted. . . ." The rain beat furiously against the windowpanes.

6

THE COLDSTREAM GUARDS

Dusk: 17 June

Cold. Bone-chilling damp cold. It swept other discomforts before it, diminished them. Teeth-chattering cold. Hands too numb to grip; feet pained with icy needles. Cold. It was all a man could think about. It came before hunger, before fatigue, before fear. Cold. And wet. The rain, unrelenting, had beaten all day. Where could so much water come from? The skies were saturated with it. Hour after hour they had poured forth their chilled contents. It drenched the hapless forms below, adding to their misery. Frigid torrents licked at every crevice of their bodies, cooled every pore of their shivering skin.

The Coldstream Guards marched north, the rain blinding their eyes to their destination. Their minds were mesmerized by the repetitive suction of sodden boots breaking free of gripping mud, step after miserable step. Chafed skin degenerated into raw and running sores. Soldiers tried to think of other things, other places: home, women, food, warmth. For a moment or two, every now and then, they would succeed in escaping the reality of their present condition. But then the pace would alter, the ranks would close, and men would bump together, evoking blasphemous oaths and evaporating the more pleasant thoughts into which they had managed to withdraw.

The Coldstream Guards formed a proud regiment that traced its heraldry back to the time of Cromwell, before the creation of the first standing army in Britain. Like all Guardsmen, they were a hardy breed—tough, unyielding, persevering against all odds, much like the hard little Scottish border town on the banks of the River Tweed from whence they took their name. But heritage and tradition could not keep out the cold. It would not shelter them from the rain. So they bent into their stride, shoulders stooped under the twin loads of equipment and misery, slogging on step-by-step in the cold, prematurely gloomy twilight.

Lt. Col. James Macdonell rode close by his column of men, the composite battalion of the Light Companies of the 2d Battalion, Coldstream Guards, and 3d Battalion, First Guards. Macdonell's large frame, lifted by his horse above the marching mass below, loomed in the twilight, a silent incentive to his men to keep up the pace. There was still some distance to go, and much work to be done before the night passed.

Macdonell watched the struggling men, heard their curses. He knew they were tired. The original order to move had come at 0130 on the sixteenth. How ironic that, just the preceding night, he had declared them at a high standard of training and ordered an extra half-ration of liquor. He had been training them hard since early March, when news of Napoleon's escape from Elba had first arrived. The leisurely garrison duties in Belgium had ended then, as the Guards division returned to the field to practice drill and tactics, fired by the energies of the newly posted commander in chief, the duke of Wellington, and motivated by increasing news of Napoleon's success in reestablishing his command of the French army.

Macdonell was a favorite of Wellington's, a veteran of hard campaigning with the duke; they had fought the French in Portugal. Macdonell had joined the army as an ensign in 1793. By now he had seen twenty-two years of service. He had risen in the ranks slowly, commanding a troop in the 17th Light Dragoons for nine years. Those had been rich years for him, and from them he had learned how to lead men, a knowledge that had stood him in good stead at the far reaches of the British empire. Time after time his mettle had been tested, and it had never been found wanting. India, Naples, Sicily, and Egypt were the hard proving grounds that predated his arrival to the Coldstream Guards in 1811. Two more hard years followed in the Peninsula, tasting battle again at Salamanca, Vitoria, Nivelle, and Nive. Then came battalion command.

It was an honor he savored. His father, Duncan Macdonell, chief

of Glengarry, the fourteenth hereditary chieftain of the Glengarry branch
of the Macdonald clan (the spelling of the last name had been changed
to distinguish its uniqueness), would have been proud of him. So too
would his brother, Alexander Ranaldson, his father's successor and a
colonel since 1803.

They were a proud family, feudal lords in their own right, but educated
men as well. His eldest brother had gone to Oxford, James to Cambridge. A few years ago, on a visit to Edinburgh, King George IV had
sworn in the two brothers along with their henchmen and retainers as
part of the royal bodyguard at Holyrood. They were a handsome band
of men, the Glengarry lot—fierce, strong, infused with the wild blood
of their ancestors, given to war and fighting, but warmhearted and
generous. These passions ran strong in James Macdonell. As the third-
born son of Duncan Macdonell, the hereditary title and all the property
that came with it could not be his. James believed, however, that an
honorable life leading men in battle would suffice. It was a tribute to
Lieutenant Colonel Macdonell and a prescience of events to come that
had brought about the creation of a battalion from the two Light Companies
of the 2d Brigade. The lieutenant colonel meant to command them well.

He had gotten them moving by 0400 on the sixteenth, within two
and a half hours of receipt of the order and in conjunction with the
movement of the division. All morning and afternoon they had marched,
covering twenty-six miles in the intense heat of the day before arriving on the battlefield at Quatre-Bras. Toward evening the Light Companies under Macdonell's command had been committed to action,
suffering seven casualties. It had been a slight bloodletting compared
to the losses of the other units on the field of battle, but it was enough
to whet Macdonell's appetite for action. The cold front that had come
in that morning—and the rainstorm accompanying it—had not dampened his enthusiasm. He had had enough experience to know that Quatre-
Bras had been only a preliminary affair; the heavy fighting was yet
to come. Already he had received indications that he would be looked
to for a major part in the action.

The thought warmed him. The clammy press of his soaked uniform
against his broad chest was forgotten as he squeezed his horse's flanks
with his heels and moved alongside the column of struggling men. They
would do well. He knew it as he knew his own strength. They were
hardened, disciplined. He had seen to that. Their curses did not matter.
Soldiers like to curse, to bemoan their hardships. But they took pride

in their difficulties. He had brought them beyond the point where they saw field life as an inconvenience. It had become their natural habitat, an environment in which they thrived, proud that they were more fit than others and able to cope with the difficulties of the soldier's life.

They were big men, larger than most. But not as big as he. At six feet and three inches, he towered above them. And his brawny arms and legs, barrel chest, and thick neck overshadowed even the strongest of them. It was not for nothing that his ancestors had been Highland chieftains. Among a warlike people, they had been the most warlike, gifted with the size and intellect to dominate other fierce and determined men. He set his jaw and moved forward in the column.

They were closing in on their destination now. The Guards Division was moving toward the western extension of the Mont Saint Jean ridgeline. Macdonell had been told there was a walled collection of buildings just to the south of the ridge, a farm known as Hougoumont. Once the Guards had settled in on the ridge, he was to take his Light Companies and occupy the farm. From snatches of conversation, he could picture the disposition of the allied army. It would form along the ridge at Mont Saint Jean from east to west, some forces left out far to the west to guard against the French swinging wide to the allies' right and cutting the British line of communication to the Channel. Hougoumont farm, off the ridge and situated between the allied and the French armies, would serve as a strongpoint. Should the French choose to attack to the right of the allies' line, they would not be able to avoid running into it.

It was just like the duke to give an eye to detail. A strongpoint at Hougoumont would break up a determined attack. The French would have to divert forces to neutralize Hougoumont before they could penetrate the main line of defense. If the outpost could exact a price high enough, the final assault by the French would be weakened. A stand at the walled enclosure would also buy time. The longer the French spent at the farm— in actuality a full-blown château—the later the main effort against the defense would come. Moreover, there was always the chance that the French would overcommit. Attacking forces not well managed had a tendency to butt up against any position resisting them. In that regard, Hougoumont offered opportunities both as an obstacle and a lure.

Macdonell imagined there were other outposts at different points along the front of the allied army. Wellington would have chosen his ground well. The duke could not be sure where the French would choose to make their main effort, but wherever it was he would be sure to make the going difficult for them. The colonel admired that trait of Wellington's. He was tough, wily. He would give up nothing without a price.

So that would be his mission: Exact a price, and buy some time. How many Frenchmen would he have to face? His own force was small, fewer than 200 men. Perhaps he would receive some attachments or at least the support of adjacent units. He had defended from buildings before. It was a tricky business. If you could make yourself impregnable to infantry assault, you stood a chance. But if there were any weak points in the defense, any flanks into which an enemy could pour, you could be cut off and defeated in detail. Even without the danger of unimpeded infantry assault, there was still the artillery to contend with. If the enemy could bring his cannon into position, the impact would be pulverizing. Buildings and walls would shatter and collapse, chunks of rock and mortar exacerbating the casualty-producing effects, tearing into flesh with shrapnellike wickedness or crushing bodies under their weight. But worst of all was fire. Eventually buildings and their contents would burn. Farms were laden with straw and fodder. These would catch and blow from building to building, spreading the fire throughout. It would drive the survivors out into the open while feeding on the wounded and the dead. Defenders were horrified by flames. The putrid smell of singed hair and burnt flesh eroded their will to fight. It was an ugly business.

Macdonell was eager to see the position he would have to defend. Every piece of terrain dictates its own conditions. There were vulnerabilities and strengths to be found in each. It would be fully dark, though, before they arrived. And the men will be tired. They will want to rest, to get out of the rain, to build a fire and dry out their clothes. They will want to eat as well. There had been no time to bring up rations since the march had begun early on the sixteenth. Unless a man had been prescient enough to withhold some edible scraps for the march, he had probably gone without eating. Macdonell's own stomach was empty, gnawing at his ribs as if to remind him he hadn't eaten in over a day.

The colonel dismissed the thought. There was no time for creature comforts now. The fighting tomorrow—fighting that will surely come—will hinge on how well we prepare our defenses tonight. What matter that we dry ourselves out and eat and sleep tonight if we are dead tomorrow? Yet, if I do not insist on work, the men will not think their way through the preparation. As hard as I've made them, the human condition will drive them to seek shelter and sustenance. But I can overcome that. They will follow my orders to the letter—because the discipline is there and because they have come to trust me. They know I will not misuse them. Oh yes, they will curse me under their breaths. But they will do what I tell them. Their officers will insist on it, and their sergeants will make them obey. And each leader will set the example; he will share the hardship of his men and work alongside them, not partaking of a meal himself before his men can be fed and forgoing any rest until the work is done. That is the way of a good unit, and that is what I have created.

The march column was slowing down, troops folding accordion-style into preceding ranks. The 2d Brigade had closed onto the Mont Saint Jean ridge. Aides were hurriedly passing orders from the division commander, showing the various Guard units where to take up position and guiding them around bodies of men already in place.

"Where is Colonel Macdonell?" The Scotsman could hear the whispered question in the growing darkness.

"Here, man. I am here."

The aide approached the burly figure sitting stoically astride his horse. "Sir, General Cooke, commander of 1st Division, asks that you move with your Light Companies to occupy the Château of Hougoumont."

Macdonell's eyes followed the pointing hand of the aide, which extended toward a barely discernible copse of trees a short distance to the south of the ridgeline. The 2d Guards Brigade was taking up position on the ridge, a few hundred meters behind the wooded area; the 1st Guards Brigade was forming a defensive line to its left. "Am I to man Hougoumont with just my small force?" Macdonell asked.

"Lord Saltoun will be posted from 1st Brigade with its Light Companies. He will set up in an orchard directly to the east of the walled château."

"Have you seen the buildings? Have you been there?"

"Yes, Sir, I have. It is quite a considerable construction."

"And is it occupied at the moment?"

"No, Sir. The family that lives there has fled. Only the gardener remains on the grounds."

"No, no. I mean, have the French occupied it?"

"Oh, no. But as you know, they are fast behind us. You must move quickly."

"Thank you, Captain. I shall." Macdonell suppressed his anger at the impertinence of the young officer. No one had to impress the urgency of the mission on Macdonell. The colonel spurred his horse through the teeming rain to find his two company commanders, Henry Wyndham and Charles Dashwood. Both were experienced hands and would be accounting for their men as they assembled in the gathering darkness. With luck—and discipline—none of the men would have dropped out from the march, although they had covered over thirty-five miles in the last two days.

He found Wyndham and Dashwood consolidating their companies on the ridgeline. He consulted with the two leaders. Tough, rangy men, they appeared calm, unruffled, seemingly indifferent to the weather. The voices of the three men rose above the storm as they coordinated their move on the château. It took another five minutes to give the orders to the massed companies and move back into march formation to begin their trek to Hougoumont. The muddied slope made the going difficult, the men slipping more than marching across the field.

Macdonell could barely make out Lord Saltoun's formations moving off to his left front, a few minutes in advance of his own companies. He made a mental note to coordinate with him as soon as it was feasible. Although a lieutenant colonel as well as a lord, at thirty years of age Saltoun was Macdonell's junior by date of rank. By tradition, therefore, command responsibility would devolve to Macdonell in the château. He would handle that arrangement gingerly, however; best not to be overbearing. Lord Saltoun was a professional officer of noteworthy combat experience in the Peninsular War. He would understand who was in charge at Hougoumont without having to be reminded of it.

As Saltoun approached the orchard to the east of the château from the direction of the Mont Saint Jean ridge, a French battalion closed in on it from the south, through a dense wood that extended for three hundred to four hundred meters. Napoleon had learned of the château from some of the local Belgians and immediately recognized its importance. He had passed orders to thrust forward and seize the farm before the British had invested it. Expecting to meet no resistance, the Frenchmen eagerly pressed on, the thought of shelter from the unabating storm hastening their steps.

But Lord Saltoun's men were a bit more determined. A few musket balls discouraged the Frenchmen and drove them back into the woods. Quickly, the Guardsmen followed up their advantage and advanced into the orchard just to the east of the château walls. A few moments later Macdonell's force entered the grounds through the north gate, occupying the interior courtyard and pushing an element of men around to the west, into the woods just beyond. Control of Hougoumont had devolved to the allies.

Even in the last light of day, Macdonell could see the possibilities. The walled garden and the tightly packed buildings offered a formidable defensive position. On the southwest corner of the château, the farmhouse itself formed a bastion that guarded the south gate. The building extended over the entranceway on either side. High walls and well-situated windows allowed for shooting down into the short open space between the woods and the château walls. A small outcropping of high wall projected from the farmhouse at a right angle before cutting to the left and extending to the garden wall. This projection would afford cover to defending troops and make any assault on the south gate difficult.

To the west were the barn and stables. Although they contained few apertures from which to fire, their high walls and enclosed roof blocked any approach from the west. With improvements, they could be converted into ideal fighting positions. There was a small side gate between the farmhouse and the barn, but if enough firing loops could be knocked through the western walls, it could be well covered by fire.

The interior of the courtyard between the walled garden and the rest of the buildings offered a warren of interior defenses. From the interior men could fight, forming a last-ditch defense should the courtyard or the garden or both be taken. The wall around the garden rose well above the height of a man. Firing platforms could be constructed from which to shoot down over the top of the wall, and firing loops knocked in the walls would afford a heavy rate of fire into the attackers. Moreover, thick hedges to the south and west of the château and garden would pose an obstacle to the French. The hedges would break up a massed formation before it could reach the walls, exposing individual rushers to the concentrated fire of the defenders. Even the north gate, away from the most likely line of the French attack, could be used to advantage by the Guardsmen as an access point for resupply and reinforcement. It allowed all other gates to be kept closed and barricaded. Certainly the French would try to force any point of entry, but with musket fire focused on these critical areas, the attackers could be made to pay a high price for their efforts.

All in all, it was an impressive defensive bulwark. But much work had to be done. Quickly, Macdonell set his men to the task. His orders were firm. There would be no fires built; the time would be better spent at work on the defenses, and fires would consume wood needed to construct the firing platforms and thicken the barricades. If the men were cold, best to keep warm by working. No one would be posted inside any of the buildings until dawn, except to chip firing holes and barricade entries. Buildings offered warmth and dryness, and encouraged drowsiness. The men could afford none of that tonight.

With few grumbles the men got to work. They trusted Macdonell, knew that he was the best leader they could ask for in a situation like this. Still, it had been a long two days, and now the storm grew worse. Lightning accentuated the heaviness of the skies; thunder deepened the sense of foreboding. The wind picked up, pressing saturated uniforms against goose-pimpled flesh and cutting deep into already chilled bones. Men struggled in the darkness, trying to find their equipment, straining to hear the shouted instructions from their sergeants above the tumult of the storm.

Macdonell himself was everywhere. He encouraged his men, gave orders for new work efforts, ensured that the north gate was guarded by an alert security force, and coordinated with Lord Saltoun in the orchard. Macdonell moved outside the walled area to inspect the defensive preparations going on in the beanfields, along the hedges, and in the woods. He climbed the firing platforms one by one to ensure that the defenders from each position could shoot over the parapets. He peeked through the firing loops, using the lightning flashes to find the dead space where a musket round could not reach and gave the orders to cover the terrain from other positions. No protection of any kind could be left for the French; every attacker must be exposed, no matter where he might go to ground. Fields of fire were cleared; the men reinforced the hedges by dragging up brush and fallen timbers, making the vegetation more difficult to penetrate.

Where he saw energy being applied, the colonel rewarded it with a compliment. Where he saw laggardness, he corrected it with a pointed remark and then a quiet reprimand to the closest officer or sergeant. He spared himself no effort, allowed himself no rest. Through the night the men worked. Slowly but surely, their positions began to take form. Their anticipation of the coming attack grew in proportion to their efforts. No longer were they reluctantly going about their duties. They had come to realize that their very survival lay in their labor, that the chances of coming through the battle rose in proportion to the effort expended. The suffering of the night diminished in importance as their eagerness to live through the following day increased.

Macdonell's leadership was having its effect. His will became the will of his men. His philosophy became the philosophy of his command. Hougoumont must be held—could be held—against all odds. Work was necessary, however. And attention to detail. Every item had to be checked. Every position had to be improved. There was no room for shortcuts. There was no time to relax. Morning was rushing toward the troops, and with it would come the attack. The French will fight desperately for this château, but they must not get it. Every man must do his duty; the failure of one will be the ruin of all. Never mind about the weather, the fatigue, the hunger. No self-pity can be allowed. Such an outlook smacks of weakness—worse, it is bound to be fatal.

The colonel had felt the transformation in his command, could see it in his men. The dejection they suffered during the march had passed and was replaced by zeal as they worked in the dark. The metamorphosis filled him with wonder. He did not know how it happened; he knew only that it was always so. Whatever is in the head—and heart—of the commander, always permeates the unit he commands. If he is depressed, his command is depressed. If he is fearful, his men are fearful. If he expects defeat, they too expect defeat. On the other hand, if he can find courage in his own heart, if he can make himself purposeful, determined, and optimistic, so too shall be his command. He had done what had to be done this night. He had made himself eager to do the labor required for a strong defense, and his men had eagerly done the work for him. Tomorrow they would have a chance. He would see to it that they got some food in the morning—and a ration of gin to go with it.

On the fields and roads around Mont Saint Jean, tens of thousands of men with less purposeful work at hand suffered through the night. The weather gave them no respite. Men who had been without food for two days or more received nothing to assuage their hunger. In the confusion of retreat and pursuit, the opposing armies had sacrificed all amenities. If there was any organization to the forces in which they served, it did not reveal itself in any alleviation of the miserable conditions.

The best a man could hope for was to find himself in the ranks of his own unit—his regiment, his battalion, his company. Miraculously, most units had held their men together despite the difficulties of the preceding two days. Small numbers of men were unaccounted for—dead, wounded, missing, or just plain lost in the confusion. But in the main, men were pleased to find themselves with their comrades in arms. There was some solace in knowing that discomfort was shared in the company of one's fellows. There was misery enough to go around, but somehow it was more bearable if a man was not alone.

Those who were alone—those sent to prepare positions, man picket lines, gather supplies, run messages, find missing elements—were not so lucky. They felt lost in the storm, unsheltered, forgotten. It was almost as if they were already dead, even before the battle had begun. It seemed they no longer counted, that they were already a faded memory to their comrades and unremembered by their leaders. The darkness closed in. The rain beating down upon them came as a personal affliction.

With few exceptions, soldiers pulled inside themselves. Men wanted to get off their feet but could not bring themselves to lie down. They wrapped wet and soiled blankets around their upper bodies and tucked their chins into their chests. Water penetrated everywhere, collected around their buttocks, drained into their boots. Men huddled together for warmth, sitting back-to-back in groups of twos and threes, mutual pressure keeping them from toppling over into the mud while the slight bit of body heat generated by their proximity fought vainly against the chill.

A few found piles of hay and snatched a few strands to lay on the ground. The hay was damp, but it raised them out of the mud—at least for a little while, until it too became inundated.

In the dark, units continued to close on the crowded fields, treading on those already arrived. Horses slipped on the muddy slopes and stepped on shivering men, drawing oaths for themselves and their riders. Tempers became short, moods surly. Hunger gnawed at empty stomachs. The world seemed a helpless morass, a cold, inhospitable swamp. Thoughts became forlorn, morbid. Many men realized that this night might be their last on earth. They yearned for a bit of comfort, some morsel of tenderness, some relief from their discomfort. They wanted the night to end. Whatever trials tomorrow might bring, at least it would end the wretchedness of the moment.

In the short space of ground between the two opposing armies rode a man well attended by a sizable entourage. He was more miserable than most. But it was neither weather nor fatigue that discomforted him, not that he was immune to their effects. He too was cold, wet, and tired. But even more than that he was fearful—fearful that his enemy would slip away from him. Napoleon, emperor of France, was looking for signs of Wellington's army.

For a while, the cannonade at 1900 the previous evening had reassured him that his opponent was there, dutifully waiting for him. But with the darkness and the fury of the storm, his doubts had returned. Wellington was a cunning foe. He had escaped from Quatre-Bras when he should have been crushed. Ney had let that happen by languishing all night and morning of the sixteenth and seventeenth. Even the vigorous pursuit of the afternoon of 17 June—a pursuit led by the emperor himself—had not been able to catch and destroy him. This Englishman had nine lives. Perhaps he had pulled away again under cover of the storm.

But where could he go? Brussels was only a short distance to the north. Would he uncover a major city? Perhaps. But he would not cut himself off from the Channel. That means he can pull back toward the coast only, away from Brussels and away from Blücher. That would be a strategic blunder. Already Wellington was separated from the Prussians, and if they were heading for Liège—as the last reports indicated—then there would be no possibility of the two armies reuniting.

But there was the rest of Europe: the Austrians, the Russians, the Bavarians, the Piedmontese, the Spanish. They were closing in to prosecute their war against a single man, against Napoleon. As long as Wellington survived, the allied nations would feel they had a chance. Numbers would be on their side. On the other hand, if Wellington's army could be defeated, they might lose their stomach for the war. Already the Prussians had been bested. If the British general—the man in whom the leaders of Europe had placed so much faith—could be destroyed, the rest might sue for peace.

Would Wellington run? Or would he stay and fight? Something was out there on the ridge. But what? Was it the entire allied army or only detachments left behind as a ruse? He had received reports that Hougoumont had been occupied. And La Haye Sainte, a farm along the Brussels road just south of the crossroads at Mont Saint Jean, was showing signs of occupation by large groups of men. Dutch and English pickets were posted, or so the French cavalry was reporting. But was it all merely a trick? Was Wellington attempting to deceive? Was he leaving behind signs of his presence just to ensure his escape?

Back and forth the emperor rode, trying to see for himself. One by one, fires began burning on the ridge at Mont Saint Jean, indicating that major forces were encamped there. But were they? The uncertainty was maddening.

At last, at 0400, the emperor tired of his reconnaissance and headed back to his headquarters at Le Caillou. There a note from Marshal Grouchy awaited him, stating that it was possible that Blücher's Prussians were not pulling away toward Liège as previously reported. Instead, they might at least in part be heading toward Wavre. The emperor was weary, however, and without giving any orders went to bed.

In his headquarters at Waterloo, the duke of Wellington had spent an anxious night. It had begun infuriatingly at 1900, when he heard an ill-conceived cannonade reveal his positions to Napoleon. It had not gotten any better when his second in command, Lord Uxbridge, came by his headquarters to inquire as to what his plans were for the coming battle.

Uxbridge had not been Wellington's choice as second in command. The cavalryman had eloped with the duke's sister-in-law, an unseemly arrangement given both their families' stations in English society. Nonetheless, Wellington had tried to put the event aside when presented with the fait accompli of Uxbridge as his deputy. Nor was there any impertinence in Uxbridge's inquiry. It was just that the duke was not given to speculating on that which he did not know.

"Who will attack the first tomorrow, I or Bonaparte?" had been Wellington's terse response to his deputy's query.

"Bonaparte." Uxbridge had given the obvious answer.

"Well, Bonaparte has not given me any idea of his projects. And as my plans will depend on his, how can you expect me to tell you what mine are?"

The curtness of Wellington's logic hurt Uxbridge, and the duke saw it in his eyes. Yielding, he added, "There is one thing certain, Uxbridge. That is that whatever happens, you and I will do our duty."

That had ended the conversation between them on a softer note, but it did little to improve Wellington's mood. His uneasiness stemmed from the disposition of Blücher's troops. Would the old man come in time? Could he come in time? The rain beating against the window did not lighten his concern. The roads and fields were a mess. Any movement would be tortuously slow.

He stayed awake until after 2300, waiting for word from Blücher about whether he would come on the morrow. When no word arrived, he went at last to bed. But he was up again before 0300, writing letters to cover all contingencies—including defeat.

It was unlike Wellington not to be able to rest when the opportunity arose. He had slept before at difficult times. This morning, however, there were things to be done. It had been a difficult night for the men, to be sure, but daylight would bring new hope, a chance to put order into the confusions of the darkness. First light comes early in northern Europe in the summer. Around 0400 the first signs of light would appear in the eastern sky. By that time the duke planned to be out and about. A momentous day was facing him.

7

THE BEST-LAID PLANS

Le Caillou: 0700, 18 June 1815

His eyelashes flickered. Dark eyes opened to the greyness of the shadowy room. Rain—not so heavy now, but still steady—splattered against the windowpane, carried by the stiffening wind directly against the side of the building. There was an undertone of murmuring from the next room. The personal staff, no doubt, preparing the preliminaries for breakfast. They would be awaiting a signal from the emperor to begin warming the food.

He moved a leg, then an arm. His joints felt swollen, his limbs heavy. For a moment he raised his neck from the hard, cylindrical pillow; lost the will; and let his head fall back to rest. He was not ready to move. His body ached; his mind felt dull. In a minute. He would get up in a minute.

He could smell the dampness in the air. It penetrated beneath his blanket, knifed into his spine, made him shiver. How swollen his joints felt. And his stomach—it hurt! A dull pain sitting deep in the pit of his belly, silently rumbling, then burning. He shifted his position—to no avail. Nausea came over him, forcing him to his side. The new position brought no relief.

Old! He was getting old. The well-being of his youth, the feeling that he would live forever—that fatigue, sickness, exposure, and discomfort held no sway over his will to thrive, to exert, to take charge—had long since faded. Now he felt only the weightiness of his position, felt it in every pore of his skin, every bone of his body. He was heavy with it—a dull, sickening load that bore down on him, slowing his movement, his thinking. He wanted to withdraw, to pull the blanket up over his face, to hide from the responsibilities he had acquired, had sought.

But there was no refuge. Only three hours ago he had assured himself that Wellington had halted, that the allied army could not escape. Now it was time to deliver the coup de grace; the campaign was nearing its climax. A few more hours and it would all be over. The Prussians had been broken the day before last. Blücher, the old fool, was crushed. Some say he was dead. Certainly, his army was retreating.

Now it was Wellington's turn, the sepoy general, that overblown tactician. Well, it wasn't tactics that mattered now. The enemy had been split. The operational concept had worked. Divide and conquer; defeat in detail. All the tactics in the world could not resist the *Grande Armée* gathered in force to deal the crowning blow. And the duke had blundered—placed his army in front of a woods, the Forêt de Soignes. There could be no retreat. Once the allies were broken, they would be impaled on the forest. It would be a battle of annihilation, the culmination of a campaign of annihilation. First the Prussians and now the British and their undependable allies. Their defeat will send a message to the rest of Europe: Do not dare to make war on Napoleon. Pull out. Save yourself. Sue for peace. I will be gracious. I will offer favorable terms. They will grovel at my feet, eager for my mercy, for my gratitude. But I will be the victor, and they will know it.

Again he raised his head and felt the magnetic pull of the mattress against his overburdened body. He almost fell back, but he forced himself to slide his legs over the side and come to a sitting position. His stomach rebelled, forcing him to hunch his shoulders over his protruding belly. With a desperate push he rose to his feet and trudged toward the window, each step sending a searing pain to his bowels.

A small hand came out, bracing his weakened frame against the wall. Watery eyes looked out into the dank courtyard at the soldiers moving back and forth. They looked wet, stiff, miserable. A few of the lancers were yet asleep in the saddle, their forms hidden beneath sodden capes. The steamy breath from their mounts encased them in small clouds of fog. There was little noise. No doubt they had been warned to keep their voices down, that the emperor lay sleeping inside. They looked half dead from fatigue and discomfort.

But they were young. They would bounce back the minute they determined it did no good to seek any further rest. They would throw off their coats, stretch their limbs, and be hard at it in no time. It was the miracle of youth, unfathomable energy. If only he could draw on it, borrow from them. He turned back toward the bed, looked at it once more with longing, then resolved to put forth a supreme effort. He would cover his own discomfort, his sense of weightiness, and face the day and all that it would bring. He called to an aide, who was waiting diligently in the adjoining room.

"Have my bath prepared. And gather the staff. I will breakfast within the hour. I would like them to join me."

The aide gave a short bow and retired from the room. Napoleon turned back to the bed and sat down. For a minute or two he stared at his feet. Over and over again he told himself it was merely a matter of will now. The plan had worked. Wellington was now drawn up before him, ready for the slaughter. It was just a matter of doing it. Once it began, it would take its own course and the outcome was inevitable. The French would sleep in Brussels tonight. There was no question of it. A cold shiver ran down his spine, raising goose bumps on his skin. Tightening his lips, he drew himself together and disrobed for his bath.

Breakfast began cheerily enough. A small group awaited him, standing awkwardly behind their chairs, ill at ease, waiting to see what mood the emperor might be in. They were relieved to observe his seemingly good humor.

He smiled as he made his way to the table. Uncharacteristically, he put his hand on the small of the backs of several of them, a show of decided optimism and fellowship.

"I have them then, these English," he exclaimed, brimming with confidence.

General Drouot, the artillery commander, caught his eye, sensed the good mood, and spoke his mind. "Yes, Sire, and the rain is letting up. With the brisk wind blowing, the ground will dry out in a few hours. It would be worth waiting for that before we begin to attack."

The emperor said nothing, sat down briskly, and reached for a glass of juice. The others took their signal from him, pulled their chairs up, and began to eat. The table was set with the imperial silver plates, covered dishes, and crystal. There was now a buoyant air in the room, and the mood emanated from the principal diner, who ate with gusto.

Only the troubled air of Marshal Soult, sitting directly across from his commander, dampened the general cheer. Napoleon had sensed Soult's pessimism from the moment he had entered, but the emperor purposefully avoided addressing it.

After a few moments, the commander spoke. "Today is a day that we shall all remember."

Smiles all around the table, except from Soult, who sat motionless, his mouth barely moving as he chewed. At last Soult spoke.

"We are outnumbered, Sire. And the ground is soaked. It will be difficult to attack." He knew that Grouchy's request for orders had yet to receive a reply, and the marshal was impatient for that oversight to be addressed.

"You are correct, Marshal Soult. The enemy outnumbers us by more than a quarter. But his position is poorly chosen, and he is reeling from defeat at Quatre-Bras. Did you not see their flight yesterday? They were desperate. Now with a forest to their backs and the initiative in our hands, taking them will be like child's play. We have not less than ninety chances in our favor, and not ten against."

He poked a piece of meat into his mouth, chewed on it rapidly, and savored it before taking a swallow from his glass. He continued, "I will attack Wellington at 0900. What is the state of the ground?"

Soult answered quickly, too quickly for Napoleon. "It will not dry before noon, Sire."

Heavy boots rang in the doorway as Marshal Ney, just returned from inspecting the line of troops, made his entry. He had heard Soult's comments. Ney made a short bow before his commander, apologized for his lateness, and said, "We have attacked with mud on our boots before. We must move before Wellington retreats."

Almost casually, the emperor responded. "Marshal Ney, you are always eager to begin. Or almost always, I should say. The English cannot withdraw; they are pinned. I have seen enough of them to be sure that they are going to fight. It is too late for them to retreat. Wellington would expose himself to certain defeat. The die is cast, and it is in our favor." From his tunic he pulled a map and proceeded to study it, purposefully ignoring the insolent look in Ney's eyes.

General Drouot spoke again, reassured by the emperor's rejection of Ney's impetuosity. "We need four hours for the ground to dry. Right now it is too soft for me to move my guns with the ease we will need to roll the enemy back."

"Four hours, Drouot? Four hours! Battles are lost and won in less time than that." The emperor enjoyed his role of antagonist to his generals.

"Unless the ground is dry, Sire, I cannot answer for my guns."

Ney looked up, his face nearly as red as his hair. "I will need little more than an hour to drive them from the ridge, whether you answer for your guns or not."

The artillery commander remained unperturbed. Staring at the emperor, he offered in a steady voice, "If Wellington were retreating, I would say go now. But he is merely sitting there, with the mud in his favor. Let us wait. Let the wind do its work."

Soult was in favor of a delay. He wanted to exercise caution. What Drouot said about the guns was true. Not only would the mud make them difficult to move, it would diminish the effects of their fire as the shot penetrated and buried itself in the soft earth. As of yet, no orders had been sent to Grouchy. It would be better if the thirty thousand troops with him joined them here, before the ridgeline at Mont Saint Jean. That would take time, but if the order could be sent immediately and the opening of the battle delayed, there was still time to mass forces. In a deep monotone, Soult spoke.

"We need to have Grouchy join us, your Majesty. With his forces, we will have the advantage. I agree that we must delay the opening until that has been arranged."

Napoleon flashed an angry look toward his chief and was about to speak when his brother Jérôme entered the room. Sporting a silken bandage from a fresh wound received two days prior at Quatre-Bras, the younger Bonaparte looked even more rakish than usual.

"Please forgive me, dear brother. I have been inspecting my division, which—it pleases me to report—is prepared for action."

"Ah, Jérôme. Welcome. It is good to see you. Please join us. You are late, but there is still some food left for you." Napoleon pointed at an empty place at the table, glanced down at his map, and went on. "We are in the midst of a discussion on the timing of the attack. Perhaps you have a view."

"We will be ready at any time you desire. But I do have some news, which was picked up over supper last night at an inn at Genappe."

"Yes. Go on." How Napoleon despised the pompousness of his brother. What airs. What could he possibly know that would affect his plan of battle?

"My waiter at the Roi d'Espagne had served Wellington and his staff only the previous evening. An aide to the duke had spoken openly of a planned juncture between Blücher and Wellington. The waiter was only too eager to report to me the full extent of the conversation, citing the aide as saying that the Prussians would come by way of Wavre."

Napoleon looked at his dandyish brother. What did he know of war? He played at it as he played at marriage—a dilettante, with no lasting grasp of the issues at hand. "An interesting plan, Jérôme. But impossible. After Fleurus, the Prussians are incapable of joining Wellington, at least anytime within the next two days. They were slaughtered there on the sixteenth, and their morale is broken. They are hardly a threat to me here."

Soult's voice rose from across the table. "That may be so, Sire. Nonetheless, I believe we would do well to call Marshal Grouchy to us."

Napoleon's eyes flashed in anger. Who were these fools to suggest what must be done? Did they not realize who had saved the Revolution? Who had rescued France from ruin, from the encirclement of her enemies? Who had conquered Europe? Where was their advice when that was being done? He raced to swallow the bite of food in his mouth so that he could speak and silence them once and for all.

But before he could, Ney, oblivious as usual of the storm rising in his commander's breast, broke in with his own comment. "Sire, do what you will. An immediate attack is what is needed. If what Jérôme says is true, then an early battle favors us and denies Blücher a chance to close."

Napoleon's head spun toward his marshal, the vein on his temple enlarged—almost bursting—from the pressure. His fists tightened in his lap, his teeth clamped together. He fought to control his rage. These idiots. How dare they tell me what must be done! Purposefully, he picked up his knife and fork and turned back to his food. All eyes looked toward him, the assembled officers aware now of the anger they had provoked. They waited for their commander to speak.

He wiped his mouth and put down his napkin, looking straight at his chief of staff. "Because you have been beaten by Wellington, you think he is a good general. I tell you: Wellington is a bad general, and the English are bad troops. We shall make short work of them.

"Wherever the Prussians have gone, Grouchy is on their heels. They will not be able to break free of him. It is his mission to pin them wherever he finds them, to worry them to death, and to finish whatever is left of them after their defeat of the sixteenth. We will face only Wellington here, and that bouillabaisse of undependable allies he has gathered about him. I will come at him straight up the middle, after feinting on his right. I will delay the main attack only long enough to allow him to send away his reserves to where I do not mean to break through. Once I commit, nothing will stop us. The English will break only a second behind the Dutch. And when they do, they will have no place to go.

"General Reille, you raise your eyebrows. Do you have something you wish to say?"

His corps commander looked caught, hesitated for a moment, then found his courage. "Sire, when the English infantry are well placed, as Wellington knows how to place them, I regard them as impregnable when subject to frontal attack; this is due to their calm tenacity and the superiority of their shooting. Before you can approach them with the bayonet, you must wait until half your attacking force is destroyed. But the English army is less agile, less flexible, less easily maneuvered than ours. If we cannot beat it by a frontal attack, we may do so by maneuvering."

A sneer crossed the emperor's face. It was all out now. They doubted him. They thought they knew better. Such ingratitude! Such impertinence! It was beyond comment, a despicable arrogance by men not fit to hold his map case. They thought themselves military geniuses.

"How dare you question my plan!" The voice was all ice, freezing those present with its barely controlled ferocity. "You advise me to maneuver. What do you think I have been doing since I returned from Elba? Everything has been maneuver, a maneuver whose sole intention has been to bring me to this place, to this point, so that I could close with my enemy and crush him. Now is not the time to maneuver. Now is the time to fight. There are no tomorrows for us—unless we win today. And we can win only by fighting. Do you expect a bloodless victory? Have you gotten soft in the year since I have been away? No, my friends, there is no avoiding it. Now we fight. I will come at Wellington with everything I have, and I will shove it right down his throat. He will not hold. This is not Spain, not Portugal. He is not fighting you this time. He is fighting *me*. And I will beat him. Tonight we sleep in Brussels. I have ordered the Imperial Guard to pack their parade uniforms. I want them to be dressed appropriately tomorrow, when I speak to my Belgian citizens. I want my imperial coach brought up and my ceremonial robes made ready. Today will bring us victory, and tomorrow all of Europe will hear my voice. They will learn that, if they make war on Napoleon, they can expect only defeat.

"Drouot, you have your wish. I will give you three hours. No more than that. A great battle awaits us. Mark my words. It will save France and be celebrated ever after in the annals of the world. Now gentlemen, this breakfast is over. I expect each of you to follow my orders. I go to inspect my soldiers."

Abruptly, Napoleon stood up and walked out of the room. His aides hurried after him, calling to orderlies to make ready the horses. The marshals and generals were left in stunned silence at the breakfast table. Awkwardly, they put down their eating utensils and filed from the room. The affair would proceed as planned.

Mont Saint Jean Ridge: 1000

"Well, Baron, I know that you Prussians would not agree, but frankly I see no sense in placing infantrymen on the forward slope to absorb the artillery."

The duke of Wellington was talking to General von Müffling. The two of them had been riding together since dawn, inspecting positions, talking with commanders, and cheering the troops. The Prussian marveled at the tonic effect his host had on the allied soldiers. It was ironic. He seemed to hold them in the greatest disdain, and they knew well the sting of his lash. But they loved fighting for him. Old Nosey was to the British what Father Blücher was to the Prussians. He was life and death itself, and their fate was in his hands.

Wellington's lean figure was modestly attired in a small hat without gilt or plumes—it was decorated with only the four cockades, one each for Britain, Spain, Portugal, and the Netherlands. He wore a blue coat, tan leather breeches, and a short cape. Even his horse, a chestnut named Copenhagen, seemed commonplace. The thoroughbred had carried him at Vitoria, in the Pyrenees, and at Toulouse. Unlike so many of the British, there was no pomp and circumstance about the man. He was all business, with as great an eye for detail as Müffling had ever seen.

In fact, Wellington had so busied himself this morning with positioning the reserves, placing units, checking defensive works, and walking fields of fire, that it was hard to envision the bigger picture, the general plan of defense. But Wellington had not forgotten it. It was his classic defense, the one for which he had so disciplined his army that they fell to it almost without instruction, each piece doing its part.

When Müffling stepped back from the events of the moment, he could see the brilliance of the plan. There were essentially three zones of defense. First came the bastions of the three farms to the front—from left to right (east to west) Papelotte, La Haye Sainte, and Hougoumont. These would serve as breakwaters to the oncoming French, positions that would draw in Napoleon's troops before they could close with the main line of defense. The three outposts would weaken and distract the attack so that its full effects could not be brought to bear in one overwhelming moment.

The second zone was the main line of defense itself, well situated along the ridge and integrated in such a way that the more reliable British units were intermingled with allied forces. When the drums had first beat shortly after dawn and the call to arms had gone out, the various units had taken up their positions with a minimum of confusion: artillery and skirmishers in front; infantry behind, on the reverse slopes, hidden from view and artillery fire; the cavalry in reserve, waiting to step in.

And the reserves—the third zone of defense—were close enough to be brought forward in short order but well enough behind to avoid taking needless casualties before being committed. Reserves placement was weighted to the right and center—to the right because of the great concern that the flank connecting the allied army to the Channel not be turned and to the center because that was the direct route to Brussels and the most likely place Napoleon would commit his main attack.

Each commander had been given explicit instructions by Wellington. There was to be no premature movement. Reserves would not rush forward, but would be fed bit by bit into the battle—and only when absolutely necessary.

Time was as important as lives in the battle that was about to unfold. The battle would be measured by the time needed for Blücher to arrive. Wellington had made sure that every possible second would be wrung from the clock, and every possible drop of French blood along with it. The duke had seen to it that the terrain was used to full advantage. The attackers would have to fight through the skirmishers and an unrelenting pummeling from the artillery before they could even close with the defenders. The bastions to the front would slow them down and, if they held, bleed them throughout. Once the attacking forces came through all of this, they would then close on an unseen enemy

who would rise at once and meet them as they crested the hill, greeting them with two feet of cold steel and a double volley from the Brown
Bess, the trusty British musket. After that would come the cavalry,
which would seek to throw the French back or pound them into the
ground if they did not retreat. Then the lines would be strengthened
and readied to do it all over again. As long as the reserves held, the
allied position would stand. The question Müffling had was how long
they could last.

"My Lord Wellington, do you think the farms are tenable? After
all, they are manned by very few forces, and wherever the French choose
to attack, they will do so in overwhelming numbers."

"Baron, the more they throw at the farms, the more I will be pleased.
My bet is that the French will overcommit. It is a natural tendency,
and once committed they will become stuck to the idea of overcoming
the outposts."

"But can the farms hold?"

"Quite frankly, I have my doubts on the left. Papelotte is poorly
situated. It is on low ground with poor fields of fire. Once my skirmishers
are driven back, I will not be able to see what the French are doing.
My artillery will be virtually useless there. Although the walls of the
farm are thick, I am not very optimistic about its chances. Nor have
I positioned many reserves there. I need them elsewhere. Somewhere
I must take risk, and that is where I choose to do it."

"And in the center?" Müffling had a special concern with La Haye
Sainte and Wellington's opinion of its capabilities. It was a battalion
of the King's German Legion that had been sent to hold it.

"We shall see. I expect it to hold, but if a mistake was made last
night in the storm, that is where it occurred. No one occupied it, at
least not with a sense to defend it. Those that went there went for shelter,
and as a result failed to preserve the essentials for a defense. But I
have seen to it that the unit occupying it now is armed with the Baker
rifle. And I have moved a similarly armed company to the sand pit
directly to its north. Marksmen there will be able to cover the eastern
walls by fire, and with the greater accuracy of the rifle they should
be able to lend great assistance. I will reinforce the farm as necessary."
Wellington was aware of Müffling's sensitivity. Therefore, he did not
add that he did not know the commander of the battalion sent to hold
La Haye Sainte and consequently could not be sure of his ability to
hold. It was a nagging doubt that troubled him.

"Surely you do not believe that Hougoumont can hold for very long. It stands alone and isolated in the midst of a thick wood. Once the French are upon it, the defenders will be lost."

"Ah, Müffling, you do not know Macdonell. I have placed him in Hougoumont. He will not yield. There is no better man in my army than Macdonell."

"I have no doubt he is a good man. I saw this morning the effort he has put into the defense. But the task you give him is great. And not all of the units there belong to him."

"Baron von Müffling, if I have learned one thing in all my time in the army, it is that the ability of a unit to fight, for a position to hold, for a mission to be accomplished, is directly proportional to the ability of the commander. If he is good, then his subordinates are good. If he is not, then the best men in the empire cannot perform. Macdonell is good. He is more than good. I have thrown Macdonell into it, and Hougoumont will hold."

The liaison officer asked no more questions. He admired the job Wellington was doing. During the morning the two men had been able to exchange views openly, and the Englishman was receptive to many of the Prussian's suggestions. The right wing had been strengthened at Müffling's urging, an abatis thrown across the Nivelles road, and the forces posted at Braine l'Alleud had been drawn closer to Hougoumont.

Some on the staff had raised reservations about the woods to their rear, but Wellington had reassured them that he knew the woods well, had reconnoitered them several times in the past, and found them wide enough to allow the passage of an army and all of its trains. Although the duke allowed no talk of defeat, it was clear that he had made his own contingency plans to draw back should the defense not hold.

The day had brightened as the morning passed. If a battle were not looming, one could almost enjoy the grandeur of the scenery and its colorful occupants. To the south of the allied line, barely a mile away, the French were on parade. It was a sight to behold: chasseurs in bright green jackets; hussars in dolmans and pelisses, with brilliant reds, greens, blues, and yellows signifying regimental affiliation; dragoons in green coats crisscrossed by gleaming white shoulder belts and with brass and leopard-skin helmets upon their heads; *cuirassiers* with steel breast-plates, crested helmets, and dark blue jackets with red epaulets; lancers in red *kurtkas* and blue pantaloons; and grenadiers in their tall bearskins. The fields were covered by a dazzling quilt of bright colors worn by the most feared fighters in all of Europe. Drums beat, bugles called, and everywhere units marched with great precision.

Wellington, mounted, watched from the southwest corner of the crossroads at Mont Saint Jean, his chestnut standing beneath the single elm tree there. His large retinue of aides had become quiet now. It was clear that the commander did not want to be disturbed. He had done all that he could this morning. Now he had only to await the opening attack.

He knew that the struggle would be bitter, that many would die. He would ask his men to hold on to this ground in a vicious fight to the end. It would be hard, unrelenting. It would be more than was decent to demand of human valor and courage. His men would fall by the hundreds, by the thousands, by the tens of thousands. But each man in his death must exact a price—and he must buy time, time for Blücher to arrive, if he would, if he could. Wellington was about to perpetrate a great cruelty upon his army—to have his troops stand in the face of massed artillery, thousands of cavalry, and the greatest infantry on the continent of Europe—with no guarantee that the outcome would be worth it. It was his duty, but he did not feel noble about it. War was a form of murder after all—mass murder. These young men—boys, many of them—would go to their deaths under his orders. That he himself might die did not diminish the suffering they would endure, did not lessen the responsibility he felt for their lives. But his duty was to command, and he would see his duty through.

At last he turned to his chief of staff. "Well, de Lancey, I think we have tended to everything. Is there anything you can think of that we have omitted?"

"No, my Lord. We are ready. God help us."

"God! I wonder. If He helps us, then who helps them? It seems that God would stay out of this. It is the devil's work that we are about to see."

"I know what you mean, Sir. However, I cannot help but think that our cause is just."

"And if it is, then what would you expect of Him, Sir William?"

"That we might win. Only that we might win." And to himself he added, Only that I might see Magdalene once more.

"Well, I hope you get your wish." With that, the duke of Wellington turned his telescope on the French parading to the south. He wondered where Napoleon might be. He would like a glimpse of his enemy.

8

HOUGOUMONT: 1130

The first cannon shot from the French passed over Hougoumont and hit the ridge behind, close to the 52d Foot. Macdonell heard it and looked at his watch, only to remember that it had quit on him some time after Quatre-Bras. He grunted, having an immediate distaste for things that did not work. He thumped the watch a few times against his palm, and then put the timepiece away. Several other shots passed. They were high and did not put the Guards within the château walls in any danger, though they were loud enough to bring up the goose-flesh on their backs. Outside the walls, in the adjacent orchard and woods, small packets of allied soldiers looked nervously skyward. Macdonell's own gaze went to the woods. The trees were thick enough to give the defenders protection from direct artillery fire. Moreover, until the French could get an observer into place, it would be futile for them to try high-angle fire into the allied positions in and around the château. By and by, the big Scotsman knew, the French would figure out how to bring their artillery in. But for a while their guns would not be a problem.

Macdonell also noted the absence of any artillery fire elsewhere along the front. So, we will be in it from the beginning, he thought, reading the enemy's intentions by the opening barrage. The rounds were all coming to his side of the line but landing behind his position. The French were trying to isolate him while softening up the main defenses for an assault. Apparently, they did not rate the toughness of the defenses at Hougoumont. Either they meant to slip around him—which would be the smarter move—or they would try to bust right through. He hoped it was the latter. He was ready to fight.

Either way, it would come to him sooner or later. That had always been the way for him. As a boy and as a man—certainly as a soldier—he had never seemed to have to go out of his way to find himself in the thick of it. He had had ample opportunity to prove himself, again and again. Just once, he thought, it would be nice if the storm broke elsewhere. But inwardly he knew he was lying to himself. He wanted the fight; wanted it badly; needed it, in fact, if he was to rest his troubled soul.

"Steady boys! It seems as if they want to try our side of the field first." The words were calm, hiding the quickened beating of his heart. He felt it unmanly, and certainly unsoldierly, to reveal any sign of concern. It would only shake the men, and they didn't need any shaking at this time. Inwardly he cursed himself for the nerves bubbling up in the pit of his stomach. But no one could detect his discomfort. Over the years he had perfected the cover of a totally unperturbed exterior.

He tried to force himself to concentrate on matters at hand. Were the positions properly finished? Did he have time to check one more time? Shouldn't he find his company commanders again to ensure that they had understood his plan? The questions raced through his mind, the speed with which he thought them making him even more aware of the emotional effects the opening sounds of battle were having on him.

Inwardly, he knew that he had already done all he could in preparation for the battle. It was time to let the situation unfold. But he needed to do something—anything—to relieve his tension. Yet, until he knew the flow the battle would take, it would do no good to dart around nervously trying to anticipate any one of hundreds of possibilities. The best thing was to show steadiness, to let his men know that he was confident in their ability to hold and in his own ability to command.

He wondered if he would ever be able to rid himself of these prebattle jitters. How many battles did it take? Does a man ever surmount them? It had been this way in Portugal every time. The inner turmoil would swell, barely contained beneath the surface, as if the anticipation of combat would drive him to distraction. He did not know what he feared most: failing his command, betraying his anxiety, enduring the terrible pain of sword and shot, suffering the loss of his men, dishonoring the regiment, losing a limb, dying? There were so many possible outcomes, almost all of them unattractive. He hated it. Yet he loved it too! Why was that? Was it the exhilaration? That must be it. Defying the odds. Standing where other men fled. Holding up where others broke. It gave him a satisfaction like nothing else—as if, through the reality of combat, he could slay all the villains of his childhood imagination. War made him free. Yet, always the fear returned—heaviest in the opening moments, then dissipating as the fighting mounted. But fear was always there, barely suppressed, and if he ever let his guard down, fear would overtake him. He wondered if his legendary courage was nothing but a charade. Behind the facade of coolness under fire hid the real Macdonell—as afraid as any man, maybe more so.

God had played a terrible joke on him, making him so big and so strong. Other men expected him to be brave. He towered above them all. His voice was deeper, his arms brawnier, his chest and neck thicker. They all said he was a born soldier, a natural leader. But he knew what he was: He was just a man, no more immune to self-doubt than any man. But he could not show self-doubt; no one would understand. They all expected him to be a rock, so that is what he would have to be. The luxury of insecurity was not for him. His was a peculiar sort of damnation, to have always to be so outwardly brave.

"Make ready your muskets and look to the south!" His voice literally bellowed from the hollow of his chest. "They will no doubt try a path through the Nassauers." There was contempt in his voice for the poorly reputed allies. Though he had said it to fortify himself, he immediately regretted the tone. Those poor devils were soldiers too, and their position was unenviable. How could they expect to hold the woods against a major advance by the French? He was glad it was they out there, and not his own Guardsmen. Macdonell immediately felt guilty for the thought.

The Guards leaned forward in their positions. They were thankful for whatever cover they could find. No one had to tell them that they would soon be attacked. Wasn't that what they had prepared for all night? Wasn't that why they had gone without sleep, why they had scraped and dug their positions through the night of rain and cold? For the first time since they had moved into the château, concern for food, rest, and warmth left them. Even the wet, soggy uniforms clinging to their clammy skin no longer distracted them. The imminence of combat focused their minds, making irrelevant any concern for creature comfort.

They had to admire their officers, moving about so coolly when it was clear that all hell was about to break loose. The soldiers had to admit that, for all their airs, the gentlemen always seemed to measure up when it came to the fighting and killing. And head and shoulders above them all was Macdonell. There was a man. How he loved a fight! It all seemed like such a great game to him. No doubt he had picked this spot because he knew it would be where the action broke. Damn him, why didn't he know fear like other men? Why couldn't he forsake the thick of it, just one time?

On the other hand, if it had to come, then it was best to have Macdonell in charge. He would know what to do. The man was unflappable. He couldn't be hurt, or so it seemed. He had survived so many skirmishes, so many battles. To have him for a commander was a mixed blessing. It meant that you were likely to have to fight hard, but it also meant that your chances of survival were better. During the night, and now again, the rank and file had both cursed and praised him. "Damn his bloody eyes, he likes this so much. But better to have him directing the action than some timid soul who would worry us to our deaths in his concern for our welfare."

The British artillery was answering now, shot flying over Hougoumont in both directions as opposing cannon searched for each other's lines. Above the din could be heard the rat-a-tat-tat of the French drum. That could only mean that infantry was on the move. Spattering musket fire from skirmishers and pickets began to chatter in the woods to the south of the château.

Macdonell peered around the side of the farmhouse to observe his men at their firing platforms astride the garden wall. They appeared ready to him, officers and soldiers in place. Incredibly, the château's gardener still tended to his plants, as if nothing out of the ordinary was about to happen. He had stayed behind when the owner and his family had pulled out, emerging early that morning to do his chores as if this were just another day. The only concern he had shown was for his trampled flowers, which he was now trying to salvage.

Cannon had opened up elsewhere along the front, covering the opening attack against Hougoumont. There must be somewhere between one hundred and two hundred guns in action, Macdonell estimated—probably nearer the latter. Rounds were falling all along the crest of Mont Saint Jean, but they still posed no threat to Hougoumont. For the moment the château was a sanctuary from the impersonal butchery of cannon fire. All right for now, the colonel mused, but we'll soon have enough to occupy ourselves. He squinted again into the thick woods a few yards beyond the wall.

"Look, Sir, the Nassauers." It was Ensign Montagu of 1st Company. Macdonell moved to where he could see outside the château walls. The Nassau troops were pulling back in considerable disorder, trying to work their way around to the north, behind the château. The Coldstream colonel was disappointed. They had not held for very long. It would have been better if the advancing French had suffered some disruption before arriving at Hougoumont. They still had the Hanoverians to get by, however, and just to the east of the walls was Lord Saltoun and his 1st Regiment of Foot Guards. With luck, they would break up the French formations before they reached the walls.

He could hear the drumbeats more clearly now, and the bugle calls that accompanied them. The musket fire in the woods had picked up tempo, although it was impossible to tell who was doing most of the firing. It could be the picket lines, but more likely it was the main formation of French trying to hasten the withdrawal of the Nassauers. Every now and then, Macdonell thought he could distinguish a chorus of "*Vive l'empereur.*" Somehow, the picture of lustily chanting Frenchmen sent a chill through his bones, as if they were a supernatural force approaching unseen in the darkened woods—a mass of demons incanting their fidelity to a devil-god.

Distracted, he looked at his useless timepiece. "Damn, what good is it? And what does time matter anyway? It could soon be eternity for the lot of us." The thought was so clear it was almost as if he were talking to himself. He shuddered, then caught himself.

Macdonell took his post, determined not to fret until the action had broken. That always seemed to be the turning point for him. The worst of battle was the anticipation; the action was never as bad as his preconception of it. During the fighting he was too preoccupied to concern himself about anything other than the battle at hand. Combat was all action and reaction, no more posturing, no more deliberating—just doing. Remembering that seemed to make him feel better. If only he could control his emotions until it began.

Use this time to think. How many of them are coming through the woods? What formation will they hold? What's the best way to stop them? Should I let them come to me, or should I hit them before they emerge from the dense underbrush? The questioning brought a certain calmness.

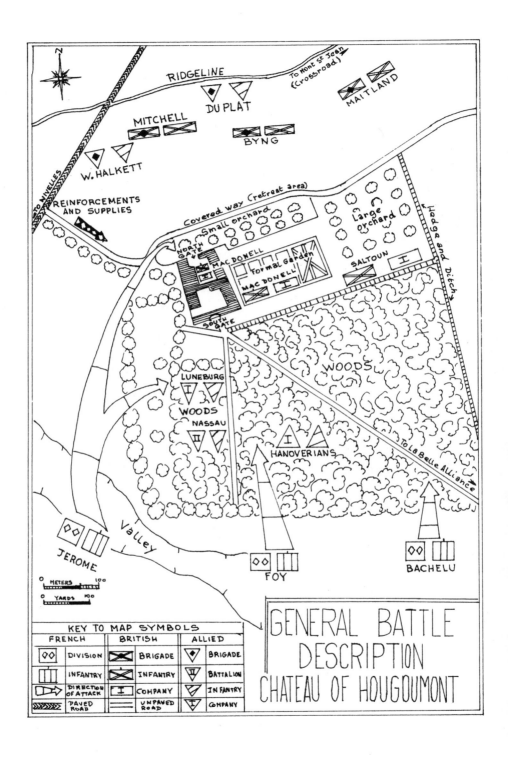

N

RIDGELINE

To Mont St Jean (Crossroad)

MAITLAND

DU PLAT

MITCHELL

BYNG

W. HALKETT

TO NIVELLES

REINFORCEMENTS AND SUPPLIES

Covered way (retreat area)

Small orchard

Large orchard

Hedge and Ditch

NORTH GATE

MAC DONELL

Formal Garden

SALTOUN

I

MAC DONELL

SOUTH GATE

WOODS

LUNEBURG

I

WOODS

NASSAU

II

HANOVERIANS

I

To La Belle Alliance

VALLEY

JEROME

FOY

BACHELU

0 METERS 100

0 YARDS 100

KEY TO MAP SYMBOLS

FRENCH		BRITISH		ALLIED	
00	DIVISION	⊠	BRIGADE	◆	BRIGADE
⊓	INFANTRY	⊠	INFANTRY	II	BATTALION
⊳	DIRECTION OF ATTACK	I	COMPANY	∇	INFANTRY
⋙	PAVED ROAD	—	UNPAVED ROAD	⊽	COMPANY

GENERAL BATTLE DESCRIPTION CHATEAU OF HOUGOUMONT

*   *   *

At that moment, General Bauduin of the 1st Brigade of Jérôme's division was pushing his seven battalions of French infantry through the woods. So far, it had been an easy go. Some of the French skirmishers had fallen—they were passing them now where they lay—but there were not so many killed as to worry the infantry formations moving forward. Most of them had seen casualties before, and these were not heavy.

Whatever force had deployed to meet them as they first entered the woods had fallen back in some haste. Jérôme, Napoleon's brother, had told the brigade commanders that the emperor thought the British army was inferior. But Bauduin harbored his doubts about Napoleon's assessment. As a brigade commander, he had heard too often of incompetent enemy troops, only to see them fight like wild men when the time came. And what did Jérôme know of battle? He was an amateur at this business, no more fit to lead a division than any of the soldiers Bauduin was now pushing before him. In fact, when you thought about it, less fit. As least those men knew what it was to fight.

What bothered Bauduin most was the lack of clarity of his mission. Jérôme had muttered something about his brigade's effort being secondary. That was a notion that the brigade commander was not about to pass on to his subordinates. What were they supposed to do with that kind of information? Soldiers in a secondary effort must fight no less resolutely than those in the main thrust. No matter a soldier's position, death strikes with the same finality. There are no degrees of death; you are either dead or you are not. You either attack or you do not. To him, an attack was an attack, to be carried forward with full fury. But he was not sure of his objective. Was it the château or was it the allied line to its rear? On that point, Jérôme had been unclear. He had merely boasted that he would roll up the allied line from the left. That did not sound like a secondary attack.

Bauduin had pressed his commander about the mission, but the brigade commander's effort had evoked only irritation, not clarity. Jérôme had told him to take Hougoumont and to press on against the main line. Which was more important was not clear. Nothing was clear about the mission. He could not even see the château he was attacking. That alone was unsettling. It was bad enough to go against an observable enemy. To move into the woods against an unknown objective was bad luck. Anything might await. Even the name of the place was confusing: The locals alternatively referred to it as Goumont and Hougoumont. Which was it anyway? And more important, what did it look like? Some of the Belgians they had questioned had given a description of its layout, but Bauduin had to wonder how much they could be trusted. They were such a contemptible people, and their French was so poor. He would feel better, Bauduin concluded, when he saw it for himself.

It was one thing to attack an enemy on the open ground. You could see, then, how he deployed himself and what shelter the ground afforded him and what obstacles it presented to you. But attacking into a woods was a cursed affair. You could see only a few meters to the front; you had to guess what lay beyond. Jérôme had allotted his brigade some cannon, but they were of little use. They could not be wheeled up through the closeness of the trees, at least not in any formation that would support an attack. Bauduin would rely solely on the infantry, and even they were difficult to keep in proper order in the tight woods. It was so like the enemy to fight from such a cowardly position. He would make them pay for such an affront.

But what was he to do after he had taken the château? The question kept nagging at him. Jérôme seemed to think that the farm itself would not be much of an impediment, so Bauduin supposed he would merely press on into the allied line that was waiting on the ridge beyond the château. But if that was the true objective, then why did he have to take this difficult route through the woods? There seemed to be room to maneuver around it to the west. That would have been a quicker— perhaps even safer—route, although so far, he had to admit, there did not seem to be much danger along the direction they were taking. But the woods could offer so much surprise. It was all very forbidding.

Belonging to the division commanded by the brother of the emperor was a mixed blessing. One might get special consideration for food and supplies, but it was difficult to question a member of the royal family. And Jérôme was such a pretentious sort. It seemed as if half the division's trains were devoted to his personal wardrobe. Jérôme liked to put on the airs of his brother, and the more it became obvious that he did not have the latter's talents, the more Jérôme blustered behind the veil of kinship. Napoleon had bestowed on his brother the pompous, silly title of king of Westphalia. With a sniff Bauduin noted that Jérôme, "His Highness," was nowhere to be seen in the woods. It was an irreverent thought, but how often the Bonapartes seemed to lead from the rear these days. Had Jérôme not been lightly wounded two days earlier in the fighting at Quatre-Bras, Bauduin would have allowed his questioning to probe further.

Bauduin brought himself back from his insubordinate contemplation. He had enough at hand to worry about. Resistance was beginning to stiffen in the woods. The first elements opposing the attacking French may have run, but whatever it was they were bumping into now was putting up a decent fight. No matter, though, the defenders were outnumbered and would quickly be outfought by the French. How much farther could it be to the château?

They had come to a beanfield now where already the small sprouts had been trampled into the mire. Obviously, a great many boots had passed this way since the heavy rain of the night before. Bauduin's concern deepened. He was liking this attack less and less.

As Bauduin's men were sinking ankle deep into the mud of the trampled beanfield, Lieutenant Colonel Lord Saltoun's two companies opened fire from the right front of the French at a range of only 50 meters. Saltoun's troops had appeared suddenly, as if from nowhere, and the effects of the massed volley were telling. The individual Brown Bess was notoriously inaccurate, but dozens of muskets aimed at several score of men bunched together were likely to hit something. A dozen of Bauduin's men were blown apart.

The attack startled the French. Faces froze in a mixture of surprise, horror, anger, fear, and revulsion. The earlier pomp and circumstance of the beautiful June morning had come to a rude end. The strutting was over now. They had closed with the enemy, who meant to stay and fight, undaunted by the parade-ground precision of the *Grande Armée*.

"Advance, my soldiers, advance!" Bauduin realized he had to get his men going again. He knew now he should have brought his artillery forward, even if it would have had to thread its way painstakingly through the forest. A touch of the grape would dampen the resolve of the defense. He was yelling to an aide to have the guns brought forward when the second volley tore into his ranks. Another score of French riflemen fell into grotesque patterns on the muddy field.

As a few French muskets answered Lord Saltoun's Guardsmen, Bauduin's officers wheeled the French infantry formation against the smaller force, seeking to overwhelm it with a larger mass. It was the only thing to do, a tactic they had drilled time and time again, normally on open ground. But in battle even the right idea can go awry. Just as the French pivoted to their right, Macdonell appeared with a small but solid detachment of his own.

The Scotsman had lost his patience. When the Hanoverians had followed the Nassauers around to the back of the château, he had come outside the walls to see if he could slow the French advance himself. Saltoun's massed volley had given him his cue, and he had pressed forward with a small contingent to see if he could contribute to his enemy's dilemma. As Bauduin wheeled against Saltoun, Macdonell leveled a volley into his flank, then charged with bayonet.

The French were caught in a cross fire. All at once the woods had belched forth death. Although Bauduin was being struck by smaller forces, the suddenness of the attack and the unexpected directions from which it had come knocked him off balance. Awkwardly, his men tried to escape back in the direction from which they had come, their boots coming off in their haste, stuck in the gluelike mud. Rear ranks pressed up against the panicked men in front, all facing different directions, unable to fire and unable to fend off the bayonets being thrust at them in their defenseless positions. Officers screamed for them to reorder. For a moment, the French had allowed their fears to overwhelm them, but quickly their discipline returned under the blows and exhortations of their leaders. Presently, they reordered themselves and turned to face their assailants.

"Pull back, lads. Pull back!" It was Macdonell, calm now, in control of his emotions. He had done what he could for the moment. It was time to pull back to better cover. Bean sprouts would not do, not against these overwhelming odds. Instinctively, Macdonell tried to estimate the number of French coming at him. It was more than a battalion, probably more than two. He spied Bauduin upon his horse and recognized the rank. A brigade commander! The colonel caught his breath.

"Steady, boys. Fall back. Give ground. But keep your order." Macdonell's clear, resonant voice eased the fear of his men. Slowly they fell back.

But the same trees and muddy ground that helped to disorganize the French made it difficult for the British to execute their normal formations. Here and there, individual soldiers broke away, not wishing to expose their backs to French musket fire. Some wedged themselves down behind trees and bushes and sought to pick off the regrouping French. Others tried to move out smartly in the direction of the château.

Lord Saltoun ordered his own men back toward the orchard. His mission was to hold there, and he knew that the French would soon be attacking. He was highly pleased with himself for drawing first blood, proud to have shown that Guardsmen could coolly break up an attack of a larger force. True, Macdonell's entry into the fray had been timely, but that was Macdonell for you. He always knew when to act. He was a natural.

Saltoun knew that Macdonell would have his hands full now, poor devil. That château would draw enemy like a dead horse draws flies. At least Macdonell would have the protection of the walls if he used them well—and Macdonell undoubtedly would. It could go a lot worse in the orchard, depending on when the French despaired of taking the château head on and decided to push around it. Hopefully, Macdonell would make that an expensive proposition for them.

The initiative had passed back to the French. Bauduin, irritated that he had been caught flat-footed in the underbrush, ordered his arriving artillery to blast away at the trees to his front. If any more enemy formations were waiting to give him a surprise, he would make it an unpleasant wait.

For the British soldiers gone to ground, the effects were terrifying. If was as if they were alone in a hostile world. The woods had become a death trap. Shot plowed through rocks, branches, and tree trunks with a sickening crack, sending splinters in every direction and adding to the deadly effects of the shrapnel. The scattered defenders responded in a variety of ways. Some put out a fusillade of musket fire with impressive rapidity, blackening their faces with repeated bites into the powder cartridges. Others merely pressed their bodies closer to the damp earth, hoping that, as in the nightmares of their childhood, the monster of death would pass them by.

But the French were thorough. They spread out through the woods, inexorably moving forward. Whenever they saw an enemy firing at them, a dozen muskets would be lowered to smite him from their path. Where they came upon a cowering opponent, a pair of bayonets would quickly dispatch the irritant. Even the dead and wounded were not left unmolested. A gratuitous chop from musket butt or heavy ax sufficed to finish off the fallen once and for all.

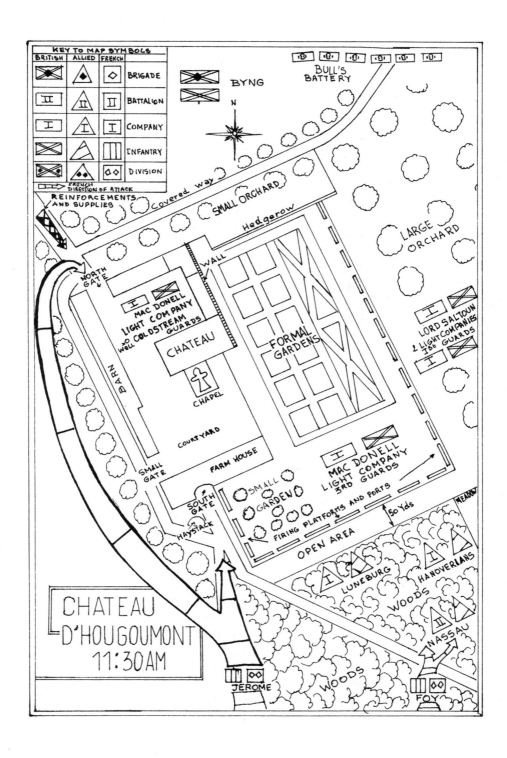

KEY TO MAP SYMBOLS

BRITISH	ALLIED	FRENCH	
⊠	▲	◇	BRIGADE
II	II	II	BATTALION
I	I	I	COMPANY
⊠	▲	|||	INFANTRY
⊠	▲▲	◇◇	DIVISION

⊏⊐⊐▸ FRENCH DIRECTION OF ATTACK

BYNG

BULL'S BATTERY

N

REINFORCEMENTS AND SUPPLIES

Covered way

SMALL ORCHARD

Hedgerow

LARGE ORCHARD

NORTH GATE

WALL

BARN

MAC DONELL
LIGHT COMPANY
COLDSTREAM GUARDS

well

CHATEAU

CHAPEL

FORMAL GARDENS

LORD SALTOUN
2 LIGHT COMPANIES
1st GUARDS

COURTYARD

SMALL GATE

FARM HOUSE

SMALL GARDEN

MAC DONELL
LIGHT COMPANY
3RD GUARDS

SOUTH GATE

HAYSTACK

FIRING PLATFORMS AND PORTS

50 Yds

OPEN AREA

MEADOW

CHATEAU
D'HOUGOUMONT
11:30 AM

LUNEBURG

HANOVERIANS

WOODS

NASSAU

JEROME

WOODS

FOY

At last General Bauduin could see the château take form through the trees beyond. "There it is. Fan out. Take it at once from all sides." He knew what his objective was now.

"Take the château. Take Hougoumont. *Vive l'empereur!*" He almost smiled with the exhilaration, just as a musket ball penetrated the side of his neck. It stung, but little more than the barb of a bee might. Without thinking much about it, he moved his right hand to the wound.

He felt a heavy splash of blood on his fingertips, and a second later yet another. He slowly turned his attention from the battlefield as he tried to comprehend what was happening to him. From the corner of his eye he saw a stream of thick fluid burst from his neck as he extended his arm to inspect his reddened hand. The realization came in an instant. The musket ball had hit his jugular.

The general's mind seemed to resist comprehending the significance of his discovery. There was not much pain, so the injury could not be too bad. Besides, he was a brigade commander, and his men were committed to action. He had to continue with his mission. But something was wrong. So much blood. How could that be, from such a pinprick of a wound? He stopped, felt the blood burst forth again. Then he admitted the terrible truth to himself. He was going to die!

He turned to call to his aide, but the young officer was nowhere in sight. He spoke anyway—to the indifferent mass of soldiers in the general direction of his voice. It made no matter. No words came out, the sounds drowned in the torrent of blood pulsing from his throat. His eyes widened in terror as he desperately tried to stem the flood by grasping his neck with his slippery hands. Fingertips frantically felt for the cut. The hole in his skin seemed so small, not much bigger than a shaving nick. The ball had not penetrated deeply enough to embed itself in the flesh, just deeply enough to puncture the vein and sail on, barely disturbed in its flight. It was enough. Already his sleeves were turning a deep purple, soaked with his own life's fluids. Slowly he slipped from his horse, his vision blurring as he turned back to glance at Hougoumont. The château had killed him. Jérôme had killed him. Napoleon had killed him. He was outraged. He was not ready to die. It was too soon. There was no pain. He could recover. If only he could stop the blood. But no one was looking, and he could not compress the wound himself. He looked up at the face of one of his soldiers and grabbed at the man's trouser cuff as he came by.

The soldier looked down, his thoughts confused. Who is this madman in an officer's uniform at my feet? Why is he grabbing at me so? Has not the order been given to take the château? And isn't that what I am doing? These officers, so contradictory. They never seem to know what they want.

The infantryman kicked loose from Bauduin's grasp. In the moment it had taken for the soldier to break free, the general had resigned himself to his death. For some reason, it was almost welcome. Where only seconds ago he was horrified at the thought, it now seemed to hold a certain appeal. He turned his face toward the château one more time. He would have liked to have gotten a closer look at the place.

Macdonell had moved to the château garden. He braced his men for the appearance of the French. Once they emerged from the woods, they would be almost at the walls. Muskets could not miss at that range. As long as the enemy did not grab the barrel of his piece, the defender could merely point and blast away. It would take discipline, though, to keep the fire up. It is natural for men to freeze when looking death straight in the eye. There is such a coldness in the stare that it seems to stop all action. But good training and, above all, discipline, would overcome that. And there was Macdonell himself. A stern glance from him could be colder than death itself.

With a roar the French emerged from the woods. The sound began deep in their chests and resonated throughout the trees, bouncing off the wall to their front. As they left the tree line, they sensed the château was theirs. Their pace quickened. From the windows, over the top of the wall, and through the firing ports, the British muskets projected at a hundred different angles. Undaunted, the French surged forward. For an instant they were spared—the British infantrymen were frozen by the shock of the ferocious attack. For so long they had steadied themselves for the onslaught; nevertheless, now they seemed not to know what to do.

"Fire!" "Fire!" "Fire!" The shouts echoed within the château walls as officers and sergeants yelled to wake their men from their trancelike state. At once the Guardsmen came alive. Fingers tightened around triggers and unleashed round after round into the oncoming French. Macdonell watched as several dozen attackers fell in a heap. How any escaped the fire he could not comprehend. There was no cover for any of them. The only hope an exposed Frenchman had was that, by some quirk of fate, no one would pick him out as a target. Even then, he was likely to be hit by a stray round. The air was thick with musket balls.

But there was no mercy in Macdonell for any of them. He wanted them all struck down. Every one that remained standing was a dire threat to his mission. They must all be slaughtered, as quickly as possible, for every second saw more and more of them emerging from the woods. Despite what seemed to be certain death, they came on.

Jérôme's troops were not fighting as individual mortals. They had become something larger than themselves, a great force whose momentum was not to be quelled by the loss of its lesser components. They pressed forward, shooting back at whatever fired at them. As some fell, others took their places, banging up against the wall, searching for a point of entry. They climbed on one another, groping for a handhold of some type in order to propel themselves over the construction before them and into the château. They slid along the wall to either side, like a flood tide breaking around an obstruction. Neither the carnage, the fire, the screaming, nor the château wall could stop them. They were a frenzied colony of fighting ants. Death did not matter. Their sole purpose in life was to get inside and kill their enemy.

Macdonell could not believe the events unfolding before his eyes. He had taken a musket from a wounded soldier and was killing Frenchmen as fast as he could fire. He could practically jam it into their teeth and pull the trigger. They were barely inches off his muzzle. Yet they did not turn back. They merely grabbed at each other, stepped over the dead and dying, and came on.

"Sir, the gate. They are through the gate!" The shout came from the courtyard. For Macdonell, it was the worst news imaginable. It must be the north gate; he had just looked to the security of the south gate. That was closed and well secured, sturdy, and blocked up with enough reinforcing material to make forcing it an impossibility. It could not have been breached.

But the north gate had been used as the entry point for supplies and ammunition. He had told his men to ensure that it was closed and bolted after each passage. Had they failed to follow his orders? What buffoonery! It could prove fatal to the defense of the entire château. He ran to the courtyard from the garden and saw the worst of his fears.

The French, led by a huge soldier wielding a fearsome ax, had come out of the woods at the back of the château and found the north gate unsecured. For a brief moment, a few determined defenders yet outside the gate put up a desperate fight. Spurred on, however, by their commanding officer, Colonel de Cubieres of the 1st Light Battalion, the French chopped them down. For a second, the gate lay uncovered. Exhorted by their colonel, a handful of attackers—the big axman in the lead—bolted inside. The officer started to come forward himself, but he took a musket ball in his face as his horse was shot out from under him.

A terrible melee unfolded before Macdonell's eyes. Almost fifty Frenchmen had penetrated inside the gate, fighting hand to hand with musket butts, bayonets, axes, and swords. The Guards were retreating back to the farmhouse steps, shooting desperately at the oncoming French, who were swarming inside the gate in ever increasing numbers.

"The gate! Close the gate before more get inside!" It was Macdonell, but no one could hear him. For a split second, he felt panic rise in his chest. He gritted his teeth and brought himself under control. His eyes narrowed into a ferocious glare of determination. He was all right now. He could sense the calm within. Calm was what it was all about. He knew what had to be done. Moreover, he was confident he could do it.

He rushed to the gate, followed by a handful of men who understood by his action what they had not been able to hear him say. They raced across the cobblestones to the half-open gate. A few Frenchmen stood to block their way, but the Guardsmen dispatched them on the run. Macdonell put his weight behind the heavy wooden gate and pushed it shut. His extemporaneous bodyguard protected him from clawing Frenchmen on both sides of the wall who knew that victory, as well as their personal survival, lay in keeping the gate open. Pushing with all of his might, the colonel felt as if his lungs would burst from the exertion. The cords in his arms and shoulders strained with the great force. The gate was shut; now if they could only keep it that way.

He spied a large timber lying beside the path leading up to the farmhouse. Yelling to his sergeants to hold the gate shut, Macdonell dashed to pick it up. A Frenchman came at him with his bayonet, thrusting at his chest, barely missing the large bulk of his shoulders and neck and slicing through a quarter inch of skin above his collarbone. The colonel grabbed his assailant's musket by the barrel, ripping it from his hands, and swung the weapon in a wide arc; the butt of the musket crashed with full force into the Frenchman's left temple. He was dead before he hit the ground. Wasting no time, Macdonell stooped to cradle the heavy wooden beam in his arms. With a grunt he lifted the beam and staggered back to the gate, where he dropped it into the latch.

The French in the inner court were caught in a death trap. Muskets blasted at them from the main house, from the barn, from the garden, and from the chapel as even the wounded sought to avenge themselves. The French tried to fight their way back to the gate or to seek refuge somewhere amongst the debris and buildings of the courtyard, but the British gave them no quarter. The large Frenchman who had led the charge into the courtyard—Sous Lieutenant Legros, known through-out Napoleon's army as The Enforcer—desperately tried to hack his way into the chapel. But his very size—his would be the largest corpse found on the battlefield—attracted the fire of a half dozen British muskets. With a snarl he smashed at the chapel door as a musket ball entered his face. A second ruptured his spleen; a third shattered his left elbow. As he went to his knees, a British saber split his skull. As he fell flat under the torrent of pain, a bayonet entered his stomach. Still he lashed out in his death throes, determined to take as many with him as he could. But his struggle was futile and with him died the last hope of the trapped French. One by one they were hunted down until only a drummer boy was left. Of no apparent threat to the defenders, his life was spared—he was the only survivor of the French force that had entered the courtyard.

Macdonell was covered in blood, only a little of it his own. But he was in complete control of the battle, fully cognizant now of how Wellington was using him to undo the French. He could hear the British artillery firing overhead and bursting into the woods beyond. It was shrapnel, seldom used over the heads of friendly troops. It was a delicate and dangerous business, but by the screams he could hear from beyond the wall, he knew it was taking effect on the attackers.

By God, the duke had starch. His plan was becoming perfectly clear to Macdonell. Bleed the French. Make them waste their men. Make them run out the clock. Use up as few defenders as possible. Trade lives for time, but make it a profitable trade. The colonel admired the simplicity of the plan, its utter ruthlessness. Well, if that was the game, he would see it through. He would hold the château until Judgment Day if necessary. As long as he lived, it would not fall.

His soldiers could see the determination in his face, and in it they read their own fate. They would fight unto death at this cursed spot.

The French were still clawing at the wall, and the British ranks had thinned. Men were crawling into the barn and the chapel for treatment of their wounds, although few anticipated anything approaching adequate assistance. There were just too many casualties, and obviously many more to come. But the chapel at least offered a sort of solace, even for the nonreligious. Perhaps it was better to die in a chapel than a barn. Those who could make it to the door of the shrine crowded inside to huddle beneath the feet of the heavy wooden crucifix hanging on the wall.

All around Hougoumont the din of battle deafened the ears. Muskets banged, cannonballs exploded, enraged men screamed and cursed, the wounded moaned, and the dying coughed and prayed while officers and sergeants shouted orders. Smoke from the muskets rose on all sides of the château, burning the nostrils and making the eyes water. The heat of the day thickened, causing parched throats to thirst for water. Macdonell's watch could not tell him, but it was a few minutes after midday.

9

COMMAND POSTS: AROUND NOON

The Allied Army

A few hundred meters to the north of Hougoumont, Wellington watched from his horse as the battle developed around the château. He heard more than he saw, but what he saw told him enough. He was watching for clues to the timing, and he found them. "Tell Colonel Woodford to move with his four companies to drive the French from the north of the château."

"Just four companies, my Lord?" It was de Lancey, his chief of staff.

"Yes, just four. This will be a long day, and I want to save a little for later. Of course, I expect Woodford to join Macdonell once he has driven the French off."

"Sir, it is at least a divison that the French bring to bear there."

"I hope that Napoleon commits more than that. He is wasting his time at Hougoumont. Macdonell won't fall, not before he's bled the French white."

Wellington surveyed the smoke coming up out of the wood around the château. "Quite a din going on down there. I think it's time to give them a bit more in the way of firepower. Tell Sir Augustus to put more of his shrapnel into action. Whose battery was it that I had Colonel Fraser position forward to support Macdonell?"

"It was Major Bull's, my Lord. The 5.5 inch," de Lancey answered, his face showing concern about firing shrapnel over the heads of their own force.

"Yes, yes, of course. Very well. We must keep the six and nine pounders firing along the edge of the wood. I want to make sure the French feel compelled to focus on the château. Pin them to it. Don't give them the freedom to detour wide around it." Wellington noticed the worry in his quartermaster's eyes. "Don't worry. Sir Augustus is very good at this business, and I shall never let it get very far away from me."

As if to punctuate his comments with irony, a French shell landed only seventy-five meters from the two noblemen. The accompanying staff hunched their shoulders, pulling their heads in turtlelike. Wellington remained unmoved on his horse. A few of the waiting British infantrymen on the ridge had fallen with the blast.

"I want all the men in ranks to move to the back slope along this ridge. And for God's sake, have them lie down. There is no return in empty-headed courage." The duke was irritated. So many of his subordinates seemed to think it was unmanly to step out of the line of fire. He was unaware that his own example was the antithesis of the caution he was urging on his army.

His staff was exhilarated to be with him in the opening moves. Wellington was as cool as ice, as if he were on an afternoon's outing in the country, not directing the climactic battle for the control of Europe. Clearly, every sense he possessed was alert. Yet he did not seem overly concerned about events. The only abruptness in his voice came in the terse orders he passed through his aides. But any agitation that could be detected was purely impersonal, directed to correct situations, not people. Most dramatic of all was his utter indifference to his own safety. The young staff members were enraptured by his iron nerve; the older ones recognized that it lessened their own probability of surviving the day. But both young and old knew that, as long as Wellington was their commander, they could show no concern for their own well-being. They were there to transmit the commander's will to his army. Their personal safety counted for nothing. They existed only to do his bidding. As a group, they followed their commander at a slow trot over to the artillery formations, where the duke could inspect the correctness of their fire.

Colonel de Lancey rode to ensure compliance with Wellington's orders. In the back of his mind was the image of his beautiful young wife, Magdalene. How concerned for him she had looked on the early morning of the sixteenth, when he took his leave from her at Brussels for the battle at Quatre-Bras. It is just as well she cannot see me now, he thought.

His mind wandered further, not without a little guilt, recalling how he had forced himself to focus on the writing of the necessary orders to the army all through the night of the fifteenth. She had stayed up with him the entire time, never speaking dare she interrupt his duties, occasionally bringing him some strong green tea to keep his mind alert. He hoped she had followed his instructions and gone to Antwerp, twenty-five miles north of Brussels. He wondered if she could hear the bombardment now taking place here at Mont Saint Jean. Probably not, he calculated, although the wind does play tricks on these warm summer days. Sometimes what cannot be heard ten miles away is quite audible at several times the distance.

He remembered, too, the wonderful night of the fourteenth, when they had lain together as husband and wife, both of them quite untroubled by the proximity of the opposing armies and the battle that was sure to come. There was a tenderness in their loving, a sweetness that lingered far into the next morning. How radiant she seemed then, completely un–self-conscious of her rapture of the evening before. She was such a beauty—doelike eyes that came alive with fire and passion; a delicate neck that flowed so gently into a strong and alluring back; tightly curled, auburn hair that, when unfettered from its fashionable bun, spilled down below her comely shoulders. They had married so recently, less than three months ago. What a cruel twist of fate that their wedded bliss had coincided almost exactly with the return of that monster Napoleon from Elba.

How had he lived before her? He could not recollect. It was as if there had been no life then—only a waiting for her. And how thrilling the discovery of her had been: a shyness at first, a self-consciousness at his attraction to her and his easily observed hope that it might be reciprocated, or at least not spurned; and then, with time, greater openness and the confessions of mutual attraction, sealed by the physical demonstration of their love. It had been exhilarating, rapturous—truly a heaven on earth. Each day seemed to deepen the love even more, and now that they were apart there was only a terrible yearning to be with her, as if nothing else in life were important, not even this battle now unfolding before him.

For a moment Sir William had forgotten the business at hand. But it came back to him in a rush as yet another cannonball bounded into sight before his eyes. He shamefacedly put his pleasant thoughts from his mind and spurred his horse forward at greater speed. He was only thirty-four years old, but he was the chief of staff of the allied army.

He should not—could not—allow personal reminiscences to distract him from his duties.

The Right Wing of the *Armée du Nord*

Marshal Emmanuel Grouchy was enjoying a late morning breakfast of strawberries at the village of Walhain, south of Wavre. Hatless in the sun, he was already suffering a reddening on his high forehead. His wizened face, weather-beaten from countless campaigns in the saddle as a cavalryman, made him look older than his forty-nine years.

Then, too, he was still smarting from Napoleon's chastisement the morning before last, at Ligny. The tight lines in his face showed the pinched state of his ego. He had been the last officer appointed by Napoleon to be a marshal of the empire. Some said, he had heard, that in the years of true glory he never would have made the grade. They whispered that it was only now, in these desperate days, that the emperor would reach down to appoint a man of his lesser stature a marshal of France.

The whispers had put Grouchy on the defensive. As it was, there was no gratitude in his breast for the trust Napoleon had shown in appointing him commander of the right wing of the army. He had not been allowed to act like an independent commander. The emperor had been overbearing, issuing orders with such minute detail as to imply that he did not trust his marshal's judgment. And the lack of appreciation by Napoleon for the bitter fight Grouchy had put up against the Prussians on the sixteenth had left a sour taste in his mouth. Even the sweetness of the strawberries could not displace it.

Sitting before him was an old friend, Commandant Rumigus, a veteran of several campaigns with Napoleon, as his missing arm could attest. Nonetheless, Rumigus was only too happy to be back in the field again. The commandant had noted, however, that the emperor did not seem the same man. Napoleon was much more withdrawn, much more tired. But, as close as he felt to the marshal and as much as he sensed Grouchy's pique with the emperor, the one-armed man was reluctant to talk further about such a sensitive subject. Even to the worldly veteran, Napoleon was still something more than a man. It was not right, nor could it be very safe, to be openly critical of him.

In the distance, some twenty-three kilometers to the west, the gunfire from Hougoumont could be heard. Above the distant horizon black smoke rose high into the sky. The marshal paid it no attention, seeming to concentrate instead on his meal.

Approaching the table across the lawn—his stride firm, determined—came the commander of IV Corps, General Gérard. During the preceding days of the campaign, Grouchy had grown to dislike his subordinate intensely. It was as if Gérard did not understand the difference between a marshal and a corps commander. All along, Gérard had barely concealed his impudence. Since Ligny he had not concealed it at all.

"By your leave, General Grouchy, do you not hear the guns firing to the west?" The words grated on the marshal. Even the lack of correct address was pointed. Why couldn't the man call him *Marshal?* Of course he could hear the gunfire. Did Gérard think his commander deaf, as well as an idiot?

"But of course, General, I do." He turned back to his strawberries.

There was a moment's awkward silence, made doubly so by the continued shell fire audible in the distance. At last Grouchy looked up. His subordinate's face was red, and it was not the sun that had caused it.

"Come, let us see if we can calculate from where the noise is coming." The marshal felt that he must give some instruction or other, even if he meant it to go nowhere. Rumigus rose with his friend, and the three officers strode from the table, through the garden, and out into a field where thousands of French infantry rested on their packs.

An aide-de-camp saw the trio approach, watched them search the horizon, and hurried over to report that a local peasant had suggested that the smoke and gunfire came from the vicinity of Mont Saint Jean. Grouchy listened to the younger man but said nothing, his face impassive except for the slight sucking in at the cheeks.

Gérard could contain himself no longer. "General, we must march to the sound of the guns. We have over thirty thousand men here, a third of Napoleon's army."

Grouchy's anger was spontaneous. "Do not presume to tell me what my duty is! You know that my orders are to keep my sword in Blücher's back. That Prussian devil is still to my north."

Gérard's eyes shot fire, his brows closed across the bridge of his nose in a tight, ferocious line. For a moment it looked as if the corps commander would strike his marshal.

Rumigus broke the tension. "Marshal Grouchy is right. Besides, an attempt to cut cross-country would put us nowhere but up to our backsides in the mud." His voice was low and throaty, the type that lends finality to the opinions it expresses.

At that moment the engineer-general, Valazé, came up and joined the conversation. "It is my opinion that we should march to join the emperor. Once we defeat Wellington, which we surely will if we join forces, then we can turn and deal with Blücher."

His words generated more discussion among the officers gathering around Grouchy. It was more than the marshal could stomach. How dare his subordinates enter into open debate, and in his presence, as if he could not decide what was the correct thing to do.

"Gentlemen, I will have no more of this. Only last night I sent a dispatch to Napoleon telling him of my intention to pursue Blücher in the direction of Wavre. That dispatch would have arrived at the emperor's camp before dawn. As you know, it is his custom to dispatch any new instructions long before breakfast. Had he cared to do so, those instructions would now be in my possession." The marshal spun on his heel and stormed back toward his breakfast table, although he had lost his taste for the meal.

His pride wounded, Marshal Grouchy would not budge. Napoleon had told him to go to Wavre. That is where he would go, the sound of the guns be damned.

The Prussian Army

"Come, my children, we must get them through this entanglement." It was Blücher, red of face and stinking of an alcohol-saturated sweat. "My word is at stake. You mustn't let the British think I fail to keep my word."

The Prussian general's manner was pleasant enough, but it still made his officers nervous. General von Bülow had been working since 1100 to push his II Corps through Wavre. His corps had been the farthest from Waterloo, but since it was the freshest—not having been at Ligny—Gneisenau had ordered it to lead the march. The first brigade had made it through Wavre easily enough. But a fire had somehow broken out and, in the narrow streets, it was almost impossible to get the rest of the troops and their artillery past it. Nor did Bülow want to detour around the town. The mud would bog him down, making the passage even slower, and the rough going would break up any semblance of a formation.

Blücher, for all his stated concern, seemed to be enjoying himself. Despite the painful condition of his leg and the bruises to his upper body, caused by the fall of his wounded horse, he was laughing and cursing with his soldiers as if he were a young recruit on furlough. The men loved him for it; he kept the entire army in good cheer as soldiers labored under their heavy packs on the overcrowded roads. His eccentric sense of humor stood him in good stead. Earlier that morning he had refused his physician's plea to rub his wounds with alcohol stating, "It makes no difference to me if I go into eternity annointed or unannoited. If things go well today, we shall soon all be washing and bathing in Paris."

Now he called to the troops. "Come my children. You must march. The British have need of some Prussian steel." It was the kind of martial clamor that the rank and file enjoyed. It made them move faster, exert themselves more. Blücher was the strong father image most of them remembered from their childhoods, feisty and irascible, friendly but firm, with enough authority behind his beckoning voice to remind them that, after all, he was a Prussian general and it would not be good to ignore his instructions.

The old marshal was eager for the fight. It had been great adventure at Ligny but, after all, he had lost that one. It was time to pay the French back. He had to chuckle at his audacious plan. His orders had put the bulk of the army on the move. Only Thielemann and his III Corps were left back to cover what was in effect a mass exodus from Wavre. It was a withdrawal of a different stripe, avoiding the threatening embrace of one army, only to turn and fight another.

"Sergeant, why do you look so glum? Do you not want to join me in a drink of some French wine, a fine red vintage?"

The struggling noncommissioned officer was compelled to look up into the leering face of Blücher. "Yes, my General!"

"Ah, a good answer. Then you must make haste. The British are no doubt drinking their fill by now. Do you not hear all the noise in the vineyard?" Blücher laughed out loud at his own joke.

He was aware that his men never knew how to take him. Even his chief of staff, Gneisenau, thought him mad half the time. But the old marshal was confident that even his brilliant, taciturn chief, for all of his punctiliousness, was as much taken with his commander—and all of his idiosyncracies—as any of the privates.

"A strange man, that one," Blücher murmured to himself as he thought about Gneisenau. "So meticulous in his planning, so detailed, so correct. But for all his thoroughness, he still needs me to make things happen. . . ." The ability to catalyze events was a gift the old man had possessed all his life, and it allowed him to get away with his many oddities. In many ways eccentricity was a perfect shield. It allowed his wild personality to become a commodity that the nation could not do without. And it allowed him to drive his army to battle when the wisest heads among his senior leaders were advising against it. He had given his word to Wellington, and he would keep it. The duke was only an Englishman, it was true. But he was a great general, and he knew how to fight. Blücher would show him it was not a skill that Wellington alone possessed.

As a series of muffled explosions reverberated to the west, Blücher urged his horse forward to help a cursing captain of infantry move his company through a muddy section of the road. With a correct nod the captain promised his general he could get things moving. The old man could not have been happier. He spurred his horse on toward the head of the Prussian column, at Chapelle Saint Lambert, halfway to Wellington's army.

As he rode past his soldiers, one of the privates slapped his knee, beseeching: "Bring us lots of luck today, Father Blücher!" The general looked down with an evil glee.

The *Armée du Nord*

With a stinging pain, Napoleon rose from the chair placed for him on the grassy knoll. He could no longer deny to himself that he had chosen a poor position from which to watch the battle unfold. Although his command post at Ronsomme was set atop a slight ridge, he could not see the breadth of the field upon which the opposing lines were drawn.

Once or twice he had mounted his horse and with the aid of a telescope had been able to discern the forward British line. But even that view was not clear, and he could not make out the movements along the ridgeline at Mont Saint Jean. Moreover, the task of mounting and dismounting his horse had been so painful that he preferred to spend as little time in the saddle as possible. It would not do to have his staff see the agonized contortions on his face. Ever since Quatre-Bras and Ligny two days ago, he could sense the doubts they were harboring. Perhaps they thought the Napoleon of old was no longer with them. Well, they had no idea of the physical exertion it was taking for him to stay on campaign. He doubted that they would have the will to withstand the excruciating discomfort he was quietly enduring. But he would not share his secret with them. They would interpret any admission as a sign of weakness. How fickle they were. Their emperor could bring them victory year after year, but one setback and they were haughtily reassuring each other that all along they had known their emperor's powers were waning.

Ney was nearby, unusually silent. The relationship between Napoleon and his marshal had been strained these last few days, and Ney had been wounded often enough by the stinging words of his commander to learn that an awkward silence was better than a direct rebuke. Not that Ney believed he had done anything to deserve a reprimand. It was Napoleon's irritability, more pronounced than usual, that had unfairly called forth repeated chastisements.

"Soult, do you detect any movement by Wellington?" Napoleon asked his chief of staff.

"No, Your Majesty. He seems to have forgotten he has an army to maneuver." Soult's comments were cautious. Reille had suggested the night before that an opening attack on the enemy's right flank would be to no avail. Napoleon had silenced him. Now that the words were proving prophetic, it would be better to recast his own views in a less critical light. Not the most subtle response, Soult thought, but Wellington's failure to react might best be attributed to his dullness, not Napoleon's. After all, had not the emperor himself assured everyone that the duke was inept?

Strange that Bonaparte would say that. Wellington had certainly acquitted himself well in Portugal. Soult knew; he had been there.

Napoleon bristled at the irony in his chief's words, but he chose not to respond. "Marshal Ney, perhaps a little more cannon would awaken the British to the fact that they are under attack."

"Yes, Sire, it shall be done." Ney was a competent general. He had anticipated the order. He had put into action what he considered to be a sufficient number of guns for this stage of the battle. But he had

also arranged for more to be brought into action if the initial allocation did not do the trick. Still, he doubted if the problem was the lack
of guns. It was more likely a question of the plan itself—and that dullard
Jérôme. What a peacock! Full of bluster, but more often to the rear
than the front. He was the last man Ney would have entrusted with
the opening attack.

Napoleon was moving toward his map table, shoulders hunched under
his coat. If he could not see with his own eyes the actual disposition
of the forces, he could at least look at their depiction on his maps.

Marshal Soult looked at the scene on the knoll, dully aware of its
pathetic nature. He could not understand why the leadership of the French
army remained here at Ronsomme. The men assembled were reputed
to be among the most courageous in all of France. Yet they could barely
see the action. God, how he hated being chief of staff. If only he had
a command, he would be much less troubled. Not that he wanted
desperately to go into action himself—that taste had left him some
years ago. Perhaps it was the recognition of mortality that comes with
age, but he no longer thrilled to personal danger. Still, he would sooner
take his chances in direct combat than serve in the thankless position
of chief of staff. He just did not have the head for it, and everyone
knew it—Napoleon perhaps most of all. Why did he make me his chief?
It was another mystery in the man. Was he afraid of being upstaged
if someone with talent had the job? It was nothing but humiliation for
Soult to go through the motions as chief of staff, and he had no doubt
his incompetence was having its effect on the army.

Take the instructions sent to Grouchy just this morning. Napoleon
had equivocated on what the right wing was to do. In one breath, he
wanted it to press on to Wavre; in the other, it was to follow Blücher
wherever he might go. There was no clarity at all in what the emperor
had told Grouchy. Soult had known what must be done: Grouchy must
come to Napoleon the instant Blücher pulled in this direction. But how
to convince Napoleon? He was insufferable. There was no talking to
him. He would not listen; he would become irritable, abusive. And
so, in the end, the orders had remained unclear. Grouchy would have
to figure them out for himself. A wave of guilt flushed Soult's face,
and he yearned once more to be free of his position. He looked away
from his leader, ashamed of his own moral cowardice.

For a few minutes the emperor stared at the red-capped pins protruding from the papers unfolded before him. Every once in a while

he moved them with his soft, puffy hands. Everything about him today seemed overblown and cumbersome. It was as if the fat rapidly overtaking his body was draining the energy that fed his mind. The quickness in his eyes, that snap of a glance that told of the remarkable engine within, had slowed with the movements of his body.

An aide came riding up, literally jumping to the ground. "Sire!" Audaciously, he interrupted the emperor's concentration, a sign that whatever it was he had to report was ample excuse for such boldness. "There is a report of movement from the east. A mass of darkly uniformed soldiers has been seen on the heights of Chapelle Saint Lambert, coming in our direction."

"What color are the uniforms?" The color would tell Napoleon whose forces they might be, Grouchy's or Blücher's.

"It is impossible to tell, Sire. In truth, there is some doubt whether or not they are troops or cattle. The distance is too great."

Ney had to admire the forthrightness of the aide. Surely he believed the sighting to be troops, or he would not have bounded in with such enthusiasm. Yet he was willing to pass on accurately the doubts expressed by others witnessing the same scene.

"Cattle. Cattle." Napoleon repeated himself, latched onto the word. "Perhaps that is what you have seen. But I need to know for certain. Let me see, where is Saint Lambert on my map?"

"Here, Your Majesty." Obviously, the aide had already checked the location of the sighting, committing it to memory.

For a minute or two, Napoleon studied the markings that indicated the folds of terrain between Saint Lambert and Mont Saint Jean. "Well, whatever it is, cattle or men, they cannot get into the battle before several more hours have passed."

He looked up into the eager face of the aide. The young man returned his gaze, enraptured, eyes afire, awaiting his task as if it were a holy beckoning. "Ride to where you can get a better look at what you have spied. When you are certain of what it is, come to me with a report. But be sure it is me to whom you come. I do not want reckless reports being heard by those for whom it will do no good." The aide saluted smartly and moved out with a sense of purpose.

Soult wondered what to make of such an order. Could the emperor mean to withhold the alarming news of Prussian reinforcements? From his own men? How long could he hope to preserve such a dreadful secret? And, when the truth became known, how greatly would the consequences be magnified by surprise? Soult knew that Grouchy was probably still at Wavre. The orders could only be reaching him now, and they lacked specificity. Grouchy was not the man to take the risky road. He would probably stay where he was as long as a single Prussian remained to his front. If the dark spot on the horizon was Grouchy marching to join them, then he must have lost his control over Gérard. Gérard would want to come. He was a warrior. The sound of the guns would be enough to spur him on to Mont Saint Jean. But Grouchy was no novice. He would not let Gérard rule the day.

Soult felt the dampness rise along his spine, the sweat drip from his armpits. He did not like the way things were going. There was an evil in the air, one that transcended the carnage on the battlefield— uglier, more repugnant, reeking of treachery and betrayal. He wanted to flee, to find a proper formation of troops and lead it into combat. Anything to cleanse himself of this foul atmosphere.

As the aide rode off to do Napoleon's bidding, the emperor climbed into the saddle and drew out his telescope. His horse shifted slightly, stamping its hoofs in the drying mud. Sharp pains shot into Napoleon's bowels. He winced and then strained to see to the east of the Charleroi road. The terrain was masked—by the distance, by the smoke, by the intervening terrain. He knew he should move, but he did not have the will. Not just yet. In a little while, he told himself. He would stay here a bit longer and trust to his luck—perhaps the dark shapes were only cattle after all. No matter. There was still time. If Jérôme conducted his attack properly, it might force Wellington to reinforce his right flank a bit more enthusiastically. The Englishman had to be worried about his lines of communication to the Channel. Sooner or later he would thicken his right. Then there would be time enough to penetrate with the main attack into the center and finish the work before anything could arrive from Wavre. Napoleon collapsed his telescope and wiped the sweat from his brow.

Jérôme's Division Headquarters

Jérôme was convinced that his finest hour had at last arrived. So much of his life had seen humiliation at the hands of Napoleon. In Jérôme's youth his brother's involvements in the affairs of state had caused their entire family to flee for their lives from Corsica to Toulon. Later, as a young man, he had chosen as his bride the beautiful American from Baltimore, Elizabeth Patterson. But even after the pope himself had refused to overturn the marriage, his brother had annulled it by imperial edict. True, the Kingdom of Westphalia had followed as compensation, but he had been made to renounce Elizabeth for the preference offered by his brother. It was degrading for a grown man to be so completely subordinate to his more famous sibling.

Weren't they born of the same parentage? Wasn't he, Jérôme, a king in his own right? The women certainly seemed to curry his favor, and not without some snickering at the physical unattractiveness of the emperor. He had especially delighted in the ladies' favorable comparison of his own manly charms to the lesser abilities—in this department, at least—of his brother.

But the unending subordination still hurt. Perhaps the ultimate insult had been 1812 in Russia. There, on Napoleon's order, Marshal Davout had relieved Jérôme of command of the right wing of the French army. Everyone had blamed him for the slowness of the advance of his forces. In turn they had named that tardiness as the cause of Napoleon's failure to defeat the main Russian army of Barclay de Tolly, before it could be joined by the forces under Prince Bagration. The outcome of all of that had been the indecisive standoff at Smolensk and the scorched-earth withdrawal of the Russian army back toward Moscow.

But that debacle was not Jérôme's doing. It was Napoleon himself who had failed there. He had let the French army advance beyond any means of support, only to be eventually defeated in detail by the Russian winter as much as by the Russian army. Jérôme bristled even now to think of it. So unfairly had they blamed him. For some time he had needed the chance to show his true generalship, lest the historical record perpetuate the injustice. Now, amidst the smoke and noise coming from the woods around Hougoumont, Jérôme could sense that his hour of destiny was at hand. He had already committed his two brigades— Bauduin's and Soye's—to the fight. He would need to commit more.

He could see his corps commander, Lieutenant General Reille, riding up to his position at the edge of the woods. His chief of staff, Lt. Gen. Pamphile Lacroix, accompanied him. Both men seemed apprehensive. Well, he could deal with them.

"Prince Jérôme, pray tell us, what is your progress?" The corps commander's voice had a hint of urgency in it, yet it remained respectful of the royal connections of his subordinate.

"The château is almost mine. A little more of a push and I shall have it."

"How much longer will it take?" The chief of staff was a bit more direct than his commander, showing less deference to Jérôme's family affiliations.

"It is less a question of time than it is of forces. You must give me Foy's division. Then I can give you the château." Jérôme's grasp was exceeding his command. Foy was a division commander in his own right, and a lieutenant general to boot.

The chief of staff looked at Reille. The latter's eyes were flicking from side to side, weighing the suggestion—and not just on military scales. "Sir, I do not see that taking the château is all that important. By containing it we can move into the main part of the allied line and there have the desired effect of forcing a reinforcement by Wellington."

"Nonsense." It was Jérôme. "Hougoumont must be taken. It stands there like a fortress astride my line of advance. Once taken, it is only a matter of a few hundred meters more into the British positions. They will not have the means to resist once we emerge from the northern edge of this infernal woods."

Reille thought that his chief of staff had a point. Taking the château might prove needlessly expensive. But then again, Napoleon had implied, at least, that he wanted Hougoumont taken. "How much more will it take?"

"General, as I said, give me only a few more troops, and it shall be mine." Jérôme's bluster should have been a sure sign of his doubts. It was the way he gambled, and the ledgers could show how misguided his wagering had often been.

"I shall order Foy to attack into the eastern half of the woods, up toward the orchard. You continue to direct your efforts against the château itself." The corps commander had made his decision.

Jérôme allowed himself a little sneer. Foy might pin down some of the defenses, but he would not take Hougoumont. That honor would fall to the best commander in the French lines—Prince Jérôme, King of Westphalia, and aspirant to the French throne. With a flourish the would-be emperor wheeled his horse and advanced into the woods, neglecting to take leave of his commander. Wearily, Reille looked at the back of his departing subordinate. He would do what he could to support his efforts, but in his heart he knew he had just surrendered the decision-making authority for the unfolding battle to Napoleon's baby brother.

Grouchy's Headquarters

The aide approached, his uniform splattered with mud, his horse frothed with a heavy white foam. The horse's sides heaved in and out, bellowlike. Grouchy looked at the aide anxiously, fingernails digging into palms.

"Marshal, I have brought orders from the emperor." The young officer said it proudly. It had been a difficult ride across the countryside, but he had made it through.

"Give them to me." Grouchy extended his hand eagerly. The parchment felt heavy and stuck to the sweat of his palm as the general fumbled with the seal. "At what time were you dispatched?"

"At 1000, Sir. I rode as hard as I could."

Grouchy did not acknowledge the answer, disregarding the defensiveness in the boy's voice, and focused on the paper. He read quickly, eyes darting over the script, searching for the key instructions. "His Majesty desires that you will head for Wavre in order to draw near to us, and to place yourself in touch with our operations, and to keep up your communications with us, pushing before you those portions of the Prussian army which have taken this direction and which have halted at Wavre; this place you ought to reach as soon as possible."

Grouchy looked up at the aide. For a moment he considered asking for a clarification, then dismissed the idea as ludicrous. What would the aide know? He was an infatuated adolescent, duped by a faded old fool who had lost his greatness in the damp mists of Elba. The order made no sense— ". . . head for Wavre . . . draw near to us. . . ." Those were contradictory instructions.

So the decision is mine. Napoleon's confusion has left me an out. The idea pleased Grouchy. He recognized the security the orders gave him. He could go either way and still be in compliance with orders.

He looked up and saw the smoke rising to the west. The deep-toned explosions were echoing off the low-lying clouds, faintly telling of the heated fighting in the distance. His mind raced.

Go to Napoleon and I risk a cross-country march that could put Blücher on my flank at any step of the way. If I get there, then I fight Wellington with Blücher at my back. If I lose, then I am court-martialed for disobeying my orders to move to Wavre. Stay here and I can be faulted for not coming to Napoleon's assistance. But my orders tell me to stay here. I cannot be court-martialed for that. And I can win here. I can beat Blücher—the more readily if he has withdrawn a part of his force

to join Wellington. And Gérard. That pompous ass! He wishes to order me, to tell *me* what I must do. There is little to decide. I stay here.
I fight the Prussians at Wavre. And I beat them.

He passed Napoleon's orders to an officer with instructions to put
them away for safekeeping. He might have need of those orders later.

Antwerp

Magdalene de Lancey had shut the windows to her apartment and pulled
the heavy curtains. Still, the noise of the cannon could be faintly heard,
like the beating of the waves on a distant shore—barely audible but
ominous and foreboding. It had been like this on the sixteenth, when
the furious sounds from Quatre-Bras and Ligny had made their way
to settlements well distant from the battles. And then, on the seventeenth, the other English ladies, on spying the increasing numbers of
wounded streaming in from Brussels and hearing rumors that the French
were advancing victoriously, had panicked and made preparations for
the flight across the North Sea.

But Lady Magdalene had vowed to stick it out, no matter what came,
and even reproached her maid, Emma, for her alarmist statements. Emma
had thereafter protested her preparedness to follow her lady into captivity
if need be. All in all, it had been a terrible scene.

Yet all the anxiety of those two days had been compensated for when
she had received Sir William's letter. He was safe and in great spirits. They had given the French a tremendous beating, he had written,
and he had come through without a scratch. She almost jumped with
the joy of his reassuring words, and she immediately took pen in hand
to tell him of both her relief and her love.

But now, barely twelve hours later, the anxiety was building all over
again. She hadn't realized how taut her nerves had become. It was as
if she had to scream. She kept pacing the floor, walking back and forth
in the darkness of the closed room.

Why did men have to fight? Why did they find such glory in war?
It was all so horrible, yet they seemed so proud of their involvement
in it.

Sir William, though, was different. He was gentle, filled with a sense
of duty. It was as if he served in the army only to make it more civilized. The night of the fifteenth had been so painful. How much she

had wanted to pull him away from his duties. A part of her wanted to lure him away forever from his sense of military obligation. Perhaps there was a way she could do it. But what effect would it have on him? Could he still love her if he felt he had failed to meet his professional responsibilities?

He had looked so handsome the morning he had left with the army. There was almost a boyish shyness, a secret delight, in going off to meet the French. Yet she knew he did not want to leave her. She could sense his body's almost visible impulse to quit his horse and hasten back to her side. It seemed to make their parting more poignant—the way he was torn between love and duty. He seemed so complete, so alive, so vibrant. That was what had given her the assurance that he could not be hurt. Yet that very fear was playing on her now.

Confused and upset, she stopped her pacing and knelt beside the bed that offered her little rest. Fervently, she prayed for his safekeeping and for the strength to do whatever she must to support him.

10
HOUGOUMONT: 1300

He knew it. It was strange, but he knew it. The closing of the gate had been the single greatest moment of his life. He didn't have to think about it; it was not a knowing of the mind. The certainty came from deep within—somewhere below his chest, behind his stomach. It made his body full, as if he had eaten a rich meal. He could feel it in the muscles of his thighs, in the sinews of his arms, across his shoulders, and throughout his thick neck. He could feel it in his organs, in every part of his being. He felt complete.

If he were certain he had one, he would say he felt it in his soul. But he had never concluded that he had a soul. Macdonell had heard all the preaching, his father had seen to that. But he harbored his doubts, keeping them to himself. Yet, he was absolutely sure that the central moment of his life had come and gone. There was no doubt. All that he had done before and all that he might yet do would not equate to that one moment.

That was what was so strange about it. He knew the battle was not yet over—not by a long shot—though he sensed now that he might live through the day. But even that did not seem so important anymore. It wasn't that he was indifferent to death; he had no desire to see an end to the life that had been so full. But if death did come, he would not feel cheated. He had had his moment.

He imagined that Wellington, if he heard of the incident, would be quite proud of him. And if they ever met again, Macdonell resolved, he would be both duly humble and proud of his accomplishment in the great man's presence. But that would be only a surface reaction. Deep within himself he would keep the significance of the moment his own secret. That moment was now a part of him; it was his very being. It was not to be shared with anyone else.

He suspected that other men with similar experiences had their own similar secrets. How many had recognized the significance of the experience? Did it impress them, as it impressed him? Did it fill them, as it did him, with wonder and self-worth?

He knew he should put such thoughts from his mind. Hougoumont was still under siege; only a moment's respite had been granted as the French fell back to reorganize. But he didn't want to put aside contemplation of his moment. It had been a great privilege to recognize the event for what it was. If you thought about it, really thought about it, nothing else mattered—at least not to him. That moment was the essence of his life. It was what he had been created for.

Slowly, reluctantly, he forced himself to come out of his contemplation. Command was still his. All those men still relied on him. They would need his leadership to get them through this fight. With an almost physical effort, Macdonell forced his thoughts back to Hougoumont. The wall of the main house came slowly into focus—then the barn, the chapel, and the farmhouse. He became conscious of the acrid smell of gunpowder and felt a trickle of blood running down his arm, its stickiness matting his uniform sleeve. His ears heard once again the terrible din of musketry, the thunder of cannon, and the mournful cries of wounded and dying men. His tongue moved inside his mouth, tasting the sawdust dryness in his throat. The wound in his shoulder ached anew. One by one, his mortal senses returned him to the responsibilities of his command. He grabbed a musket and moved toward the south wall, stopping to take a ladle of water from a bucket outside the chapel.

"You, soldier, what are you about?" Macdonell yelled at a frightened-looking youth stumbling from the barn.

"Nothing, Sir. I was trapped outside. I've just made it inside the walls."

"Did you come in through the gate then?"

"No, Sir. There was a door in the barn. I ran for it, and it opened."

"Damn! Then we should bolt it. I'll have no more of easy entry for our enemies." He yelled to a nearby sergeant to see to the barn door, then turned his attention back to the soldier, letting the water from the ladle slip down his parched throat.

"What's your name, soldier?"

"Clay, sir. Private Clay."

"Well, Private Clay, I see by your blackened face that you have been doing a little shooting. Good lad. Get yourself up in the attic of the main house. I'll be wanting you to do some more firing for us."

"Yes, Sir." The private moved out, seemingly glad to have orders to execute. The colonel watched him go—a boy really, so skinny, so frail. Yet he had done his duty, one man among many, pitting himself to the cause at hand. He would need some help, Macdonell reckoned, and set about finding his officers in order to have them push more men up into the main house.

A great roar arose in the large orchard beyond the château wall. Macdonell raced across the garden and peered through a firing loop in time to see a large formation of French—elements of a brigade, he figured—emerge from the woods and rush Lord Saltoun's defenders. The attackers, from Jérôme's 2d Brigade, were moving quickly forward in tightly packed battalions configured to allow the maximum rate of firepower to the front.

As Macdonell watched, a French officer shouted an order that gave rise to a storm of musket fire from the brigade. For a moment Jérôme's men were hidden by a cloud of smoke. Undaunted, the British fired their own muskets back into the puffs of thick haze as fast as they could load. Wounded men cried out in English and French, appealing to a common God for mercy. A wave of attackers emerged from the smoke, bayonets at the ready, and charged the British.

"Pour your fire into them. Support the Guards!" It was Macdonell's booming voice rising above the din. All along the south and east faces of the château wall, musket fire crashed into the flanks of the attacking French.

But the advance was more than Saltoun's men could withstand. Men discharged their weapons, then were bayoneted and clubbed before they could reload, falling like overripened fruit beneath the orchard trees. An Englishman fired his weapon directly into the face of an attacker, clubbed another, and turned to withdraw—only to be run through by two French bayonets. The blade of one pinned him, face to bark, to the trunk of a nearby tree. The owner of the bayonet braced his foot

against the dead man's back and withdrew the blade. For every Frenchman that fell, three more emerged from the smoke. Despite the odds,
Saltoun withdrew his men in order, losing far more than he could afford
but exchanging their lives for a few precious minutes.

It seemed to Macdonell that the orchard was certain to be overrun.
This would mean that the château would be encircled on three sides,
making further resupply untenable. He strained to calculate how long
he could hold out with the ammunition he had on hand.

As he struggled with the sums, a shout could be heard from the north.
Four companies of Coldstream Guards from Byng's brigade counterattacked under the command of Colonel Woodford. Macdonell saw the
colonel's strong face through occasional gaps in the clouds of smoke.
He watched Woodford's mouth forming the orders, and Macdonell saw
his eyes piercing the fog of war with a cold glint of steel.

"Now boys! Now! Pour it into them!" Macdonell urged his command to intensify their supporting fire. Simultaneously, the British
artillery shifted its fire into the trees. Shrapnel burst everywhere,
shredding flesh and bark alike as it filled the air with deadly iron balls
packed 153 to the shell. Death rained on the French from every direction. Jérôme's 2d Brigade fell back before the onslaught of men
and fire, hastily retreating over ground they had only just won.

Macdonell had to marvel at the allied response. It had the touch of
Wellington in it: scant defenders left to hold ground against all odds
but reinforced at precisely the last moment, when the attack was on
the verge of succeeding, the defense stiffened by the delicate placement of exploding shrapnel. It was a bloody business that killed and
maimed not only Frenchmen, but any wounded or straggling British
left in the orchard. The response worked, however, and the clock moved
forward another precious few minutes, the defense still in place.

"Sir, reinforcements are approaching by the barn door." A burly British
sergeant, his jacket soaked with his own blood, called to his commander
as he ran to unbolt the recently secured door. Macdonell moved to get
a better look.

The first of Wellington's installments was arriving. More Guards,
together with elements from the King's German Legion, were entering the courtyard. Colonel Woodford followed them in to meet with
Macdonell.

A seasoned soldier, Woodford could see in a glance that Macdonell
had tight control over the situation. Despite the carnage inside the

courtyard, soldiers were going about their business crisply. Watering parties were dousing flames, ammunition was being run up to the defenders, and sergeants and officers were regulating the rate of musket fire. He considered his options as the senior officer present, then made his decision.

"Colonel Macdonell, let me know where you want me to put my men." With only a moment's hesitation to size up the situation, Woodford had subordinated himself to the nominally junior man. Protocols of rank would be suspended. Macdonell had obviously thought through a plan of defense, knew the ground well, and was up to the task.

"Thank-you, sir. I think the French will be back at us in a moment. If you would leave one of your companies by the north gate, I would feel a bit more secure. We only recently had a close call there."

Colonel Woodford saw the dead Frenchmen in the courtyard and appreciated the understatement. He had long been impressed with the Scotsman's coolness under fire. With a quick nod he agreed to the request.

"The rest," Macdonell continued, "should move to the attic of the main house and reinforce the survivors along the garden wall. The French will soon test us again."

"That is what I am told Wellington anticipates—and why I am here."

"Aye. I am glad you have come. Will there be more?"

"I believe so. As I left to come forward, orders were being passed to Colonel Hepburn of the 3d Guards to make ready seven companies. I also believe that du Plat is standing by to send four Light Companies upon order. I would not expect any of them, however, until things get absolutely desperate. The duke is using us sparingly, you know."

Macdonell was trying to keep up with the information Woodford was giving him, adding up the figures in his head. Mathematics had always been difficult for him. The trick would be to translate all of those units into numbers of companies and multiply by a hundred.

Woodford could see him struggling and offered some assistance. "I don't know what you have left, but if all of those units are sent, there would be over two thousand fighting men in the area."

"Well, that sounds like a great bit. But we will need all of them during the course of the day, if not all at once. I have lost a great deal already, and more will be lost in equal proportion. The problem is, I cannot take many more inside the château." He paused to contemplate his options. Woodford remained silent, respecting Macdonell's status as commander of the position.

"Do you know if Lord Saltoun is still alive? He was commanding in the orchard outside the wall when the battle broke. Perhaps you saw him on the way in."

"I did not see him, but I am told he survives. I understand his horse was shot from under him." Woodford was careful to give an accurate answer.

A sudden surge of shouting rose from outside the wall, along with a reinvigoration of the firing. The French were back. Macdonell heard it and looked up, then turned toward Woodford. "Perhaps you could pass the orders to your men. I need some time to consider the best way to reorder the defenses. I fear it will be a long afternoon."

"Of course." Colonel Woodford glanced at Macdonell's wound, concluded it would not disable him, and moved to counsel his officers. Rising shouts of *"Vive l'empereur!"* came from beyond the wall.

For a few minutes, Macdonell watched to ensure that his orders were being followed. He sensed that the command relationship was a delicate one, and he respected the dignity with which Colonel Woodford had conducted himself. But he knew that Hougoumont was his to defend, and he had to be certain his orders were both clearly understood and properly executed. The attack had been much greater than he originally feared. He would have to rethink the defense plan.

Here and there men were falling from their firing positions, but he could see that as long as the French attacked as they now were, the defenses were in no danger of a sudden collapse. It was the unexpected that worried him most. The north gate was a good example of that. It would matter little that the majority of the defense was holding if suddenly a major advantage fell to the attacker in a particular spot. Macdonell knew that was the greatest danger. He would need a reserve force to hedge against the unforeseen, but a force that would not necessarily have to be inside the walls.

That was the answer to his problem. As long as the bulwarks held and the French did not alter their attack, he already had enough firepower inside the walls to keep the attackers from penetrating. What he needed was the other half of the equation—a maneuver force. The two together—firepower and maneuver—were the essence of battle. Each by itself was inadequate, incomplete, but the enemy could be beaten by the combination of the two. One maneuvered to put firepower on the enemy, and the other used firepower to gain the freedom of maneuver.

It made no sense to race outside the walls to get at the French. That would only put the retention of Hougoumont at risk by creating a meeting engagement in the vicinity of the gates, the most vulnerable points of the defense. He had gotten away with it once, early in the battle, before the French had closed on the walls en masse. But he could not risk it again. It would make it an equal fight in the open, without the advantages of the defender, and the heavier numbers would win.

But what he could do was leave the bulk of the reinforcements outside the gate. They could find cover in the woods behind Hougoumont, away from the French. If the pressure against the château became too great at any point, the reinforcements could emerge from their covered positions and beat the attackers back before they achieved a penetration. The fire from within the château would assist the maneuvering of the reserve, pinning the attackers from multiple directions.

To the east, Saltoun would have to be reinforced as well. He was dangerously exposed in the orchard. The last attack had shown that. Only the musket fire from Hougoumont and the flanking fire from Bull's artillery battery were keeping the French from concentrating overwhelming force on that side of the château. It was a battle of attrition out there, and in time the defenders would be worn down beyond the point at which they could still hold. The idea was to make the attackers pay dearly for their efforts, then reinforce the defenders at the last minute, so that the French would have to start all over again.

The key to the entire allied defense was holding Hougoumont. The French were impaling themselves on it. There was no sense in it, but that is what they were doing. Let them come then, by God, but don't let them get by. Suddenly, it all seemed so simple to Macdonell.

Jérôme could not contain his mortification. The strutting peacock in him had been humiliated. Hougoumont had not yet fallen. It was impossible for him to blame himself for the failed attack. Just when he had swept the orchard, he had been denied his victory. His men had lost their nerve, General Foy had failed to mount a coordinated attack on the château, his brother had been too slow in sending him the artillery he needed. All of these reasons, as well as many others, were the cause of his setback. In no way—at least not in his mind— could the failing have been his own.

The younger brother of the emperor was beside himself with anger. He snapped at his aides, scoffed at his staff, swiped at his retreating soldiers. Their repeated shouts of allegiance to Napoleon added to his fury. With an intensity that defied all reason, he had grown to hate the adulation paid his brother. He was chagrined to realize that the world thought there was only one great Bonaparte. It made him want to try all the harder to prove his own comparable abilities. That had become his overriding objective in this attack.

If there had been any military rationale for attacking Hougoumont in the first place, it paled next to Jérôme's personal need for victory at the château. The measure of Hougoumont's value did not lie in its tactical contribution to Wellington's defense. It was only as a worthy objective of his military genius that the château mattered at all to Jérôme. He would give no consideration to bypassing it in order to more successfully turn Wellington's flank and force him to reorient his overall defense. His reputation was at stake. Hougoumont must be taken at all costs.

Jérôme dispatched an aide-de-camp with an urgent message for Napoleon. The note requested howitzers with which to bombard the buildings where the allied infantry was entrenched. Only a combined-arms attack of artillery and infantry, working together, could take the strong defensive position. If only he had thought of it sooner. Jérôme spurred his horse toward General Foy's command post.

"General Foy. General Foy! What have you been doing?" Jérôme's high-pitched voice grated on his fellow division commander, putting him immediately on the defensive.

"I have been looking for a way around that fire sack of a château." Foy's answer was straightforward, but his voice belied irritation. Unstated but implied in his tone was the query, "Why, and of what do you accuse me?"

"Around! A way around? Do you not understand? I have spoken with General Reille, and we have agreed that you must support me directly in my attack on Hougoumont." Jérôme knew that the words were an exaggeration of the circumstances of his earlier discussion with the corps commander, but he allowed himself to believe what he had said. Step-by-step, as was his custom, his embellishments and interpretations of events would meld to become his mental image of reality.

"My dear Prince, I am not in receipt of such instructions." Foy's voice was uncertain, betraying his lack of resolve in resisting Jérôme's onslaught. He did not like the unsoldierly dandy before him, but he well understood the importance of Jérôme's family connection.

"As soon as I am able to reorganize my regiments, I plan to strike again at Hougoumont. I have already sent to my brother for artillery support." Jérôme was quick to emphasize his tie to Napoleon. "If you will take your battalions into the orchard to the east of the château, I can concentrate on the buildings themselves. With the artillery in support, I cannot fail."

In Foy's timidity before the barrage of stinging words, Jérôme gained all the encouragement he needed to continue. "If you fear that the orchard is too formidable, then you must have General Bachelu's division assist you. We cannot expect to fulfill our duty if we allow any portion of our forces to stand by idly while others go in to the attack. You will note that I have left the most difficult objective to my own command—the taking of Hougoumont itself."

For an instant the insulting words tempted Foy to strike out in anger. But he held himself in check, and by so doing capitulated to the harangue. Not only would he attack into the orchard—against his better judgment—he would do so at Jérôme's bidding while seeking to bring Bachelu's battalions into the battle with him. Elements of three divisions would attack where a single one need not have gone. Jérôme had instigated a trite exchange of heated words with a fellow commander, but the fate of thousands—and perhaps the battle itself—were sealed in their utterance. The two division commanders parted company to give the necessary orders.

Wellington had noticed the activity unfolding in the French center and sensed that his attention must now shift to the middle of his line. The battle at Hougoumont had developed about as well as he could have expected; it still stood. More important, Macdonell was still alive. His presence in command made all the difference. It allowed the allied leader to move on with confidence that his plan for holding the right of the line was still intact. Under Macdonell, Hougoumont would continue to resist as long as humanly possible.

Before riding off on Copenhagen, Wellington paused to write a short note to Macdonell. Should the buildings catch fire, he was to keep his soldiers among the smoldering rafters until the very last moment. Only then should he order his men out, to return again as soon as the heat of the fire had passed.

Macdonell received the message without surprise, without slight. It was typical of Wellington to think of every small detail. It was not lack of confidence in a subordinate that prompted him to send the instruction. It was his way of making sure his intention was understood. The colonel would have insisted upon that tactic anyway, even without the note. After all, he had not served under the duke in the Peninsula without learning from him. The two men thought alike, had a common feel for both terrain and men. The note confirmed that and reassured Macdonell that he was key to Wellington's plan. They were brother warriors. Both of them knew how to get the most out of men. Both of them knew when to spare soldiers and when to expend them. And both of them knew that they could expect nothing but loyalty from men who understood that they would be made to do only what was absolutely essential. In the end, their soldiers would do whatever was asked of them, no matter the price.

Jérôme timed his next offensive to coincide with d'Erlon's attack into the center of the allied line. Jérôme pressed forward in three directions simultaneously—one thrust coming directly through the woods to the south, a second cutting a short angle through the woods to the south gate, and a third hooking around from the west to try the barn and north gate once again. At the same time, battalions from Foy's and Bachelu's divisions attacked from the south toward the large orchard.

Macdonell could hear them coming. He steadied his men and had them withhold fire until the French appeared from the brush and came into range. Again it was a butchery. Muskets roared into life, tearing the French ranks apart. It was a repeat of the earlier attacks, the only difference being that more Frenchmen in the attack meant more dying at a faster rate. But the increased weight of numbers was telling—the defenders in the orchard were forced to give ground, however slowly.

Nonetheless, the château walls remained impregnable. All exits and entrances had been secured and reinforced. Weapons protruded in a multitude of angles from the double tier of firing loops chopped in the walls; from windows in the buildings rising over the parapets; and from atop the walls themselves, as soldiers stood on makeshift firing ports to look down into the snarling mass of French below.

Only in the orchard did it prove to be an equal contest. But just as the British were about to give way before superior numbers, a counter-attack by du Plat's brigade drove the French back.

Jérôme, unmindful of his own safety, was up and down the line, exhorting his men to drive home their charge. His courage fortified by his fury, he was determined to take Hougoumont at all costs. With great effort, he placed a battery of howitzers into action at the edge of the woods and ordered them to fire directly into the château.

The direct fire of the heavy guns introduced a new horror to the battle. In a few moments the thatched roofs of the farmhouse and the barn caught fire. Fanned by the afternoon breeze, the flames quickly spread to the surrounding buildings and straw. The air filled with pungent smoke. Men were unable to see the enemy. They struggled to catch their breaths amidst their labors. Fresh air could not be found. Temperatures became unbearable. In the burning buildings, officers positioned themselves by the exits, shouting orders to keep up the musket fire.

Here and there, under the cover of smoke and confusion, Frenchmen began to find their way over the wall. But the same fire that afforded them entrance into the château barred their way from quickly exploiting their advantage. They could not mount a coherent effort inside the walls. Leaders were separated from men who consequently huddled individually or in small groups of two or three, unsure of their next move. Terror overtook discipline. The ferocity that had propelled them over the wall now turned to desperation as they realized their plight. There could be no going forward. The instant they emerged from the smoke, they would come face-to-face with the muskets and bayonets of the defenders. If they stayed where they were, they would suffocate or be burned to death in the fire. If they withdrew, they would be caught up in the savage fighting before the wall, as likely to fall victim to the frantic firing of their own countrymen as to the musketry of the defenders.

The situation was little better for the defenders. Made to stay and fight amidst the flames until the last possible moment, scores were succumbing to heat exhaustion. The wounded suffered the worst of all. Many who fell abandoned all hope of extricating themselves. Furniture, support beams, staircases, straw, and all manner of battle debris were feeding the flames. The cries of the wounded caught up in the raging fire filled the air with horror. Sergeant Graham, who earlier had helped Macdonell close the north gate, begged his commander to allow him to run to the barn to save his brother. Conscious of his debt to this valiant soldier, Macdonell gave his permission and Graham's brother was saved. But few of the wounded were so fortunate.

In the chapel—where so many had crawled seeking sanctuary—the tightly packed men stared in horror as the flames crossed the courtyard inch by inch to lick at the door of their makeshift hospital. The wooden frame caught fire, as did the hay that was strewn about. Smoke filled the crowded interior. Men clawed at each other in a futile attempt to make their way outside. The smell of singed hair and flesh filled their nostrils. The wounded screamed in pain and anguish. A great tongue of flame leaped to the wooden crucifix and slowly began to burn the cross from the wall. The fire consumed the feet of the

Christ figure—then, strangely, went out. Those who survived swore they had witnessed a miracle. But it was no miracle to the many who died.

"Out of the farmhouse. Now!" It was Macdonell, following his orders to the letter.

Men raced down the burning staircase. Officers and sergeants immediately put them to work breaking apart the burning embers and scattering them so they might be more easily extinguished. Survivors were dispatched to thicken the defenses along the wall; work parties were formed to douse the fire and prepare the buildings for reentry. Any French that had entered the interior grounds of the château were methodically hunted down and killed. None of the defenders were allowed to care for the wounded. The fight was too desperate.

"Quickly! Move lively there. Get some water onto the wood and then back to your battle stations." Macdonell's voice rose above the noise of battle as he moved here and there, cajoling, threatening, leading, and setting the example. His men followed his orders unhesitatingly.

Outside the walls, Jérôme continued to blast away with his howitzers. The terrible truth had begun to dawn on him. He would not take Hougoumont. The fire that had at first given him hope was forming an impenetrable barrier. The discipline of the defenders was too great, their preparation too thorough. They would not break.

For a moment, Jérôme paused to wonder what manner of man was leading the defense. Then the face of Napoleon appeared in his mind, and he returned to his high-pitched exhortations. As long as life breathed in a single one of his soldiers, he would continue the attack.

11

THE CENTER: 1400

It was more than Ney could stand. This was not his type of action. The battle had been going on for over two hours, but still there was no progress on the left. What was Jérôme doing at Hougoumont? It was just a farmhouse, an isolated château! Surely those rabble British could not be putting up much of a fight.

Yet more and more of Reille's corps were sifting into the woods, disappearing from view to the south of the billowing smoke rising from Hougoumont. Why can't we get on with it? Ney asked himself. This was not a battle. Battles were shock action and violence, a terrible meeting of sword and flesh, before whose savagery the weaker side must give way. That was the kind of warfare for which the French were famous. But what had happened to French generals? Had they forgotten how to fight?

And the damned artillery, Napoleon's chosen arm. The emperor was relying on it for results, but Napoleon could not even see what effect it was having. What was wrong with him today anyway? Where was his starch? And where was he? Why was he not up where he could observe the battle, see the wasted efforts of his brother on the left flank? The emperor had seemed so strange this morning, so distant. He had come forward as far as La Belle Alliance to take in the entire array of deployments but then had retired to Ronsomme before the battle had begun. Surely he could see very little from there. Ney did not like the way the day was going, not one bit. The more the marshal thought about the events of the morning and the mood of his superior, the less he liked them. He was impatient for action. That would relieve the tension.

For thirty minutes the artillery had been raking the ridge at Mont Saint Jean, but even Ney in his forward position could not see the effect. The smoke was too thick upon the battlefield, and in the stillness of the hot June afternoon the musket-fire haze was obscuring the marshal's vision.

Wellington's placement of his forces had not helped to make anything clearer. The majority of the allies were out of sight, behind the crest of the ridge. How could the artillery know if it was hitting anything at all? Even if the French did find the range, the allied formations could quickly move out of the impact area, without being observed. The artillery fire was a waste of ammunition and a waste of time. So far the whole day had been a waste: Jérôme preening before an insignificant farmhouse, hoping to gain glory by pretending it was a formidable obstacle, and Napoleon listening to the pleas of his artillerymen to wait until the rain-sodden fields would dry.

Where were the real soldiers, the ones who knew the meaning of personal combat, of the point of the bayonet and the charge of the cavalry? Demonstrations and indirect fire did not win battles. It was the attack—the unrelenting crash into a wall of human flesh by horse and by blade and by shot—that broke the defenders' will to resist. That is what took away their backbone, by God, and it was time to be on with it. The adrenaline coursing through Ney's veins seemed to brighten the marshal's already fiery red hair. To relieve his own anxiety, he desperately needed to get into action.

Ney's hopes were about to be fulfilled. At long last Napoleon had become aroused. At about 1330 he had ordered thirty minutes of artillery preparation, which was to precede the attack on Wellington's center. D'Erlon's corps would do the honors. Four divisions of over 4,000 men each had positioned themselves in the valley between La Belle Alliance and Mont Saint Jean. They were waiting now for the cannonade to run out its clock. It was an imposing sight: four large columns of tightly packed men, brightly bedecked, weapons at the order, deployed as battalions in line to a depth of three ranks. Only six paces separated the four battalions of each brigade, stretching to a front of 90 men, each brigade joining with its sister to give the divisions a front of 180 men across and 25 to 30 men deep.

To their front were hundreds of *tirraleurs,* the individual skirmishers who would drive back the British pickets and throw the fear of imminent contact into the waiting allied line. Already their muskets were firing; for Marshal Ney the sound was a welcome addition to the maddening whistle and crash of artillery. But most thrilling of all—the force that touched the marshal's cavalry soul—were the French *cuirassiers* forming now on the left flank of d'Erlon's corps. Ney conceded a little respect to his commander—the emperor still knew how to stack the deck.

Napoleon had ordered General Milhaud's cavalry corps and Major General Dubois's brigade of the 13th Cavalry Division to support the main thrust. The 1st and 4th *Cuirassiers* along with Major General Travers's brigade of the 7th and 12th *Cuirassiers* would deliver the primary attack. All in all, eleven squadrons of the French heavy horse were going in, a total of 1,700 steeds ridden by big, powerful, armored men—each cavalryman with the strength and will to smash an opponent into the ground or cut him in two with a single swipe.

The marshal's heart jumped as he considered the prospects. There would be action now; blood would flow and unleash a tide that could carry the battle to victory. At last the waiting was over. Marshal Ney, commander of the left wing of the *Armée du Nord,* placed himself astride his horse at the head of d'Erlon's corps. He would lead his men into battle as he had done so many times before. He would show Napoleon that he was the best of his marshals. He would make the emperor swallow the critical words he had uttered at Quatre-Bras. How dare he question my nerve, my initiative? How many times do I have to prove my courage to that ingrate? Ney's bitterness had not only reddened his face, it had colored his thoughts.

The allies could see them coming. Wellington had moved back to his position at the center of the line, by all outward appearances as yet unfazed by the great battle that was unfolding. Peering between the spiraling clouds of smoke, he could distinguish the maneuvers of the French forming at a distance of one thousand yards amidst the high stalks of corn. The French artillery continued to test the nerves of the duke's troops as it randomly chose its victims from the formations. Death was so fickle. A whistle and a bang, and three men would be disemboweled, leaving a fourth untouched except for the soft splash of his comrades' vitals against his legs.

The British infantry was lying down in formation. How peaceful they appeared, like so many children napping at midday rest in school. Only the smoke and noise and blood gave hint of the terror raging in their breasts.

Whistle, bang! On came shot and shell like a horde of heavy, razor-toothed insects infecting the air. The thoughts of the survivors echoed a common theme: Let it miss. If someone must die, let it be another. A twinge of shame followed—until the next sound of incoming artillery. Then the prayer that it be for someone else rose again.

Whistle, bang, a scream, and a curse. Cannon shot came hissing amongst the men lying prone on the ground—a storm of iron, a hurricane of death. Desperate thoughts raced behind their stoic faces. How much more? Can my luck hold? Please let it hold! Please let this murder end before my luck gives out.

The waiting soldiers could hear the screams of the hurt and dying. They could sense the broken bodies being pulverized into gore. Their eyes dared not look up because of the horror they would see and the exposure it would bring. Only the press of breathing flesh to either side reminded them they were not alone in this nightmare.

General Bijlandt's Dutch-Belgian brigade had spurned Wellington's orders to retire behind the forward ridge and take to ground. The brigade stood alone on the forward slope. The price was high. Compared to a man lying prone, a man standing offers a much greater profile to the inverted umbrella arch of bursting case shot.

Even worse than case shot was the round shot, the heavy iron ball that flew through the ranks with unstoppable momentum. A standing man might absorb the projectiles unleashed from case shot, thereby sparing his neighbor. But round shot had been known to plow through a line of fifteen men, pulverizing bones and sending parts of bodies every which way.

The only unit visible to the French gunners, Bijlandt's brigade became a magnet for death. For the Gaullist artillery it was great fun to watch the effects of the fire—the brigade wilted in formation like a rose past its prime, succumbing to the violence of a heavy rain, the petals relentlessly beaten into the ground. And the proudest petals of the Dutch-Belgian brigade had by now fallen beneath the torrent of fire. The senior leaders were all gone, as brave and as useless in death as they had been in life. Now, with the remorseless French infantry coming on, the futility of standing there in the face of it all came home to the brigade. The rank and file could not hold up before it. The Dutch and the Belgians broke and ran to the rear of the allied line, despite the wrath of their junior officers and the disdainful looks of the British.

General Picton, commander of the 5th British Division, had anticipated the event. He had doubted all along that Bijlandt's troops could take the punishment. He had readied his men and, when the anticipated breakdown of the Dutch-Belgian brigade left a dangerous hole to the front, he ordered forward General Kempt's 8th British Brigade composed of the 28th Foot (North Gloucestershire), the 32d Foot (Cornwall), the 79th Cameron Highlanders, and part of the 95th Rifles. They repositioned themselves barely in time.

The French infantrymen were picking up speed, slipping and sliding on the muddy slopes as they descended into and then rose out of the valley. Cries of *"Vive l'empereur!"* could be heard above the musket and artillery fire. The British artillery was ranging d'Erlon's corps now, but with twenty thousand men on the move toward the allied line, it seemed to Picton that the effects of the shelling could be of no consequence. If he could have seen the carnage in the French ranks, however, his opinion would have been different. But despite the suffering it was enduring, the French infantry remained formidable.

On its left rode the *cuirassiers,* engulfing La Haye Sainte. Major Baring and the King's German Legion held against them, but the *cuirassiers* shattered a battalion of Hanoverians from Kielmansegge's brigade, which had been sent forward to reinforce the farm. The French cavalrymen continued to come on hard, riding through the British shelling toward the rise of Mont Saint Jean, crossing the Brussels road as they swept by La Haye Sainte. Nine squadrons cut around to the west and two cut to the east. In the smoke and confusion they interjected themselves behind the British first line of defense and in front of the British second. It was the worst place for them to be.

The French artillery momentarily lifted to allow d'Erlon to close on his objective. In this reprieve the British infantry rose from the ground en masse and poured a deadly point-blank fire into the French cavalry. Caught in a veritable killing zone between the two lines of infantry, men and horses were shot to pieces.

The slaughter of the cavalry on the reverse slope of Mont Saint Jean had gone unobserved by the French infantry, who were momentarily deluded into believing that their objective had been swept clean of defenders. Euphoria swelled in the ranks of foot soldiers as they swept forward at a charge. Drumbeats quickened; officers raised their voices in exhortation. As the French rapidly closed the final two hundred yards, the British artillerymen fired the last cannisters and fled the field. The British infantry on the reverse slope of the ridge had not yet appeared in the attackers' view. D'Erlon's men could see they would have to pursue quickly to gain their reward for withstanding the deadly advance through one thousand meters of muddy fields. No matter. The ridge was there for the taking, the enemy nowhere to be seen.

Now Picton the warrior came into his own. Summoned from the duchess of Richmond's ball two nights before, he had taken to horse with his top hat and umbrella. Still in his evening clothes, his beefy arms and thick legs strained the fine material, the threads rubbed ever thinner as he shifted and chafed in his saddle. He simply had not had time to change. At the ball he had been out of place, but this was a different sort of dance, one that he had mastered and so relished.

His heavy eyes gleamed self-satisfaction. They wouldn't laugh at him now; here uncouth manners and profanity were in fashion. This was fighting and killing—making men who would rather flee and hide move forward into the face of battle; grabbing the enemy by the throat and making him play your tune; sticking and hitting and yelling and growling, the blood up in your veins and your voice bellowing with determined resonance. The old warrior relished the carnage that turned other men's stomachs and wilted their backbones to jelly. This was the dance for which Picton had been born.

With a glance at the cool and composed Wellington, Picton moved his division to its feet and ordered his men to fire into the French who now appeared over the crest of the ridge. Three thousand muskets exploded into the surprised faces of the leading French ranks, the sounds of the blast echoed several times over by a series of half-company volleys. The French wavered for a moment, but came on again. Picton muttered an oath and moved his 5th Division forward. He knew that for a fleeting instant—before the French *cuirassiers* could get their bearings, before the British cavalry could pick their point of countercharge, and while the artillery of both lines lay still—it was bayonet and musket ball that would determine the flow of the battle.

"Into their flank! Get a flank! Move you bastards, move! Rally the Highlanders." This was Picton's moment, the one he savored, the one he loved more than anything in life. His will was moving an entire division; his will was challenging an enemy that outnumbered him four to one. He filled his lungs with breath in anticipation of his next bellow and turned majestically in his saddle to point the way forward just as a French ball pierced his top hat and blew his brains out his ear. Barely missing a step and totally uninspired by the general's soldierly end, a British infantryman stooped to snatch Picton's purse.

"Get back in line, you bastard!" It was Captain Seymour, Picton's aide, smacking at the soldier with the flat of his sword. Cowering, the infantryman turned his attention back to the French.

Seymour yelled for two grenadiers from the 32d to take Picton's body out of the battle. Kempt, the brigade commander, came riding up. "How bad is it, Captain?"

"He is dead, Sir." The words sounded devoid of emotion; reality had not yet touched the young aide's consciousness.

Without hesitation, Kempt raced forward to take charge of the division. The French *cuirassiers* had reorganized their misdirected charge and were now riding straight at the British infantry, which was trying desperately to hold the ridge. The allied line was wavering, pressed hard by four divisions of infantry and eleven squadrons of cavalry. From his vantage point only a few dozen yards from where Picton fell, Wellington sensed that the battle was hanging in the balance. He had seen his division commander fall and knew there was nothing he could do to alter the momentum of forces now in motion.

Wellington allowed himself a moment's sympathy for his old friend. Poor Picton, I could use him now. No matter, the immediate engagement would take the course already set. He forced himself to think ahead to events yet to unfold.

"Baron Müffling, take yourself to the left of the line. I must have the Prussians in place. Get them into the battle. By God, I must have Blücher and I must have him quickly!"

"My Lord. You need hold only a little while longer. General Blücher said he will come, and he shall." The Prussian was proper, but his voice was strained by the thought that the word of his commander could be doubted.

"Of course, my dear Baron. So he shall. I wish only that you be there to greet him and expedite his integration." Wellington remained composed, his thoughts darting to the youthful, inexperienced prince of Orange, the commander of the 1st Corps and the senior officer now holding the left half of the line. Why did they send me a twenty-two–year–old prince? Were they mad? Did they have no idea of what it is like in this furnace? Youth is so volatile, so untempered. It would take an experienced leader to deal with the situation on the left, should it develop as it had here in the center.

"Once the Prussians are in place, please coordinate the efforts of the left wing." Wellington was giving Müffling the authority to assert himself in the prince's sector. There could be no greater demonstration of trust in an ally. In truth, the outcome of the battle hinged on that trust.

For all their arrogance and bloodiness, Wellington concluded, these Prussians were cool heads in a fight. The duke wanted a little insurance that the left would hold. Müffling could handle it. He had a warrior's head. The baron wheezed, embarrassed by the flattery bestowed on him, and moved off to the east on his heavily laden horse.

But if the Prussians were to have any impact on the field, it could only come later. In the meantime, the battle was on a knife edge. Already the French thought they had won the field. Picton's division had momentarily checked them in front of the hedges along the crest of the ridge, but no longer would the French be compelled to rely on the musketry of the few front ranks while the great mass moved forward, impotent behind them. Now it would be the sure and true bayonet, the cold steel easily penetrating the soft cloth of the enemy's uniform, cutting through yielding flesh to reach the vital organs beneath. The French front expanded to allow musket and bayonet to come to the ready.

It was the moment of crisis for the allies. The *cuirassiers* had at last gotten their bearings. General Travers, the French cavalry brigade commander, could see the British infantry faltering before the much larger mass of Frenchmen stabbing and hacking their way through the hedges. With a throaty roar and a point from his saber, he directed his horsemen into the fray. He itched to strike back at his enemy. His beloved cavalry had been blooded enough. Filled with rage at the enemy for the suffering endured by his unit, the French commander wanted his revenge. All the pain his men had endured under the British guns would be paid back with interest. This ragtag bunch of British scum could not hope to withstand the onslaught of the cream of the French cavalry, whetted now for the kill.

Lord Uxbridge saw it all. He had ridden to the right of the line to supervise the placing of Dörnberg's and Grant's cavalry brigades. Now he waited, along with Lord Somerset, for news that would cue the counterattack of the British cavalry. Uxbridge himself was primed for

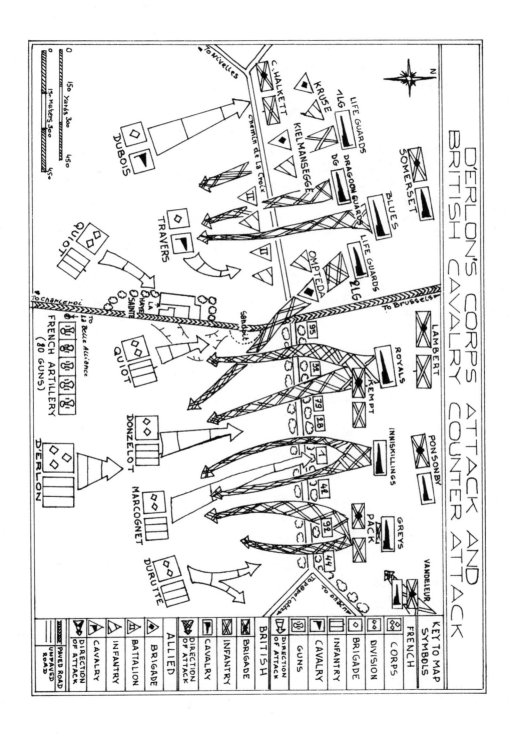

D'ERLON'S CORPS ATTACK AND BRITISH CAVALRY COUNTER ATTACK

N

To Nivelles

C. HALKETT
KRUSE
7LG
LIFE GUARDS
KIELMANSEGGE
DG
DRAGOON GUARDS
BLUES
LIFE GUARDS
2LG
OMPTEDA
SOMERSET
Chemin de la Croix
TRAVERS
DUBOIS
QUIOT

To Charleroi
To Brussels
Sandpit
LA HAYE SAINTE
To La Belle Alliance
QUIOT
FRENCH ARTILLERY (80 GUNS)
D'ERLON
DONZELOT
MARCOGNET
DURUTTE

LAMBERT
ROYALS
KEMPT
95
34
79 18
PONSONBY
INNISKILLINGS
1
42
GREYS
PACK
92
44
VANDELEUR
To Papelotte

0   150 Yards 300   450
0   15 Meters 300   450

KEY TO MAP SYMBOLS

FRENCH		
CORPS	⬠⬠	
DIVISION	◇◇	
BRIGADE	◇	
INFANTRY	▭	
CAVALRY	◇◇	
GUNS	⊗	
DIRECTION OF ATTACK	▽	

BRITISH		
BRIGADE	⊠	
INFANTRY	⊠	
CAVALRY	▼	
DIRECTION OF ATTACK	▽	

ALLIED		
BRIGADE	◆	
BATTALION	△	
INFANTRY	△	
CAVALRY	▽	
DIRECTION OF ATTACK	▽▽	

PAVED ROAD
UNPAVED ROAD

action, having taken all he could stomach of the loss of horses and men before the merciless artillery barrage of the French. The men had dismounted to lessen their exposure, but the poor dumb animals absorbed the hot iron with no understanding of why any living thing would want to hurt them. They had been taught to trust humans, and it made no sense to them that the very men who lavished such care on them would bring them to such terrible suffering. Already much of the finest horseflesh had been destroyed, and riders had switched to substitutes to be ready for the countercharge that seemed forever in coming.

Uxbridge's fellow cavalryman, Lord Edward Somerset, had posted a quartet of subalterns from the Household Cavalry Brigade to the front line. They were to observe the movements there. Their very arrogance was a defense against admission of their own vulnerabilities to the terrors that stalked lesser men, who were rooted to the ground. They fervently believed that their noble mounts elevated them above the baseness of the foot-slogging infantry. The four young men had seen the British infantry falter and recognized that the critical moment was at hand. They had eagerly raced each other back to their commander, who now received the news with grim satisfaction. It was at last time for the decisive arm to commit. With a flourish Somerset ordered his regiments to form line and make ready to charge the rampaging French *cuirassiers.*

"My Lord, are you ready to advance?" Uxbridge looked Somerset in the eye.

"That I am." Somerset's voice was steady, but his eyes belied his eagerness.

"Be sure to hold the Blues in reserve. You will need a supporting force to help with the recovery. Await my final order. I will go and prepare Ponsonby." Uxbridge spurred his horse across the Brussels road as Somerset readied his own men.

It was six hundred yards to Ponsonby and the Union Brigade. Uxbridge had time to think, but he found that concentration was almost beyond his will. His heart was racing. He could see the great infantry battle on the crest of the ridge, he could hear the great din of the melee, the shrill voices of French and British throwing insults at each other, praising their emperor, their regiment, their standard—praising anything that would give them identity with a cause greater than themselves, an identity that would transcend the imminent specter of death. They were seeking immortality at the very moment their mortality would be undeniable.

Think, Uxbridge, think! Damn you, discipline your emotions. His mind was speaking to his heart, but his heart was taking control. The adrenaline pulsed through his veins, fed by the thundering hooves of the French cavalry that pounded into sodden earth and fallen bodies. And now the French artillery began again, killing friend and foe alike.

What kind of beast is Bonaparte, raining artillery on his own men? Napoleon would do anything for victory. Individual lives were not important; only the emperor's own glory mattered.

Uxbridge's mind raced. A madman! Napoleon is a madman. He spends their lives like so much filthy coin. Well, I will help him spend them, the faster the better. At least from my countercharge they will die at the hands of an enemy. Surely there is greater glory in that. He spurred his horse over the remaining distance to the Union Brigade.

Uxbridge could see Ponsonby now. The latter was astride a small bay hack. Though his charger had been butchered in the shelling, Ponsonby's dignity was preserved by a fur-trimmed cloak and a great cocked hat.

"The Royals and the Inniskillings will charge, the Greys support." Uxbridge was barely audible above the din. But Ponsonby was waiting for the words, so he heard them well enough. Somerset's Household troops had already advanced to the summit. Ponsonby had seen them move forward and was determined not to be outdone by his sister brigade. With a wave of his saber, he set the Union Brigade in motion. What began as a walk quickly turned into a trot.

The British infantry were recoiling into squares, bracing for the impact of the French cavalry. The fight atop the crest of the hill and along its northern slope had taken on a direction of its own. Individual battalions parried and moved as though in drill, discipline overcoming fear. The French infantry wavered yet again, just as their cavalry lost formation in their sprint for the British infantry. Into this confused scene charged the Household and Union brigades, racing each other in their quest for glory.

The timing could not have been better. Into the already wild entanglement—the smoke of thousands of muskets and artillery shells, the roar of tens of thousands of blood-lusty voices, the screams of death from man and beast, the thunder of hooves and the crash of steel on steel—the British cavalry countercharged at precisely the right moment. On they came, in one glorious rush. Nothing was held back.

In went the Life Guards, the Dragoons, and the Blues. In went the

Royals, the Inniskillings, and the Scots Greys. No verbal orders were possible. It was all screams and bugles. Napoleon's *cuirassiers* were caught in the flanks and driven into the ground. The French mounts—spent by their charge up to the ridge, from being caught between the two British lines, and by a charge into the British infantry to the east of the Brussels road—were too weary to turn and meet the oncoming British. French officers yelled—unheard in the melee—and went to their deaths, examples of courage and fighting spirit.

A British sword sliced through a decorative headdress, separating flesh from bone, bone from bone, head from torso, and man from horse. It was an orgy of killing, of laying men open, of kicking and trampling, of thrusting and punching. Some men took on a horrible look of finality as they crumpled before a terrible blow. Others stared with mute but overpowering sadness as they witnessed the severing of their own limbs from what a moment earlier had been a complete, healthy, and virile body.

Lieutenant General the Earl of Uxbridge could not help himself. He was in the thick of it, out in front in the finest tradition of the cavalry. He saw the standards of the Royal Horse Guards and the Scots Greys, the designated reserves, racing out to the front, and he knew he should have stayed back to ensure that they followed his orders and remained in support. But he could not stop himself; it was as if his horse and saber had taken hold of his body. He had to lead the attack. French horse came at him; he cut them down—first one, then another. Their numbers seemed limitless. For every one he split, two more would appear. He was like a boy playing at battle. It was exhilarating, made more so by the cheers from fellow cavalrymen on his left and right.

"To the guns! To the guns!" shouted a colonel of the Scots Greys. He had slashed his way through cavalry and infantry only to see the French artillery on the ridge beyond. The French guns were firing again, bringing back all the colonel's anger and frustration from the earlier barrage. He could think of only one objective: Even the score!

"To the guns. Charge the guns!" The colonel roared just as a *cuirassier* came up beside him and crashed his saber down through his left forearm, laying it open and cracking the bone beneath. Tightening his legs around his horse, the colonel ignored the pain and thrust his saber out and up, cutting off the Frenchman's chin to the teeth as easily as an apple is sliced to the core.

But the *cuirassier* had fight in him. In his agony he thrust wildly with his saber, embedding it in the right shoulder of the British cavalry colonel. For an instant each looked into the contorted face of the other. Then the Frenchman sank from his saddle, his disfigured lower face cupped in his hands.

"Charge the guns! Charge the guns!" the colonel shouted again as he struggled to place the reins in his teeth before use of his right arm was gone. His left already hung limp, squirting thick red blood over his elegant uniform and brightly blanketed horse.

Uxbridge knew the instruction to charge was the wrong order as well as he knew he was to blame for placing his forces in a situation where it could be given with such immediate, disastrous effect. There was no sense in going after the guns. They were too distant, and a charge that far could not possibly be held together in any kind of order. His cavalry would be laid open needlessly to a French countercharge. The British cavalry units had already done their job. The French cavalry on Mont Saint Jean had broken; the British infantry had held before d'Erlon's attack. There was no need to push his own cavalry charge any farther.

Uxbridge yelled a counterorder, but it was to no avail. His voice cracked, impotent in the frenzy of the charge. The lead British horsemen turned their mounts in the direction of the French guns and were off in a fury. As one, Uxbridge's two brigades followed.

The earl pulled in his horse just as Lord Ponsonby came rushing by, his little bay hack wheezing from the strain of the unaccustomed exertion. A young boy charged alongside, straining hard to keep up with his lord. To Uxbridge the scene epitomized the futility of the charge at the guns: the brigade commander racing in to do personal combat on the back of an unfit mount, accompanied by a mere youth.

How innocent they are, the boy and the bay hack. Why have I allowed them into this business? The thought filled him with guilt.

Uxbridge could see now that nothing had been held back. He had given the order to maintain reserves, but the order had not been obeyed. Instead of ensuring compliance, he had set his forces in motion, had become a part of the attack himself. In so doing he had relinquished whatever control he might have maintained over his cavalry. Neither Ponsonby nor Somerset—even less their regimental colonels—could be faulted for their zeal. Uxbridge himself had set the tone by going forward. Courage had come before any other consideration. Courage was manhood, and manhood was everything. Go forward into battle.

Better to die a brave man in defeat than to win a battle with one's bravery in doubt. That is where his heart had led him. And so too it had led every last one of his cavalry.

What had been gained? A reputation for great valor, a lifetime of parlor admiration for an act of personal courage? At what cost? The battle might be lost. He had certainly wasted the lives of many brave and trusting—and perhaps a little too foolish—young men. Uxbridge called for a bugler to sound recall, even though he knew it would do no good. He needed to make the gesture—if only to soothe his own conscience. Predictably, the bugler's notes were lost in the excitement of the charge as hundreds of cavalrymen sped off, riding hard for the French guns.

From his position at Ronsomme, Napoleon could not see what was happening. His keen battle sense allowed him to surmise that he had suffered terribly on the ridge. He had received reports that his infantry had wavered, regrouped, attacked again, and then wavered once more as the British cavalry and infantry came on. With callous disregard for his own troops, he had ordered his artillery back into action, calculating that a little more confusion—a little more carnage—might be enough to give his massed infantry the added weight to break the defenses on Mont Saint Jean. But when he learned of the British cavalry attack, he feared that he had lost the moment.

He could picture soldiers falling on both sides, victims of the grand indifference unleashed by close quarters' fighting. He knew that the formations would fall apart; that the infantry would shoot in every direction, hitting friend and foe alike; that the horses would trample freely, without concern for uniform or standard. The momentum of the struggle had already become a macabre dance of death, moving alternately from attacker to defender. The emperor sensed more than observed that the dance was moving against him. Wellington was holding, that much he knew for sure. As Napoleon's eyes burned into the distant ridge, a fierce pounding seized his chest.

"Sire, the allied horse is attacking our gun line!" It was an aide galloping in from his forward observation post at La Belle Alliance.

"At last," Napoleon muttered, "Wellington has made a mistake. Damn him, he has made too few. But this one will cost him."

He knew instinctively that the British cavalry had gone too far, out of support of its own infantry and most likely uncovered by any horse held in reserve. Through his telescope he could discern the mounts racing into the valley and up the near slope toward the French guns, his "beautiful daughters." Now the mud would work for the French and against Wellington. The British horses would slip and slide in the morass, bursting their lungs over a thousand-meter charge.

Napoleon would add to their difficulties. "Tell General Jacquinot to send up Gobrecht's Brigade of the 3d and 4th Lancers. Who are the colonels in command?"

The young aide answered eagerly, pleased that he had been called upon to make a contribution. "Colonels Bro and Martigne, Sire. They are already moving forward."

"Yes, of course, and they are brave men are they not?"

"Oh yes, your Excellency, very brave indeed." Perhaps, by stressing the bravery of others, the aide could show that he knew what it meant to be brave.

"Very well. Have them move quickly. I want them to greet Wellington's horse and show us how brave they really are." Napoleon fed the aide's ego, knowing that it was not bravery he needed now so much as the ruthless slaughter of the heavy cavalry of his enemy.

Eagerly, the captain galloped toward General Jacquinot. The emperor dispatched a second aide to ready two more regiments of *cuirassiers* from Milhaud's 4th Cavalry Corps.

The British cavalry arrived at the guns, stabbing and slashing men and horses in furious abandon. Neither the beardless faces of the youths—many of the gunners were mere boys—nor the fearful, innocent eyes of the horses deterred them from their gory revenge. For the most part, the artillery pieces themselves were ignored. It was easier to sink sword into flesh than to disable iron guns. Horses cried out in terror and pain under savage cuts. Artillerymen fought desperately, then fell beneath the blows.

Too late to save them, in came the French lancers and *cuirassiers*. They swept across the front, well to the south of Papelotte farm, catching disorganized packets of British horsemen preoccupied with killing gunners. The French cavalry fell on the frothing mounts of the Household Brigade. Long lances thrust into the surprised and short-sabered Scots Greys, Inniskillings, and Royals. Powerful *cuirassiers* shattered the spent Guards and Blues. The British were hopelessly outnumbered. Individual fights raged at odds of five, six, or seven to one. For the British, totally disheveled by their mad rush at the artillery, it was every man for himself.

Lord Ponsonby commanded only his exhausted horse and his aide. Frenchmen were all around him. He turned and slashed with his chipped saber, its edge red with blood. The aide moved in to parry an enemy lance, was not strong enough, and took it through his leg. The limb was pinned to his horse.

"Run, boy, run!" Ponsonby kicked the youth's mount in the flank. In terror it reared and kicked out in desperation. Another lancer speared the boy in the groin while a third thrust his weapon into the side of the aide's face. Ponsonby lashed out, but saw he could do nothing. The young man looked around in terror, slipped from the saddle, and lay still in the mud.

The general slipped under a lance and slashed at the midriff of an attacker, catching him across the brass buttons of his jacket. Before he could recover he felt an unseen lance sink into the soft underside of his armpit, driving his shoulder bone up toward his neck, splintering it as it went. With grim determination he spun his horse out of the muck and momentarily broke away from his attackers, blood drenching the right side of his torn and muddied coat. A look over his shattered shoulder told him he had but a moment before being overtaken again. His thoughts fled back to his wife, and he groped with his usable hand for the locket holding her picture. He held it tightly in his fist.

Time. Time. If we only had enough time. Where did it all go? His fingers probed into his coat, looking for his pocketwatch. Suddenly, the watch seemed very important to him. He pressed locket and watch together in the palm of his hand—the symbol of love and the symbol of time. Five French lancers rode him down, spearing and respearing general and horse, mixing the blood of animal and man together on the soft earth.

Wellington was sickened by the utter carnage of it all. He knew he had held the ridge, but the cost had been enormous. His face impassive, his soul tormented, he watched from the crossroads the mayhem all around him. All the plans and the preparations, all the posturings and the parades, this is what it had all come down to. In the end it was just killing and dying.

The day was a long way from being over. He had stopped d'Erlon, but it had cost him the best of his cavalry. He would have to recover what horse he could. Napoleon had held a great number of his own cavalry back. No doubt they would soon enter the battle—and still the Prussians had not arrived. The duke wondered how much longer he could hold out.

All along the crest of the ridge and down the slope on either side, infantrymen were picking themselves up from the mud. It was amazing how many could stand after the trampling they had taken from the cavalry of both sides. Full of curses and contempt for the rude treatment they had received, they could take some comfort in the knowledge that their own coolness under fire had kept them alive. For many of them, survival had come from playing dead, allowing man and beast to tread on arms, legs, torsos, and heads—without so much as a flinch. Here the mud had been a blessing. Many had withstood the trampling only because of the soft ooze of earth beneath; a hard crust would have finished them. Not that bones weren't broken, and in many cases damage to internal organs would cause death eventually. But the fact was that many could rise from the ground to fight again. After such a pounding, the infantry took heart that a few more moments of life remained—at least until death came once more.

For the French who had not managed to flee the ridge, it was all over. They suffered wounds and death no more or no less than the British, but the ground remained in allied hands. Unless they could dart away and hide in whatever stalks of corn and rye had not been flattened, they had little recourse but to surrender. They had no organization left to them: So many of their officers had fallen, and the fight had taken them in every direction. Nor was there much desire to re-form and fight again. Without the driving force of their officers to compel them to reorganize and devoid of regimental colors to rally behind, many were content to turn their fate over to their captors.

In this the duke found some hope. If only the cavalry situation were not so pathetic. The attack on the French guns had been a poor exchange. Perhaps thirty artillery pieces had been put out of action, but at enormous cost. Two great brigades of British cavalry were now but tattered remnants. By small packets—sometimes in ones and twos—they made their way back to Mont Saint Jean. Those coming back by La Haye Sainte fell prey to the intense fighting raging there, and so the number of survivors was diminished further. The French infantry troops impaled before the farmhouse, maddened by their inability to penetrate its walls and gates, had vented their frustrations on the horsemen. The infantrymen's instinctive hate for cavalry allowed them to show no mercy. Torn and bloodied cavalrymen, their horses white with sweated foam, were shot to pieces as they came past La Haye Sainte.

A small band of Life Guards rose into view, passing within a few yards of Wellington. Concealing his great sadness, he paid them a compliment: "Guards, I thank you." They smiled and nodded in return, a little sheepishly perhaps, but proud nonetheless. The duke cocked his hat and gave a grand wave.

Wellington assessed his cavalry losses. Perhaps two thousand had fallen, maybe more. And the officers—they led the casualty lists. What grand foolishness. How can I fight without them? He made a mental note to admonish the cavalry when the battle was over. Outwardly, he continued to smile and nod at the small groups of survivors drifting back to allied lines.

It was still early in the afternoon. In this first main attack of the day, the losses had been enormous. At Mont Saint Jean alone, almost 4,500 British and Dutch-Belgian infantry had died. About 2,500 allied cavalry had evaporated, almost a quarter of the whole. Easily, over 1,000 horses had fallen on either side; many still cried out in their death throes.

The French had lost a good part of a corps, but the survivors would be reorganized to fight again. At that the French were very good. So too would their cavalry be recovered and reorganized. They would end up a few thousand short in either category, but Napoleon still had the greater part of the strength of his army to call upon.

Neither side could spare men to care for the wounded. Although surgeons on both sides were at work in whatever primitive shelters they could secure, those benefitting from such care were only the wounded who could get to them under their own power. For both allied and French soldiers, the most advanced means of evacuating a casualty was transporting him in a blanket held taut by two or more men. The small number of ambulances—and only the French had them—were reserved for officers. The order given before the battle had been firm: Casualties would lie where they fell. Men would not be spared to assist in the evacuation of the wounded. In the aftermath of the first great clash, the order applied even to those who had given it.

Desertion added further to the losses of the early afternoon. Despite the emphasis on bravery, there remained within each soldier enough of an instinct for survival to inspire a desire to be elsewhere. If anything held them in place, it was discipline—a discipline that came from the habit of following orders, an allegiance to the regiment and the comrades therein, and the hold and the example of the officers and sergeants. Though there were severe sanctions against breaking ranks, when all around was blown asunder, when the havoc was so great that all organization was lost, the urge to flee was strong. A deserter could invoke one of many excuses later on—confusion, enemy pressure, the evacuation of a beloved officer, the pursuit of a fleeing enemy. If there was any wonder at all, it was that so many held fast.

For the allies, there was enough opportunity to make good an escape. They were in friendly territory—friendly as long as the local Belgians concluded that the allies were going to be the winners. But for the French, desertion might put them at risk from a hostile population. Dying in battle was a terrible thing, but being picked apart by enraged peasants was more terrible yet. To varying degrees, soldiers from both sides endeavored to make their escape. But, for the most part, they stayed on to meet their fate on the battlefield.

The two antagonists, Wellington and Napoleon, gathered in their resources and prepared for the next phase of the fighting. The affair had just begun.

12

LA HAYE SAINTE: 1445

Maj. Georg Baring could not afford the luxury of watching the rout of the French at the center of Wellington's line. He was at La Haye Sainte, a bare two hundred meters forward of the line, and the storm had broken all around him. In the brief respite in the aftermath of d'Erlon's failed attack on Mont Saint Jean, Baring hastened to assess his situation and brace for the next wave he felt sure was coming.

Like Hougoumont, the farm at La Haye Sainte had offered a strong outpost to the front of the main allied defensive position. The farmhouse and its adjacent high walls had become a barrier to the flow of the French attacks. La Haye Sainte sat beside the main road to Waterloo and Brussels, just where the ground began to steepen before it rose to the ridge, two hundred yards to the north. Baring's battalion of the King's German Legion was armed with Baker rifles. From their posts on the roof and in the windows of the farmhouse, his soldiers had been able to sharpshoot the French infantry and cavalry as they passed by on their way to attack the center. Like Hougoumont, La Haye Sainte had become a magnet for French forces.

It was only that morning that Baring had been ordered to occupy it—he had spent the night with his 2d Light Battalion on the ridge, shivering with his men in the rain. Colonel Christian von Ompteda, the brigade commander, had spent part of the night with them before moving on to his other battalions. The colonel, in his great blue coat, had gone from watch fire to watch fire, cheering his men as best he could.

Major Baring, like his men, had a great deal of respect for Ompteda. The colonel had a youthful attitude toward his command, as if the army were a great adventure that he had only recently discovered. But he was not a young man; he was fifty years old and a veteran of many campaigns; the most brutal of them, Spain, had eventually brought him to a nervous breakdown. If the army had a particular appeal to him, it was because no other aspect of his life had brought him any joy. After two unsuccessful romances he had resigned himself to bachelorhood, although his preference would have been marriage and family. He liked children and had brought his two young nephews with him on campaign. His servant had procured shelter for them out of the cold, rainy night, but Ompteda preferred to share the discomfort of his soldiers. They had become his family, more so than his own kin.

His nervous breakdown had nearly cost him his one great happiness in life—soldiering. But his reputation in the army was so great that he had been allowed to return to command after some rest and whatever little treatment was available. His brooding eyes, set above high cheekbones, gave only a hint of the psychological unrest seething inside of him. His command authority was what most impressed his men. Here was a man they were ready to obey. When he told Baring to move with his 376 men to the farm of La Haye Sainte in the early morning drizzle, the battalion accepted the order without reservation. If Baron von Ompteda told soldiers to hold the farm, then they would hold it.

Baring was experienced enough to realize that the order had come too late to develop fully the advantages the farm offered. The night before, his own sappers had been detached from him to help Macdonell over at Hougoumont, and with them had gone their axes and spades. Worse yet, La Haye Sainte had attracted large numbers of allies who were seeking shelter during the miserable night. With no one in charge, the natural quest for comfort by so many soldiers had confounded any preparation of defenses. Men had drifted to the inner courtyard without orders; none entertained any thought of holding the place during battle. Concerned as they were with the needs of the moment, the men had burned any wood they could get their hands on. All carts, crates, and barrels in the courtyard had been sacrificed for a few moments' warmth. Then the great wooden door in the archway between the stable and the barn was removed from its heavy hinges and offered up to the fire.

Without tools or wood the best Major Baring could do was scrape a few firing loops in the wall surrounding the farm. Since the wall itself was too high to fire over and there was no way to construct firesteps, he had sent the majority of his men out to the hedge at the edge of the orchard.

The first test of the 2d Light Battalion had come about noon, when a swarm of French skirmishers had probed toward La Haye Sainte. Not being regular infantry and armed only with muskets, the skirmishers contented themselves with taking potshots at the defenders. For the riflemen crouched behind the hedge, this was little threat, but for the officers perched upon their mounts, it was deadly. Baring's own horse had been killed in the first volley, and a few minutes later Major Bosewiel, Baring's senior assistant, had been mortally wounded. But officership has its price, and the battalion leaders continued to sit stoically on their horses until the superior rifle fire of their men drove back the skirmishers.

The attack of the French infantry at 1400, however, had been a different story. They had come on in such numbers that Baring had brought his men back inside the cobblestone courtyard. A high rate of rifle fire, along with timely reinforcements of Hanoverian militia—countrymen of the King's German Legion, though not as militarily proficient— had kept the French from getting inside the wall. Baring had wisely posted Lt. Georg Graeme's company of Legion sharpshooters on the roof of the farmhouse, and their murderous fire had dropped several score of the French in their tracks. Nonetheless, the multitude of French would have surely broken through had not the British cavalry coun- terattack on d'Erlon broken their attack in the nick of time. But after the heavy fighting, in the confusion of the reorganization, the Hanoverian militia had fallen back to the ridge, leaving the survivors of the 2d Battalion alone at the farm.

"Sergeant Major, give me a count of the dead and wounded." Baring's boyish mop of black hair was matted with gunpowder and sweat.

The sergeant major made a quick survey, concentrating less on who was missing than on how many were left. He carefully noted that three of the officers were dead and another six wounded. Only two hundred of the soldiers were fit for further combat. After arranging for the redistribution of ammunition among the survivors, he brought his report to Baring. "Herr Major, we have the strength of only two companies, and I would estimate that fewer than one hundred rounds per man re- main."

Baring peered into the sergeant's beet-red face—the result of too many nights in the open and too many schnapps to help withstand them.

It was impossible to tell his age, but no doubt it was much less than his appearance implied. "Very good, Sergeant Major. Send a runner to Colonel Ompteda with a request for reinforcements. Have him tell the colonel how many of us remain. And order the men to conserve their ammunition as best they can. God knows where our resupplies are, and if they can ever get up to us in all the confusion."

Raising a gnarled hand in salute, the noncommissioned officer moved out to comply with the orders. Baring watched him go for a moment, then turned to look for his officers. He found Lieutenant Graeme by the opening under the archway, where only last night a door had stood.

"What are you doing, Lieutenant?" It was less a reproach than honest curiosity. Graeme was a good officer, Baring knew, and his initiative in the recent fight had been commendable.

"Oh, excuse me, Sir." The sincere face of the eighteen-year-old lieutenant had a troubled look about it. "I have been watching that man there. Do you see him? He is still alive."

Baring allowed himself the distraction. A short distance away, in the orchard, lay a French infantryman. His uniform was torn and bloody, and his pale face had a strange determined look to it. The man's legs had been shattered, either by shot or saber or both, and he was painfully trying to position his sword so that he could impale himself on it. But he could not raise himself high enough off the ground to gain the momentum he needed. Again and again he tried to no avail while around him other wounded Frenchmen were calling out encouragement, *"Vive l'empereur. Vive l'empereur."*

"I have never seen such resolve, Sir. He does not have the strength to ram it home, yet he wishes so much to die for his cause that he keeps jabbing himself with it, adding to his pain." Baring looked at the desolate scene, unable to find the words to respond.

"Sir, may I have your permission to send my servant to remove his saber? Although I have been killing Frenchmen with all of my energy this day, I cannot bear to let that man torture himself so."

"Of course, but do not dally. His cousins will soon be back to try us again."

The two officers separated, struck by the scene they had witnessed but aware that they had little time to dwell on it.

Already the French were regrouping a short distance to the south. Baring estimated that his position was strong enough, with an opportunity to bring rifle fire to bear four hundred yards in all directions. The woods to the south was the only cover the approaching enemy could take. Unfortunately, that route took them straight to the opening left by the missing door. The major hastened to position riflemen to cover that vulnerability in his defenses. He regretted that he had no debris from the courtyard to place in the archway.

As the 2d Light Battalion readied itself, its youngest officer, sixteen-year-old Lt. Georg Franck, tried to steady himself. Before today, he had never seen a man killed in battle. Now, looking for his missing soldiers, he picked through more dead and wounded men than he could count.

Franck heard the sound of running men approaching from the north. He looked up in dread, afraid that the French had surrounded them and were attacking from a new direction. "Don't worry, Lieutenant Franck." It was Major Baring. "Those are our own soldiers—the reinforcements from Colonel Ompteda." The major's voice held a ring of hope. Ompteda had sent two companies from the 1st Light Battalion. Baring calculated that they would bring his strength back up to around four hundred men.

"Lieutenant Carey, take one of those companies and station them on the roof of the farmhouse. Have them train their rifles on the front gate and the Brussels road." Major Baring was addressing one of the English officers in the King's German Legion. "Move 2d Company to the barn, where they can add their strength to the defense of the west portal. Have them share their extra rounds. I want each man to have an equal number of rounds."

"Sir, the French are coming again! One column is approaching through the woods, another from the direction of the road." It was the sergeant major.

The news spread quickly among the defenders as the new arrivals were hastily put into position. In the few minutes they had to wait, men did whatever they could to ready themselves, sometimes performing little acts that did nothing but consume their nervous energy. They tightened their muscles under their dark green coats, they wiped the dust and mud off the stocks of their .60-caliber Baker rifles, and they tried to find a vantage point from which to see the enemy approach. Talking fell to a whisper, then died out altogether. Each man was alone with his own thoughts.

"Vive l'empereur! Vive l'empereur!" The harsh battle cry of the French announced their arrival at the main gate. Musket fire began to pepper

OVERVIEW
LA HAYE SAINTE

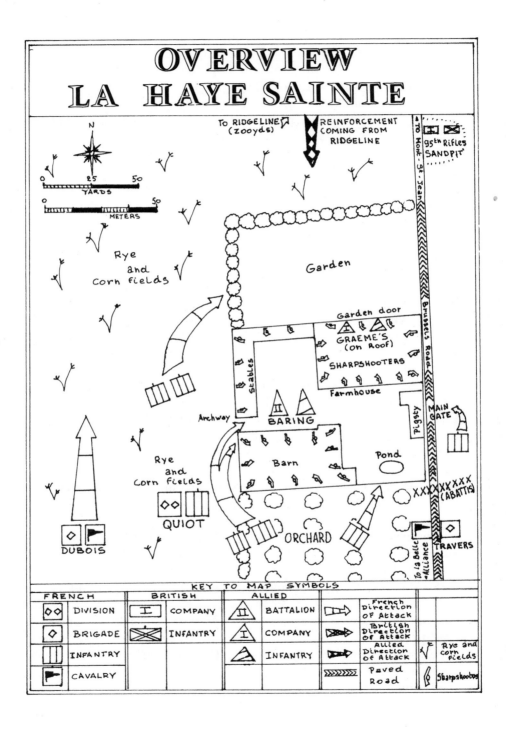

TO RIDGELINE (200yds)

REINFORCEMENT COMING FROM RIDGELINE

TO Mont-St.-Jean

95th Rifles
SANDPIT

N

0   25   50
YARDS

0   50
METERS

Rye and Corn fields

Garden

Garden door

GRAEME'S (on Roof)

SHARPSHOOTERS

Farmhouse

Brussels Road

Pigsty

MAIN GATE

Archway

Stables

BARING

Rye and Corn fields

Barn

Pond

QUIOT

XXXXXXX (ABATTIS)

ORCHARD

To la Belle Alliance

DUBOIS

TRAVERS

KEY TO MAP SYMBOLS

FRENCH		BRITISH		ALLIED					
◇◇	DIVISION	I	COMPANY	II	BATTALION		French Direction of Attack		
◇	BRIGADE	⊠	INFANTRY	△	COMPANY		British Direction of Attack		Rye and Corn fields
	INFANTRY			△	INFANTRY		Allied Direction of Attack		
	CAVALRY					>>>>>>	Paved Road		Sharpshooters

the roof and the windows of the farm; it was answered by the more accurate and much more deadly rifle fire of the defenders. Frenchmen fell in bunches, but they took not a step back. They continued to clamor at the wooden door and to grab for the weapons of the King's German Legion, which protruded from the firing loops.

"Sir, the portal!" Lieutenant Franck's adolescent voice cracked on the final word.

Baring mounted his second horse of the day and moved behind the ranks waiting just inside the archway. There was an underpass of six yards, which was formed by the stone arch that joined the walls of the barn and stable. The French saw the opening. They came on in a rush, directly into the massed fire from the Legionnaires waiting just inside the courtyard.

It was no contest. The first rank of French fell in a heap, causing the following ranks to stumble and lose their momentum. Their officers came up behind them and yelled, punching at them with the flats of their sabers. Men scrambled forward, only to be shot dead a few steps into the sally port. More Frenchmen came forward, stepping over the dead, discharging their muskets, and rushing in with bayonets. Here and there, unlucky Legionnaires fell from the random musket fire. But others filled the holes and poured their fire into the attacking French.

Major Baring counted seventeen dead Frenchmen in a heap just inside the sally port. They formed a barrier about a yard high and made it difficult for the attackers to pass. Where they could, the wounded tried to drag themselves out of the way. Some came toward the waiting defenders, who either bayoneted or clubbed them; others pulled themselves back outside the farm, where rifle fire from the roof and windows finished them off.

Baring sensed that for the moment his men could hold the vulnerable archway. But for how much longer? The main door along the Brussels road still held, although the din raised by the firing, screaming, and clawing on the far side of the wall was ominous.

The major's jaw muscles tightened. If that door gives way, we don't have a chance. We must conserve our ammunition. But how can we? Our rifle fire is all that stands between us and defeat. If only I had a door in the archway. A barrier at least. Those French bastards are throwing everything they've got into it. They have no fear of death. I have never seen such fanaticism.

He was about to shout an order for his men to consume their ammunition sparingly, when another French surge into the sally port drew his attention. A musket ball struck his horse in the chest and brought it crashing down to the cobblestones. Baring was pinned beneath the beast as it thrashed out wildly, hooves flailing viciously. A soldier ran toward the major to lend assistance but was hit by a musket ball in midstride. Baring could see him fall, rise as if to get back in motion, then stagger headfirst into a face-shattering kick from Baring's dying horse. The major beat at the terrified animal with his saber, at last dragging his bruised and lacerated leg from beneath its weight. He looked up in time to see a small group of Frenchmen penetrate the inner courtyard, there to be riddled by flanking fire from Legionnaires in position by the front of the farmhouse.

The major knew that this desperate struggle could turn against him at any moment. Inch by inch the French had penetrated the portal, littering it with their fallen as they came through. But as they fell, their bodies offered cover. Now the French could come the entire distance under the archway with less chance of being hit. True, once they emerged into the inner courtyard, concentrated fire from the defenders within would stop their advance for a while. But each Frenchman who fell offered further cover to those coming behind. The attackers would eventually be able to fan out to the point where they could dash into the barn or rush the farmhouse itself.

"Major Baring! Major Baring!" It was Lieutenant Graeme running over from the farmhouse. "My men on the roof tell me that they can see French cavalry forming to our southwest. Do you think they mean to come at us?"

Gathering his thoughts, the commander stared at the young officer. No, that did not make sense. Cavalry would not attack a walled farmhouse. They would be forming for an attack on the allied line. "No. It must be Mont Saint Jean they are after. Have your men tell me when they are formed for the attack. It may mean a respite for us."

The lieutenant raced back to pass the order. A dead soldier on the roof pitched forward, slid down the steep incline, and fell with a thud to the courtyard. Baring turned his attention once again to the sally port. He regretted that he did not have another horse. It seemed so undignified for the battalion commander to have to fight on foot.

From his position by the tree at the crossroads, Wellington could see the battle raging at La Haye Sainte. It was a sturdy-enough position, but he was uncertain of the ability of the defenders. He did not know Major Baring well; Colonel Ompteda, although a brave officer, was a question mark because of his past breakdown. The duke had felt that he was well enough to resume his command, but he had not bargained for fighting as intense as this. He was glad that supporting fire from across the Brussels road was helping in the defense of the farm.

The night before, Wellington had noticed the sand pit across the road from La Haye Sainte and ordered the 95th Rifles to send three companies to occupy it. From there riflemen could bring flanking fire down the Brussels road right at the main gate, which was only one hundred forty yards distant. The duke had a keen eye for ground. This little outpost of one hundred men or so had gone largely unnoticed in the grand sweep of the battle, yet it was contributing a great deal to the critical defense of La Haye Sainte. It was a key to the entire allied center. Before the weight of d'Erlon's attack, the companies from the 95th Rifles had given way. But in keeping with their regimental discipline, they had reoccupied the tiny but critical position as soon as the French fell back. In such ways, Wellington reflected, does terrain count for so much in battle. But men count more, and he knew that Baring would need reinforcements if he was to hold out much longer.

"Colonel de Lancey, what troops can we spare for La Haye Sainte?"

"Perhaps we could have Colonel Ompteda send another battalion forward, my Lord."

"No. That won't do." Wellington was thinking ahead. "We have yet to see the worst of it against our main line. I will need his Germans."

"Then perhaps we could send up the Nassauers. It would be Germans reinforcing Germans. But as you know, Sir, we have not seen much staying power in the Nassau troops. And their weapon is the musket, not the rifle."

"Very well. Send them in. They will do me little good here, and perhaps their encouragement to the defenders will compensate for their paltry fighting skills. As to the rifles, have Ompteda send forward some of his skirmishers."

"Yes, my Lord." De Lancey was amazed once again at the rapidity with which Wellington could assimilate a myriad of details and make a sound decision. He felt a little intimidated. Details were the business of the chief of staff, after all. He made a mental note to locate the wagons carrying the .60-caliber rounds for Ompteda's troops. At the moment they were lost somewhere in the traffic jam between Waterloo and Mont Saint Jean. At the rate they were firing in La Haye Sainte, the King's German Legion must be running low. He spurred his horse and raced to pass the orders. A French round shot crashed into the ground where only seconds before he had been standing.

Wellington watched him ride away, noting the round shot impact and bury itself in the ground. His expressionless face momentarily showed a bare flicker of concern as he stared after de Lancey. I hope he makes it through this battle. He is a fine officer and a loyal friend as well.

The allied commander surveyed the battlefield, trying to take stock of the situation. Hougoumont is holding out, leaving the right wing of my line essentially unopposed. That gives me an opportunity to bring reserves over to the center. If Napoleon ever gets by Hougoumont, then I will have my problems. But Macdonell will not let him by, not if I can continue to feed him reserves—bit by bit. That is the answer— bit by bit. Enough to hold on the right, but only enough so I can yet reinforce the center. On the left though, Papelotte has fallen. Even as I stopped d'Erlon in the center, his right wing was able to press through to my leftmost outpost. The ground is bad there—too low, with no view of what is coming at you. That tends to unnerve defenders, making things seem worse than they are. That is probably why Papelotte did not hold. But the ground doesn't go anywhere there, just back up the ridgeline to the center. Napoleon won't press on my left. He is too afraid of the Prussians coming on. He has got to be thinking of that. That means he will keep pressing in the center. But as long as La Haye Sainte holds, it will foul his formations. It will split the mass of any attack in two directions—east and west—without giving them any distance in which to rejoin before I can meet the two parts of his main attack, each one weakened by its separation from the other. The center, then, remains the decisive point. If the center holds until Blücher arrives, I can lose everything else. I only need to make sure that, whatever I lose, I lose it slowly. He turned to his aides to pass his orders. Artillery was bursting all around.

Major Baring cold not believe that he still held the farm. The French had pulled back again, this time before the sudden arrival of the Nassauers—the reserves Wellington had released to the King's German Legion. The Nassau troops did not constitute much of a reinforcement, but with the French attack focused on the sally port and the main gate, the sudden appearance of what seemed to be fresh counterattacking troops had stampeded the French infantry away from the walls. The interlude would not last long, Baring figured, as he hastened to put the Nassauers in place. He had found another horse, was relieved to be properly mounted at last. It made him feel more confident in his ability to hold the farm.

A French prisoner was brought before him. "What division are you with?" Baring spoke in French.

"I am with the division commanded by General Quiot."

"And is it with his orders that you attack my position?"

"That I do not know. I take my orders from my captain."

"And where is your captain?"

"He lies dead in the orchard just beyond the archway."

"Then why do you attack?"

"Because it was my captain's wish."

Baring ordered him to be moved to the rear, along with the few other prisoners that could walk. He regretted having to spare any of his men to herd prisoners, but decided that the alternatives of slaughtering them or turning them loose to attack again were not acceptable at the moment. He recognized the strong possibility that before too long he might be a prisoner himself.

"Sir, they are coming again!" It was Lieutenant Franck.

In the orchard where he had posted them, the red-coated skirmishers of the Legion opened fire on the advancing columns, giving ground slowly back toward the sally port. The French came on in the same old way, slowly walking in formation to the beat of the drum. Again they advanced in two directions. This time, however, the greater mass headed toward the opening between the barn and the stables.

It was a repeat of the earlier scenes—a fierce fight at the sally port, pressure all along the wall, a clamoring at the roadside gate—only this time even more dead littered the ground. The main door held. Frenchmen pressed up against the wall, taking shots at the Legionnaires every time one revealed himself to draw a bead on the attackers. Rifle fire poured down from the sand pit, chewing up the French pressing in from the Brussels road along the eastern walls of the farm. The only progress was in the west. Step-by-step, attackers there penetrated deeper and deeper into the archway, advancing behind the ramparts of their dead.

Baring recognized the familiar pattern of the struggle. Inch by inch the French would press forward behind their dead. Body by body, they would consume his bullets. For a while it would be sheer suicide for the attackers, but eventually the defenders would run out of ammunition. Then it would be saber and bayonet, few against many.

The major's eyes narrowed. He called out to no one in particular. "What is that smoke? It is a different color from the gunpowder. My God, the barn has caught fire!"

The French saw it at the same time, and they realized the advantage it gave them. At first singly, then by twos and threes, they tried to squeeze by their dead and get behind the smoke. Some snatched at the burning straw and flung it toward the stables on the other side of the sally port, trying to spread the fire. Many were shot dead for their efforts, but somehow or other the attempts succeeded. Soon both barn and stable were raging infernos.

Baring could not abandon his position, for it would give the French access to the courtyard. He knew that no water barrels were available— they had been burned the night before. But the Nassauers had large cooking kettles secured with their kits.

"Sergeant Major! Have the Nassauers take their kettles and form a line from the pond at the southern edge of the courtyard to the barn. Put out the fire there first, and then move to the stables."

"But Sir, they will be standing directly in the line of fire from the portal."

"Do it, Sergeant Major. I will have the officers keep the Nassauers in line. It must be done. Do you understand?"

"Yes, Sir." The square-built man moved out at a trot.

Within minutes the line had been formed. The French were now holding a position a few feet inside the courtyard and were probing toward the barn door. Not having time to reload their muskets, they charged with bayonet into the Nassauers. From their covering positions Legionnaires shot them dead at point-blank range. The Nassauers were terrified by both the determined Frenchmen lunging at them with bayonets and the heavy fire from the half-crazed Legionnaires. Only with great exertion did the officers keep the Naussauers in line.

Suddenly a large group of French rushed through the archway, fired their muskets, and dashed for the barn. The Nassauers fell back, preventing the Legionnaires from sighting their targets. In an instant the French held the barn.

Lieutenant Carey saw what had happened and brought his men forward from the relative safety of the farmhouse. Into the barn he raced behind the French and engaged them there in a fight at close quarters. Men fell dead on one another in the suffocating stench of the smoldering fire. Friend could barely be distinguished from foe. There was no halfway measure. Soldiers fired, stabbed, clubbed, and hacked at anything that threatened them. Within a few minutes of the start of this desperate struggle, all the French within lay dead. A few Legionnaires emerged from the barn and helped get the Nassauers back into their firefighting line.

For a few minutes more, the French tried to break through. But the slaughter was too great. They lost heart and withdrew from the courtyard. Rifle fire from the roof chased them back through the orchard.

Baring surveyed the grisly scene. More than half the battalion lay dead or dying around the littered courtyard. Very few officers remained on their feet. Lieutenants Graeme and Franck were still standing, but Carey was near collapse and losing blood at an alarming rate. One or two of the Nassau officers were still unhurt, but it seemed that only their bodies were whole. Their minds were numbed by the ordeal; the men were unable or unwilling to give coherent orders.

Yet the major felt strangely elated. His heart was full of boundless joy. He had held. He had held. He wanted to grab his men and kiss them. They had fought like lions. He felt that of all the fighting on the battlefield this day, his was the most crucial, the most valiant. He felt invincible, immortal. He was prepared to hold on forever. The great numbers of his own dead at his feet seemed to be unreal, inconsequential. Although he thought himself a decent man, their lying there did not diminish his joy. They were not alive, so they did not matter. The only thing that mattered was holding the farm, and that he had done.

"Sergeant Major, find out how many rounds we have remaining."

While he waited for the count, he set to reorganizing his defenses for the next onslaught.

Marshal Ney was furious. Everything was going wrong today. Everything was out of his control. He bit his lower lip and turned his head furiously left and right, trying to find order somewhere on the battlefield. But there was none.

D'Erlon's corps was shattered. It did not have to be. We almost went over the top at Mont Saint Jean. It was that confounded formation. How come the order was garbled? I told them to attack in columns of division by battalion—checkerboard fashion in battalion columns, each with a two-company frontage of almost seventy men. It would have left enough room between each column for the battalions to deploy in line when we closed on the ridge. But almost half of my forces, a full two of my divisions, went in columns of battalion by division—those damned immobile columns with 200-man fronts and a depth of up to nine battalions. What is wrong with our generals? Have they been away from war too long?

And Napoleon. Still he remains at Ronsomme. He is in control of nothing. But he thinks he is! He gives me orders as if I were a subaltern. "Take La Haye Sainte without further delay." What does he think I am trying to do?

Why has he suddenly taken a personal interest in the farm? Does he want an example for Jérôme? That pretty boy is still languishing in the woods around Hougoumont. At least I have taken a whack at the main line. I think Jérôme must be looking for a new kingdom, and any château will do.

Perhaps the emperor's impatience is not with Jérôme. It could be Grouchy. He wants to use me as an example for Grouchy. Where is Grouchy? I know where he *should* be. He should be under my command, not out chasing Prussians. And where are the Prussians? I thought they were pulling back on their lines to Liège. Let them go. Let them run to the Rhine. Wait. What did Jérôme say last night? Blücher plans to join Wellington here! How can that be? Can it be he is coming? Impossible. But maybe that is why taking La Haye Sainte is so urgent.

His temper was fogging his thinking. All the insults and hurt from Napoleon's mocking manner of the past days were mixing with Ney's natural excitability, already fired by the combat of the day. His arms shook with the urge to do something, to take action, to end the battle. He could not grab a thought and hold it for more than an instant. His instincts told him to fight, to move in for the kill, to smash the enemy. But it took more than instinct to organize thousands of men in the correct formation, to coordinate the artillery and the cavalry with the infantry, to wait for the exact moment. There were days when Ney was good at that—he had proven his mettle time and time again. But today was not one of those days and he knew it.

Was it Napoleon's doing? In times past he would tell Ney what to do, when to do it. And when he could not, the orders were clear enough and the plan unfolding well enough for Ney to follow through as expected.

But Napoleon was not clear today. He had lost his touch. Worse, he had belittled his marshal—and his marshal could not stand it. He had been dared to undo his humiliation but given no guidance about how to do it. Only more chastisement, more humiliation—the taunting, sneering smile of Napoleon behind every shift in the storm.

But Ney thought he knew what to do. The allied line was moving, and much of it was going to the rear. He could see infantry, cavalry, and wagons—all moving back. They were losing their stomachs for the fight. They were about to cave in. La Haye Sainte was not the place to invest; it was a sideshow. The main prize was the allied line. It had taken enough. It was about to break.

He would give the line a little push. It would not take much. The signs were there. The allies were crumbling.

Wellington sat impassively astride the chestnut Copenhagen. The horse was a study in serenity, stoically surveying the battlefield with its master as if there were not a single disturbance in the atmosphere. Like its master, it seemed to know when to move, when to remain still. All things in their time.

The artillery fire had thickened. The duke again reminded his subordinates to pull their men out of the fire and lay them down. Small parties were moving prisoners to the rear. Supplies had been brought up to the battalions, and the wagons were now being herded back out of range. Though the fighting continued to rage at Hougoumont, La Haye Sainte, and Papelotte, in the respite on Mont Saint Jean Wellington had relented and allowed casualties to be evacuated to where they might receive some aid. All in all, there was a great deal of movement, but it was only the activity of a great army getting ready for its next battle— shifting, reorganizing, and sheltering itself from the fire, bringing up supplies, and evacuating wounded. It was not a retreat.

"Look, Sir," said de Lancey, pointing. "There is a large formation of infantry coming up toward La Belle Alliance. And I think I see a command group riding with it. Could it be Napoleon?"

"That is who it is. And that would be the Imperial Guard on the march. Boney has at last arrived. I did not think he was overseeing the battle in person up until now. There has been too much impetuosity." It was the duke at his impassionate best, no excitement in his voice. It was almost as if he were making an observation he expected to be of no interest to anyone hearing it.

He went on. "We will not have to worry about him for a little while yet. He is moving slowly today. It is Ney who will make the next move. Did you see him in the infantry attack? He came on like a mad dog. It was unseemly—a marshal fighting like a common soldier. I caught a glimpse of his red face. It was terrifying. He must be sending in the attacks at La Haye Sainte. I can only imagine how flushed his face has become now. No, it is Ney who will move next. Mark my words."

De Lancey noted that the tone of his commander's words had finally picked up a measure of emotion—an icy tone that spoke of terrible resolve.

13

THE CENTER: 1600

It began with a single brigade. Ney was so certain that the allied line had broken that he ordered Milhaud to send his *cuirassiers* across the Brussels road and attack. But the movement drew other cavalry units, and they in turn drew still more.

Had Napoleon seen it forming, he might have stopped it before it was too late. Had Ney been less certain that the allied center was folding, he might have hesitated. But Napoleon did not see it, and Ney was fast losing control. In fact he had never really had control. All day he had hovered at the ragged edge of rage. Now he was about to fall into the abyss.

Squadron by squadron, the French cavalry joined the forming mass, like souls assembling for Judgment Day. An invisible force pulled them together. Eternity hung in the balance. Seeking an unimpeded route of attack, the French would now pay the highest price of the day for not taking Hougoumont and La Haye Sainte. They would approach the allied line through the nine hundred meters that separated these two citadels. To give a wide berth to the musket and rifle fire emanating from both, the horsemen would squeeze themselves in tighter still, cutting their frontage down to a mere seven hundred meters.

The hundreds of thousands of tons of horse and man thus compressed into the soggy ground quickly turned the field into a morass. They could gain no momentum in the charge. The soaked field would not allow more than an ungainly trot.

Still they came. Ney watched the numbers mount and his blood rose.

Could Napoleon have seen what he had in mind? Did he approve? Yes. Yes. That must be it. That is why more are forming. That is why the cavalry from the Imperial Guard has joined. The emperor must have ordered them to the charge. So he agrees with my plan. He knows the enemy is breaking. And he knows the cavalry will smash them once and for all. The more the better.

The marshal did not notice that the dense formations were masking his own supporting artillery fire. He did not think of using horse-drawn artillery to support the attack he was about to unleash, and he did not consider involving the infantry that remained under his command. If Napoleon had felt it necessary to integrate the artillery and the infantry, he would have done so. He had not, so Ney dismissed it from his own consideration.

His mind had completely accepted his delusion that Napoleon was in charge of the attack. In his mind the responsibility to organize it had been lifted from his own shoulders. Ney was its leader, but Napoleon had endorsed it and in so doing had accepted responsibility for its coordination. Ney would drive it home. He had only to fight; there was no need to manage. He would take his place at the head of the formation and lead it into victory. The initiative was his. He had seen the opportunity. He had set the forces in motion. It was just like Napoleon to take credit for his subordinate's ideas. Well, let him take the credit for the plan. I will get the credit for the execution. It will be Ney as history should remember him: the bravest of the brave, the most valiant warrior.

In grand self-delusion the marshal drew himself to full stature astride his horse and started the cavalry up the hill toward Mont Saint Jean. Over five thousand horse—both heavy and light—were pounding toward the crest. The formation was so compact that several mounts were squeezed completely off the ground, their hoofs flailing in thin air as they tried to comprehend how they could be moving forward with no contact with the earth.

Wellington watched in disbelief. Cavalry never attacked without infantry and artillery support. It must be a ruse. Perhaps Napoleon planned a flanking movement, maybe around the right of the line, past Hougoumont to the west. He sent an aide to order a brigade of cavalry to screen the right flank. But the formation to his front thickened and kept coming straight toward the allied center.

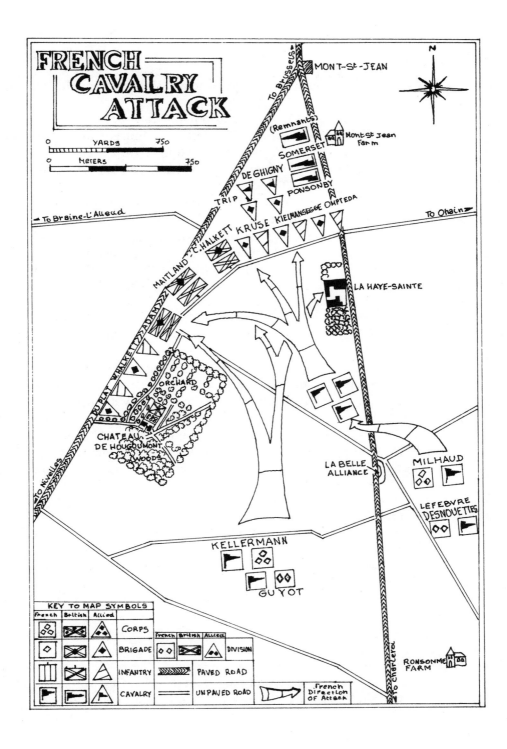

"De Lancey, do you see what he intends to do? Damn it, the fellow's a mere pounder after all."

"You are right, Sir. That is not the Napoleon we expected. This is pure madness." Wellington's chief of staff readied himself to receive his commander's orders. He would not hasten him. De Lancey knew that up to this point, the duke's direction of the battle had been flawless. The man wasted no energy. The chief watched as Wellington calmly surveyed the cavalry to his front, then turned in his saddle to observe the formations in his own line.

Once more the allied line had been withdrawn out of direct fire behind the crest of the ridge. There the French artillery had reached for them, occasionally striking home, fouling a portion of the line with blood and gore, then reaching out again to find some more fodder for its cannon, like a blind man stomping on an ant hill, seeking to smash the massed insects, sensed but unseen, into the ground.

"Have them form square." Wellington condensed his order to a mere four words.

In an instant, aides rode out along the line, spreading the word, "Prepare for cavalry!" The cry was met with incredulity by all ranks, from general to private. They all knew the tactics of the day: Cavalry did not attack unsupported. It would be a suicidal gesture, a duck shoot for the defenders. But the call was repeated. Anxiety passed to anticipation. At last! The rank and file savored a revenge for the brutal pounding from the artillery. Battalions raced to form square, the brightly uniformed units creating a dazzling checkerboard on the ground behind Mont Saint Jean. It was a breathtaking scene.

At the allied command post, de Lancey broke the momentary silence. "Sir, do you wish me to tell Lord Uxbridge to ready his cavalry? We may be able to mount a. . . ."

The round shot had struck a mere ten meters from Wellington, glanced against a flat rock, and careened into the air with a heavy whump. It caught the colonel in the back and propelled him over the head of his horse. The impact took the wind out of him, but in the first second there was no pain. He felt himself flying, could see the ground coming up. Sounds seemed to blend together into a meaningless hum, a sort of background to the slow-motion scene in which he found himself. His left shoulder hit first, a second later the left side of his forehead. His upper body followed his shoulder into the ground; his head ricocheted slowly off the damp earth, coming back down as his legs and arms came to rest behind his torso. Grass and mud wedged between his lips. Slowly he brought his right arm up to catch his face before it fell back into the soil from the apex of its second bounce.

The arm movement brought recognition of pain. It came from deep within his chest and went down his spine to just above his stomach. He felt a terrible stretching, as if the movement of his arm was tearing his right side from its skeletal frame. Then, suddenly, a sharper pain high in his chest, as if he had been stabbed from within. He let his hand fall to his side, bringing his body to rest where it lay. He did not want to move just yet. He would rest for a moment, then face whatever he must.

Members of the staff dismounted and ran to the side of their chief. The duke rode the few meters to where de Lancey was lying. The wounded man looked up and softly said, "Pray tell them to leave me and let me die in peace."

Wellington studied the handsome face. Not him, he thought. He is such a good man. It is too high a price. Not him. So many have already died today. So many more will fall; surely this one can be spared.

He turned to an officer. It was de Lancey Barclay, the cousin of the chief of staff, who had seen him fall and had run to his side. "Carry him to the rear. And be gentle. I want no further pain brought to him."

"But there is no blood, my Lord. Perhaps he will recover in a moment. The wind has been knocked out of him."

"I wish it were so. But look into his eyes. There is something terribly wrong there. If he could get up, he would. Do as I say, and be quick about it. I do not want him ridden over when those blasted French arrive."

Barclay turned back to the injured man as the commander turned his attention to the battle. "Come, dear cousin, let me take you away from this place. We can find some shelter only a little distance back."

"Nay. Just let me rest a while longer. Please, I do not want to be moved."

"But you must. It is too dangerous here." Barclay motioned to a sergeant nearby to form a litter and gather some soldiers.

De Lancey asked Barclay to come closer and whispered in his ear. "Write to Magdalene for me, please. Say everything kind, and break the news gently."

With those words he seemed to drift away in thought. The eyes remained open, but they were no longer looking at the fields of Waterloo. He had passed to more serene contemplation.

✳   ✳   ✳

In her tiny apartment in Antwerp, Magdalene turned with a start. She felt a moment of panic seize her. It was followed by a frightening emptiness and, an instant later, by a sudden overflowing of love. She knelt and prayed for the strength she had known all along that she would need. Her beauty, which had momentarily faded behind a veil of morbidity, returned on a shroud of serenity and resolve.

Suddenly, the French artillery stopped. To the infantry waiting behind the crest of Mont Saint Jean, it was a blessed event. They did not believe that anything could be worse than that awful pounding. Friends had disappeared in horrible bursts. The sounds had been deafening. Above the din, a macabre humor had made the rounds.

"By Jove, that's his head. He'll complain no more of his rotten teeth."

"I say, could you wobble that stump a bit. I'm getting it all, you know!"

It did little to steady the nerves.

The waiting infantry could see that their own artillery had not stopped. At rapid fire, round after round was pumped down the far side of the ridge. Although they could not see what their artillery brethren were firing at, the infantrymen could tell by their frantic pace that whatever it was, it was coming at them fast.

An old rumor spread through the ranks: Musket balls could not penetrate the breastplates of the *cuirassiers*. It frightened the youngsters, and unnerved the veterans. Above the shouting and the racket of the allied artillery fire, a deep, thundering sound of thousands of hooves could be heard on the far side of the ridge. It was like a tremor deep in the bowels of the earth. The vibrations could be felt even as the sound deepened—all the time drawing nearer and nearer.

Suddenly the artillery stopped firing. Gun crews dropped the wheels of their carriages so that the field pieces could not be towed away. Then they raced wide-eyed down the hill, for the shelter of the squares. Men stepped aside and let them in. In the next instant a horrifying spectacle broke over the crest of the ridge.

The French cavalry appeared in all of its terrifying glory. Thousands upon thousands of horses and men came crashing over the hill, like a tidal wave ready to sweep everything away in its fury. Thousands of infantrymen cursed under their breaths and swallowed hard, trying to seek courage where there was overwhelming fear. Sergeants muttered, "Steady, lads," scarcely believing in their ability to stand in the face of this monstrous attack.

The French were as shocked as the allies. They had been told that the enemy was routed. They believed themselves to be coming at broken infantry. They did not expect to see them in orderly squares, waiting so steadfastly for the attack.

Only Ney remained nonplussed. This was what he wanted. There was the enemy. They were in reach now. A quick rush and they would be his. Bareheaded, he turned and waved his squadrons forward. His sword arched skyward, then fell in a determined point at the nearest square. He spurred his horse and charged forward. The great wave of cavalry followed in his path.

To observers farther back, it seemed as if nothing could survive this onslaught. As far as the eye could see, more and more horsemen came pounding into the waiting troops. The ground was swallowed in the churning, crushing flailing of hooves. The sun reflected in a thousand crazy angles from darting forests of saber and lance. White smoke rose in plumes from belching firearms. Leaden musket balls crashed into heavy chest armor, beating like a deluge of metal darts on sheets of tin. Demonic sounds echoed from the mouths of men and beast. Cries of anguish rose from the injured.

But the squares held, like so many outcroppings that broke the oncoming wave. The storm of cavalry separated around the individual formations, beating an ever deeper path through the checkerboard maze of battalions. Like rocks in a frenzied sea, the squares were momentarily submerged and lost from sight. Then they rose again to turn the frothing cavalry from its wild run.

The horses could not be made to charge into the waiting bayonets of the forward troops. Cavalrymen came up and slashed with their sabers; many of them were shot dead at point-blank range. Lancers jabbed at the stalwart ranks, trading their lives to carve a minuscule opening in the solid squares—an opening that was quickly filled. Wounded horses out of control crashed into the formations and fell amidst the waiting men, thrashing out wildly and forcing men to scatter left and right. Infantrymen tossed out their dead, passed their wounded to the rear, and closed ranks. Bit by bit, the squares shrank, their four-sided front-ages becoming ever smaller. French cavalry wheeled round and round, probing for weak spots, trying to break the disciplined formations before them.

Lord Uxbridge watched wave after wave come crashing in; saw the French lose their organization in the mixture of chasseurs, lancers, and *cuirassiers;* and noted the aimless circling around the successive lines of squares. Remembering the fiasco of his own earlier charge, he chose his moment carefully. When the confusion of the French seemed at its worst, and before the squares broke under the pressure of so many thousands, he unleashed his counterattack.

He was missing his Household and Union brigades, which had been decimated in the earlier fighting, but the shock of his counterattack was great enough to throw the enemy into panic. Then a terrible cavalry battle ensued. It was a masterful display of horsemanship and swordplay. Powerful thrusts lopped off limbs and separated heads—yet encased in their helmets—from torsos. Horses pitched over in the mud; men were trampled to death. One group of *cuirassiers* ran headlong into a sunken road behind the British squares into a steep-sided pit that the allies had created, filled with branches and brush as a trap. Horses panicked in their terror, kicking each other and their riders to death in their frenzy to get out. Elsewhere, the French began to give ground, retreating over the slippery, corpse-strewn ground back from whence they had come.

As the ridge cleared of cavalry, the allied artillerymen emerged from the squares and raced back to their guns. In their haste the French had overlooked one of the basic maneuvers of the day: They had failed to spike the guns. A headless nail and a swift blow from a blunt hammer would have finished the artillery. But no one had expected the infantry to be lying in wait; the French had assumed the guns were theirs for the taking. Now they would pay a heavy price for their presumption.

Gun after gun went back into action as Uxbridge pulled his cavalry out of the way. Round after round caught the French trying to re-form in the low ground to the south of the Mont Saint Jean ridge.

Ney's horse was shot dead from under him, bringing the marshal to the ground with a crash. Quickly he grabbed the reins of a riderless steed and remounted. With a wave he started his cavalry back up the hill. Again the artillerymen dropped the wheels of their carriages and ran for the squares. In a moment, the second wave of the attack crashed into the waiting formations.

From his command post at La Belle Alliance, Napoleon watched in dismay. "What is he doing? Has he gone mad?" He was talking to no one in particular. With his telescope he had caught a glimpse of the bareheaded Ney, red hair blazing in the sun. He was poised over a British gun, furiously beating on its barrel with the flat of his sword.

"Is that my cavalry? That cannot be my cavalry."

"Yes, Sire, it is." It was Soult. "Victory is won. We hold the ridge."

"We hold nothing." Napoleon spat the words at his chief of staff like poison from a viper. "It is a premature movement that augurs fatal results in the course of the day."

"Yes, your Majesty, Ney has moved too quickly." Soult was changing his view, or at least his articulation of it.

"It is an hour too soon. But we must stand by what he has already done."

"What would you have us do, Sire?" asked Soult.

"Send in the squadrons of Kellermann and Guyot from behind the left wing. I see that my Guard cavalry has already joined."

"But Sire, that will put over ten thousand horse into the battle." Soult was quick with figures.

"Thank you, dear Chief of Staff. I can count too. But we have no other choice. That fool has committed us. We must dare all, now. It is not what I would have done, but he leaves me no choice."

Soult looked hard at the ground in the distance. He kept his thoughts to himself, but he was experienced enough to know that they were sending 10,000, maybe 12,000, horse into an attack that could justify only 1,000 at best. He passed the order.

In the center, the infantry took the second wave of the attack. It was a repeat of the first. Conditions inside the squares were unbearable. The carnage and, above all, the thirst, seemed more than a man could stand. Still they held. And again the French fell back.

But a moment later, the French cavalry appeared again, this time with even more horsemen to drive home their attack. Ney had finally thought to bring up horse artillery, and the crews were now unlimbering their guns, looking for an angle of fire from which to deliver grape into the already suffering defenders.

"Fire at the horses!" It became the order of the day. To those inclined toward the beast, it seemed a monstrous thing to do. These were noble animals, scarcely less intelligent—the infantry maintained—than their riders. The horses seemed so pathetic in their agony. They whinnied and snorted, looked at their own mangled bodies, and raised their heads to seek the owners who had brought them to this terrible fate, as if in forlorn hope that somehow their masters would rescue them. The horses died in droves. But men fell even faster.

The tactics of attacker and defender were becoming more and more deliberate. The infantrymen were loathe to discharge their muskets, knowing that the cavalry would charge in the wake of the firing before they had a chance to reload. The cavalry was wary of charging until the muskets had been discharged, preferring to rely on the notorious inaccuracy of the Brown Bess at a distance rather than rush in and raise the probability of being hit at point-blank range. So the French would circle, attempting to panic a square into firing, then charge pell-mell into the ranks, trying to force the horses to overcome their fear of being impaled. For the French the goal was to undo the formation.

Again and again the French attacked. A fourth wave broke, then a fifth. Two more horses were shot from beneath Marshal Ney, but each time he rose again in the saddle and rallied his troops forward. He brought his artillery into action, and finally remembered to order up the eight thousand waiting infantrymen from the unused portion of Reille's corps. (The balance was still desperately trying to take Hougoumont.) But still he neglected to spike the allied guns, and every time he was forced back down the ridge, he paid the price.

The sixth and seventh attacks almost broke the squares. With grape pouring in, ammunition running low, casualties mounting, and water becoming scarcer and scarcer, infantrymen were becoming crazed with delirium. Their actions became mechanical. They lost all awareness of time. Discharge weapon, steady bayonet, withstand charge, reload weapon, tighten ranks; discharge weapon, steady bayonet, withstand charge—and so it went. All the time, the squares became smaller and smaller.

The artillery was the worst of it. The infantry could see the French gunners sighting at them directly over the tops of their guns. A belch and a puff of smoke; a second later a whizzing burst of shrapnel in their midst. Men screamed, clutched at their wounds, flailed at their comrades, or were silently metamorphosed into grotesque hunks of meat. As fast as the squares could close up over the tangle of mangled flesh, the enemy artillery raced to repeat the horror.

Leaders begged for relief. Senior officers rode up and told them there was no relief to be had. Commanders swore to die in place. Often they did.

An eighth and a ninth attack. Now Reille's infantrymen added to the carnage, rushing up, firing their muskets, and tearing into the squares with their bayonets. But still the allies held. The discipline of the defending infantrymen remained unbroken. They held their ground. Friends who had joked with them at the beginning of the attack began to grow stiff in death. Water was completely gone now. The wounded men remained untreated, and were wounded again and again. There was no respite. Still they held.

A tenth charge, and the allied cavalry was almost gone. A regiment of Cumberland Hussars broke, quietly making its way to the forest to the rear. Uxbridge saw them slipping away and sent an aide in pursuit. It was to no avail. They had seen enough. They would fight no longer.

Wellington continued to reinforce where he could. Artillery was about all he could add, and he had to play that carefully, so he did not add to the suffering of his own men. As it was, the allied survivors were coming to welcome the cavalry attacks—they brought respite from the artillery.

The cavalry attack now degenerated into small individual fights. Friend and foe came to know the faces of one another, having seen them so close so many times before. A reluctant camaraderie began to develop. The infantry had to admire the courage of the cavalry. They had been ordered to attack, and they did so without question, even though their numbers were dwindling at alarming rates.

The battlefield had become a mosaic of the dead. Men and horse were strewn everywhere. The squares had become morgues. Cavalry could not move faster than a trot, lest a horse break a leg stumbling over the multitude of cadavers.

An eleventh and twelfth charge. Ney still screaming, yelling, beating with his sword at anything within reach. As squadrons died out, he rode to find more. Whatever he could scrape up, he threw into the battle, himself at the head. He no longer wanted to live. He knew he had lost. If he could not carry the field with the cavalry he had massed, nothing could. He had lost. He preferred death. But it had to be honorable death, death at the head of a charge, death in the manner of a cavalryman.

In the end, he could find no more cavalry to lead to its ruin. All the squadrons were gone. It had been a grand attack, exceeding the limits of glory, surely the grandest cavalry attack the world had ever seen. But it had been to no avail. Not a single square had broken, not even those now populated for the most part by the dead. Reluctantly, in a rage even more seething than the one with which he had begun the attack, Ney withdrew his survivors from the field.

Wellington knew that the battle was at last turning in his favor. At the start of the attack, he had despaired. The loss of de Lancey had been a bad omen. So many of his personal staff had fallen that day. He shuddered to think of it. But so many of every unit had fallen across the battlefield. Why should his headquarters have fared any better?

But he still held the ground. It seemed incredible. How had they withstood so much cavalry? He had never seen anything like it. Time and time again he had moved among the squares and seen French horse intermingled with his own troops. Yet the squares had held, even acknowledging their commander as he rode by—as if to thank him for putting them into this hell.

"Silence! Stand to your front. Here's the duke." They looked at him with reverence. He could not understand it. He had led them to this slaughter, knowing all along that it would be a butchery. He was buying time with their lives. There was no point to their dying, other than to let the clock tick out. And all the while he had shown them such disdain, never concealing it from them, even relishing the denigration he heaped upon them. Yet they revered him. It made no sense. He used the infantry as he used de Lancey. Or Macdonell. Or Baring. He asked of them the impossible, then demanded that they perform. It was a strange hold he had over men, and it frightened him. Yet he had always used it. And he always would.

The only salvation was that he was no less severe on himself. He had not rested on this campaign. Yes. Yes. He had taken his favors where he could. There were pretty girls everywhere that had to be attended to, and he had. But so had his men. That was part of being a soldier. Otherwise, he had spared himself no hardship, no danger.

He was amazed he had lasted so long this day. His dazzling, impressive staff of the morning was worn away now. He would do the bitter accounting later. For now, he was aware that many were not riding back from the missions he had sent them on. Still others had fallen within his sight. So much for the privilege of higher headquarters. But he had lasted. No shot had touched him, no saber had drawn his blood. How could that be?

Perhaps because he had been too busy. Fate did not seem to interrupt a preoccupied man. Maybe he had not been touched at any given moment because his thoughts were so seldom on that moment. They were always looking ahead. Even at the worst of the recent cavalry attacks, he had been looking into the progress of the Prussians. That was what was important. That was the hinge upon which the battle hung.

And at last they had arrived. Sometime in the midst of the attacks, a rider had brought word that the Prussians were entering onto the battlefield at Plancenoit. That would be Napoleon's right rear, as good a place as any. So Blücher, the old rascal, had come through. Wellington had figured that he would. Now if only the Prussians could fight as well as their commander. They were a bloody bunch. Strange allies, but better an ally than an opponent.

But whatever they do, it's not finished here at Mont Saint Jean. Napoleon is not out of it. He has had a bad day so far, but his record shows that he has been losing at 1700 before, only to seize a victory by 1900. I don't have much left, but whatever I have, it will have to hold again.

The duke turned to organize his survivors.

Colonel de Lancey had been moved to a barn a short way from the rear of Mont Saint Jean. He remained conscious, although the depth of his pain mercifully had caused him to fall into something of a stupor. He was waiting his turn among the wounded to be seen by the blood-soaked surgeon working frantically over his patients. The doctor's operating table was constructed of four barrels supporting a piece of the barn door. He was an older man, endowed with thick shoulders and strong forearms, their sinews exposed and veins engorged by the pressure of rolled shirtsleeves tightly encircling his elbows. His beard was matted with sweat and dried blood.

His eyes held a fierce indifference, the pupils widened by the darkness of the interior of the barn. A shaft of light cut through the gloom to illuminate the yellow-red straw beneath the operating table. Two orderlies, equally as brawny as the doctor, only more indifferent, stood sullenly nearby.

A young captain of Hussars lay on the table. His brightly colored uniform looked somehow incongruous in the dismal surroundings of the barn. His blond hair was glistening with sweat, which dripped into the dust and dirt adorning the barn door beneath him. His left knee was protruding from his tightly fitted breeches, which had been ripped from midcalf to thigh on the one leg. A pulp of muscle and tissue, rent by a protruding section of bone, had further ruined the fine material of his uniform. The frayed gold braid of the officer's stripe running down the side of his trouser had stuck to the jellylike mess at the joint.

"Cut away the trousers above the wound and peel back the cloth." The surgeon was giving quick instructions to the orderly, who roughly grabbed the broken leg of the Hussar captain.

The officer grunted from the pain and lifted his head sharply from the table. His eyes caught the glint of the light as it reflected off the greasy saw the second orderly was passing to the surgeon. The captain understood the meaning of the transaction and turned his face to the side. There in the corner of the barn he could distinguish a pile of bloody arms and legs, the remainders of previous operations of the afternoon.

"Lie still," the doctor reprimanded the captain. "You there, orderly, hold that leg steady." The Hussar began to tremble. The quiver began in his shoulders, then spread in all directions through his torso to his head, arms, and legs.

Colonel de Lancey looked away. He did not feel particularly sorry for the officer. Even when the young man's screams mixed with the dull grinding of the saw blade ripping through the man's thigh bone, the colonel remained distant. He was captured within his own thoughts. He could see Magdalene standing beside his table in the apartment in Brussels, holding a steaming cup of green tea, looking shyly at him as he worked over the orders for the army. He could see himself reaching up for the tea, feel a smile lighten his face, and the pleased reaction in her eyes. Their fingers touched for an instant, a spark flew between them; he forced himself back to his work. Suddenly there was a great pain and he looked back up. She was crying. Her face was filled with alarm. He tried to say something, but he could not be heard above the screaming. What was that screaming? He looked back at the table. The captain had arched his back and was straining his head toward the rafters of the barn. His mouth was wide open, his cheeks flexed concavely into the hollowness of his mouth. His bright blue eyes bulged from his head. A terrible sound emanated from his throat. Another orderly had appeared, and the three of them hunched together over the captain's shaking body, pinning the critical parts in place as the surgeon cut through the last few inches of meat. Abruptly, the leg broke loose at midthigh.

The orderly nearest the severed limb pushed it off the table as the surgeon prepared to cauterize the stump.

De Lancey closed his eyes and tried to find Magdalene once more. But she was gone. He felt his own pain and focused on that for a while. After a few minutes he became aware once again of the operation going on a few feet from him.

"No. No. Please. No. Please." It was the Hussar talking to no one in particular. The surgeon had already turned his attention away from him as two orderlies roughly dragged the captain from the table, carrying him rudely toward the barnyard outside. The third orderly stooped to pick up the severed leg. He spied the gold braid that had stuck to the joint and attempted to pull it off. His attempts failed after repeated tugs, and in disgust he flung the limb across the barn to the pile in the corner.

The doctor wiped his hands on his smock and looked toward Colonel de Lancey. "Bring me that one over there," he instructed the two returning orderlies.

Wearily they approached the colonel from either end, dragged him a few feet out onto the open portion of the floor and jerked him up to where they could get a grip under his arms and legs. De Lancey could feel a ripping in his lungs and a terrible stabbing throughout his back and side. Yet he could not muster the wind to call out his discomfort. Momentarily, he went unconscious from the pain, only to be jarred awake by the heave onto the table.

The surgeon probed under his shirt. "You have no wounds that show. Where are you hurt?"

De Lancey only looked at him. What reason would there be to explain. It would only take an effort he could ill afford, and to no avail.

"Who are you? I have seen you before? You are on the duke's staff, are you not?"

"Yes, Doctor, I am Colonel Sir William Howe de Lancey, quartermaster general." How strangely formal and elaborate the title seemed, as if mocking the wounded wreck of a man lying on the barn door.

"Yes, of course. You are the chief of staff. And how is the battle going? Are we winning?"

De Lancey sensed the facetiousness of the surgeon. It seemed a cruel question to ask of him.

"Well, win or lose, it is a high butcher's bill we're paying. There will be much room for promotion when this is over." He continued to press at the colonel's chest.

"I am going to bleed you. You have been injured deep inside, and although I cannot tell what the condition is, we must relieve some of the pressure." For a moment de Lancey felt he detected a note of kindness in the doctor's voice. He felt the incision of the sharp knife, and could feel the warm blood flowing freely to the back of his shirt.

"There, that should do it. I will be truthful with you Colonel. There is much damage inside of you, but I can do nothing about it. If your wounds were in a limb, I could cut it off. But where you are hurt, I cannot cut. We will see if we cannot get you to a quiet place and let you rest. Maybe some good will come of that." As he spoke, more wounded were brought inside the barn. One of them, a mere boy, was moaning for his mother.

The plaintive cries in the youth's voice caused de Lancey to turn his thoughts to Magdalene again. He considered asking the doctor to reach her for him, then saw again the hardness in the man's eyes. The two orderlies lifted him from the table and carried him to a straw-filled wagon waiting outside. The Hussar captain was lying to one side of the wagon bed, silently sobbing into the wooden frame as a swarm of flies picked at the quickly fouling bandages around the stump of his left leg.

14

PLANCENOIT: 1730

It had been a brilliant march. Blücher was immensely proud of it, though he had felt every step. His leg throbbed. His back and butt were sore. His stomach growled with hunger. Like his soldiers, he had had nothing to eat all day. There had been no time. His head ached from lack of food and the exertions of the day. The drinking of the night before had not helped, but the field marshal had allowed himself that one small indulgence. After all, he was not as young as the soldiers he was leading. He would share all of their hardships—hard marching, lack of food, lack of sleep, exposure to the elements, the danger of battle—but every now and then a field marshal ought to be able to take a little privilege unto himself.

At that moment, however, he was unmindful of his physical ailments. The day had been too exhilarating for any self-concern. It was the kind of day that the commander of an army lives for. The old Prussian knew that few besides himself could have done it. Most would have faltered. The march was too difficult; the soldiers too spent.

Nothing had gone smoothly. Getting through Wavre had been only the beginning. It seemed then that the four corps of his army would never get untangled. But by cajoling and exhorting, Blücher had gotten them on their way and kept them moving. The Bois de Paris had been another obstacle. The woods were so thick it was hard to move the artillery and the baggage trains through. But he had kept pushing, and his corps had begun to pick up momentum. Bit by bit the battalions fell into place, finding order among the brigades and pressing on in the intended directions.

Again and again Blücher had sent orders to his corps commanders, making sense out of what seemed at first to be aimless meandering. Von Bülow's IV Corps had cut southwest out of Chapelle Saint Lambert, then hooked west at the town of Lasne, looking for a crossing over the river by that name before turning again to the southwest. The lowland by the River Lasne had been abominable. The boggy ground had sucked the boots off the weary soldiers. Many had expired in the exertion, falling facedown in the mud, only to be run over by the following artillery or trampled down by their fellow infantrymen.

The decision to head down into the valley had been difficult. For a while, the lead elements had hugged the slopes on the south side of the river. But Blücher calculated that, to deploy for attack, a crossing would have to be made. This necessitated a move into the bottomland, a position that would be sure to slow the movement down and expose the entire column to an attack if the French should suddenly appear.

Gneisenau had articulated his opposition to the move. "Field Marshal, we must not proceed with this march. There is too much danger."

"Nonsense, my friend. Our scouts have reported that the way is clear."

"But there is nothing to keep the French from coming against our flank. They could come from either direction—Grouchy from the east or Napoleon from the west."

"You worry needlessly. Grouchy has shown no fight all day. Why would he trouble himself now? And Napoleon is preoccupied with my friend Wellington. He cannot come."

"Sir, you know that either one can make a decision to move against us at any time. If they catch us in this swamp, we are finished. Let us turn back. You call Wellington your friend, but look how he abandoned you at Ligny."

"Ah, General Gneisenau, you are too unkind. The duke had troubles of his own at Quatre-Bras. He could not come to us. Why are you so hard on him?"

"My Field Marshal, it is not a question of friendship. Our very army is at stake. You take too many risks. I beg of you, reconsider."

"No. It is out of the question. I ask you to trust me. I know what I am doing. I mean to crush Napoleon. I cannot do that if I allow myself to sit where nothing happens. I tell you, if I do not get to Wellington, it is all over for him. And if he goes, there goes our efforts to crush the ogre once and for all."

"But Field Marshal, there will be another day. The army is tired. We have barely rested in three days, and virtually none of the men have eaten for over twenty-four hours. We cannot continue to push ourselves like this for an uncertain ally."

"Oh, Gneisenau, you know that I love you like a son. You are a great soldier. I marvel at your capacity for generalship. But of this I am certain. I have given my word to Wellington. Let there be no mistake about it. I shall keep my word." The discussion had ended with Blücher overwhelming his chief of staff. IV Corps descended into the valley and all of the hardships that followed.

II Corps, under General Pirch, was close on the heels of IV Corps. For Pirch's men the marching conditions were made even worse by the churning caused by von Bülow's men to their front. Thousands of boots can turn wet ground into a pudding. Men sunk into the muck up to their waists, unable to pull themselves out without the concerted efforts of their fellow soldiers, who formed human chains to extricate one another. Those who faltered drowned in the bog. Those that struggled free were rewarded by being able to take a few difficult lurches before becoming mired once again. Step-by-step, the maddening march sapped the energy from the exhausted men.

To the north, I Corps under General Zieten followed the Wavre–Braine l'Alleud road toward Ohain and the left flank of Wellington's line. Even there the trek was made difficult by the worn condition of the road and the muddy fields to either side. Wellington, who had first spied the advancing Prussians as early in the day as 1400, was distraught at the slow progress they were making. It seemed to him as if both his watch and the advancing Prussians were frozen in time, while the French continued to hammer away at his thinning defenses.

Blücher was doing all that was humanly possible to fulfill his promise to Wellington. Only his energy kept the columns moving. Only his daring allowed him to risk everything to come to the aid of his ally. Gneisenau marveled at the generalship of the old man, though he doubted the wisdom of the move. Even III Corps under Thielemann, tasked to hold Grouchy in place, had been denuded of its brigades at Wavre so that they could follow IV and II Corps down the valley of the Lasne. Blücher's plan was to swing IV and II Corps out to the left flank and aim them

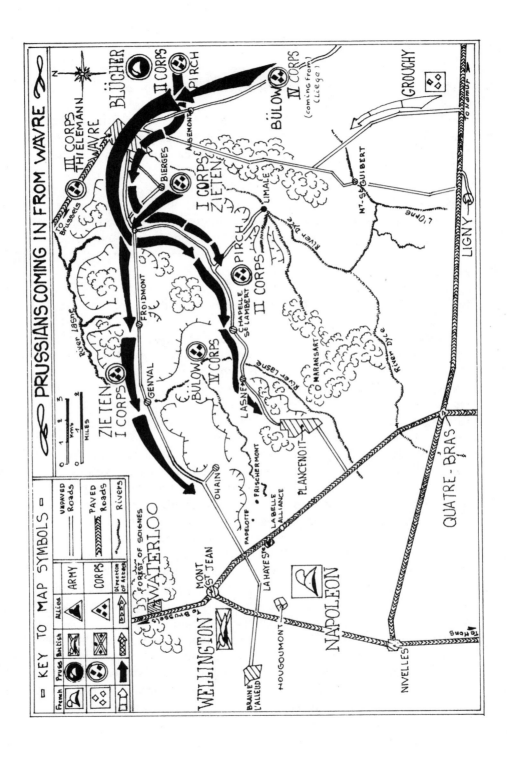

PRUSSIANS COMING IN FROM WAVRE

at the town of Maransart, so that the greatest power could be focused
on the village of Plancenoit. Increasingly, Blücher's attention had been
drawn to the small cluster of buildings near Napoleon's right flank—
the buildings that more or less defined Plancenoit. It was there that
he meant to concentrate the bulk of his army.

The Prussian commander was risking everything to crush the French.
The smallest French force could have stopped all movement. If Napoleon had blocked the Lasne, it would have taken the Prussian corps
twice the time to get through, if they ever did. If Grouchy came alive
and detected Blücher's departure, he could slip to his left and catch
the Prussian movement in the flank. Strung out as Blücher's troops
were along the route of march, an attack from Grouchy could have
been fatal.

As it was, Grouchy gradually pressed forward at Wavre, timidly at
first, not understanding that most of the Prussian forces had left for
the sound of the guns over at Mont Saint Jean. Before taking his leave,
Gneisenau had spoken with Thielemann's chief of staff, a seemingly
intelligent officer by the name of von Clausewitz, and worked out a
contingency for the push by the right wing of the French army. Elements
of III Corps closed back into Wavre to hold Grouchy by the nose while
the rest of the Prussian Army continued its march to attack Napoleon.
To compensate for the loss of the forces he had wanted to swing wide
on the left flank, Blücher ordered II Corps to detach a brigade to close
on Maransart. The die was cast. It would be all or nothing at Plancenoit.

Blücher sat upon his horse at the edge of the Bois de Paris, waiting for the lead elements to move into attack formation.

"Field Marshal," said the Prussian adjutant, Count Nostiz, "the gunfire
at Wavre is increasing. Can you hear it?"

"Of course I can hear it, Count. Do you think, because I am old, I
am deaf?"

"But General, if Grouchy is successful there against Thielemann,
the French can roll us up from the rear. Are you not concerned?"

"My dear Count. Can you not see? This is my lucky day. Everything
is going my way. Look how the French failed to block our approach.
I could not believe my luck when your reconnaissance told me these
woods were devoid of French. It is not like Napoleon to make an error
as large as that. When he does, I cannot deny that it is unusually good
luck for us.

"And Grouchy. Yes, he is attacking now, but it is too late. I have made my decision. We cannot turn back. Thielemann is on his own now. In truth, it matters little what happens to him at Wavre. If he holds, then good fortune to him. If he falls, then Grouchy will have to follow in our tracks. Have you not seen the route? There is nothing left of it. I doubt if we could go back over it, even if I should order it.

"But I would not order it. That would be a loser's choice. Do you not like to gamble, my good adjutant? All day long Gneisenau has worried over what to do. Great mind that he is, he has failed to see that the moment we left Wavre to come to this spot, our wager was set. Either we win here, or we lose everywhere. No, there is no turning back now. It matters not that Wavre falls, or even if Thielemann is crushed. Not a horse's tail shall he get. I will take my revenge here."

The field marshal fell silent, his watery eyes surveying the battlefield. Nostiz was not sure how much his commander could see. Yet, it did not seem to matter. Somehow Blücher knew what was happening— sensed the key terrain, found the route to it, knew where to commit his forces and how to inspire his subordinates. It was a genius that was different from the detailed brilliance of his chief of staff. The two men complemented each other. The field marshal could motivate men to do the impossible. They loved him—a father-warrior who would take them to glory and victory. He was outrageous, bold, bombastic, loveable, even zany. Yet he knew how to lead, knew how to fight.

The chief of staff could take the intentions of the field marshal and convert them into a detailed order in a matter of minutes. As much as the rank and file loved "Alt Vorwarts," they depended on the chief to keep them fed and supplied. Gneisenau too had a genius for war. Taciturn, even dour, he was nothing if not thorough. For all the gambling ways of the commander, the chief would leave nothing to chance. Every detail would be looked to; every order double-checked for understanding and compliance.

A strong bond had formed between these two very different professional soldiers. Each recognized the strengths of the other, as well as the limitations. Each tried to augment the genius of the other without altering his own unique character. And, despite their differences in temperament, both men had a similar grasp of the essence of battle—find the center of gravity of your opponent, control it, and destroy him.

That is why there had been no disagreement between them on Plancenoit. It was the logical choice for the point of attack. As soon

as Blücher had ridden up to the edge of the Bois de Paris he had recognized it. The whole panorama of the battle had appeared before him.
He could see the French hammering away at Wellington's center. He
could see Napoleon's reserves waiting behind La Belle Alliance for
their moment. He could see the smoke and hear the firing over by
Hougoumont on the left, telling him that the French were wasting precious
resources on a secondary attack that pulled them ever farther away
from the locus of essential action.

Instinctively, Blücher had already set in motion the forces that would
capitalize on the weaknesses in the French dispositions. Zieten's I Corps
was on its way to reinforce Wellington's center. This should be enough
to keep the line from cracking, but would not denude the powerful
thrust that best go deep. That is why he had sent two corps, the IV
and II, to the southwest. The way to beat Napoleon was to catch him
in his rear, where he could least afford to turn his attention. This late
in the day, all of the French leader's effort would be directed forward
to deliver the coup de grace against Wellington. If suddenly he was
forced to divert his attention to his flank and rear, it would cost him
his momentum. Better yet, it would unnerve him. Even that battle-hardened
ogre had nerves. All men had nerves, no matter how they might pretend
to rise above them. It would take courage to pound away in one direction
when threatened so severely from another. That was the courage Blücher
was displaying in his own movement to contact, although he did have
the buffer of several kilometers of trackless wilderness between him
and the consequences of a French success at Wavre. Napoleon had no
such luxury at Plancenoit. If the Prussians could penetrate there, it would
be a lance stuck deep in Napoleon's side. Unless he turned to it, it
would soon bleed him to death. And when he did turn to it, it would
be a desperate struggle to the finish. Blücher didn't know how that
would turn out, but he was up to the risk. All day he had sensed his
luck was running strong. Now was not the time to falter.

"Count Nostiz, have you delivered to von Bülow my orders to attack?"

"Yes, your excellency. I spoke to him about forty-five minutes ago
now." Blücher's lapses of memory always shook the adjutant.

"Yes. Yes. Of course. And he complained that his 13th and 14th Brigades
were yet to come up?"

"Correct, Herr Field Marshal. Just as you anticipated. But, as instructed,
I told him that your orders were to attack forthwith, nonetheless."

"Good, Nostiz. Good. You see, the French have formed a defense now. There are two divisions of cavalry there on the Frischermont heights. And now an infantry corps is coming up. Lobau's no doubt."

"That would be the French VI Corps, Field Marshal." As a good adjutant should, Nostiz was attempting to assist his commander's thinking.

"My IV Corps against his VI Corps—a good match, don't you think? But I don't want to hit them square. We must slide to our left, toward Plancenoit. That is where it will all happen."

"I am sure Bülow understands that, Herr General. You can see how he has extended his line to the left."

"Yes, I can. Return to him, Nostiz. Tell him I am pleased with his dispositions, but add that he must close with his 15th and 16th Brigades against Lobau's corps while he passes his following brigades to the left at Plancenoit. I will have II Corps reinforce that effort as soon as they can come up. Go quickly now, and have my aides close in around me. I have several orders to give in the next few minutes."

For a moment the adjutant stared at the old man, surprised at the field marshal's total comprehension at the very moment he had begun to show forgetfulness. A dark glance from Blücher's face brought the count from his reflections and sped him on his way.

General Lobau, at the head of the first-rate regiments of his corps, had sensed the danger to his right flank and was slowly withdrawing his corps to the heights of Plancenoit. He was careful to send one brigade into the town itself, in the low ground, so that the Prussians could not seize Plancenoit without a fight.

The Prussian infantry made good use of supporting artillery and cavalry to apply continual pressure. They pushed the French back farther and farther along the critical high ground all along the front. Blücher was trying desperately to uncover Plancenoit for a direct attack.

The French defense, however, was nothing short of brilliant. From Papelotte farm forward to the Frischermont heights, then down through the Lasne valley to Plancenoit, Lobau's stalwart resistance forced the Prussian IV Corps to fan out in an increasingly thin line. Nowhere could von Bülow gain enough of a concentration to drive home a winning attack.

When the opportunity to attack Plancenoit came at last, it came to the weakened battalions of 16th Brigade, under Colonel von Hiller. Reinforced by two battalions from the 14th, Hiller's troops went into the crowded village, where Frenchmen fired from every conceivable nook and cranny. Crammed into the tiny passageways, the Prussians, many of them green militia unaccustomed to street fighting, were slaughtered in droves, the dead in the lead ranks being propelled steadily forward by the onrushing mass behind. Twice the Prussians were driven back by the ferocity of the French defense. On the third try—under the exhortation of Gneisenau, who personally threw his weight into the attack—they succeeded.

Colonel von Hiller was proud of his troops. For many of them, this had been their first engagement. They had been on the move since 15 June, practically without rest, on a forced march from Liège to Gembloux, then back toward Wavre. Since 0400 on 18 June, they had been through a forced march again, after which they had attacked into the teeth of the ferocious defenses put up by the French. Now sixteen hours after the grueling day had begun, the 16th Brigade had a toehold in Plancenoit.

Napoleon could no longer ignore the threat to his right flank. He had watched Ney impale himself on the allied center time and time again and had observed, to his dismay, that Wellington had not yet cracked. Once, when Ney had despaired of the ability of his own forces to take the center unassisted, the marshal had sent a request to his emperor for more troops.

Napoleon's answer had been harsh: "Where do you expect me to get more troops? Should I make some?"

But now the French leader could withhold his reserves no longer. He recognized that if the battle did not turn in his favor quickly, all would be lost. The morning's lethargy long behind him, Napoleon quickly calculated his chances for success. There were three critical points on the battlefield to be considered.

First, Plancenoit must be retaken immediately. The Prussians had it now, but it was evident that they could not hold the town in the face of a counterattack. The lead Prussian elements had exhausted themselves in their efforts to take the position. An entire corps had been expended and, although it stood momentarily on key terrain, it could be shattered with a determined push. The remainder of the Prussian army had not yet arrived in force. When it did, the French would have no chance of retaking Plancenoit.

Second, La Haye Sainte must be taken. All day it had stood like an obstacle in front of the main French attack. Ney had wasted his attacks on the farm through piecemeal efforts. Not only had he expended disproportionate numbers of troops trying to take this one outcropping, but his failure to take it had split his main effort time and time again, never allowing him to concentrate for a forceful push along a continuous front in the center of Wellington's line. Infantry and cavalry had been split apart, and only a paltry amount of artillery had been brought forward around the farm to bring the allied squares under concentrated fire. What little artillery had made it forward had battered the allied squares brutally, but artillery had not been enough. Despite all the expenditure of blood to crack the allied center, French efforts had never been properly coordinated—a failure that could be traced directly to the resilience of that single outpost in front of the middle of the line.

Third, the allied center must be cracked. All day that had been the goal. In the beginning, it had been the objective of choice. Now, it became an imperative. The allied right was inconsequential at this point. The failure to take Hougoumont had left that part of the line untouched. Hougoumont had been an overpriced affair: the better part of a French corps for one or, at most, two allied brigades.

An attack on the allied left was also out of the question. It would send the few remaining French forces into the oncoming Prussians. The middle of the line was key. The center must be taken, and it must be taken quickly. It was still possible to defeat Wellington and Blücher separately. Although the Prussians were closing, they had as yet failed to join. There was still time, but it was fast evaporating.

The problem was finding enough men. The Imperial Guard was Napoleon's reserves. The infantry portion of the Guard consisted of the Young Guard, the Middle Guard, and the Old Guard, approximately four thousand of each; the latter were the cream of the French army. They had never lost in battle. Every time the Old Guard had been committed, it had won. The entire army stood in awe before the men of its battalions. So confident was Napoleon in these elite soldiers that he had ordered them to carry their dress uniforms in their knapsacks so they might be properly attired for the victory parade in Brussels.

But the cavalry of the Imperial Guard had been prematurely used earlier in the afternoon, when Ney had rushed pell-mell into an unsupported attack up the middle. Its four thousand horse could have been well used now, but they were ruined, so much flotsam dashed upon the allied squares. It would have to be the infantrymen that did the job. Napoleon's task was to decide how to divide them up in accordance with his priorities. With the proper allocation of reserves well supported by massed artillery, the battle might yet be won.

"Soult, have Lieutenant General Duhesme take his Young Guard into Plancenoit. Support the attack with twenty-four guns. I must have that village. To the north, send word to Ney that he must take La Haye Sainte at all costs. I will take no excuses from him. It shall be taken. In the meantime, have the Imperial Guard form squares along the Brussels road between La Belle Alliance and Ronsomme. I must protect the rear while I prepare for the final push. Let me know when the orders have been received." The emperor spurred his horse forward to check his line of attack to the north.

It was short work for the Young Guard. Eager to prove themselves worthy, the guardsmen rushed into the burning village and quickly dispatched the remnants of von Hiller's brigade. For a few minutes the Germans resisted, but they were up against well-fed and rested troops, overflowing with zeal to bring victory to their emperor so that they might be deemed worthy in his eyes. Before their vigorous attack the Prussians withdrew to the east.

Once again Blücher saw his objective fall from his grasp. It was maddening. If only he could hold the village. It was crucial to his plan to undo Napoleon. For the first time he despaired of achieving a victory, and in the moment's disillusionment he gave his worst order of the day.

"General Gneisenau," he called to his senior staff officer. His subordinate appeared winded, having just withdrawn before the attack of the Young Guard. "I must have more troops, and I must have them now."

"Yes, Field Marshal, I know. But von Pirch is coming up from the south even as we speak. Soon we will be able to commit the bulk of his II Corps into the action."

"No. It is not enough. I need to ensure victory. Send word to Zieten. He must come south across the Smohain Creek and join us here."

"But General, he is just now closing on Wellington's left flank. He will never get to us in time. Moreover, he is needed to the north. Just as it matters not that Thielemann is beaten at Wavre if we win here, it matters not that we win here if Wellington is shattered."

"General Gneisenau. Do not argue with me. Plancenoit is the decisive point of this entire battle. We must win at Plancenoit. Until that confounded village is ours, we are in danger of losing everything."

The chief of staff thought of responding once again to his commander, then reconsidered. Perhaps the old man was correct. So far today his instincts had proven him right. Besides, he did not seem in a mood to be trifled with. Their argument about the crossing of the Lasne still stung. Gneisenau rode to a nearby aide, Captain von Scharnhorst, and told him to find the commander of I Corps and pass the order.

In the meantime, General von Pirch continued to move his II Corps forward through the Bois de Paris. Blücher gave orders to von Bülow to coordinate yet another attack into Plancenoit. The two corps commanders worked out a plan. Bülow would send forward two brigades from his corps while Pirch massed his newly arrived brigades. Together they would attack in three columns, supported by six batteries of artillery. All would converge on the bloody ruins of Plancenoit.

In the face of this onslaught, the Young Guard made a bold stand. For a few minutes they held the attack in check, but the Prussians poured in from every angle, outflanking pockets of resistance in the disheveled battlefield. The fighting at the church and in the cemetery was the worst of all. Smoke filled the air, from the musket firing as well as from the burning buildings. Defenders hid behind anything they felt would protect them from the fury of the attack—walls, carts, dead livestock, even fallen comrades. Within the rooms of the dwellings, frantic defenders fired from behind tables, chairs, looms, mattresses—anything that might slow the trajectory of a musket ball or deflect the lunge of a bayonet. Still the French died. At last, fearing that they would be cut off, the survivors of the eight French battalions withdrew before the combined attack of two Prussian corps.

Napoleon watched it all, seemingly unperturbed. Mentally, he added and subtracted the forces he had remaining in reserve. It was now the turn of the Old Guard. "General Count Morand, take two battalions of your men and show the rest of my army how it is done."

"Gladly, Sire. It will be my pleasure."

The gigantic men of the Old Guard majestically swung into action. All day they had awaited their turn. Now they would go in: twelve platoons in all, half grenadiers and half chasseurs. One battalion was led by a major; the other a general. The prestige of leading a formation of the Old Guard made rank immaterial. Unhurried, with an air of overwhelming self-confidence, they deployed into formation. Their front extended to thirty files; their depth to thirty-six ranks. On their faces, a look of grim determination. Never defeated in battle! It was a legacy.

The movement forward began in silence. In perfect synchronization they moved toward Plancenoit. Fourteen battalions of Prussians waited in the ruins, not yet reconsolidated from the efforts of their recent attack. As individuals, then in small groups, their attention turned to the wall of big men coming at them. It looked unstoppable—like death itself. Imperceptibly, the Old Guard picked up the pace of the march. Bit by bit, their momentum grew, until at last they were moving at double time. Not a shot was fired. Bayonets stood at the ready.

The bayonet charge was pure, beautiful, and frightening. The distance closed rapidly. The Prussians became unnerved as the massive men swept forward in determined stride, their eyes cruel and cold, their long bayonets gleaming in the fading light of evening.

The Young Guard saw them go in and took heart. Some felt ashamed that they had given up the village so readily, although God knows they had fought stubbornly. Lobau's corps also saw the Old Guard go in. In the wake of the glorious bayonet charge, the Young Guard and the survivors of VI Corps streamed back toward Plancenoit. The Prussian battalions fell back, terrified, not stopping until they had retreated five hundred yards from the village. Cold steel had taken Plancenoit—cold steel and the ferocious reputation of the Old Guard.

Blücher stared, demoralized by the disintegration of his fleeting hold on what he considered to be the key terrain of the entire battle. Evening had come; it was now almost 1900. Victory seemed to have eluded him. In his mind he could see Napoleon sitting on his horse, as yet unmoved, his opportunity to strike with the last of his reserves into the center undiminished. All of the old general's bones seemed to ache. His leg began to throb. At once he felt old and tired. It had been a terribly hard day. And to what end? His heavy head drooped upon his chest.

The old man could not know just how effective he had been. Plancenoit might not yet be his, but he had accomplished one of his major objectives. Napoleon was shaken. The emperor had recognized the threat to his right flank for what it was. If Plancenoit fell, there could be no retreat. Defeat at Waterloo would now turn into nothing short of a disaster.

For that reason Napoleon had begun to siphon off his reserves. At one fell swoop, the Young Guard had been committed—one-third of the infantry of the Imperial Guard. When the young Guard had failed to hold on to the contested village, another two battalions of the reserves—this time the elite Old Guard—had been sent in. They had succeeded, but the reserves had been diminished by another critical portion. At Le Caillou yet another battalion, which had been guarding the imperial coaches and treasury, was now forced to turn and face the Prussians swarming out of the Bois de Chantelet. The cavalry was already gone. The uncommitted infantry battalions—the Middle Guard and the remainder of the Old Guard—had been forced to form square along the Brussels road.

In the meantime, Pirch's II Corps continued to emerge from the Bois de Paris. Blücher was coming into action with elements of three infantry corps, along with strong supporting forces of artillery and cavalry. Forming against Plancenoit were no less than 31,000 infantry and 4,800 cavalry. Blücher had 110 artillery pieces in action. Against them were arrayed 12,500 French infantry. Napoleon could muster perhaps 2,000 cavalry. Only 52 French guns were in action.

The old man could not know this. He knew only that Plancenoit was not his. It had almost broken his heart to see it fall to the French a final time. He had forgotten that this was to have been his lucky day.

The day was not yet over. Nor had Blücher's luck abandoned him. Maybe it was not luck. The cross-country move certainly had been an act of calculation and will. True, the French had not put a blocking force well forward, where it would have done the most good—for example, in the valley of the Lasne. But they had sent the right wing of their army against the Prussians to fix them in place. The withdrawal of the Prussians before that force after the defeat at Ligny the night of the 16th and all day on the 17th had not been luck; it had been leadership, discipline, and training. That Grouchy was timid could not explain it all. Every enemy has his shortcomings. It is not luck to capitalize on them; it is generalship in its purest form. Now another type of generalship would come into play—the kind that shows itself in the training and discipline of subordinates who understand the intention of the commander and can take appropriate action to fulfill that intent, even if it means disregarding clear orders from the commander himself.

Captain von Scharnhorst had made his way to the head of I Corps, but it was not Zieten he found. Baron von Müffling, sent over earlier by Wellington to take charge of the left wing and coordinate the arrival of the Prussians, was already giving orders for their placement. Zieten's chief of staff, Colonel von Reiche, was with him.

Müffling, looking up from his discussion with Reiche, recognized Scharnhorst. "How goes it with Blücher at Plancenoit?"

"Not well, my dear Baron." The captain's eyes blazed with intensity. "He cannot bring enough forces into play to concentrate an attack. That is why he has sent me here, with orders for General Zieten." Captain Scharnhorst's excitement said much about the manner in which he had received his orders. Junior officers so readily pick up the mood of their commanders.

"What orders do you have, Captain?"

"He says that I Corps is to turn south, across the Smohain and on to the Frischermont heights, from there to devolve upon the village of Plancenoit." The captain had the message right; he had been well trained.

Reiche was the first to answer. "But that will be a difficult move. Already the lead elements of 2d Brigade have passed the fork where they would have to turn off to march to the south. I can send them back, but before we can order them to march in a different direction, I will need the confirmation of General Zieten."

"It is worse than that," added General von Müffling. "I have taken it upon my own initiative to order the allied brigades of Vivian and Vandeleur to move from the left of the allied line to relieve the center. Though the order stems from Wellington, I have advised them to go now, in anticipation of General Zieten's arrival."

"But I must point out, gentlemen, that Field Marshal Blücher is in terrible straits. All will be lost if you do not comply with his orders." The captain made a strong case, adding as the final weight, "General Gneisenau was there as well. He urged me to bid you hasten to Plancenoit."

A pained look crept over the faces of the two senior officers. Here was an order that was hard to deny. If either Blücher or his chief of staff had given the order, there might be grounds to question it. But when both of them reinforced the other, the odds were that it was an appropriate order.

But how could it be? Müffling thought to himself. It is at least two kilometers from the turnoff to the Frischermont heights. Then it is another kilometer at least to the village of Plancenoit. And if the situation is as desperate as the captain implies, then it will be a flanking march across the front of the French defensive line. Such a movement would be impossible without accepting major casualties. The route of march, therefore, would necessarily take I Corps farther to the southeast, back into the Lasne valley, where it would most likely run into elements of II Corps still closing on Plancenoit.

"What is the route like in the valley of the Lasne?" Müffling asked the captain.

"Sir, it defies imagination. It has been the most difficult march I have ever seen. The ground has disappeared beneath the muck."

"Then we cannot expect to make much time if we go that way, can we?" Müffling was asking no one in particular.

He continued, "Chances are, we would have to either expose ourselves as a target to flanking artillery fire or we would never arrive in time. Does that sound like the wishes of General Gneisenau or Field Marshal Blücher to you, my Captain?"

Scharnhorst looked disconcerted. "No, of course not. But his orders were clear. You are to come to his aid immediately."

Von Müffling jumped on the statement without hesitation, "Yes, we are to come to his aid, but we can best do that here. Look, you can see that Papelotte is once again in French hands. The entire left of the allied line is under pressure, and I have just weakened it further to buttress the center. It is the center that is most crucial. If it collapses, we lose the battle. It is no longer a matter of time there. But at Plancenoit, we still have time. If we cannot take it now, we can take it later. In either position we threaten Napoleon. But if he senses he can crush Wellington's middle, it is all over for us. What do you say, Reiche?"

In all the years of his service, Colonel von Reiche had never been challenged as much as by this question. He could see the logic in it, but the orders had come from both the commander in chief of the army and the chief of staff. He was just a corps chief of staff. How could he disobey? Yet if he obeyed, then by his lack of resolve he could be sealing the fate of his army. He hesitated, then gave his answer.

"The decision is not mine. I know that what you say is true, but I cannot doubt that Blücher and Gneisenau do not see it that way. I am duty bound to defer to my own commander. But I promise you that I will support you, and take full responsibility for my actions. In the meantime, I have no option but to prepare the corps for compliance. That means that I must redirect the lead elements from this location back to the fork in the road by Ohain."

It was an eloquent speech, and Müffling admired the colonel for it. He was a brave man, and his stance had been utterly correct. The Prussian liaison officer to the allied army had no recourse but to bide his time and wait for Zieten to make the right decision. Müffling was sure it would come; but would it be in time? In the meantime, the lead elements of the Prussian army would reverse march, having just failed to link up with Wellington's line.

15

LA HAYE SAINTE: 1800

Major Baring listened to the sergeant major's report. "Three to four rounds each. That's all we have, Sir. Three to four rounds each."

"Thank you, Sergeant Major. Our mission remains unchanged. Ready the men."

The battalion commander was bone weary. He almost welcomed the musket ball that would bring him some rest. Anything to get him off his feet would have been a relief. His back hurt, his chest felt constricted, the pain inside his head was so great that he dared not think about it. As if in a fog, he surveyed the inner court of the farm. Smoke burned his eyes, distorting his vision, adding to the surreal effects impacting upon his senses.

For a moment he felt concern over how much blood he might have lost, then dismissed it as a trivial worry. Why did a man need blood if he was not going to live? It was no longer a question of death. It was just a question of when it would come.

"Sir, two enemy columns are approaching from the south." The voice came from an unidentified soldier, reaching the major as if in a dream. He could picture leaden-footed infantrymen making a painstakingly slow approach toward La Haye Sainte. They seemed in no great hurry, impervious to artillery and musket fire, and indifferent to the killing that lay before them. Their faces held no expression—neither fear nor anger, sadness nor joy. They were merely machines of death, like

Baring himself—told to do something unspeakably brutal, against all odds, with no reprieve possible.

"Sir, the enemy is coming. They will be on us soon."

The second warning stirred the major from his stupor. His tongue felt grotesquely thick, as if he had fallen into a deep sleep only to be awakened before the slumber could have any restorative effect. He shook his head and wiped his blackened eyes. He felt a desperate desire to douse himself in water, as if that might refresh his zest for life.

But there was no water. The pond was fouled with the dead, and there was no time to remove them before the next attack would hit.

Baring swallowed hard—a dry, grating swallow that vainly tried to wash some spittle down his constricted throat. He put any thought of personal need from his mind and focused on his tactical situation.

There was not much hope. Hardly sixty men remained on their feet, many of them several times wounded. Among the officers, only Baring, Lieutenant Graeme, and Ensign Franck, the sixteen-year-old, were left. The sergeant major was there too, but his left arm had been mangled by a musket ball. He had tucked his arm limply into his jacket pocket. In his right hand he held a walking cane. This had become his weapon.

The farm continued to burn; none of the survivors had the energy to fight the fire, and the attackers found it in their interest to let it burn. Most worrisome of all was the lack of ammunition. Devoid of obstacles to throw up against the French by the open archway, the only recourse was firepower. But now the firepower was gone. Only cold steel could stop them, and not for long.

Somehow, Major Baring found his voice. "You are brave men. We are not yet done. Use your ammunition with care, but do not let the devils pass. Wellington is relying on you. Let every man do his duty."

His voice was notably strained. The words cracked, almost choking in his mouth. It was a feeble attempt to rally men facing death. But somehow, the very frailty of the effort touched the tired men yet responding to his orders. They had to admire their commander. He had spared himself nothing. He had held them together through terrible fighting, against impossible odds. They could see the blood drenching his uniform, his thin form almost waving in the draft of the smoke searing his eyes. Despite their own dire condition, they could not fail to be moved by his allegiance to the cause and his unstinting efforts to lead.

A soldier broke the awkward silence in the courtyard, "Do not be concerned, Sir. No man will desert you. We will fight with you—and we are prepared to die with you."

A few men muttered their agreement. A few grunted. Most remained silent. It was not much as spontaneous rallies went. But it was enough. No man would move from his position. As one, they were wedded to the mission to defend La Haye Sainte. They braced themselves for the French, now only a minute away.

The major swelled with pride. He could not have been more elated. His men inspired him. They would do as he asked. They would fight to the death, without complaint, without reproach. He knew that they trusted him completely. It was all that an officer could ask for. A tear formed in the corner of his eye.

Then the French were at the gate. Axemen chopped furiously at the wooden door while their comrades threw strands of burning straw over the wall in hopes of spreading the fire. A rush by the attackers in the archway was met with one stiff volley of fire that piled more Frenchmen onto the corpses already crowding the passageway. It was the last volley for the defenders. From now on, they would pick and choose their targets with great care, saving the one or two rounds remaining until it was a matter of life or death.

The axemen were making progress in hacking through the main gate. With no rifle fire from the roof to hinder their efforts, the work proceeded unimpeded. Baring knew it was only a matter of time before they would burst through.

"Sergeant Major, get a dozen men over here by the gate immediately! We will be fighting from two directions in a minute. Do not let the French advance past you to fall upon the backs of the defenders at the archway."

"No, Sir. I mean, yes Sir, I won't." The sergeant major squared himself to a proper position, angry at himself for the momentary fluster in his words.

"Good man. Be sure to greet them with the bayonet the instant they break through." Baring had no concern about his subordinate's confused answer, knowing full well that the sergeant would follow his orders to the last. The commander helped the sergeant grab men and push them into a screen line just inside the gate, then turned his attention to the desperate fighting going on at the archway across the courtyard.

Almost all the rounds were gone now. A few of the men were frantically calling out for resupply, forgetting in their desperation that there was no hope of obtaining any more .60-caliber ammunition. French soldiers sensed the lack of fire and cautiously began to inch forward into the courtyard.

"The bayonet, men. Give them the bayonet!" Baring raced to the front and swung his saber at a terrified Frenchman, striking him high on the shoulder, driving him back into his comrades. A dozen Hanoverians lunged forward behind their commander, jabbing with the bayonet, then grabbing their weapons by the barrel and swinging them like so many clubs. A few of the Germans were shot dead at point-blank range, but they drove the French back into the archway.

At that instant the axemen splintered through the remaining strands of wood at the gate. The first of the French riflemen attempted to force their way through the opening, only to be met by a dozen bayonets. Three of them fell dead from multiple stab wounds as the remainder pulled back, yelling for the axemen to widen the breach. A minute later the entire door crashed to the courtyard. From opposite directions two avenues of approach opened upon the defenders.

"Fall back, men. Fall back. Cover each other." Major Baring had seen the gate fall. Only fifty of the King's German Legion were left to respond. From the portal, the Legionnaires pulled back in order, Lieutenant Graeme and Ensign Franck guiding them from either flank. Warily, the French watched them fall back, not wanting to be the first to rush in through the archway only to join the growing pile of dead.

At the gate, the sergeant major could see that there was nothing that could stop the rush. Rank upon rank of Frenchmen were lined up, waiting to charge past the door.

"Fall back on Major Baring!" he yelled as he rushed headlong into the gateway, brandishing his cane with his one good arm. He smashed it full force into the face of a startled Frenchman, then brought it back to strike again and again. In a rage the first rank of French fell on him, discharging their muskets directly into his powerful frame, catching him in midswing and driving him to the ground. A half dozen soldiers gathered around him, sticking with their bayonets and smashing his head with the butts of their muskets. The screen line of Legionnaires fell back to the center of the courtyard.

The French scrambled by the defenders and made for the farmhouse.

Their plan was to make for the roof where they could avoid the bayonets of Baring's men while firing down into the dwindling survivors.

Baring watched them race past. He anticipated their plan and realized he was powerless to prevent it from unfolding. Once the French were on the roof, it would be certain death for him and his men.

"When I give the order, I want all of you to race as one for the house. From there we will make our way into the garden and back to our own lines. We must move as a unit or we will be slaughtered like sheep."

He allowed them a second for the order to sink in, then gave the order. "Now! Move!" It was all that was required. Together they darted toward the house.

The French were startled by the sudden movement, but only for a moment. In a flash, they followed them to the farmhouse, shooting the slowest of the Legionnaires before they could make it through the door.

But the remainder passed quickly through the interior of the house and emerged into the outer garden. Baring yelled an order to put them on line, then charged with the bayonet at the surprised French blocking the way. But it was the French following in pursuit and those firing from the roof that were the greatest threat to the King's German Legion. Several more of Baring's men fell dead before the onslaught.

Without a word, Lieutenant Graeme turned back toward the farmhouse to meet his assailants. Franck saw him turn and dropped back to cover his friend while Major Baring continued to press toward the allied line with the survivors. The ensign could see a French soldier drop to one knee and level his musket at Graeme. The distance from the end of the weapon to his friend could not have been five yards.

"Look out, Graeme! You will be shot!"

"Let the blackguard fire!" was the lieutenant's only comment.

On the run, Franck unleashed a ferocious swipe with his saber at the soldier about to shoot his friend. The blade caught the man above his mouth and sliced cleanly through the top of his head.

A musket shot rang out, and Franck felt a ball smash into his ribs and penetrate deep into his side. A split second later, a second ball entered his neck and exited through his shoulder, splintering the collarbone on the way. Reeling from the twin impacts, the ensign lurched back into the farmhouse and staggered into a side room. Blood flowed heavily from both wounds, causing him to worry about his ruined uniform, which had recently been purchased at an exorbitant price. Through glassy eyes he spied a bed lying in a tangle in the corner of the room, apparently moved there in haste by a soldier seeking protection from the shooting. With his energy fast ebbing, Franck fell to the floor and crawled beneath the bedding.

Outside, Graeme had seen his young friend hit and raced at his antagonists before they could finish Franck off. The group, a French officer and four soldiers, now turned their attention to Graeme. The officer circled wide and came at the lieutenant from the rear while his men approached with fixed bayonets. Graeme moved into a half crouch, prepared to saber the man that approached first.

A Frenchman lunged. Graeme parried and stepped to the side, catching the soldier high on the ear with a back swipe. In this instant of distraction, the French officer made his move, grabbing Graeme from behind by his collar.

Unable to break the hold, the lieutenant parried the bayonets of the remaining three soldiers. The five of them lurched around in an awkward dance—the French officer afraid to let go of his grip but concerned that his captive might be able to reach him with his saber, the soldiers doubly wary of the energetic movements of their antagonist and the risks of stabbing their own officer, and Graeme fighting for his life.

The struggle continued until at last a bayonet found Graeme's left arm, stabbing deep into the flesh, finding the bone, and breaking it. The French officer saw it go in, heard Graeme cry out in pain, and released his grip, prepared to watch his enemy fall. It was the Legionnaire's chance. He cut a wide arc with his saber and raced for the heels of Baring and his men. The French fired twice and missed, but they did not pursue. There was too much fight in that one, they had concluded.

Inside, Ensign Franck was fading in and out of consciousness. He could hear Frenchmen everywhere. Occasionally he would recognize the voice of one of his own soldiers pleading in anguish, followed by a French curse and the heavy sound of thick wood smashing repeatedly against skull. Realizing that the wounded were being systematically slaughtered, he buried himself deeper into the bedding and tried to control his breathing. Terror welled up in him. It was the worst nightmare of his life. At last he passed out from loss of blood and fell into troubled dreams, from which he would be awakened later that night by his countrymen.

On the ridge, Major Baring gathered his men together for an accounting.

He had forty men left, and he could see Lieutenant Graeme approaching in the distance, his crippled arm cradled by his good hand. La Haye Sainte had fallen; it now belonged to the French. Baring was disappointed with himself for failing to accomplish his mission, but he knew he had done his army a service. For six hours he had held that inferno, and by so doing had preserved the center of the allied line. It had cost him 90 percent of his battalion.

"I thank you men for a job well done. The fighting is not yet over, however, and now you must take your places in line. I will see that you are given some ammunition." Ever the dutiful officer, he turned to get support as his men took up firing positions in a hollow.

Colonel Christian von Ompteda, Baring's superior officer and commander of the King's German Legion, was having a busy day. He had been watching the fighting at La Haye Sainte all along and, at the critical moments, had rushed up reinforcing units from his brigade. He not only admired Baring and his 2d Battalion, but he understood the crucial defense the farmhouse was providing for the center of the allied line.

One by one, Ompteda had sent in his battalions to help keep Baring and his stalwart resistance alive. In turn the 1st, 8th, and 5th Battalions had been committed to action. The latter was reputed to be one of the best in the entire British Army, having fought most recently in Portugal.

Ompteda's own horse had been shot out from under him, and each of his battalions had suffered horribly. The 8th Battalion, relatively inexperienced, had withered away by midafternoon, the slaughter among soldiers and officers reaching appalling levels. The 1st had been consumed at La Haye Sainte. Only the tough 5th Battalion had survived in any kind of strength.

Ompteda loved his men. They were his life, and he looked to their care and safety with the manner of a kindly father. At around 1700 he had received an unreasonable order from an English aide-de-camp: Ompteda was to deploy into line and advance. At that time, the French cavalry was still pounding into the defending squares. At first Ompteda had resisted the order, but when the aide insisted that the orders were firm, he complied.

The 5th Battalion had no sooner deployed into line when a French cavalry squadron fell upon their rear. Just in time, the battalion commander re-formed square and stopped the cavalry attack at the distance of only a few paces. For the next hour and a half, Ompteda was not bothered by unreasonable orders, and he continued to contribute to the battle by staying on the defensive.

But the fall of La Haye Sainte began to make his position untenable. No longer hampered by the fire from the farmhouse, the French were able to bring up horse artillery and range directly into the allied squares. Ompteda's men, exposed at the point of main effort, suffered disproportionately. The brigade adjutant was killed. The squares became increasingly smaller. Eventually, Ompteda himself was forced to abandon his horse, since there was no longer any room within the square for a mounted man. Nonetheless, his troops held and continued to deny the French a concerted attack in the middle.

It was late in the day, however, and the twenty-two–year–old prince of Orange was concerned that he had yet to make his mark on the battle. He knew there was little glory to be gained in the defense, and the fall of La Haye Sainte had given him the opportunity he was looking for. He spurred his mount over to Ompteda.

"Why are you standing here in square?" The youthful corps commander's voice held an air of impertinence that irritated the veteran Ompteda.

"My Lord, we are resisting the attacks of the French." The brigade commander was self-conscious about giving so obvious an answer to a seemingly senseless question.

"But can't you see that La Haye Sainte has fallen? It needs to be retaken."

"Retaken! But I have lost the bulk of my men trying to defend it. It cannot be retaken now. Look at the fluidity of the battlefield, my Lord. To move out of square would be suicide." There was a desperate plea in the colonel's voice. He was asking that his men be spared. The only sensible response was to allow them to remain in square.

But the prince of Orange was smitten with the terrible arrogance of youth in authority. He would not listen to the voice of experience. All of the aged—and Ompteda, at fifty, was extremely aged in the eyes of the corps commander—had this detestable air of caution about them. They did not seem to understand that glory in war was only for those bold enough to seize it. They needed encouragement. More than that, they needed to be told what to do.

"Perhaps you do not understand me, Sir. I want La Haye Sainte retaken."

"But, Prince. . . ."

"I repeat my order, Colonel Ompteda. You will take the King's German Legion and attack. I will allow no laggards in my corps. My orders are firm, and I will listen to no further arguments on the subject."

The words stung Ompteda as if a whip had lashed across his face. In his rage he could only mutter, "Well, I will." The prince rode off, a look of disdain on his face, self-assured that he had shown the middle-aged colonel who was in command.

Ompteda knew it was over for him. That he did not regret. His whole life had been the army, but if mere children were allowed to spring into command at the head of men they were not fit to lead, then he had had enough of it. Since there could be no life for him outside the army, then this was as good a way to end it as any. He did regret his brave men having to suffer such nonsense, but he could do nothing to save them now. The prince had impugned their honor. At least that much would be regained. But at what cost!

There still remained the problem of his young nephews. He should never have brought them to this place. Somehow they had survived the day's fighting. But this final exposure would be too much.

"Lieutenant Colonel Linsingen," Ompteda called to the 5th Battalion commander, "try and save my two nephews. I will lead the battalion in the attack."

"Yes Sir, I will do my best." Although preferring to lead his own battalion in the final charge, Linsingen understood the depth of feeling in his brigade commander's last request. He could not deny him.

The two hundred survivors of the 5th Battalion deployed into line as Ompteda remounted his horse. His two nephews were protesting the grip that Linsingen had them in, pleading with their uncle to let them go forward in the attack. The colonel ignored them.

"Forward the Fighting Battalion!" The men of the 5th Battalion squared their shoulders at the sound of their nickname and started forward.

The French infantry turned to meet them. One thousand stood ready for an assault by two hundred men. The soldiers of the King's German Legion picked up the pace, moving at double time as bugles sounded along the line.

The French had time for one volley before Ompteda's men were on them. With a vicious clash the lines closed. It was all bayonet—on guard, thrust, parry, jab, extract, pivot, butt stroke, jab, parry, wheel, jab, parry, slash. The French were good, but the Legionnaires were better. They were punching a hole through an enemy five times their size.

For a brief moment the prince of Orange prided himself on his order. It seemed as if the 5th Battalion would make it through to La Haye Sainte.

But it was not to be. As the brigade colonel had anticipated, the French cavalry was only waiting for the right moment. Like a cat watching a mouse emerge from its hole to go after the cheese, the *cuirassiers* allowed their prey to become fully engaged before making their move. Suddenly they were upon them, rolling them up from the rear.

The Legionnaires gave a shout. "The cavalry! The cavalry!" But nothing could be done. It was a massacre. Colonel Ompteda gave one last order: "Follow me, brave comrades!" Then he rode forward into the French lines, his white plume marking his passage to those survivors able to watch him go. French riflemen drew a bead on him, but their officers knocked the barrels up into the air. It was a show of respect for his courage, allowing him to close on his enemy with dignity and bearing. For a few moments he proceeded with a steady, unhurried pace, then was seen to sink from his horse. As he preferred, he found his resting place beneath a soldier's blow.

Lieutenant Colonel Linsingen still held the two nephews tightly. They had grown quiet now, awed by the terrible scene they had just witnessed. The few Legionnaires who were left straggled back into a shrunken square. The French did not follow. Fresh troops were arriving on the battlefield and taking up positions. They wore uniforms of a color different from those of the allied forces they had been fighting all day. Until they were sure who the troops were, the French decided to wait.

Lady Magdalene and her maid, Emma, were quietly sitting by the open window of their room in the apartment in Antwerp. It had been an uncomfortably hot afternoon, so different from the chill of the night before. Below them, in the street, the traffic had taken an ominous turn.

Stragglers from the allied army were making their way to the port. Some were wounded, although all were ambulatory. Most, however, seemed unharmed. Yet all had a wild stare—as if they could not focus on anything close. They seemed to be a particularly unsavory lot, somewhat deranged, rude of manner, and intent on continuing their flight no matter what or who got in their way.

"Lady Magdalene. I have heard some of the ladies talking downstairs. They have inquired of the men how the battle goes." Emma spoke to her mistress with care, not sure that she wanted to be interrupted in her thoughts. Her lady's brow seemed so tight that it had frightened the maid. There was an unnatural serenity in Magdalene's eyes. Emma had never seen them like that before.

When Lady de Lancey did not answer, Emma continued, although now more tentatively than before. "They say the men in the street speak of a defeat. They say that Brussels has fallen and nothing can stop the advance of Napoleon."

"Emma!" It was almost a cry. "I do not want to hear any of that. Colonel de Lancey told me such things would happen. It is all nonsense. These are the weaklings, the ones who would not fight. He told me they would come, that they always do. And they always speak of defeat, as if to justify their cowardly withdrawal. Shameful. They are utterly shameful."

Magdalene became quiet once more. She glanced at the men below her. There were few officers among them. Though she had silently condemned the lot, she found herself secretly wishing that she might see Sir William among them. If only she could see his face, know that he was safe. All day long she had been hearing the intermittent boom of cannon in the distance. Sometimes the better part of an hour would pass in silence, and she would begin to think it was over. But then there would be a few more minutes of resonant thumping before the sounds faded out once more. Every time she heard the cannons, her terror increased.

A part of her believed everything her husband had said. He had been so correct all along. He had said there would be a battle—and there was. He had said there would be a second—and now that was happening. He had said there would be deserters streaming to the rear with exaggerated tales of ruin. That had occurred on 16 June and was happening again today. And he had said he would not be hurt. For the first battle that had been true. Certainly it would be true again today.

Do not move until you hear from me, he had said. How confident a signal that was. To hear from him, she would have to receive a message. To receive a message, he would have to send one. And it could only be sent after the battle. Therefore, by the end of the battle he would have to remain unhurt. It all seemed so logical. He was so sure he would not be hurt.

He had explained that the role of the quartermaster general was to move the forces, to write the orders, obtain the supplies, and bring everything together in compliance with the commander's wishes. It all sounded so administrative—as if, in a rainstorm, he would have to seek shelter to keep the ink dry or, in a wind, to move indoors to keep his papers from blowing away. He had even implied he regretted having so inglorious a post. While his friends and peers were out gaining honors, he would be performing clerklike functions far from the scene of action.

"Emma. Do you know much of men?"

"My Lady, what do you mean?"

"I mean, why is it that they seek to be so noble, so heroic?"

"Well, Lady Magdalene, I suppose because they think it makes their women think so well of them."

"But if we told them it did not matter, would it make a difference?"

"Oh no, Madam, because they would not believe it."

"But if we could convince them. Then would they still take such chances? I mean, would they thirst so much for battle?"

"If you mean would they still want to go to war, I think so. It seems to be an important thing to them. As if it were the most important thing that a man could do."

"And your men, do they feel that way as well?"

Emma thought this one over. "Do you mean those that aren't gentlemen? I suppose it's different with them. They don't seek it out, but there is a code that seems to run among them. They don't want to be found wanting by their fellows."

"But if they didn't have to do it, would they want to prove themselves?"

"Oh no, my Lady. That is a habit of the gentlemen. I suppose it has to do with proper breeding and all that. I can't understand it myself. It seems like such a beastly thing to do."

Lady Magdalene became quiet again. She was sorry she had started the conversation. A tone she did not like had crept into Emma's voice at the end. It was probably improper that a lady of her breeding had raised the subject. Yet it was all so perplexing. Colonel de Lancey was such a gentleman. He was so kind, so considerate. Why would he elect to spend his life as a soldier? And her own family. The men were such proper sorts. They were warm and tender, loving and humorous. What drove them to serve in the ranks, to seek battle, to relish the risks of combat?

She found herself hoping that this would be the last of it for her husband, that he would tire of it and find some other occupation. There was enough money between the two of them. Certainly they could do without his military pay. Besides, how many days like this could she stand? And what of the children when they came? She could not follow him about as she had this time. It would not be fitting for a mother to do that.

There it was again. That awful booming in the distance. So the battle was still going on. There would be such sad news tonight. So many of the wives with her here in Antwerp would be grief stricken by the news of their husbands' deaths. So many more would be sick with worry upon reading their loved ones' names on the lists of wounded. It had been like that the night before last. What kind of wound did he have? Would he recover? Would he be maimed for life? What would he look like? How would he act? It was all so terrifying. She hated to go through it again—suppressing her own joy at the sparing of her husband in order to comfort those who had lost theirs.

She had not noticed that she had stood up and was pacing back and forth. Nor that her youthful forehead had once again compressed into a tight pattern of deep, furrowed wrinkles. Emma noticed it though—but said nothing.

16

LA BELLE ALLIANCE: 1900

Long shadows fell across the blooded fields as the sun sank low in the sky, its rays cutting brilliant lanes through the scattered clouds. A solitary figure sped his mount down into the valley between La Belle Alliance and Mont Saint Jean, racing directly at the allied lines. A hail of musket balls from skirmishers of the 52d Regiment flew at him, causing no damage as they passed by harmlessly on either side. The rider held his right hand aloft, palm open. His saber was sheathed, and his face displayed the determined look of one who had made a resolute decision and was prepared to see it through no matter the cost. Only as the distance closed to the last hundred meters did a British sergeant major comprehend the intent of the oncoming horseman and order his men to hold their fire. The Frenchman passed through the lines and dashed toward the nearest mounted figure, assuming correctly that it would be an officer.

"By the grace of God, I swear my allegiance to the cause of King Louis XVIII and repudiate the butcher Napoleon." Nobly did the officer declare his traitorous purpose.

"Identify yourself." The regimental major tried to hide his disgust for a leader who had abandoned his troops in the midst of battle.

"I am Captain de Barail of the 2d Carabiniers."

"Well, Captain! Had enough have you? You are a prisoner of the 52d Foot. Thank your God that you yet draw breath. We have spared few of your countrymen today."

"I have information regarding the emperor's plans. I request safe passage so that it may be delivered."

"Safe passage is it? This is a queer day for anyone to be asking for safe passage. I will grant it, however, provided that you speak quickly. Come with me."

The two officers rode at a trot toward the commander of artillery, Colonel Fraser, as the British rank and file regarded the plumed captain with a baleful stare. Several considered the consequences of a quick shot at their visitor. It did not sit well with them that even in battle the officer caste preserved for itself special privilege. A private soldier would not have gotten away with running into the enemy lines, better yet prancing around with the opposing force like some kind of rare gift. "At least make the bugger walk!" was a common thought. But the very strength of the despised class system stifled the urge to kill the French officer. Sullenly, the British riflemen returned their gaze to the front, where thousands of the traitor's countrymen clamored for more direct attention.

"What have you there, Major?" Colonel Fraser eyed the enemy prisoner.

"Sir, this gentleman wishes to render a report in keeping with his recently altered fidelity to his monarch." The word "gentleman" was glazed with ice.

"And what is that message, *monsieur*?"

"If you please, Colonel, I am Captain de Barail. Long live the king! You must prepare yourselves. That bastard Napoleon will be on you with the Guard within the half hour."

Fraser fixed a steady gaze on the Frenchman's eyes. They had the self-righteous look of a man who had stifled his own sense of shame with an overzealous public commitment to what was probably an intensely personal decision. Such a man would not lie at a time like this; but would he recognize the truth?

"The Guard, hey? Have they not yet been committed?"

"In part. But the bulk of them remain. They will come at the center, where Ney has been all day."

A cold chill ran down Fraser's spine. He was a hard man by nature, and his ferocity had not been dimmed by the rugged fighting of the day. But he knew the reputation of the Guard. If they were coming, it would be the heaviest push yet. And the Guard had never lost. The colonel's steady gaze disguised the deep concern the Frenchman's news had given him, allowing him to settle himself before he spoke.

"We welcome the opportunity. It has been long awaited—a final act to bring this troubled day to a close."

The French officer returned Fraser's look with a studied curiosity, uncertain as to what sort of a finish the day might see. For a moment he wondered whether he had made the right choice in his allegiance. But, completing his assessment of Fraser, he concluded that the colonel, at least, would stand his ground. The captain was eager to be moving on.

"Come with me to find Wellington," said the colonel, who seemed to be in a hurry as well. He wanted to be back by the guns in time for the action.

Napoleon sensed the moment. His experienced ears had detected the slackening of the musket fire. It was always so at the penultimate phase of battle. It was less a reflection of the dwindling of ammunition stocks—although he calculated that on both sides they had indeed run low—than it was the waning of human energy for the fight. The combat had lasted for almost eight hours, with no appreciable gains for either side—none, at least, that was apparent to the combatants. The emperor—now fully alert, his agile mind more capable of dealing with the rush of events than it had been all day—could see what his soldiers could not. The morning's odds for victory, which he had estimated at nine to one in his favor, had dwindled. The truth, which he dared not share with his subordinates, was that the odds had reversed themselves.

He could hear the continued firing in the woods surrounding Hougoumont. What an expensive diversion that had become—more costly, he knew, to himself than to Wellington. Although his forces once again held Papelotte, on the right flank, he had no faith in their ability to keep it. The terrain was too poorly situated. Whoever wanted Papelotte could have it for a price, and he had little doubt that the bloodthirsty Prussians who continued to arrive in force at the left of the allied line, as well as at Plancenoit, were prepared to pay. The fighting in the center was desultory, the infantry of Quiot, Donzelot, and Marcognet merely skirmishing on the slope before the Ohain line. Behind them, in the valley, lingered the weary and dispirited remnants of the cavalry. Disorganized and dejected, they were contributing nothing to the battle. The mood settling on the *Armée du Nord* was one of defeat.

Napoleon had just learned that the commander of chasseurs had already taken it upon himself to send to the rear the entire train of carriages and wagons left in his charge. He ordered that the imperial carriage be halted at the lower end of Genappe. This pullout was hardly a move to hearten French soldiers at this critical juncture, but the emperor did not overrule it. Instead, he tucked the knowledge away for future reference. It might prove useful.

The battle, Napoleon calculated, was not yet lost. Wellington had been stubborn, but he had bled all day. It was not possible that he had much blood left. The Prussians had not yet reached the center, and it was the center that was key. La Haye Sainte had fallen at last, opening the way. Ney had certainly failed him there, never putting together the right package of combined arms until late in the day. The fool! Where was his mind today? Maybe Davout had been right all along. After Russia, Ney had never been quite the same. Except for his courage. One could not deny that he had courage.

That was why I chose Ney, Napoleon remembered. My instincts have been right all along. It comes down to courage now. The side with the greatest courage will win. All of the strategy, all of the tactics have brought the battle to this—a question of courage. The plan has not gone awry. I meant it to be a bloodletting on a massive scale. So far the British have not faltered, and their allies, amazingly, have stayed with them. But they are close to the edge—the British, the Dutch, and the Belgians—they are close. They must be!

The Prussians are a different story. They drink blood, those barbarians. But they are not the target. The objective is Wellington and his motley allies. Somehow they have held up, but they have yet to see the worst of it. They will crack when it comes, and then even the Prussians will hesitate. Grouchy is coming. Where is he? He must be close. So much of Blücher's force has arrived. The old drunk has brought everything with him. Nothing is left to delay Grouchy; he has to be nearby. With the allied line shattered and Grouchy on Blücher's back, the battlefield will be swept clean. The plan has worked. All along it has been the right plan. Now it comes down to courage.

Courage. And will! Yes, that was it—the will to win. I shall not be beaten, not by this charlatan Wellington. Not by that maniac Blücher. Not by any of them. They are not good enough. I am Napoleon. I am emperor, master of Europe.

My men, my generals, are not what they once were. They have grown soft on the fruits of my victories. They have degenerated in my absence. They lack fortitude.

Davout has failed me. He has sent me boys, boys that are yet fat from their mothers' milk, from which they are barely weaned. Soult has failed me. That imbecile! He forgets what I tell him. He cannot comprehend the details. He has been useless to me, worse than useless. He is an impediment, an obstacle to be overcome. He does not use his head. He cannot see what orders need to be given. And, when he does, he is unclear or does not check to see that the orders have been carried out. He has been an anchor on the movement of this army.

Grouchy has failed me. A marshal of cavalry who moves like a snail. My orders were clear. He is to throw his weight here, at Mont Saint Jean. Where can he be? I will court-martial him when this is over.

And Ney. Oh, Ney, Ney. You idiot. You have run around all day like a decapitated chicken. You do not understand victory. Russia has wiped it from your memory and replaced it with tragedy. Tragedy is what you seek. You do not recognize winning. You threw it away at Quatre-Bras, and here you cannot find it. It was there at La Haye Sainte, but you never took it. It was in my cavalry, but you wasted it. It is at the center of the allied line, but you can't put together the arms that I have given you to take it. You are mad, absolutely mad. You seek death. That is the only victory you desire.

No matter. The battle can yet be won. My will is too great. It cannot be resisted. I can motivate these boy-soldiers to a final effort; I can bring them fire. I can inspire them to victory as I inspired their fathers, as I have inspired all of Europe. Nothing can stop me! My chief of staff cannot botch it any more than he already has. The battle has moved beyond administrative concerns. Soult can no longer hurt me, nor can my marshals. The whole affair is now in the hands of the commander in chief—in my hands. Ney can be led. He can be told where to go, and his thoughtless courage will inspire his men to follow his reckless example. That is the extent of his contribution, and I can exploit it, as I always knew I would. But where is Grouchy? Where can he be? He must come. I must use him. I cannot use him if he is not here.

A glint appeared in the emperor's eyes that hinted at the sinister thought registering behind their filmy veil. He took on an evil countenance. His lips curled up slightly at the corners, as if he were smiling at a private joke he dare not share with anyone around him. His presence evinced an aura of complete self-satisfaction, an intense pride that he alone possessed the ruthlessness to see this battle through. It was a look of complete resolve, utterly devoid of morality. A watching aide-de-camp shivered at the coldness in his commander's eyes.

"General, is the Guard ready?" Napoleon spoke to Lieutenant General Drouot, commanding the Imperial Guard in place of the ailing Marshal Mortier.

"Yes, Sire," he answered in a quiet voice, put off by the remorseless stare of the emperor.

"Then move them into attack formation. I wish to speak with the soldiers of d'Erlon's corps, after which I will speak to the Guard. All depends now on how well they heed my words." With that he spurred his horse forward to position himself for his oration.

For the soldiers in ranks, it was difficult to hear the speech. Officers and sergeants were giving orders to form for the attack. The curses and grunts of the repositioning men added to the noise of restless horses responding to the tugs of their riders. Musket fire from the skirmish lines continued to the front while, in response to Napoleon's orders, the artillery fire intensified, seeking to achieve a softening of the defenders before the next attack. Despite the noise, however, the emperor knew that his words would have an effect on the soldiers and be crucial to the outcome of the battle.

"Soldiers of France, now is your finest hour. All day our enemies have sought to overcome your patriotic defense of our beloved country. But your ardor has been too great. Now is the time to deliver the coup de grace. For the sake of your country, for the safety of your families, and the preservation of your homes, you must surpass yourselves. For the glory of France, I beseech you to carve a way through the enemy line so that I might march into Brussels before you in victory. The hour of glory is upon us. Marshal Grouchy has arrived upon the field to join us with thirty thousand men. March with me to victory!"

Only those soldiers nearest to the emperor heard the complete message. It was enough. Their spirits rose with the strength of the impassioned plea and the grotesque lie. The effects rippled through the ranks like an irrepressible wave. "Grouchy has arrived. Grouchy has arrived. The new formations you see entering the fighting are our own. Victory is ours!" Those were the words passed on from soldier to soldier. They believed in their emperor. He had delivered them. Now they would share in his glory. The thought fired their imaginations.

Napoleon could see the confidence rise in his men. With a reproving glance he silenced the nearby members of his staff whose shocked looks revealed their consternation. Only Soult found his tongue.

"Sire," he began in a hushed tone, the air escaping from his lungs in a shallow, prolonged breath, "Grouchy is nowhere to be seen. The only forces arriving on the battlefield are Blücher's." The chief of staff was staggering under the pain of the emperor's blatant dishonesty. He could not bring himself to believe that it was intentional. Perhaps someone had misinformed the commander in chief. He felt compelled to speak out, to correct the error, but found himself almost unable to speak. Deep inside, he feared it had been no mistake. He dreaded the possibility of having the suspicion confirmed.

Napoleon stared at Soult with a look of utter contempt. Here was his chief of staff unable to grasp the importance of the moment, unable to comprehend the significance of what had just been done. He despised Soult for his weakness. "Silence. The message that Grouchy has arrived will be passed to all taking part in the attack."

"To all, Sire? Even to your generals?"

"Yes, to all. It is a question of will, and will must be powered by faith. The belief that Grouchy has arrived will bring faith. With that, I can direct the will of this army to victory."

"But Sire, Grouchy has not arrived. You cannot mislead your own soldiers—your generals—on so obvious a falsehood."

"You will do as I say, Soult. You know nothing of what you speak, and I would be the biggest fool of all to listen to you. Dispatch riders to my corps commanders. They will be told as I have declared. If you are troubled by that order then console yourself that, if you had passed my earlier order properly, then Grouchy might well have been arriving at this very moment." The emperor turned his horse toward the next formation. The grand lie would be repeated again and again, until its retelling convinced everyone of its truth.

Soult sat upon his horse in muted shock. All of the pain and wretchedness of the entire campaign was nothing next to this. He despised himself for being a part of it, yet knew he did not have the courage to override his orders. The final words had been too cutting. He knew he shared responsibility for Grouchy's absence. He had never asked to be chief of staff, had resisted the imploring of his emperor to take the post. But, in the end, he had capitulated. He had wanted so much to be a part of the campaign. He had agreed to serve in a capacity for which he knew he was unqualified. That was the real beginning of all this dishonesty. He was already tainted. He could not extract himself now. He called in the aides to have them spread the falsehood, heartsick at his own culpability in the plot.

The attack began with great spirit. The French could sense the climax coming and felt that victory was within their grasp. Movement began all along the line as the Guard band struck up the sprightly tune, *"La Marche des Bonnet á Poil."* D'Erlon's corps marched once more against the Ohain line while, on the left, Reille's men again rallied against Hougoumont. In the center, Napoleon cried out to the five Guards battalions gathered for the assault, "Everyone behind me!" The emperor himself was going to lead the attack.

With a steady gait they closed on the allied center. Bodies lay everywhere—on the valley floor, on the slopes, along either side of the Brussels road, before every clump of trees, in front of the burning farmhouses. Undaunted, the Guards moved forward, eyes fixed on the ridge of Mont Saint Jean. Behind it lay the enemy. And victory! Resolutely they moved up the rise from the valley.

Ney, now astride his fifth horse of the day, rode beside Napoleon. He was moved by his leader's presence. Napoleon had never lost his power to quell the rebelliousness in his marshal's breast. Ney could hate this man with a passion, but when the great general spoke to him directly in a kindly fashion and took a soldier's stance, Ney could do nothing but worship the ground on which he strode. Now he was here to lead the attack in person. The marshal was both proud and humbled. He could not shake off an extreme self-consciousness. Above all, he wanted to please his emperor, to show him that his subordinate was worthy of his trust. Ney could not look at him. Instead, he locked his eyes on the ridge to his front and tried to keep his horse abreast of his leader's.

La Haye Sainte was close by now. The fields thickened with corpses all about. Soldiers on the near edge of the formations could feel the heat from the flames engulfing the farmhouse. The road was littered with the debris of war. Mangled horses not yet dead filled the air with woeful cries of anguish. It was a somber scene, full of foreboding and dark premonition.

"Marshal Ney, continue with the assault. I will pause here to rally the troops as they deploy." Napoleon gestured toward a nearby gravel pit, his personal staff officers immediately grateful for the reprieve they had been granted.

Ney gave his commander an incredulous look. The old doubts welled up once again. What was this cunning bastard up to? Now that the ridge was only moments away, he saw fit to "rally the troops." Well,

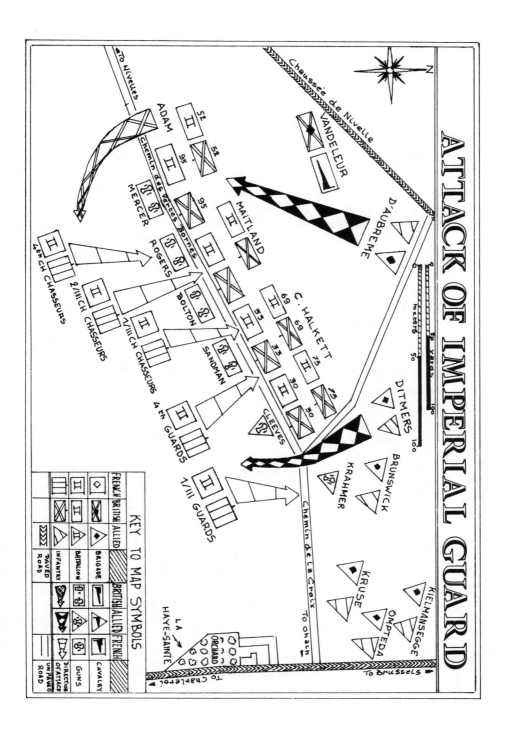

ATTACK OF IMPERIAL GUARD

To Nivelles

Chaussée de Nivelle

N

VANDELEUR

D'AUBREME

ADAM

52

58

95

MERCER

95

Bornes

Chemin des Vertes

ROGERS

MAITLAND

BOLTON

C. HALKETT

69

69

33

33

30

30

SANDMAN

73

CLEEVES

4/Ch CHASSEURS

2/III Ch CHASSEURS

1/III Ch CHASSEURS

4th GUARDS

DITMERS

meters

50

yards

50

100

100

BRUNSWICK

KRAHMER

KRUSE

KIELMANSEGGE

OMPTEDA

1/III GUARDS

Chemin de la Croix

To Ohain

To Genappe

LA HAYE-SAINTE

ORCHARD

To Brussels

To Charleroi

KEY TO MAP SYMBOLS

FRENCH	BRITISH	ALLIED		BRITISH	ALLIED	FRENCH	
			BRIGADE			CAVALRY	
			BATTALION			GUNS	
			INFANTRY			DIRECTION OF ATTACK	
						PAVED ROAD	
						UN PAVED ROAD	

so be it. I have enough leadership left in me to take us over the top. It's not as if it were a new experience for me. I have already been there many times today.

"Yes, Sire. Of course. I will take them the last short distance." He cut the satire in his voice down to an inaudible undertone.

The emperor's staff peeled off as the attacking battalions kept on their march. "On brave soldiers!" Napoleon called out his encouragement to infantrymen not a little startled to discover that their commander in chief was no longer to the front.

D'Erlon's corps was becoming engaged to the west of La Haye Sainte, the musketry rising in volume, overpowering the French shouts of allegiance to Napoleon. Ney pressed on with his attack. He planned to take the Middle Guard in slightly to the west of the allied center. Five battalions would attack in echelon, the right echelon leading. Artillery—eight pounders, under command of Colonel Duchand—had been placed between the battalions. The cavalry was missing, but the emphasis was to be on combined arms. In the lead was 1st Battalion, 3d Grenadiers.

Along the top of the ridge, the British artillery mixed with the infantry brigades to form a waiting concave line, a snare waiting to be tripped. Above the opposing armies floated clouds of sulphurous smoke, dispersing the deeply angled rays of brilliant sunlight into an eerie glow. With impressive precision, the French closed the distance between the two forces.

Napoleon noticed that somehow Ney had shifted the attack far to the left. He had seen the merging of two battalions, inadvertently cutting the five-echelon formation to four, and immediately thereafter witnessed an oblique turn to the northwest. It could not have been intentional. He had told Ney where to put the attack. Ney was much too cowed at this point to put his own interpretation on those orders. Probably the change had been caused by the number of casualties on the ground toward the middle of the line where the great cavalry charge had been aimed. That was where the bulk of the killing had taken place. The sudden turn must have been caused by the need to circumvent the horrible pile of dead and dying to the immediate front of the attackers. The redirection was understandable, but it must be straightened out before the final charge into the line. For an instant, Napoleon considered riding up to take personal charge once again, then reconsidered. Weren't his loyal aides always imploring him not to expose himself to the fire?

"For the safety of France and the army," they had repeatedly told him, "you must not risk yourself needlessly." The emperor looked up and dispatched an aide to Ney—an aide who had remained quiet about his commander's safety.

With a flash and a roar, the British artillery opened up on the leading battalion, which was hit in the flank with a double salvo of cannister shot from over thirty guns. There were barely 200 meters to go. Ney's horse took a large chunk of shrapnel between its shoulders, staggered a few meters forward, and fell to the ground. The marshal sprang to his feet, unsheathed his sword, and on foot continued to lead his men forward.

The grenadiers closed ranks and pressed on, the shot and shell ripping through their number like giant meat cleavers. Determined, they closed on the forward elements, driving back the Brunswickers and seizing guns temporarily abandoned. Musket fire belched forth death from all around. General Friant fell from his horse, was grabbed by a soldier, and spirited away to the rear. Ney continued to march forward, bringing his forces in against Halkett's brigade. The 30th and 73d Regiments retired before the determined onslaught of the French. Only a vicious bayonet charge by a brigade of General Chassés's division—he was a Dutchman who had once fought for the French but now commanded at a critical point in Wellington's line—combined with savage artillery fire to slow the relentless advance of the French.

The second unit of the French formation, the 4th Grenadier Battalion, arrived on the scene and attacked the righthand square of Halkett's brigade. Its two regiments, the 33d and 69th, savaged by the cavalry attacks earlier in the day, were on the verge of snapping. So many of their best had fallen. This final grinding seemed to be more than they could stand. Their commander sensed the depth of their morale and raced forward to seize the regimental standard of the 33d. For a moment or two he stood waving it above his head, then fell mortally wounded, a nearby soldier catching the colors before they hit the ground. Colonel Halkett was out of the battle, but not before inspiring his brigade to hold its ground. For a few minutes, the face-to-face butchery continued, then the attackers backed away to catch their breaths.

On came the 1st and 2d Battalions of the 3d Chasseurs, their point of aim being Maitland's brigade. In the valley behind, Napoleon was urging on the advance of the three battalions of the Guard. He sensed that at last the battle was going his way. The wounded General Friant had been carried to the emperor's command post in the gravel pit, where he reported that the Guard was breaking through Wellington's line. Blooded and hurt though he was, a smile crossed the wounded general's lips as he reported that victory had been achieved.

If it was victory, Wellington had yet to concede it. He had seen the attack of the Imperial Guard. The men looked big, made larger yet by their shoulder-broadening epaulets and towering bearskin hats. His own line looked small before them, thin and tattered from the pounding of the day. The awful drumbeats of the French musicians added to the menace. Nothing seemed able to stop the rhythmic cadence carrying up and over the Mont Saint Jean ridge, nor the men it urged on.

The duke had seen the cannon pour into the French grenadiers, had seen them waver in the face of the deadly firestorm, then close ranks and come on again. Neither cannister nor musket shot seemed to deter them from their resolute march. He had seen Halkett's brigade bend before their onslaught, had seen Halkett himself waving the standard, then fall to the ground.

He had watched the Brunswickers break into flight, galloped over to them himself, and placed his own cavalry in their way. He had then moved to the front to steady them and re-form two of their battalions. Every moment seemed a crisis. He could not linger a moment at any single point in the line. Urgently, he spurred Copenhagen to Maitland's brigade, the last hope of the thin line of defense.

The French chasseurs were coming on rapidly, making their way over the ridge. The only thing visible to their front were the British guns, their crews now frozen in fear by the onrushing Imperial Guard. For an instant, the battlefield went silent save for the relentless drums. Sixty meters separated the French from their objective. The leading officers could see the lone figure of Wellington, his head and shoulders visible over the rise of the hill. The symbolism struck Ney. It was as if the duke himself was all that stood in their way. What the attackers could not see were the Guardsmen of Maitland's brigade lying prone behind the crest.

The commander of the allied army stared at the big Frenchmen. To their front he could see Ney, who at six feet tall was dwarfed by the ranks that he led. How small and insignificant he looked. Only the red hair gleaming above his smudged, blackened face served as a reminder of the ferocity of the man. For a moment, Wellington stood motionless, as if admiring the scene before him. Then he gave the order.

"Now, Maitland. Now's your time." The French rushed in yet another twenty meters. "Up, Guards, and make ready!"

As one, fifteen hundred men rose from the ground. The sight of it stopped the French in their tracks for a split second. Then the line of blue overcoats started forward again.

"Fire!" Four hundred muskets roared a welcome, and three hundred Frenchmen fell to the ground. Simultaneously, the British batteries opened fire once more, just as the survivors of Halkett's brigade sent in a hail of musketry from the flanks. The French were trapped. Death rained on their close formation from multiple directions. The way ahead was blocked by the broken bodies of their comrades. They hesitated another instant, tried to press forward, and were gunned down again by the hundreds.

It was enough. Those left standing among the French realized that to move forward was suicide. Soldiers will fight unto the death, but only if they believe there is some chance of survival—no matter how remote. That small sense of hope enables them to carry on against all odds. The 3d Chasseurs of the Middle Guard had abandoned all hope. Each man knew there was no longer any question of survival if he persisted in the attack. Each man, therefore, had to face the inevitability of his own death. The attraction of life was too great. En masse, the battalion turned and ran.

Quickly, Wellington turned to Lord Saltoun and ordered him forward. The Guards savored their revenge for the hard fighting they had undergone all day along the part of the line from Hougoumont to Mont Saint Jean. With a roar they were on the French, driving the chasseurs before them in scattered groupings.

But on came Ney's next—and last—battalion, the 4th Chasseurs. Uncomprehending, its soldiers watched their brethren flee before their common enemy. It was an unfamiliar sight. Shaken, they pressed forward by habit, their spirits weakened by the scene unfolding before them. Saltoun's Guards drew back to the allied line, like lions awaiting fresh meat at feeding time.

Wellington felt a momentary twinge of pity, then caught himself with a silent reproach. Let them die; there's yet room in hell. He gave no orders. He trusted to his army. They had done everything he had asked of them all day. The final option was theirs. Stoically, he watched it all develop.

Maitland's Guards and Halkett's brigade—the latter's commander bleeding to death from a gunshot wound to the mouth—awaited the last of the Middle Guard. The Hanoverian brigade emerged from Hougoumont to come up on the rear of the French. From the two directions, the three brigades began the systematic slaughter of the best of France.

Sir John Colborne, the commander of the 52d Light Infantry, watched from the reverse slope of the allied line, to the right of the Guards. As the French reached the summit, still moving forward despite the terrible butchery, he wheeled his regiment upon its left company, bringing his entire line parallel with the left flank of the attacking battalion. At the prime moment, he ordered his men to open fire. It was as if a terrible blow from a demon's hand had fallen on the entire left flank of the Middle Guard. Men were flung into the air from the impact of multiple hits. For an instant the survivors reeled to the left and returned fire, but the allied line intensified its onslaught from three directions.

As the French staggered under the hail of fire, Wellington sprang back to life. "Send Colborne in with the bayonet." An aide raced to carry the message.

In a flash, the 52d swept forward. The last of the Middle Guard broke for the rear. All along the French line to the adjacent corps, the movement was detected. *"La Garde recule! La Garde recule!"* "The Guard has broken!" Never before had that cry been heard. It darkened the soul of every last combatant remaining in the *Armée du Nord*.

Now was the terrible lie realized. It was not Grouchy arriving from the heights of Ohain; it was the Prussians. The enormity of the betrayal sank in. The French soldiers fled to the rear, uttering a mournful cry, "We have been deceived. There is no hope. Every man for himself!"

A surge of elation filled Wellington. At last. At last. It had been eight hours of relentless pounding, but the storm had broken. It was all but finished. Now not to let them get away. Silhouetted against the bright sunset on the crest of the ridge, he raised his hat and waved it toward the south, toward the backs of the retreating enemy.

The entire line understood the gesture. Officers gave orders, drumbeats reverberated, bagpipes exhaled, and the survivors of the allied army swept forward. The pursuit was on.

The duke went forward with them, ignoring the pleas of his surviving aides to remove himself from danger. "So I will when I see those fellows driven off," was his calm reply.

As he came by the regiments the men stopped to cheer, raising their muskets by the stock high into the air. "No cheering, my lads, but forward and complete your victory. Don't give them time to rally. Go on! Go on!"

Baron Müffling came riding over to report the status of the Prussian forces. Wellington caught his eye with a smile and gestured toward Hougoumont, still burning in the valley to their front.

"You see, my dear Baron, Macdonell has held Hougoumont."

The Prussian gave a short bow of respect as Wellington rode Copenhagen toward his command tree at the crossroads.

17

PURSUIT: 2000

The duke eyed the battlefield with a grim air of satisfaction. He was confident that he had gotten the timing right. Colborne and his 52d Regiment had been the final catalyst in turning the battle, but Wellington knew the call had been his own. In fact, it had been so the entire day. For every correct decision he had made—and he sensed that he had made several score of them—there had been at least a half dozen options that would have led to disaster.

Lord Uxbridge, the commander of cavalry and second in command of the allied army, sat quietly on his horse not far from the duke. With his telescope Wellington surveyed the field. All day long Uxbridge's commander had kept his own counsel, and although he had felt left out of the critical decisions, the cavalry chief could not help but admire the masterful way in which the duke had handled himself.

Again and again, Wellington had appeared at the critical juncture on the battlefield, said the right words, given the right orders, and steadied the course of the allied effort. Even when blunders had occurred, blunders such as Uxbridge's own disastrous loss of the heavy cavalry in the early afternoon attack of d'Erlon's corps, the duke had calmed rather than harangued.

How the commander had been everywhere without being hurt was unfathomable. Uxbridge noticed that virtually none of the aides remained. A few feet from Wellington's side rode young Colin Campbell, one of the very few left uninjured. It seemed as if Providence had protected the duke—not just in regard to his personal safety, but in his conduct of the battle. Even now, at a moment when Uxbridge would have yet urged caution, Wellington was exhorting every commander he could reach to move forward without restraint. Uncannily, that seemed to be working as well.

"Lord Uxbridge, I believe it is time to commit the rest of the cavalry."

"So I shall. Vivian's Hussars are making their move now. I will join them."

"Very good, Uxbridge. I will come partway. There is little more I can do here. All of our forces are on the move now."

"Sir, once again, I beg of you to be careful," said Colin Campbell.

"You worry too much, Sir." Wellington was tiring of all the concern being shown for his safety. "Their artillery fire is all but ended."

Campbell reddened and fell silent as the two generals spurred their mounts forward. At that moment a French cannon in the distance discharged a single round, which flew over the duke and struck Uxbridge in the leg. The cavalry commander winced as the heavy ball crushed his right knee, tearing the flesh from the bone. His hand tightened around the reins as he braced himself to inspect his leg. With great trepidation he leaned over and peered at the wound. The worst of his fears was realized.

"By God! I've lost my leg!"

Wellington lowered his telescope and stared at his second in command, first at his pained eyes, then shifting his gaze to the red blotch staining his trousers.

"By God! So you have!"

The duke rode over to Uxbridge and grabbed his upper torso in the crook of his right arm, supporting him upright in the saddle. No words were spoken—the cavalry commander fighting hard to keep himself from going into shock; the army commander unable to find a way to console him. For a few seconds they remained locked in an awkward embrace until some soldiers came up to carry Uxbridge away.

For a moment Wellington watched his deputy's broken form. Then, turning his face toward the battle, he rode out to spur his soldiers on.

Napoleon had read it clearly. The instant the battle had broken, he had sensed it. Even before he saw his men running back, he had known it was all over for him. The turning was like a ball tossed high into the air. It seemed to soar ever higher and higher, until—imperceptibly at first, then more and more dramatically—the momentum slowed. At last the orb lay frozen in space. Then the forces of gravity took over, drawing it back to earth with ever increasing speed until it returned to the starting point with as powerful a thrust as that which launched it.

Now his soldiers were falling back toward him, terror in their eyes. And behind the army came the British, the Dutch, the Belgians, and the Prussians. The emperor could make out a figure on horseback, his hat raised on his sword, exhorting his men on. Wellington, no doubt. So he has beaten me after all!

With lightning speed Napoleon analyzed the situation and gave his orders. Lobau was to hold at Plancenoit at all costs, keeping the Brussels road open. Once the French had withdrawn, Lobau could fall back toward Ronsomme. But he must keep Blücher off until then. An aide rode away with the order.

The three battalions of Guards nearby were to form square immediately. That would be 1st Battalion, 2d Grenadiers under General Christiani; 2d Battalion, 1st Chasseurs under General Cambronne; and 2d Battalion, 2d Chasseurs under General Monprez. They were to tie their right shoulder into the Brussels road. A fourth battalion—2d Battalion, 3d Grenadiers, under Lieutenant Colonel Belcourt—was to hold open the westernmost extent of the line in the vicinity of Hougoumont. Three aides rode off in different directions to pass on the instructions.

Napoleon moved with General Drouot, the acting commander of the Imperial Guard, to Christiani's battalion. Outwardly, the emperor appeared cool. Inwardly, his stomach twisted into a tight knot. Allied cavalry was all around the grenadiers' square, looking for a way to penetrate. The tough Guards held them at bay, but their perimeter was shrinking as more and more of them fell under the force of a thousand blows. On either side of the road and across the flattened and blood-soaked fields, Napoleon could see his soldiers streaming south. Very few of them were fighting now. Over the crest of Mont Saint Jean flooded more and more enemy soldiers, a high-pitched roar emanating from their throats.

"General Drouot, have the Imperial Guard move back slowly toward La Belle Alliance and from there to Ronsomme. The men should not hasten their march. They are to draw as many of the enemy unto themselves as they can while I extract my troops and re-form them as an army. You are to stay with me. I depend on the Guard, and you must help me organize them."

"Certainly, Sire. As you command. The Guard will not fail you."

The general passed the orders, and good to his word, the Guard was able to break the cavalry attacks, despite the repeated and spirited nature of the allied rush. But before too long the infantry and artillery closed in, and it became a much harder defense. Nonetheless, the Guards slowly made their way toward the south, keeping their formation as they went.

Napoleon spurred his horse down the Brussels road to Ronsomme and fell in on the two Guard battalions he had posted there earlier. "Steady, my friends. The army looks to you now for example. Show them how the Guard fights!"

The big men held up under the deluge, but if they were setting an example, their countrymen fleeing the battle did not seem to notice. The latter had eyes for only one thing: escape. And so did their emperor. But he would do so with dignity. For a few more moments he would take in the spectacle of a defeated army. Then he would make his move.

The final debacle of battle lies in the pursuit. Glory and discipline pass to stark terror and murderous chaos. Military ardor evaporates before the compulsion to flee. Honorable combat is displaced by wanton sadism. Humanity departs both pursuer and pursued. The latter reverts to a panicked animal, desperate in its quest to survive, prepared to scratch and gnaw its way through any animate or inanimate obstacle in its path. The former degenerates to a blood-bloated ogre, insatiable in its demonic drive to destroy and devour. The beast rises in both. Their faces distort with depraved zeal—the one to escape, the other to punish.

Across the front the French had broken, no less in those areas where they were uncontested than in those places where the allies had directly counterattacked. Panic had spread like a cancer. Nothing could stem it.

At Hougoumont the French attack ceased as if an invisible hand had smothered its last vestige of aggressiveness. The French survivors of over eight hours of incessant attack on the impregnable walls of the château now streamed back from the bastion as if the very structure were about to rise and pursue them. Officers shouted commands to halt, imploring their soldiers to maintain order and explaining that no one was after them. It was all to no avail; they could not be stopped. Back they fled through the woods around the château—tripping over the dead, becoming entangled in the undergrowth, throwing down their arms, discarding their haversacks, and abandoning anything that would slow them in their flight. Officers were able to subdue, at the points of their weapons, a few men, but the great mass of Jérôme's division and Reille's corps fled wildly across the fields. They ran as long as their legs could move and their lungs could sustain the strain of the exertion.

In the center and to the east of the Brussels road, it had become every man for himself. D'Erlon's corps had ceased to exist. In its place a mob of survivors raced each other to the rear. Men ran headlong into the muddy and broken valley where earlier they had marched as an organized army. They plummeted southward, slowed only by the suck of muddied and broken fields into which they sank, sometimes to their knees. They clawed their way over broken carcasses of horseflesh and mounds of dead and dying combatants who lay indifferent to the desperate flight.

Beneath the darkening sky soldiers could not distinguish friend from foe. A Prussian artillery battery from Zieten's oncoming corps crested the ridge at Mont Saint Jean and proceeded to rake a British battery that had withstood the entire day of battle. For a while the latter returned fire, but when the commander was informed that he was firing upon an ally, he sank into a weary indifference and had his guns cease work. The Prussians, however, had not received the word and continued to pound away until a drunken Belgian battery arrived on the scene and fired into them, forcing them back over the ridge and sparing the few remaining English survivors.

Here and there, extraordinary units of the defeated French struggled valiantly to maintain some semblance of order in the midst of ruin. On the French right, Count Lobau fought desperately to hold his infantry in place and prevent the Prussians from closing on the Brussels road and cutting off all hope of retreat. In Plancenoit, the heroic stand of the Young Guard saved what little French integrity remained. House by burning house they retreated slowly through the town, counterattacking at every opportunity, keeping Blücher's forces off balance and buying the escape of their countrymen down the Brussels road. Bravely they met their fate, and earned with their deaths the right to bear the legacy of the Imperial Guard.

On the slopes to the south of La Haye Sainte, a single brigade of French held out under the leadership of General Durutte. It was Brue's brigade, but General Durutte, the division commander, had been the inspiration that rallied what was left of it to the colors.

D'Erlon, the corps commander, had failed to stem the flood of his men to the rear. Carried along by the surge, he was propelled into the path of Marshal Ney, who was watching the rout with a sense of doom.

"D'Erlon, all is lost if you cannot rally your men." Ney stood bareheaded, his face black with powder and his uniform torn and blood-stained.

"I understand that. I am doing all I can, but they have seen the devil. I cannot stop them. Grouchy, the emperor said! He told us that it was Grouchy arriving on the battlefield. Look, they are not French that have fallen upon us. They are Prussians!"

Ney had a crazed look on his face. His eyes darted back and forth across the dim battlefield, trying to see into the gloom. "D'Erlon, if we live through this, we can expect only one outcome. We shall be hanged."

D'Erlon turned to answer, but Ney was gone. The marshal had spied Durutte standing with the remnants of Brue's brigade, the only French formation with any semblance of order within sight.

Durutte did not see the commander of the left wing of the *Armée du Nord* approach. He was preoccupied with holding his men together. His tight uniform stuck to his sweaty back like a damp cloth. Blood flowed freely from a gash below his hairline, where a saber had penetrated to his skull before being deflected. Durutte was shouting encouragement.

"Hold, men! Steady now. Give ground slowly. They cannot penetrate if we hold together. Steady. That's the way." They were a rock in a stormy sea, awash with attackers but ever emerging from the swell intact.

"Durutte! Fine job. It is good to see a French general who knows how to hold his men together." Ney approached with the wild look still frozen on his face. It was an unnatural grimace caught between excitement and terror.

"Marshal Ney, are you hurt?" Durutte felt uneasy about the approach of his superior. Instinctively he knew that, as bad as things were, they could yet get worse.

"Hurt? I am not hurt. I am Ney, prince of Moscow. I can be killed, but I cannot be hurt."

A squadron of cavalry charged the formation, which shook before the onslaught, caught itself, and brought its formation more tightly together. The cavalry took a few swipes, then moved on after easier prey.

"Durutte, soldiers of the *Grande Armée!* Follow me." Ney's voice rose above the din. "I will show you how a marshal of France dies on the battlefield."

Before Durutte could countermand the insane order, the men dutifully followed Ney back up the muddy slope. They were met by hordes of

Prussians and British troops. Ney, on foot, slashed and parried with his saber. Durutte, now mounted, rode forward to cover him, knocking several of the enemy aside before the Frenchman's horse was brought down in a heap. The fall deepened the cut in Durutte's forehead; blood gushed from the wound. Horse and rider rose from the mud just in time to escape a thrusting bayonet, but an onrushing horseman struck at the general from above. Durutte threw up his arm to protect his head as the saber descended in full arc, neatly slicing off his hand at the wrist. He spun his horse toward Ney as if to ask for help, but the marshal was caught up in his own battle, hacking and stabbing at anything he could reach. Durutte ebbed into unconsciousness as his mount was carried rearward with the English charge.

For as long as the formation held, Ney fought like a madman. But one by one the soldiers of Brue's brigade perished. The scattered survivors lost all unity. Ney himself yet stood, but found it necessary to fight his way back into one of the few remaining French squares left on the battlefield.

The three battalions of the Old Guard left by Napoleon below La Haye Sainte were among those few French units still holding together. Slowly they retreated back toward La Belle Alliance. Attack after attack had reduced their number until so few remained that they could no longer form square. Instead, the survivors drew three double lines together in triangle, crossing their bayonets together to lock themselves in from attack.

Moved by their gallantry, an English officer approached on horseback. "You have fought well, but you have fought enough. Surrender and you shall keep your honor. Fight on and you shall die."

Their commander, General Cambronne, understood English. He glared back, his eyes hardening into black coals. Steadily, he gave an answer. *"Merde."*

The English officer returned to his ranks. "What did he say, Sir?" A sergeant posed the question.

"He said, 'Shit.' "

" 'Shit,' Sir?"

"That's correct. 'Shit.' "

"Very good, Sir. What shall we do?"

"I'm afraid we have no choice. We must slaughter them. Prepare the men."

"Yes, Sir."

The firing began, and in an instant General Cambronne was hit in the forehead by a round and fell to the ground unconscious. In droves, his men fell with him, but not before they had bought a few precious moments to cover the retreat of their countrymen.

With the fall of Cambronne, only three battalions of the Old Guard remained intact. These were the two battalions of grenadiers at Ronsomme. They had been joined by Napoleon and the 1st Chasseurs, which had remained at Le Caillou all day. As the Prussians at last dislodged the Young Guard from Plancenoit and General Lobau's troops from the heights above it, they moved on to attack the battalions at Ronsomme. The grenadiers did not move except to close in over their dead. For a desperate few moments the Brussels road still remained open, and thousands of French broke out of the trap. But they were not an army any more. They were merely survivors fleeing for their lives.

Napoleon stood with his chief of staff within a square of the grenadiers as the soldiers beat off attack after attack. After each encounter, they were fewer in number and the wall of men covered a smaller and smaller area. Suddenly, Lobau burst through the perimeter.

"Sire, we could not hold at Plancenoit. All is lost."

The emperor looked at him impassively. "Is it? Perhaps."

Soult looked at his commander in chief. How small and insignificant he looked. All around them the storm was breaking, and he seemed powerless to do anything about it. He was no longer a general in command of an army. What army there was—and, as far as Soult knew, the army could be only the perimeter of the square he found himself in—existed only to save the person of its commander.

"Sire, what shall we do?" It was Lobau again, taken aback by the indifference of the emperor. Surely they must do something, he thought. It was madness to stand here in the midst of this ruin.

"What shall we do? What shall we do? What can we do! My army is ruined. There is nothing left to fight with. I must get back to Paris. Davout will raise more troops. I will move in forces from other outposts. We can reconstitute and come back. I have bled Wellington all day. Surely he cannot fight again."

Soult stared in disbelief, pausing before he spoke. "Sire, you must leave this place. Your carriage awaits you back at Le Caillou. A battalion of chasseurs is there, waiting to speed you to safety."

"You are right, Soult. I must go. Mount an escort. You must come with me. And you also, Lobau. I will need you again. You fought well today."

There was a scurry of activity as a half dozen chasseurs were readied. General Drouot, acting commander of the Imperial Guard, fell in with them, and in a moment ten men, including the emperor of France and his chief of staff, fled for their lives from the onrushing allies. To their rear, the two battalions of grenadiers continued to cover their escape, retreating slowly, still in order.

The Brussels road, the main axis of advance, had become the lifeline out. But it was a lifeline marred by the flotsam and jetsam of war. The worst of it was between La Belle Alliance and Ronsomme. The headlong flight of thousands had littered the route with all types of equipment. Fleeing *cuirassiers* who had lost their horses had thrown down their heavy armor so that they might run on foot more easily. Wagon drivers had cut the traces of harness and galloped off on horseback. Supplies had been dumped unceremoniously. Thousands of wounded had been abandoned on the road and left to the mercy of the pursuers now falling on them.

Nightfall had brought on a terrible thirst for revenge. Men who had fought nobly and gallantly all day now became enraged in their efforts to secure the victory. Their appetite whetted by blood and fired by a long day's suffering at the hands of the French, they sought satiation in wanton killing. Blood begat blood; brutality fired brutality. The stench of the dead strewn everywhere along the road reminded the living of their own mortality. To those running away, it made them more desperate to disregard anything but their own survival. To those running them down, it made them want to kill everything in their path lest they succumb to the unavoidable eventuality of death themselves. It was an orgy of stabbing, of bayoneting, of sabering. Every fleshy object was skewered, bludgeoned, or butchered. In the dark, no chances were taken. The lame, the hurt, the forlorn, the wounded—none was spared. Arms grew weary with the constant slashing and thrusting. Salty sweat poured into the eyes of the pursuers, making them blind to their own inhumanity. The pleas of the hurt only antagonized the allies and exacerbated their bloodlust. Otherwise decent men excused themselves from all acts of mercy and bathed themselves in gore. In daylight, it would have been a sight too horrible to behold. Only the darkness veiled the terrible evil and justified its remorseless prosecution.

Just ahead of this scene fled its author. At Le Caillou he fell in momentarily with the square of Imperial Guards. Behind him he could hear the screams of his dying army, but they moved him not at all. He could think only of himself. It was Russia all over again. Then he had dared all and taken a half million men to their deaths. But in the end he had escaped to Paris, only to rise again from the ashes and lead forth his armies to victory once more. Great men do not steep themselves in pity. Their destiny is to lead others to their fate, not to question it. If they did so, they would not be great. With a clear conscience he turned to the commander of the 1st Chassuers. "Take me to Genappe. I count on you."

Immensely pleased with these words of honor, the officer brought his saber to a rigid salute. He would take his emperor to safety or die in the attempt.

The retreat was an hour old as the duke of Wellington rode up to La Belle Alliance. He was sickened by what he had seen in his path. As bad as the killing had been all day, this was worse. Already the ghoulishness had begun. He had seen soldiers stooping to rob the dead. He had heard the harsh, pitiless cries of the Belgian peasantry as they picked over the fallen. The soullessness of it had chilled him to the bone.

"My Lord, Blücher is nearby. He has just come in from Plancenoit." Campbell, his aide-de-camp, was speaking.

"Where? I must see him. We must talk." The duke sounded groggy.

From the darkness appeared the old man, similarly alerted that his counterpart was nearby. Wellington could see his dark outline as he straightened himself in the saddle and could smell the alcohol on his breath. Blücher was the first to speak.

"Mein lieber kamerad." And then in French: "Quelle affaire." Finally falling back into German: "Ich stinke!"

Wellington spoke no German and Blücher spoke no English, but they understood one another. Their common language was French, the language of their enemy, and even at that they were not very good. But they were comrades in arms, and the language of command in war had brought all the eloquence between them that their alliance required.

The two men leaned forward in their saddles and embraced one another. Blücher reeked of liquor and linament. But Wellington did not mind.

He held Blücher affectionately, smiled into the old man's watery eyes, and patted him heartily on the back. With the help of their aides, they set the course of the evening's events.

"My dear Wellington, there is too much confusion in the dark. Only one of us must continue the pursuit lest we kill each other off in our eagerness to finish the enemy."

"You are most correct, Field Marshal. If it is all right with you, I would rather bring my own men to a halt. They have fought all day and could use a bit of a rest."

"Naturally. And they have fought well. Our day has been none too easy, but we would not mind a little more French meat. I would be delighted to take the honors of the pursuit."

"It will be a dangerous business. Please exercise care for your own safety."

"Many thanks for your concern, my dear duke, but I will turn the management of it over to my confederate, Gneisenau. I assure you there is no more fit man than him for a hound's chase by moonlight. It will be a cavalry affair. There is no fight left in the French at this point."

"That is true, General Blücher. But we have suffered much at their hands today, and we need to ensure that they cannot re-form and come back. I trust, however, that you will take them prisoner whenever possible."

"Of course. But of course." For the first time in the conversation, Blücher's eyes evinced a glimmer of insincerity.

"Well, then, our business has been successfully concluded. I cannot thank you enough for your steadfastness. I could not have asked for a finer ally."

"Nor I. Go with God. You have had a fine day. Now I must finish the business."

The two commanders parted company. Each had met his obligation to the other.

As the imperial party pulled farther away from the Prussians, the emperor parted company from his escort of chasseurs so that he could make better time. Through the darkness Napoleon galloped with his small party of fugitives. Among them was a Belgian peasant, Decoster, who had been captured by the French early that morning for information about the terrain in the vicinity. The emperor needed him, for the main road was choked and haste was possible only by way of adjacent secondary roads.

Although the enemy was momentarily beyond striking distance, the danger to Napoleon was great. His own army had become a howling mob. The soldiers would show no respect to their emperor as they struggled to save themselves.

The royal party pulled to a halt just north of Genappe to observe how events were proceeding there before entering the town. The road narrowed as it approached the single bridge over the River Dyle, allowing the passage of only six men abreast. But the large number desperately rushing toward the crossing had greatly exceeded the capacity of the small bridge, and the men were jammed hopelessly into a massive blockage.

Napoleon watched in silence, afraid to show himself. The French soldiers were out of their minds with fear. The stronger among them were hacking away with their sabers and bayonets, trying to carve a path across the bridge. The road was cluttered with abandoned equipment. Men were trampled in the crush, adding to the blockage as they fell beneath the boots of their comrades.

From the darkness, an officer emerged. For a few seconds he exhorted the crowd to get themselves under control and listen to the orders of their superiors. His voice could barely be heard above the clamor. Suddenly, a soldier lashed out with the butt of his musket and knocked him unconscious; the crowd surged ahead, tossing the officer to the side of the road. Napoleon recognized the officer as his provost, General Radet.

"We cannot go that way," the emperor commented to no one in particular. "That mob knows no respect for rank. The only distinction they make is between the living and the dead, and they hold neither in any regard."

Then to Decoster, "There must be another way across this river into town. You must tell us how to proceed."

The Belgian peasant grunted and motioned for the small party to follow as he led the way to the edge of town to a ford of the shallow river. The emperor of France found himself wading in the dark, muddy water, as much afraid of his own army as he was of his enemy.

The Prussian drums could be heard closing from the north. From the nearby bridge Napoleon could hear the panicky screams of his countrymen as they pressed forward with renewed urgency to get out of the path of their enemy. A shiver went down his spine as he scrambled up the riverbank.

Somehow, the small party found the emperor's coach, which had been positioned in Genappe. The gilded carriage offered the trappings of regal office, briefly reassuring its owner that he still reigned triumphantly. But the sensation was short-lived. As the imperial party made its way through town, the Prussian cavalry under Gneisenau closed in. One of his officers seized the door of the carriage as Napoleon scrambled out the other side. Momentarily protected by his personal guards, the emperor mounted his horse and sped for safety.

Behind him raced the remnants of his army. Between thirty thousand and forty thousand Frenchmen were in full flight—cavalrymen on worn-out horses, infantrymen without burden of weapon or haversack, officers mingling with privates, the wounded abandoned where they lay. A full moon shone down on the fleeing hordes, lighting their way south along the Charleroi road and on every byway running away from Mont Saint Jean back toward France. The invasion was over.

At Wavre, General Grouchy continued to press against the rear guard of the Prussian army. He had no knowledge of the events at Waterloo and along the Brussels road. Grouchy, in fact, was quite pleased with himself. He had followed Napoleon's orders to the letter and now, late in the evening, was beginning to develop the position much to his advantage.

The bridgehead across the Dyle around the town of Limale was holding, and with the help of the cavalry he had been able to expand it. He expected that, by morning, conditions would be ripe for continued attack, and—given the weakness with which the Prussians seemed to be holding the line—he had little doubt that he would break through.

All day General Gérard, the commander of Grouchy's IV Corps, had been surly. But that would pass with victory. Grouchy had little doubt that his subordinate would be quick to claim what credit he could for the decison to continue the attack at Wavre. No matter, the commander would be the one who rightly received credit or blame for victory or defeat. By deciding to stick to his original orders, he had developed the situation so that a victory could be concluded shortly after daybreak. When the news was received by Napoleon, Grouchy thought to himself, what grounds could he have for denying him any longer the full respect that came with a marshal's baton? The commander of the right wing of the *Armée du Nord* drifted off to sleep, content in the belief that he had done the right thing that day.

Wearily, the duke of Wellington rode back up the road to his headquarters at Waterloo. Now and then he would pass a group of soldiers who recognized him in the dark. Fatigued as they were, they would rise to their feet and give a hoarse cheer. Old Nosey had brought them through it. It had been a terrible day, but they had won. Those who were still alive to appreciate it instinctively knew that the battle could have turned with a single bad call. Their commander, as fatigued as they, returned the respects with a wave of his hat, then moved on his way, aching to climb out of the saddle and wanting to remove himself from the terrible battle he had directed this endless day.

At his headquarters in Waterloo, he dismounted Copenhagen and patted him affectionately on his hind quarters. The horse started and lashed out with both hooves, but the duke's luck held. Untouched, he entered the building.

A servant stood by and, noting the exhausted look of his commander, asked, "Sir, do you wish to have your supper now?"

"Thank you. I am hungry. But let us wait a few moments for the others to return." The last few words drifted off as the duke realized that perhaps very few would be returning. Alone, he climbed the stairs to his room and sat down at his table. For a few minutes he just sat there, staring at the window and the moonlit darkness beyond. Then an orderly approached.

"Sir, Colonel Gordon has arrived. He is by the front door, but he is badly hurt."

Wellington lifted his tired frame from the wooden chair and made his way back down the steps. Outside in a litter lay his closest aide, whose leg had been amputated a few hours earlier on the battlefield. The duke bent over him, placing a hand gently on his shoulder.

"Alexander, it is good to see you. I'm glad you are back."

The younger man turned his head toward his commander. "Thank God you are safe," he whispered.

Tenderly, Wellington looked down at him. "I have no doubt, Gordon, you will do well."

But the pain was too great, and Colonel Gordon did not reply. After a brief pause, Wellington turned to the attending doctor. "Have him carried to my bed. Do everything that you can for him."

Quietly, the little procession made its way into the building. Wellington was walking more slowly now. For a little while longer he awaited the arrival of his aides-de-camp, then asked for supper.

Only Gen. Miguel de Alava, a friend and aide since the Peninsular days, joined the duke at his table. It was a solemn occasion. Each time the door opened, Wellington looked up, hoping it might be one of his personal party. The table was set for all, but the places remained unfilled. At last, the duke raised his hands in resignation and said, "The hand of the Almighty has been on me this day."

A few moments later he raised his wineglass and drank a toast with General Alava. "To the memory of the Peninsular War." Then he moved to a pallet and fell asleep. Alexander Gordon lay dead in his bed.

18
THE COST

Antwerp: Monday, 19 June 1815

"Madam. It is Captain Mitchell. He begs to see you."

Emma looked eagerly at Lady Magdalene, hoping to see some alertness in her after the long, wearisome night of mindless pacing. Her mistress had been distraught since the sounds of battle had begun to be heard in Antwerp, shortly before noon the previous day. Again and again her lady's neck and shoulders had shaken violently as the sounds of the cannonades echoed off the atmosphere and were made more ominous by their distant reverberations—fading out to silence, then picking up again and increasing in resonance until they had seemed to touch the very marrow of the young wife's soul.

The morning had brought no respite from the tension. Throughout the apartments of their dwelling, in the parlors and hallways, the ladies and civilian gentlemen of the aristocracy of the allied army awaited news of the battle. They spoke to each other in whispered breaths, groping for a hint of what had become of a loved one, trying to discover who might know something and who might be withholding information in misguided compassion. Magdalene had stayed apart, sensing the terror the others held within themselves, afraid that her own might overwhelm her should someone say something disturbing in the course of an unguarded conversation. The waiting was like trying to avoid looking at a repulsive sight, knowing it was there but desperately trying to avert your gaze lest it capture you in all its horror. Even the early morning symphony of cheerful birdcalls failed to lighten the oppression. Something terrible was lingering nearby—something cold, clammy, silent, wicked.

"Lady Magdalene. It is Captain Mitchell. He wishes a word."

"Oh, yes. Of course. By all means." She seemed startled, even afraid. Straightening her dress, she went to the door.

The young officer stood a few feet back, his hat in his hand, respectfully keeping his distance from the lady's chambers. His head nodded in an abbreviated bow. "Good morning, Lady de Lancey. I bring good news."

Good news. Good news. Magdalene's heart jumped. He had said "good news." She fought to retain her composure. "Out with it!" was what she wanted to cry, but no lady would do such a thing. Trembling, she looked into his eyes.

He saw her anxiety, cleared his throat and went on. "Madam, the battle is over. The French have been entirely defeated. Sir William is safe."

The first two bits of information meant nothing to her. It was the last four words that forced the breath from her body. Her legs weakened, almost buckling at the knees. "Are you sure? Have you seen him? Has he sent you a message?"

"No, madam. I mean yes. I am sure. I have not spoken with him, nor received a dispatch. But I have read the list of killed and wounded. Sir William is not on it. I can assure you of that."

Her soft brown eyes became pools of tears. Her breath came in shallow gasps. Captain Mitchell disappeared from her consciousness. She could see only Sir William before her. He was alive. He was unhurt. She was sublimely happy. A delirium came over her. The tempo of her pulse jumped dangerously high. Her delicate hand reached out for the wall, allowing her to keep her balance.

He was alive! Her heart burst with love. Life was so wonderful. She would be with him, for years and years to come—forever. They would have children. He would be so proud, standing beside her, watching admiringly as she presented the children to him, well scrubbed, immaculately attired, bright eyed, all looking like him. Him. He was so handsome. So good. She wanted to go to him immediately, to kiss his face, to feel his arms, to be pulled to him, to make love again and again. There was no shame in her, no self-consciousness. Only bliss.

And passion! She felt her color heighten, her body flush. She filled with joy. It was all so wonderful. Alive. She had never felt so alive.

Awkwardly, Captain Mitchell withdrew unnoticed by Lady Magdalene. She had turned and walked back the few steps to her apartment. Emma came out, shutting the door behind her, leaving her mistress to herself.

"Thank you, sir. You have brought wonderful news." The maid was appreciative of the captain, yet embarrassed at the boldness of her own words. She knew she was overstepping her station, but she felt that something must be said to relieve the awkwardness of the moment. And it was such wonderful news!

"I am glad, Emma. I have never carried a happier message." He sensed Emma's self-consciousness and continued. "I understand completely. Do not be concerned. It is best we leave her alone. See what you can do for the others whose news is not so cheery. There will be much misery in Antwerp this day." With a short bow he walked off down the hallway.

For two hours Magdalene wept and smiled. A great load had been lifted from her heart. She had denied to herself the extent to which depression had gripped her since the morning of the fifteenth. There was no need to deny it anymore. The trial was over and she had passed. Again and again she went to the window and looked at the sky. It was a beautiful day.

A knocking at the door awoke her from her reverie. "Who is it?"

"Lady Magdalene. It is Emma. May I come in?"

"Yes, Emma. Of course."

The door opened and the maid primly entered. "Madam, Lady Hamilton is in the parlor with Mister James. She begs a word with you."

"Yes. Yes. Has she news of her nephew?"

"I do not know, madam. She does seem distraught, however."

"Then I will go. Oh, Emma, we must help those around us. We have been so fortunate." She stooped in front of the mirror, smoothed her hair, adjusted her skirts. In a flash she was out the door.

Lady Hamilton sat on the sofa, her face expressionless, as if in a mask. Nearby stood Mr. James. Magdalene noted the sorrow in his eyes. It disturbed her. Never had she seen such a sad countenance. She remembered that his brother was with the army.

"I trust your wife is well?" Magdalene felt a need to say something to the man, something safe. A wife was a safe subject; surely *she* could not have been hurt in the battle.

"She is, thank you." The voice was low, pained. Just to hear it caused sadness.

Instinctively, Magdalene sought to counter with a happier remark. Before she could silence herself, the words were spoken: "I have had news to rejoice in. Sir William is safe."

The man recoiled from the words as if he had been shot. He turned his face away and quickly stepped from the room. Magdalene was alarmed. Clearly something was wrong.

"Lady Hamilton. What is it?"

"Poor Mister James. He has lost a brother. And I a nephew. It has been a terrible battle. So many are dead."

"I am sorry, Lady Hamilton. I am truly sorry." It was not entirely true. Lady Magdalene was angry as well, angry that they would deny her her own happiness. Why did they ask to see her? So that they could burden her with their grief? Did they not realize she was entitled to her own joy? That, until a short while ago, her own burden had been unbearable? How mean of them. She caught herself in midthought and reddened at her own selfishness.

"I am sorry. I have no right to express my own joy. My heart goes out to you both."

"Have you heard from Sir William?" There was an odd coldness in Lady Hamilton's voice.

"No." Magdalene was confused. "Has he sent a message?"

The older woman ignored the question. "Will you leave if the fighting continues? Will you go back to England?"

"But Captain Mitchell said the fighting was over, that the French were entirely defeated."

"Will you leave?" There was a harshness in the question.

"No. I will stay until I hear from Sir William. I expect he will call for me soon." The younger woman was annoyed. This was getting to be an inquisition.

"He is not well."

"What?"

"Sir William. He is wounded."

"No. He is not. Captain Mitchell told me. He has seen the list."

"Oh, Magdalene. I wrote the list that he saw. A general came from the field during the night. He told me the names of the English officers. Sir William was among them. I could not bear to have you hear of it in that way. I omitted his name. Forgive me. Please forgive me." The coldness on her face had fled, giving way to a profound remorse. Lady

Hamilton, who had meant only kindness, now realized the enormity of the harm she had done. The woman before her was reeling from pain and shock, both made worse by the earlier belief that she had escaped tragedy.

"No. No. It cannot be. How bad is his wound? Do not lie to me. I can bear no more lies."

The words stung more than a rebuke. Lady Hamilton shrank before the seething rage in the woman before her. No tears came to Magdalene's eyes, just a wild hurt, like an animal caught in a deathly trap from which there was no escape.

"His wounds are desperate."

A gasp escaped the lips of the young woman. For an instant she remained frozen. Then, in a voice barely audible she said, "Help me to go to him."

"Yes. At once." Lady Hamilton did not hesitate to agree. Not because such a journey made sense—there was enormous risk for a woman to be travelling alone to a recent battlefield. She agreed because she could not bear to look in Magdalene's wounded eyes, knowing how much she had deepened the wound. The older woman went out momentarily to help make arrangements for the trip. Lady de Lancey put her hand to her mouth, biting down on it sharply. A terrible pain seared through her chest. Emma came quickly to her side.

While a carriage was readied, Emma packed a small valise. As she gathered her belongings, Magdalene seemed oblivious to the commotion around her. She tried desperately not to face her own thoughts. Once she stopped for a moment and asked Lady Hamilton if what she said now was the truth. Having been deceived so deeply, she could bring herself to trust nothing she heard. When the older woman answered that it was true, regretful as it was, Magdalene hurried on with her preparations. Every second counted. Sir William was hurt. She must run to him.

Some of the men entreated her to reconsider. The rabble of the army was still streaming up the Brussels road toward Antwerp. They were a desperate lot, exposed as deserters—and worse—now that the news of victory was becoming increasingly clear. No doubt there were some among them who would not take pity on a woman alone. Lady Magdalene refused all such advice.

When at last it was clear that she would not be deterred from going, Captain Mitchell sent off his friend, Captain Hay, to seek news of Colonel de Lancey. He would ride as fast as possible to Brussels, find out what he could, and then return, attempting to intercept the carriage at the halfway point.

After what seemed to Magdalene like an eternity, she set off with Emma and a driver. They immediately ran into the crowds of men and materiel jamming the roads. Everywhere the ruins of war lay in their path. It seemed as if the whole world was streaming north, against them. The men on the road looked surly, menacing. Emma pulled the blinds shut and beseeched her mistress not to look out. The maid had secreted a knife beneath her skirts, so desperate was her fear of the mob.

An hour past the gates of Antwerp, two wretches pulled themselves onto the rear of the carriage. The driver called to them to get down, but a barrage of curses and threats soon silenced him. Neither woman dared speak, cringing in the darkness of the interior, hoping that the men would not try the door. The vagabonds spoke in the clipped tongue of the Flemish—throaty, hoarse voices that seemed to gloat over some secret treachery, their gruff conversation punctuated by mirthless laughter. Once or twice Emma heard them moving forward toward the carriage door, and she gripped the handle of her knife.

Two miles short of the prearranged meeting point at Malines, a small town north of Brussels, Captain Hay came riding up. From their darkened cabin the two women heard an English voice call out, "Get off that carriage, you vermin!"

There was a guttural response from the two men, then the sound of a drawn saber and a sudden swaying of the carriage as the two men quickly unloaded themselves and took off running across the fields. Capt. William Hay presented himself.

"Lady de Lancey, I bring you news of Sir William."

The young woman threw open the blind and looked at the downcast face of the officer. Again, the sadness in his eyes betrayed his message even before he spoke. "Please. Tell me quickly," was all she could manage.

"Madam. It is over." He sat on his horse, drawn saber resting lamely across his leg, wishing with all his heart he were somewhere else. His own brother was among the missing at Waterloo. Still, this moment was at least as difficult to bear as that knowledge. Magdalene looked back at him blankly. For an instant she opened her mouth as if to speak, then fell silently back inside the carriage. After a minute the captain instructed the driver to turn around. There was no use in going on.

The rest of the afternoon they made their slow way back to Antwerp.

Once or twice a sob came from the enclosure holding the two women, a cry that gripped the officer's heart. Captain Hay was a veteran of the Peninsula, and his own kin was likely lying dead on the fields at Waterloo this very moment. Yet the heartbreak of the woman inside the carriage was more grief than any man could bear. He would keep to himself the reports he had heard at Brussels—stories of robbing and mutilating the dead, of stripping the wounded even before they died, of terrible carnage, of piles of human and animal corpses mixed together, of stink and rats, of grotesque wounds and savage inhumanity. The poor woman. She had sorrow enough. No need to dwell on what terrible things might have happened to her husband before he died.

Once back at Antwerp, Lady Magdalene returned immediately to her room. A number of the ladies stood by, ready to go to her. But she showed no sign of recognition. Once a friend of Lady Hamilton's knocked at the door, but Magdalene was so distraught that her cries frightened her away. Inside the apartment she paced restlessly, returning to the window again and again where for two blessed hours that morning the world had seemed so bright. The memory seemed only to mock her now. How woefully ignorant of the truth she had been. How could she have been so joyous then, when Sir William lay mortally wounded, probably dead even as she was thinking of a beautiful and long life together? If only she had been able to see him. Five minutes. Only five minutes. Oh God, if you had only given me five minutes it would have been enough. To see his face again, to console him, to tell him how much I loved him—it would have been all that I asked.

Around midnight Emma arrived with her bedding, prepared to spend the night in the room with the grieving widow. The maid did not want to leave her alone; she was afraid for her lady's health. Never had she seen anyone so distraught. It was as if demons were racking the very soul of her mistress. Lady Magdalene would lie in bed for a few moments, return to the window, look up at the dark sky, and see nothing except a vast emptiness. Long, quiet moans occasionally came from deep within her. The moans frightened Emma more than anything else.

Shortly before dawn there was a rapping on the door. "Send them away," was the only response from Lady Magdalene.

Emma got out of bed and went to the outer chamber, returning a moment later. "Madam, I—"

"Hush. I do not wish to speak. Leave me alone."

"Madam, please! I have news."

"I want no news. I have heard enough news today, enough to last me my lifetime."

"But madam, it is *good* news I have."

"Emma, how can you be so cruel? What can be good now?"

"But—Sir William is not dead."

"What!"

Emma bubbled with joy. "Yes. He is alive. There was a gentleman at the door. A general. General McKenzie I believe. He told me that Sir William was alive. Wounded, yes, but alive. And there were even hopes that he might recover."

"Oh Emma. Emma! Can it be? Is this yet another falsehood? I cannot take any more lies. How does he know?"

"My Lady, it must be so. Would the commander of Antwerp, for that is who it was, come to your apartment in the middle of the night with such news if it were not so?"

The logic of Emma's last statement sank in, flooding Magdalene's heart with hope. Magdalene had to believe it. If she did not, she would go mad. "Emma, we must leave at first light. And this time, I shan't go back, no matter what we might hear on the way."

She put on a robe and fled to the parlor, where the general awaited her. They spoke a few words and he gave her a letter. She pored over the words, which were written by a staff officer who had seen her husband alive. They stated that he was being tended to by a competent surgeon. The message, dated seven o'clock in the evening of the previous day, was carefully worded so that undue hope might not be raised. But it clearly said Sir William was alive. And he might recover! Magdalene's heart soared, then fell back to earth. The thought occurred to her that the news might be stale, that the worst might have already happened. Her emotions ricocheted until finally she got a grip on herself. It was enough to know that he had lived through the battle. She would go to him, appealing to the general for assistance, which he promptly gave. Again the carriage was made ready, and this time an officer of dragoons was sent along as escort. At nine in the morning, the two women set off again for Brussels and a small town beyond it by the name of Mont Saint Jean.

The trip this time was no less terrifying than that of the previous day. The stream of undisciplined men moving up from the Brussels road had slackened, but in their place came even harder men, men who had survived the battle and had business to attend to. Many saw no need for a civilian carriage to be on the road. Several scuffles ensued in which sabers were drawn. On one occasion a Prussian officer stopped the carriage, determined not to let it pass. He menaced the driver for a moment or two, but the desperation in Lady Magdalene's voice softened his demeanor and he let them go on.

Captain Hay was waiting for them in Brussels. He had returned to the battlefield the evening before, still searching for his brother. Early that morning a rider from Captain Mitchell had sent him a message that Lady Magdalene would be making the journey a second time.

"Madam, I have good news. I have seen Sir William, and he is asking for you. I came at once. You will find it difficult to proceed by carriage from here on. The road remains badly congested."

Magdalene alighted from the carriage. The air was heavy with the smell of gunpowder. Everywhere soldiers were moving equipment and wagons. Cartloads of wounded men were still arriving from the direction of the battlefield. "Mister Hay. You are very considerate. Can we go at once? Can you take me to him?"

"Yes, I can. But I must tell you that the way will be dangerous. And there will be some terrible sights, madam. The corruption will be offensive. Even the horses balk before it."

"I shall pay it no mind. God bless you, sir. Please, take me to Sir William without delay."

Drawing his sword, the captain led the two women and their carriage into the crush of the crowd. Slowly they made their way south, covering nine miles in three and a half hours. The stench of decomposing bodies was horrible. The two women tried to avert their eyes, but the longer they rode, the less able they were to avoid seeing the sources of the smell. Just as the captain had said, the horses tried to turn away from it and had to be forced to go forward. Death frightened man and beast alike.

At last they came to a small cottage at the edge of a village alongside the dusty road. Here the smell was worst of all for, in addition to the great numbers of dead, scores of wounded lay about. Many were without limbs. Some lay naked, their bellies torn open, their bodies mutilated in frightening ways. Magdalene braced herself. This was where she would see her husband.

"Lady Magdalene?" A tall man in a surgeon's smock approached her carriage.

"Yes."

"My name is Scovell, madam. I have attended your husband."

"Is he alive?" The doubt was still there.

"Yes, alive, and we are of the opinion he may recover. I regret how you have suffered."

"My suffering matters not. Please, take me to my husband."

"I must warn you first, madam, that his condition is delicate. His life hangs on a slender thread. Any agitation could be fatal. We have not told him that you were informed he was dead. I beg of you not to mention it. It could be fatal."

"I promise I shall not mention it. Just take me to him, please." She was fully composed now. All that had come before mattered not. Her prayer had been answered. Five minutes. Five minutes. Oh, please let me be with him for five minutes. I would never complain again.

They entered the cottage. She remained in an outer room while her escort went ahead. An instant later she heard a voice, "Let her come in." It was her husband.

She walked through a rough doorway and entered a little room. He lay in a rumpled heap upon a tiny bed wedged wall to wall at the end of the enclosure. A pale face looked up at her, the eyes heavy with pain, a frail smile across the lips. His legs, cramped by the lack of space, bent up toward his chest; his head lay back on a filthy sack that substituted for a pillow. For an instant his neck tensed as he tried to rise in greeting, but the pain only worsened and he fell back with a grimace. She controlled an urge to run to him, to cradle him and shower him with kisses.

"Hello, Magdalene. This is a sad business, is it not?"

She was overcome with grief and joy—grief at his pitiful state; joy that he was alive and she with him. Saying nothing, she walked to his side and took his hand. It seemed so soft, so lifeless. All the strength had left it, this soldier's hand that had impressed her so with its touch, its manliness. They looked into each other's eyes. Both had resolved not to cry, but there was no threat of that. There was only total joy, a deep and abiding love that knew no distraction, no unhappiness, no regret. The seconds turned to minutes and still not a word was spoken. Yet the communication was intense, an exchange of souls, a tender loving that needed no signature of outward appearance.

After a long while he spoke. "Are you a good nurse, my love?"

"I have never been much tried," she answered with a low sweetness, still clinging to his hand, "but I shall endeavor to be one for you."

"And I shall try to be a good patient." He smiled, a deeper smile now, and it touched the strings of her heart. "Thank you for coming, Magdalene. Oh, thank you so much."

Bending gently from the waist, she kissed his brow as his eyelids closed. After a few moments he fell asleep, a peaceful look crossing his face in repose.

Magdalene now took stock of their situation. He looked terrible, but not as bad as she had imagined. Would he recover? She could not know. The doctors themselves apparently had been unable to say, although they did offer hope. Hope! It had been given to her then dashed so repeatedly in these last few days. One could not base a plan on hope. Whatever she did now must be based on reality. Her assessment of that reality must be absolute.

The first and most important point was that they were together. Even if he died, they had this time no matter how short it might be. She must savor every moment of it. No matter what happened in the future, this time of theirs could not be changed. She would remember every second of it, regret nothing, and embed it in her heart as a cherished event to carry her through whatever years lay ahead.

The second thing was that she would devote her energies to make this time as comfortable for him as it could be. He was suffering much, that she could tell. But if she could bring him love, solace, companionship, and as much creature comfort as possible, he would know relative peace— and she would be reassured for the rest of her life that she had done all that she could have for her love. Her own needs were unimportant. She would stay by his side until he recovered or until he died. There was no question about that, no room for self-pity.

She could see that those around her had little time to devote to concern for his—and therefore her own—ordeal. There was just too much misery, too much work, for the surgeons or the military officials to occupy themselves with the plight of one man, even if he was the chief of staff of the army. She would find out how he might best be cared for and see to it herself that it was done.

She had asked for five minutes. That was all. The Lord in his grace had given her that. It seemed that He would give her more. Every minute would be a gift. She must do everything to make it a lasting gift. She must do nothing to agitate him, for if it shortened his life by only one hour it would fill her life with reproach the rest of her days.

Finally, the conditions under which he was housed were positively abominable. They must be improved, no matter the meager resources at hand to do so. The bed was little more than a wooden frame, attached to the wall on hinges, and unable to accommodate the length of his body. The rags covering him were infested with vermin, and the dust in the sack of chaff that was his pillow must be disturbing his already labored breathing. A proper bed must be brought in and turned the length of the room so he might lie down and unbend his legs.

The lack of cover on the window made him susceptible to all the noise and disturbance in the courtyard outside, as well as to the prying eyes of every passerby, some of whom might have less than noble motives for looking after the incapacitated. He must be bathed and made comfortable, although to move him without pain would be difficult. By keeping a washbasin handy and wiping him often she might keep him reasonably clean while at the same time cooling him from the stifling heat of the tight enclosure.

Most of all she would stay with him constantly, even when he was asleep; he might awake and need some assistance or be desirous of her company. Only God knew how much time they had together. She would not lose a minute of it.

With the most profound clarity she had ever known, Magdalene thought of how to implement her plans. A peace came over her soul—not from a knowledge that easy days lay before her, but from an assurance that, whatever came, she would do the right thing for the most powerful force in her life: the love of Sir William. Carefully, she laid his hand by his side and went out to speak to her maid.

"Emma, bring me a cushion from the carriage. We must make him a pillow. And bring what clothes I have. I need to see what I can construct for Sir William from the material."

And so began a week together at Waterloo for Lady and Sir William de Lancey—a week of suffering, but also a week of tenderness, of tranquillity, and of love. Lady de Lancey, the delicate young bride who knew little of life and only lately of war, stood courageously by her plan.

Sir William's wounds were grievous and gave him great pain. But he complained not at all, save when he fell into a fever and spoke unconsciously of what he felt. She stayed with him always, seeking advice from the doctors when they came by but understanding when they gave her little attention.

Bleeding was the only treatment for fever, and she saw to it that whatever had to be done was tended to. The purplish swelling beneath his skin frightened her, but she kept her fears to herself. Whatever desires he made known to her she did her best to fulfill. When he could no longer stand the foul water, which had been polluted by the passing of three great armies and the ruin they left in their wake, she sent a servant to find a cow and bring him milk. When he asked that his infested room be fumigated, she devised a contrivance of hot irons and bellows, which did the job without disturbing him. When the swelling became more than he could bear, she obtained leeches and applied them to the wound to relieve the pressure.

She fed him, bathed him, talked to him, brought him his medicine, or merely sat beside him while he slept. Practically every moment of the day she gently held his hand, softly speaking to him. Only once— on the fifth day—did she leave him to obtain some sleep in an adjacent room. She quickly gave up her desperate need for rest when she heard his voice call her name. From then on she left him not at all.

His appetite weakened day by day. And as he lost interest in food, so did she. Often her mouth was parched, but she would drink nothing so it might be available for him should he suddenly regain his thirst and want to drink.

He became increasingly unable to sleep. Clearly, the pain was becoming worse and his breathing more and more labored. Nor would she sleep, preferring to soothe him through the short periods of darkness in the Belgian summer. On the sixth night he appealed to her to come lie down beside him to help shorten the night. With great fear of causing him pain, she at first refused. But when he asked again and again, she at last contrived a way to wedge her body onto the narrow bed by placing a chair beside it. It was a gift for them both: They drifted off into a badly needed sleep, comforted in repose by the presence of one another, a facsimile at least of the wedded bliss they were due.

On the seventh day his breathing became even more difficult, but still he did not complain. At five in the morning, she had risen from the bed and tended to his wound. He said that it barely disturbed him— merely a trifle. But she could see the discomfort, and by late morning an ominous coughing had crept into his breathing. Quietly she sat, endlessly stroking his hand, listening to the fluid rattling in his throat. By three in the afternoon, his suffering had intensified to the point that she felt compelled to call for a doctor.

While they waited she continued to hold his hand.

"Magdalene, I wish you would not look so sad."

The young bride, her face now aged with fatigue and pinched with grief, could say nothing. She had never known such total and complete sadness. But it was not just for them. Her own prayers had been answered. She had had a few moments with her husband, to savor, to cherish, forever and ever. But in the long hours she had stood by him, the enormity of the loss on this battlefield, on this campaign, had sunk in. How many thousands—no, how many tens of thousands—had been lost by this enterprise, by this war? How could the waste be measured? How many loves were trampled into the dirt? How many mothers had lost the babes they had brought into the world and raised with such tender affection? How many children had lost their fathers? And for what? For glory? For politics? What a terrible waste. Silently she put her head into his palm and wept. The tears ran softly down her cheeks and onto his limp hand.

"Oh, my love. My darling. I have never known such happiness. Such peace." In a fading voice he repeated every term of endearment he could utter.

"Magdalene. Kiss me. Please kiss me. I want to feel your lips on mine. Once more, dear Magdalene. Let me kiss you."

She lifted her head. While still holding his hand, she looked into his eyes and drew her face close to his. Her eyelids closed, and she brought her lips to him. Softly he responded to her and brought his own lips together.

"Magdalene!" It was his last word. The breathing stopped. He was gone.

Again she pressed her lips to his. Then she sat down and remained beside him for a long, long time. Never had she seen such a sweet, serene countenance. It gave her pause in her own sorrow. She did not want him to sense her grief, lest it disturb his peaceful rest. Finally, as the sun sank low beyond the ridge of Mont Saint Jean, Lady de Lancey left his side.

EPILOGUE

Seldom does a battle so conclusively set the terms of peace. France is defeated; Europe resets the balance of power at the resumed Congress of Vienna, being careful to include France in the postwar settlements. For forty years there is no great war involving two or more of the major powers of Europe. The Continent has had enough, the blood-soaked fields of Waterloo a grim reminder of the costs of international folly.

Napoleon: Forced to abdicate on 22 June, he attempts to strike a number of deals for his safe passage to the United States. This the British will not allow, and on 15 October Napoleon disembarks on the remote island of Saint Helena in the South Atlantic. A small group of loyal retainers voluntarily accompanies him into exile.

His daily routine becomes monotonous. He rises late, breakfasts about 1000, and seldom goes out, although he is given freedom to range over the small island as long as he is in the company of an English officer. Dinner takes place about 1900, followed by an evening of reading aloud and card playing before going to bed at midnight. The majority of his time is spent writing and talking, much of it dedicated to absolving himself of any blame for the defeat at Waterloo.

He receives no word from his wife, Marie-Louise, who begins a liaison with the Austrian officer appointed to watch over her. Eventually she secretly marries him, not waiting for her husband's death. Nor does Napoleon receive any word of his son, the former king of Rome, who now lives in Vienna as duke of Reichstadt. Napoleon's confidant is Emmanuel Las Cases, a former chamberlain who has followed him into exile. After the arrival of Sir Hudson Lowe as governor of Saint Helena in April 1816, Las Cases is arrested and expelled from the island. Napoleon's only remaining emotional outlet is his hatred for Lowe, whom he sees as his jailer. The sentiment is returned.

At the end of 1817, a terminal illness begins, its origins becoming the stuff of legend, like so many of the tales surrounding the fallen emperor. Whether it is cancer, a stomach ulcer, or strychnine poisoning is not clear. What is clear is that his inactivity contributes immeasurably to his rapid decline. Napoleon's doctors are summarily dismissed by Lowe until an acceptable incompetent is found to administer a diet of useless potions. On 5 May 1821, the deposed emperor dies, mumbling on that day only a few coherent phrases, which include, "My God . . . the French nation . . . my son . . . head of the army."

Wellington: After Waterloo, his revulsion for war is complete. "I hope to God that I have fought my last battle. It is a bad thing to be always fighting." But if the years of the sword are behind him, he cannot deny his place as a hero of Britain. Idolized by his soldiers, he now becomes worshipped by the public. His modesty, however, remains intact, though he cannot deny the ground swell of support that propels him toward political office. By 1828 he is summoned by the king to take over as prime minister. His years in office are tumultuous, his marriage unhappy. Although he declines in 1834 to sit again as prime minister, he continues to serve in high office as foreign secretary and later as minister without portfolio.

In 1846 he retires from public life, although he continues to be consulted by all parties. To the end of his days, he remains a humble man, shunning any glorification for his flawless day at Waterloo—or for all his years of fighting. His watchword, "I am but a man," is his response to the undiminished adulation he receives from around the world. He despises vanity and offers that each man in his own right— carpenters and shoemakers and farmers—could beat him on his own ground.

He dies in 1852 from a stroke and is given a monumental funeral, the last heraldic one in Great Britain. He is buried in Saint Paul's Cathedral, at the center of the British empire.

*   *   *

Blücher: In the hours and days that follow the battle, the old field marshal continues to savage the retreating French relentlessly. Two more horses are shot from under him during the pursuit, but on the day after Waterloo he is proudly wearing Napoleon's hat and sword, recovered for him by his soldiers. On 22 June, the day of the emperor's abdication, he writes his wife, "If the Parisians do not kill the tyrant before I get to Paris, I will kill the Parisians."

For all his bluster, however, his health is waning, broken in the end by the exertions of the campaign. His delusions deepen; he reiterates again and again that he is pregnant with an elephant, fathered on him by a French soldier. He too has had enough of war. "I am sick of murder," he says in July. Gambling becomes his major preoccupation; he throws his money around with the same abandon he did his army and himself on the field of battle. In October he enters a horse race outside Paris, despite entreaties from Wellington and his staff. Blücher is thrown to the ground and reinjures his shoulder, which had never fully recovered from Ligny. He returns home to Berlin with his arm in a sling.

Over the next three years he turns his attention to farming, seemingly content with life, but saddened by his son Franz's progressive fall into dementia. Blücher's love for his young wife, Katarina, remains undiminished, and he pours what energies he has into his farm. In the fall of 1819, Silesian troops begin field exercises near his home in Krieblowitz as he takes to his bed one final time. His aide, Nostiz, is still with him and suggests the troops move on lest they disturb him. "What on earth for?" is his reply. "I have heard plenty of cannon fire in my lifetime—surely I can stand some more now." As the days pass and he grows weaker and weaker, he adds, "They have learned a great deal from me. Now they must learn from me also how to die peacefully."

He dies in his bed on 12 September 1819, his wife by his side. In summing up his career, he answered the question as to what he owed his victory: "It was my resolution, Gneisenau's wisdom, and the compassion of Almighty God."

Ney: In the end, his deathwish is denied him at Waterloo. Major Schmidt of the Red Lancers obtains for him another horse—his fifth of the day—and spurs him on his way toward Paris, where he arrives on 20 June, the day before Napoleon. That he has lost all coherence is evident when he speaks before the Chamber of Peers on 22 June and attempts to put blame for failure on Napoleon, for committing the Guard too late.

He cannot make up his mind to go into exile. He remains in Paris until 6 July, then goes into hiding at an isolated château in the provinces. On 3 August he is arrested by the restored Bourbons, who are mindful of his unfulfilled promise to bring Napoleon back in an iron cage.

His lawyers attempt to save him from prosecution under French law by dint of the fact that his birthplace, Saarlouis, was no longer in France. Springing to his feet in the courtroom, he cries out, "I am French. I shall know how to die like a Frenchman."

He is found guilty of treason and sentenced to death. On 7 December he is taken to the Jardins du Luxembourg in Paris to appear before the firing squad. Noble, calm, and dignified, he chooses to address his executioners directly. "Soldiers, when I give the command to fire, fire straight at the heart. Wait for the order. It will be my last to you. I protest against my condemnation. I have fought a hundred battles for France, and not one against her." Eleven bullets bring him down; one goes wide of the mark and embeds itself in the wall above his head. To the end, he is "the bravest of the brave."

Grouchy: Unaware of the defeat at Waterloo on 18 June, he fights well at Wavre the following day against Thielemann's III Corps. At 1030 on 19 June, he learns of the disaster of the left wing of the *Armée du Nord* and skillfully extricates himself, slipping away toward Namur. His army remains intact, ready to fight on. On 20 June, he stops the pursuing Prussians dead in their tracks. On 22 June, he learns of Napoleon's abdication and moves his forces into France, heading first for Rheims, then for Paris, where he turns his army over to Marshal Davout.

He sails for America, where he takes up residence in Philadelphia. His battles continue on paper as he engages in a war of polemics to justify his actions at Waterloo. Both Napoleon and Grouchy's own subordinate, General Gérard, publish telling condemnations of his failure to move to the sound of the guns.

In 1819 he is amnestied as a lieutenant general. The following year he returns to France. After the Revolution of 1830, he is reinstated as a marshal by Louis-Philippe, and subsequently raised to the Chamber of Peers in 1832. To this day he remains a prime example of a general following the letter of his orders, though the great doubt of whether he did his duty remains.

Soult: In the breakdown of the *Armée du Nord* he once again realizes his remarkable powers as a commander—as opposed to a chief of staff—and is able to rally the fugitives near Laon in France. It is clear, however, that the emperor's rule is disintegrating, and Soult retires to his estates in his hometown of Saint Amans–Labastide. His reputation as a Bonapartist, however, plagues him, and he narrowly escapes lynching before fleeing to his wife's home in Germany. There he undertakes to write his memoirs.

Gradually he is insinuated back into French politics, becoming minister of war in 1830 and again in 1840. His energies in the halls of government grow legendary as he throws himself into his duties, beginning his workdays at the unheard-of hour of five o'clock in the morning. Four years before his death in 1851, he is appointed a marshal of France once again. To the end no one doubts his capacity as a commander. However, to this day the reasoning behind his disastrous selection as chief of staff to the *Armée du Nord* remains a mystery.

Jérôme: After the debacle at Waterloo, Jérôme, his wife, and his son are imprisoned in Württemberg by Jérôme's father-in-law. The older man is motivated more by the desire to force his daughter to divorce her wayward husband rather than by a wish to hold a rampant Bonapartist in check. She refuses, although Jérôme remains an incorrigible rake. Eventually, the three of them are released on the provision they live in exile in Austria. Despite his fickleness, utter unfaithfulness, and complete selfishness, Jérôme becomes the heartthrob of countless women of nobility, who underwrite his spendthrift ways. They also legitimize his return to the corridors of power, and with the resurrection of the Napoleonic legend he finds himself welcome among the royalty of Europe.

In 1848 he is reinstated as a general of division with full pay. Shortly thereafter he is appointed governor of the Invalides; later he becomes president of the Senate. Finally, he is promoted to marshal of empire and given the Palais Royal, all this as the beneficiary of a nephew now the reigning monarch of France. His sexual promiscuity continues until the last decade of his life, scandal following scandal, until his state funeral in 1860. His almost eight hours of continuous attack at

Hougoumont stands as a monument to dogged persistence—and a tragic waste of life.

Baring: He survives the battle at Waterloo and continues to soldier on, although war in Europe wanes for almost half a century. His honors abound, and he rises in rank to become a major general and the military commandant of the city of Hanover. In January 1834, he is knighted.

A rumor grows that his failure to hold at La Haye Sainte was a disappointment to Wellington. Regimental rivalries and nationalistic sentiments point out that Hougoumont, the first of the farms to be attacked at Waterloo, held out to the end under continuous siege from the better part of two divisions. In comparison La Haye Sainte fell at a critical moment in the fighting, allowing Napoleon to set up his final attack by the Imperial Guard. Wellington's public praise for the steadfastness of Macdonell and the lack of the same for Baring are further cited as proof of this discontent.

Yet Baring faced even more impossible odds than did his fellow commander in the Guards Division. Denied the opportunity to occupy his defensive position at a time when its ramparts were still intact, stripped of his sappers (who were sent to buttress Hougoumont), given the order to occupy and defend at the last possible moment, armed with the slower-loading—though more accurate—Baker rifle, and not resupplied with ammunition, Baring's defense at La Haye Sainte remains one of the more valiant episodes in the history of warfare. His subsequent career bears testimony to the esteem in which he was held. So too does his presence as an honorary pallbearer at Wellington's funeral in 1852.

Macdonell: He receives, along with all ranks who took part in the battle, the Waterloo Medal—the first general issue made to the British Army. He is quick to share the credit for his successful defense of Hougoumont with his fellow Guardsmen. Nine other men are cited for closing the gate: From the Coldstream Guards, Captain Henry Wyndham, Ensign James Hervey, Ensign Henry Gooch, Sergeant James Graham, and Corporal Graham (his brother); from the Third Guards, Sergeant Fraser, Sergeant Brice McGregor, Sergeant Alston, and Private Lister. As British pride in the conduct of the battle surges in the years that follow, Sergeant Graham and Sergeant Fraser are awarded a special medal for their gallantry at Hougoumont.

Graham is additionally nominated by Wellington for an annuity of ten pounds a year, offered by a patriot—the Reverend John Norcoss of Framlingham Rectory in Norfolk. Unfortunately, the fund expires after only two years upon the bankruptcy of the reverend, but when Norcoss dies he bequeaths 500 pounds to be given to "the bravest man in England." Wellington is asked to choose from among all the brave men who fought on that day. He answers: "The success of the battle of Waterloo turned on the closing of the gates at Hougoumont. These gates were closed in the most courageous manner at the very nick of time by the efforts of Sir James Macdonell." Upon award of the money, Macdonell promptly shares it with Sergeant Graham.

Macdonell continues to serve in the Coldstream Guards. In 1825, ten years after the Battle of Waterloo, he is honored with the title of regimental lieutenant colonel. Later the same year he is named regimental colonel. The honor marks him as the officer who signifies, more than any other, the traditions of the regiment. In July 1830 he is promoted to major general and subsequently commands in Ireland and Canada, where his legend continues to grow. Repeatedly knighted, he is eventually promoted to lieutenant general and then full general. He is known throughout the empire as "the bravest man in the British Army." He dies on 15 May 1857, in London. He was unmarried save to his profession.

Lady Magdalene: In the hours that follow the death of Sir William, she fights to hold back her overwhelming grief, lest it "disturb his tranquil rest." Her resolve turns toward profound reflection as she remembers the prayer of her journey to Mont Saint Jean: that she be given but a few more moments with her beloved.

> As I drove rapidly along the same road [Antwerp–Brussels–Waterloo], I could not but recall the irritated state I had been in when I had been there before; and the fervent and sincere resolutions I then made, that if I saw him alive, I never would repine.
> Since that time I have suffered every shade of sorrow; but I can safely affirm that except the first few days, when the violence of grief is more like delirium than the sorrow of a Christian, I have never felt that my

lot was unbearable. I do not forget the perfection of my happiness while it lasted; and I believe there are many who after a long life cannot say they have felt so much of it.

She arranges for the body to be brought to Brussels, where it is laid to rest on 28 June. She has a small inscribed stone emplaced to distinguish his grave from the forty other new graves in the cemetery and arranges with the caretaker to maintain it. Struck by her tragic beauty, he promises to plant some roses around the site. On the Fourth of July she visits the grave of her American-born husband one last time before departing for England, three months to the day of her marriage.

For her brother, Captain Basil Hall, Royal Navy—a friend of Sir William's and the source of their introduction—she writes an account of the last days she had together with Sir William in Belgium. The captain is deeply moved by the intensely personal narrative. While he respects the privacy of his sister's emotions, he lends it sparingly to those on whom he believes its meaning will not be lost. Again and again, the comments he receives as to its merits indicate so great an impact that he is motivated to pass it to literary figures of his acquaintance.

Among the more renowned of these is the Scottish novelist, Sir Walter Scott, who remarks in 1825 that the account of Lady Magdalene is among the more moving documents he has ever read on the woes of war: "I never read anything which affected my own feeling more strongly, or which, I am sure, would have a deeper interest on those of the public." With some caution expressed to shield the personal emotions of the family, he recommends to Captain Hall that he consider publishing it.

Sixteen years later the diary is passed to the great English author, Charles Dickens, who is compelled to write of it:

> To say that the reading of that most astonishing and tremendous account has constituted an epoch in my life—that I shall never forget the lightest word of it—that I cannot throw the impression aside, and never say anything so real, so touching, and so actually present before my eyes, is nothing. I am husband and wife, dead man and living woman. . . . What I have always looked upon as masterpieces of powerful and affecting

description, seem as nothing in my eyes. If I live for fifty years, I shall dream of it every now and then, from this hour to the day of my death, with the most frightful reality.

Ninety-one years after the battle, an abridged version—the original having been lost to time—is published in London. Entitled *A Week at Waterloo,* it receives little circulation.

Of the young woman herself, she marries another soldier four years into her widowhood. She dies in 1822. Perhaps more than any of the thousands who fought and fell on the fields of Waterloo, she best defined the limits of glory.

Selected Bibliography

Adair, Major P. R., "The Coldstream Guards at Waterloo," *Household Brigade Magazine*, Summer, 1965.

Anglesey, Marquess of, "The Allied Cavalry in the Waterloo Campaign," *Household Brigade Magazine*, Summer, 1965.

Barnett, Correlli, *Bonaparte*, George Rainbird, Ltd., London, 1978.

Barrès, Jean-Baptiste, *Memoirs of a French Napoleonic Officer*, Greenhill Books, London, reprinted 1988.

Beamish, North Ludlow, *History of the King's German Legion*, 1832.

Bernard, Henri, *Le Duc de Wellington et La Belgique*, La Renaissance du Livre, Brussels, 1983.

Bukhari, Emir, *Napoleon's Cuirassiers and Carabiniers*, Osprey Publishing, Ltd., London, 1977.

Bukhari, Emir, *Napoleon's Dragoons and Lancers*, Osprey Publishing, Ltd., London, 1976.

Bukhari, Emir, *Napoleon's Hussars*, Osprey Publishing, Ltd., London, 1978.

Bukhari, Emir, *Napoleon's Line Chasseurs*, Osprey Publishing, Ltd., London, 1977.

Chalfont, Lord, editor, *Waterloo: Battle of Three Armies*, Sidgwick and Jackson, London, 1979.

Chandler, David, *The Campaigns of Napoleon*, New York, Macmillan Publishing Co., Inc., 1966.

Chandler, David, *The Hundred Days*, Osprey Publishing, Ltd., London, 1980.

Chandler, David, *Napoleon's Marshals*, Weidenfeld and Nicolson, London, 1987.

Cotton, Sergeant Major Edward, *A Voice from Waterloo*, J. H. Baird, Brussels, 1854.

Creasy, Edward S., *Fifteen Decisive Battles of the World*, Military Heritage Press, New York, 1987.

Cronin, Vincent, *Napoleon*, Penguin Group, London, 1971.

D'Aguilar, Lieutenant General Sir George C., translator, *The Military Maxims of Napoleon,* Macmillan Publishing Co., Inc., New York, 1988.

Dalton, Charles, *The Waterloo Rollcall*, Arms and Armour Press, London, 1971.

Daniell, David Scott, *Cap of Honour: The Story of the Gloucestershire Regiment (The 28th/61st Foot), 1694–1975*, White Lion Publishers, London, 1975.

De Callatay, Philippe, *Quelques Souvenirs d'Epoque a Propos de Lord Uxbridge en 1815 et de la Jambe Qu'il Perdit aWaterloo*, The Waterloo Committee, Brussels, 1983.

De Lancey, Lady Magdalene, *A Week at Waterloo in June 1815*, edited by Major B. R. Wood, John Murray, London, 1906.

De Las Cases, Emmanuel, *Mémorial de Sainte Hélène*, Gustave Barba, Paris, undated.

De Norvin, M., *Histoire de Napoleon*, Furne et Compagnie, Paris, 1847.

Duffy, Christopher, *The Military Experience in the Age of Reason*, Atheneum, New York, 1988.

Elting, John R., *Swords Around a Throne*, The Free Press, New York, 1988.

Epstein, Robert M., *Prince Eugene at War: 1809*, Empire Games Press, Arlington, Texas, 1984.

Fisher, John, *Eighteen Fifteen*, Cassell, London, 1963.

Fortescue, Sir John, *The Campaign of Waterloo*, Greenhill Books, London, reprinted 1989.

Fosten, Bryan, *Wellington's Infantry, Vol. 1*, Osprey Publishing, Ltd., London, 1981.

Fosten, Bryan, *Wellington's Infantry, Vol. 2*, Osprey Publishing, Ltd., London, 1982.

Fraser, Brigadier D. W., "The First Guards—2nd and 3rd Battalions, 16th/18th June 1815," *Household Brigade Magazine*, Summer, 1965.

Gaillet, Gérard, *Le Journal de Napoleon*, Denoel, Paris, 1978.

Gates, David, *The British Light Infantry Arm c. 1790–1815*, Batsford, Ltd., London, 1987.

Gérard, Jo, *Napoleon: Empereur des Belges*, Editions J. M. Collet, Brussels, 1985.

Gow, Lieutenant Colonel J. M., "The Third Guards at Waterloo," *Household Brigade Magazine*, Summer, 1965.

Griess, Thomas E., editor, *Atlas for the Wars of Napoleon* (West Point Military History Series), Avery Publishing Group, Wayne, New Jersey, 1986.

Griffith, Paddy, editor, *Wellington: Commander*, Anthony Bird Ltd. of Strettington House, Sussex, 1983.

Haythornthwaite, Philip J., *British Infantry of the Napoleonic Wars*, Arms and Armour Press, London, 1987.

Haythornthwaite, Philip J., *Napoleon's Military Machine*, Hippocrene Books, New York, 1988.

Haythornthwaite, Philip J., *Wellington's Military Machine*, Spellmount Ltd., Kent, 1989.

Herold, J. Christopher, *The Age of Napoleon*, American Heritage Publishing Company, Harmony Books, New York, 1962.

Hofschröer, Peter, *The Hanoverian Army of the Napoleonic Wars*, Osprey Publishing, Ltd., London, 1989.

Hofschröer, Peter, *Prussian Cavalry of the Napoleonic Wars: 1807–15*, Osprey Publishing, Ltd., London, 1986.

Hofschröer, Peter, *Prussian Line Infantry, 1792–1815*, Osprey Publishing, Ltd., London, 1984.

Houssaye, Henry, *Waterloo 1815*, Christian de Bartillat, Étrépilly, France, 1987.

Howarth, David, *Waterloo: Day of Battle*, Atheneum, New York, 1968.

James, Haddy, *Surgeon James's Journal 1815*, Cassell, London, 1964.

Jones, B. T., editor, *Napoleon's Army: The Military Memoirs of Charles Parquin*, Greenhill Books, London, reprinted 1989.

Keegan, John, *The Face of Battle*, Military Heritage Press, New York, 1976.

Kincaid, Captain Sir John, *The Adventures in the Rifle Brigade and Random Shots from a Rifleman* (abridged), Richard Drew Publishing, Glasgow, reprinted 1981.

Lachouque, Commandant Henry, *Waterloo*, Arms and Armour Press, London, 1972.

Lawrence, William, *The Autobiography of Sergeant William Lawrence*, Ken Trotman, Cambridge, reprinted 1987.

Leach, J., *Rough Sketches of the Life of an Old Soldier*, Ken Trotman, Cambridge, reprinted 1986.

Logie, Jacques, *Waterloo: L'évitable défaite*, Duculot, Paris, 1989.

Longford, Elizabeth, *Wellington: The Pillar of State*, Harper and Row, New York, 1972.

Longford, Elizabeth, *Wellington: The Years of the Sword*, World Books, London, 1971.

Lucas-Dubreton, J., *Le Marechal Ney*, Libraire Fayard, Paris, 1941.

MacKinnon, Colonel, *Origins and Services of the Coldstream Guards*, Vol. II, Richard Bentley, London, 1833.

Mann, Michael, *And They Rode On*, Micheal Russell Publishing Ltd., Great Britain, 1984.

Margerit, Robert, *Waterloo: Trente Jours qui ont fait la France*, Editions Gallimard, Paris, 1964.

Mercer, General Cavalier, *Journal of the Waterloo Campaign*, Greenhill Books, London, reprinted 1985.

Nicolson, Nigel, *Napoleon 1812*, Harper and Row, New York, 1985.

Nosworthy, Brent, *The Anatomy of Victory: Battle Tactics 1689–1763*, Hippocrene Books, New York, 1990.

Page, Brigadier F.C.G., *Following the Drum: Women in Wellington's Wars*, André Deutsch, Ltd., London, 1986.

Paget, Sir Julian, *The Story of the Guards*, Michael Joseph, Ltd., London, 1979.

Palmer, Alan, *An Encyclopaedia of Napoleon's Europe*, St. Martin's Press, New York, 1984.

Parkinson, Roger, *Blucher: The Hussar General*, Peter Davies, London, 1975.

Rafter, Captain, *The Guards*, Clarke, Beeton, and Company, London, undated.

Ribbons, Ian, *Waterloo 1815*, Penguin Books, Ltd., Middlesex, 1982.

Saunders, Edith, *The Hundred Days*, Longmans, Green and Company, Ltd., London, 1964.

Seward, Desmond, *Napoleon's Family*, Viking Penguin, New York, 1986.

Siborne, Captain W., *History of the Waterloo Campaign*, Greenhill Books, London, reprinted 1990.

Siborne, H. T., editor, *The Waterloo Letters*, Arms and Armour Press, London, 1983.

Smith, Frederick C., *Waterloo*, Award Books, New York, 1970.

Sutherland, John, *Men of Waterloo*, Prentice-Hall, Englewood Cliffs, New Jersey, 1966.

Thorton, James, *Your Most Obedient Servant*, Webb & Bower, Exeter, 1985.

Von Pivka, Otto, *Brunswick Troops, 1809–15*, Osprey Publishing, Ltd., London, 1985.

Webster, Sir Charles, *The Congress of Vienna*, Thames and Hudson, London, 1963.

White, Arthur S., compiler, *A Bibliography of Regimental Histories of the British Army*, London Stamp Exchange, London, 1988.

Wise, Terrance, *Artillery Equipments of the Napoleonic Wars*, Osprey Publishing, Ltd., London, 1979.

The Author

Jim McDonough is a colonel of infantry in the U.S. Army. He has had a lifelong interest in the traditions, history, and values of the military. As the son of a career army sergeant he lived abroad as a child for seven years in Europe and the Middle East. In 1969 he was an honor graduate and boxing champion of the United States Military Academy at West Point. Training in the U.S. Army's paratrooper, ranger, and jungle warfare schools and a short assignment in the 82nd Airborne Division preceded a combat assignment to Viet Nam with the 173rd Airborne Brigade in 1970 and 1971. His book *Platoon Leader* is an account of that experience and is currently required reading in many of the military's schools for small unit leadership.

Subsequent tactical assignments as a company and battalion commander and staff officer in Europe, the United States, and Korea, interspersed with temporary duty with the State Department and Department of Defense, and high level staff assignments—to include a stint as military assistant to the Supreme Allied Commander, Europe— deepened and broadened his perspectives on the military profession. In 1988 he published *The Defense of Hill 781,* an allegory of modern mechanized warfare set in a desert environment. This book became recommended reading for the U.S. Army's preparatory course for brigade and battalion command.

He is currently assigned as the Director of the School of Advanced Military Studies at Fort Leavenworth, Kansas, an institution dedicated to the education of a select group of Army, Air Force, Navy, and Marine Corps officers in the operational level of war. The mission of the school is to produce officers able to integrate the tactical missions, actions, and dispositions of disparate air, ground, and sea forces into campaigns designed to accomplish strategic objectives. It is also the proponent agency for the coordination, writing, and publication of the U.S. Army's central warfighting doctrine.

Colonel McDonough's interest in Waterloo was heightened by a three-year assignment to Belgium and by the fact that it represents a case study that combines the tactical, operational, and strategic elements of war with an immense human drama of courage, passion, and tragedy.

He is married to the former Pat McKenzie, herself the daughter of a career Air Force sergeant. They met as children in Damascus, Syria, in the early 1950s and were married four days after graduation of the West Point Class of 1969. They have three sons, Jim, Mike, and Matt.